Elizabeth and After

Elizabeth and After

Matt Cohen

PICADOR USA

New York

Picador® is a U.S. registered trademark and is used by
St. Martin's Press under license from Pan Books Limited.

ISBN 0-312-26151-9

First published in Canada by Alfred A. Knopf Canada

First U.S. Edition: August 2000

10 9 8 7 6 5 4 3 2 1

for Daniel and Madeleine,

and with thanks to D. M.

"All happy families resemble each other, but each unhappy family is unhappy in its own way."

LEO TOLSTOY, *Anna Karenina*

Elizabeth and After

The West Gull Cemetery announces itself with a twenty-foot-high stone archway of quarried limestone. Its gates are black wrought iron with silver tips and fittings, and the matching fence stretches hundreds of yards along the highway. Located on a high and windswept plateau, it offers a unique and flattering perspective on Long Gull Lake, the town of West Gull itself and the rich surrounding farmland. Even a stranger would be impressed.

Once Elizabeth McKelvey was such a stranger. On a certain spring day that marked the end of a long winter, both real and metaphorical, she passed through the archway, drifted a palm along the silky-slick surface of the limestone, stepped gingerly onto the moist dense grass. The sky was blue, the light a sparkle of sun and budding leaves. Soon she could hardly see the car in which she had arrived, and the man who brought her had receded to a shadow. As she lost herself in this new world, the idea that she might one day be buried there seemed almost natural.

But when that time actually arrived the word everyone used was not "natural" but "unexpected." Unexpected. *Like the woman herself, like the accident that killed her.*

On the day of the funeral Long Gull Lake was a distant stretch of snow dotted with fishing huts merging into the grey sky. The town, so picturesque in summer, was just a jumble of metal and asphalt roofs, columns of smoke rising straight into the still air. The fertile farmland was a barren waste with a few clusters of houses and barns.

Halfway through the ceremony, the sun surprised everyone by coming out. By that time Elizabeth, encased in her chrome-trimmed oak coffin, had been placed in the hole all eyes were trying to avoid. The sun melted the frost in the top layer of the mounded dirt beside the grave and tiny rivulets of water began to form. Gerald Boyce, who had dug the grave and whose head was still ringing with the brain-jarring experience of sitting on the front-end loader while its bucket smashed into the half-frozen ground, reached out in wonder to squeeze this suddenly pliant and beautifully glistening soil.

"Elizabeth McKelvey. An extraordinarily generous woman with an uncanny ability to touch and shape the lives of those who knew her — her students, her family, her friends. For all of us, Elizabeth passed through our lives like a dazzling shooting star. And in the way the light from a shooting star stays visible long after that chunk of rock has disappeared into its own nothing- ness..." And so on and so forth until Dr. Albert Knight's eulogy to his friend and patient ended in a heartfelt burst of tears. But despite the fact that he'd compared Elizabeth to a chunk of rock, not exactly flattering the deceased, many residents of West Gull felt he'd hit the nail on the head with the bit about the light: a rich and haunting green-blue glimmer had emanated not only from Elizabeth's eyes but seemingly from her entire being. "Like an electric shroud you would be afraid to touch," alleged one of the spiritually minded Ladies of the Inner Circle old enough to have witnessed her testimony.

According to the coroner's report, at the time of her death Elizabeth McKelvey was 51 years old, a white female 66 inches tall and weighing 128 pounds, the possessor of chestnut hair and 27 teeth.

The cause of death was deemed to be "shock and massive hemorrhaging due to multiple fractures of the skull." This event was accompanied by tears in the skin, including one over the right ear where a section of scalp was actually stripped from the bone, fractures of the nose and both cheekbones, internal injuries unenumerated since an autopsy was not deemed necessary, and other outrages to what had been a healthy living body before it took an unplanned trip through a suddenly stationary windshield attached to a car that had accordioned into a large oak tree.

Nothing was said about the blood in the snow but there was a lot — more than you would think a body could hold. In some places it had clotted into frozen puddles, in others it was scattered in long splotched whips like scarlet maple taffy. Perhaps in deference to those who had seen it, and to ease the suffering of relatives and friends, the report added that "death was almost certainly instantaneous."

At the funeral, following her father's eloquent eulogy, Maureen Knight remarked that "my father was always one to exaggerate." This statement was left to hover uncontradicted while those who had heard quickly whispered it to those who hadn't.

PART I

ONE

As William McKelvey lay twisted in his bed, grizzled barrel chest barely moving, each drawn-in breath rattled like a truckful of gravel being poured through a giant tin culvert. There followed a brief moment during which the echo grew as hollow as a horror-movie tomb, then the gushing exhalation began: a long moist flushing out of spongy lungs clogged by decades of tobacco and woodsmoke.

Asleep, as awake, William McKelvey made a large ungainly lump. But in his dream McKelvey was all air and fire, a sheet-wrapped ghost drifting through West Gull, a small farming centre and tourist town that for almost two centuries had been clinging to the shore of Long Gull Lake, an elongated granite-shored dip on the southern edge of the Precambrian Shield. The sky was black and moonless, the street lamps off. But in the residential area where William McKelvey slept, the tended streets with the expensive homes between the highway and the lake, most of the doors had amber-lit brass coach lamps showing the way for horses that would never come, and through the windows of their glassed-in solariums could be seen the glowing numbers of VCRs and digital clocks and sometimes the trembling green and red lights of fax and answering machines.

The main street brought more lights — the white fluorescent glow of the big glass-doored refrigerators in which the convenience store kept its milk and juice, the tricoloured neon pop sign that burned day and night over the counter of the Timberpost Restaurant and the light Luke Richardson kept on at the Richardson Real Estate office. Luke Richardson. There was a man who could turn a dream into a nightmare. These days he liked to come up to McKelvey and stand too close, his lank black hair shining with grease. "Hey, Bill," he would start, his jaw dropping to reveal the dark poison hole of his mouth. "How's my man? Where you been hiding?" William McKelvey, convinced eight years ago by Luke Richardson to sell his house and farm to the West Gull Rest & Retirement Villa in return for the privilege of resting and retiring there until he died or became a vegetable, would turn and walk away.

The dream-ghost of William McKelvey was looking for fresh brownies in the bakeshop when the radio woke him up.

"Five a.m. at TWANG FM," rhymed the all-night DJ, his tinny voice emerging discreetly from the clock radio William McKelvey kept under his pillow.

He rolled onto his back and began to massage his bad knee. It was late June. The sweet smell of clover and fresh-cut hay lay across the township and filtered through McKelvey's screened window, along with the beginning ripples of birdsong and the restless trembling of the poplars that stood in the yard of the R&R, originally the home of Luke Richardson's great-great-grandfather and now the penultimate residence of two dozen officially ambulatory souls whose bodies, like the slowly collapsing barns that dotted the landscape, now gave only the most provisional shelter to anyone trapped inside.

McKelvey pushed away the covers and silently dressed in the clothes he had laid out. Soon he was padding downstairs, shoes in hand.

Once in the kitchen, he opened the refrigerator door and helped himself to a package of sliced salami and a square of cheese, both of which he stuffed into his fishing vest, a beige labyrinth of pockets and zippers sent to him by his son on the occasion of his seventy-fifth birthday. From one of the pockets within a pocket, he withdrew a key he'd confiscated the afternoon before and used it to unbolt the deadlocked kitchen door.

By now there was just enough light to make silhouettes of the surrounding trees and nearby houses. Even in the few minutes it had taken him to dress and get outside, the birdsounds had grown more complicated, new calls and songs crowding into the pre-dawn sky. He crossed the grass to the sidewalk. A few steps took him to the delivery lane that emerged on Main Street. There, standing beside the real-estate office, the same one his dream-ghost had passed, he peered across the street to Richardson's New & Used. Beside the garage, parked where it had been for the last week, was the white Pontiac.

The white Pontiac! There was a ghost worth catching. He'd first seen it when he was out for an afternoon apple pie and coffee at the Timberpost. Something about its tilt made him think that his own old Pontiac — a gold-orange dinosaur he'd long ago sold for scrap — had somehow wound its way back from wherever it had been, got itself painted, then settled in Luke Richardson's car lot to wait for him.

Unable to believe such a gift, he'd approached it slowly, telling himself that if the upholstery was the same mesh polyester, the steering wheel faded on the left side by sun and sweat, the corner of the glove compartment bent where he'd had to pry it open with a crowbar...

But this ghost Pontiac had upholstery of gleaming white leather, a white suede-covered steering wheel, a glove compartment that resembled a strongbox. This Pontiac was lower to the ground, equipped with twin stainless-steel exhausts, hood and fenders shaped in expensive aerodynamic curves. This Pontiac was no ghost, it was a bomb — a white bomb — and underneath that hood was most likely some kind of fuel-injected V-8 nuclear power plant that would send the car smoking along on the oversized tires that bulged out from beneath the fenders.

McKelvey wished he'd woken up an hour earlier. He had his old car keys with him, not the exact ones but copies he'd made before selling it. Just in case. Of course this was a different car. But those manufacturers were cheap bastard fools and his key slid unresisted into the lock.

No one was watching. He pretended to be looking through the window as if he, seventy-six-year-old William McKelvey, had won the lottery at five in the morning and decided to spend it on this bomb that had a price of $34,999.99 crayoned in red wax onto its windshield. The key was in the lock and now he tried to turn it. No luck. No matter how carefully he jiggled, it wouldn't work. Then, just because he was a stubborn old ass and he hadn't gotten out of bed for nothing, he tried the passenger door. The lock yielded with a smooth oiled click. McKelvey opened it, leaned across to release the driver's side. He walked around the car and let himself in. Being surrounded by the white bucket seat was like sitting in a cloud of whipped cream. He took the key and carefully, a tiny wiggle at a time, hardly daring to hope, inserted it so-slow-slowly into the ignition. "Please go," he said, twisting it. The engine caught immediately, a deep and powerful purr.

Two seconds later he had adjusted the driver's seat to accommodate his long legs, reversed out of the lot, turned the corner and was cruising down Pine Street, fat tires humming in tune to the engine's low growl. His foot barely touching the accelerator, he floated past the cop shop, then the Brewer's Retail at the edge of town. The light made a narrow red-yellow band along the horizon and the car was skimming towards it; then gravity and impatience grabbed his foot and rammed it to the floor. The big Pontiac rocketed forward, pinning him back like an astronaut in his seat. McKelvey was laughing. Again he stamped the pedal and this time the bomb exploded, shooting him over the hill and into the sun.

After a few miles he turned off the highway and stopped to wipe the price off the windshield. As the sound of the engine drained away, a nearby crow cawed; its sharp wild call tore through the air and McKelvey looked up to see the bird gliding to rest on the top branch of a dead elm. "Good morning, crow," he said. The crow looked down at him, startled, then flapped away cawing into the morning sky. McKelvey began winding his way through the back roads, his window open. The air here was sweeter than town air could ever be, the grass thick and tangled, the maple and oak that lined the fields heavy with their brilliant loads of green, the rising light.

He rounded the corner that the swamp flooded every spring and suddenly his chest filled up with a terrible homesick feeling he wouldn't have known he could still have. Even before the house, his eyes went to the sign. It was centred in front of the row of pine trees he and Carl had transplanted one day when Carl was just six years old and happy to go anywhere with his father in the big pick-up. That summer Carl was always playing in the truck, jumping in and out of the box, trying to climb into the front seat to get at the radio. Evenings at twilight McKelvey would find his son stretched full length in the truck seat, baseball glove clutched like a teddy bear to his heart, listening mouth open and mesmerized to the country music flooding through the oversized Motorola AM/FM McKelvey had hung beneath the dashboard of his old Ford.

RICHARDSON REAL ESTATE, the sign read. Big black letters against a green background with a telephone number beneath. At the side of the front yard, near the road and where the bugs were always the worst, was a set of swings that hadn't rusted yet.

The house. Like the Pontiac it had turned white: the straight polished gleam of its new aluminum siding taunted him like the echo of a two-handed slap. "Tastefully renovated" was how the ad described it. Reading the description of his old farm had made him so angry he blushed.

> Country hobby waterfront jewel. Tastefully renovated century home near tourist town offers rural playground for young family. Safe swimming in Dead Swede Lake, outbuildings that could be converted for offices or horses, drained fields, vintage maple bush.

"Country waterfront jewel," he had read aloud, sitting on the porch of the R&R. "Century home." He remembered hanging from his father's huge hand as they wandered through the house for the first time. The damp musty smell of the wet basement rising through the rotting pine-planked floors he would eventually replace with hardwood. The peeling mildewed wallpaper. The windows with more spiderwebs than glass. *Waterfront jewel ... rural playground ... safe swimming in Dead Swede Lake.* He'd cut the advertisement out of the newspaper, put it in his fishing vest, then kept pulling it out to see if it was still true — like a love letter or a bottle of rye that knew how to fill itself in the dark. A couple of days later the Pontiac had appeared.

A black chain was draped between the gateposts. He undid it, drove in, put the chain back in place. He cruised slowly down the driveway, approaching the metal-clad box that had once been his house with all the caution due an enemy fortress, continued past the kitchen door and parked behind the chicken coop so the car wouldn't be visible from the road. The sun was fully up now, sending brilliant shards of light from the new aluminum windows, the shiny metal door, the white siding. It was amazing that they could buy a man's life like this, then turn it into a tin box looking like it needed to be kicked in. *Century home.*

This was as far as he had planned: to get the car, drive it to the old farm, park where he couldn't be seen.

But now he was at the house itself, at the doorway he had passed through so many tens of thousands of times. Despite everything they'd done to the outside of this tastefully renovated waterfront jewel, he could feel his mouth forming into a stupid grin, his eyes closing as though inside this bizarrely deformed memory-house his youth was waiting to be stepped into again like an old coat miraculously converted into a handsome new garment. He was sweating and clinging to the brass handle of the new door with its matched metal-vinyl self-hung casing. He was wishing he was back in bed at the R&R

listening to the news and the birds squabbling in the feeders. If only Elizabeth would suddenly appear.

The thought of Elizabeth steadied him. He straightened up, looked at the white panelled door with its half-ring of half-moon peek-a-boo windows. Like the swings, the siding, the newly shingled roof, the door made him wonder about the people who'd lived there. Of course they had ripped out the old hand pump in front of the house — a man couldn't even get a drink of water without going inside. He turned away from the house and went to the chicken coop. The electric meter was still there. He threw the master switch. The previous owners had used the coop for storing wood and at one end of the small woodpile they'd left a splitting axe. It had a long hickory handle, the varnish still unworn, and a good solid weight that swung like a comforting pendulum as he limped back across the grass towards the new door.

His shoes were soaked through with dew and he had a sudden memory of himself as a boy, a day like this, barefoot in this very grass, grass so wet he could feel the juice squirting between his toes as he ran.

The rotting wooden steps had been replaced by poured concrete. McKelvey positioned himself carefully, stiffened his bad knee, swung back and then torqued his two hundred and forty plus pounds into low gear as he powered the butt end of the axe into the gleaming brass handle. The lock gave way but when the door swung open McKelvey saw not his nostalgic old kitchen but a great sweep of whiteness that looked like an oversized bathroom in search of a piss-pot. White tiles, white counters and stove, white-enamelled sink, white walls and ceiling, even a white ice-making refrigerator.

McKelvey went to the sink and pulled hard on the new tap. It shot out a thick stream of water that ricocheted off the bottom of the sink and into his face. The telephone rang. A loud old-fashioned bell that started his heart racing and for a moment he was sure that if he picked it up he would hear Elizabeth. For the first time in a decade, he could remember her voice: dry, affectionate, yet with a built-in twist that announced — or was it insisted? — that between her and every other living being was a space that could never be crossed. Then he wondered if the telephone meant someone was calling who had reason to expect an answer. Frightened, he grabbed the axe and bolted outside.

By the time he was back in the comforting whipped-cream leather of the driver's seat, had the big motor purring and awaiting his orders, his stomach was going again. But instead of returning to the road, he drove into the heart of his old farm, going between the barns to pick up an old tractor trail that wound between the fences of two hayfields, through the *vintage maple bush*, down into the swamp between the maples and the lake. The trail was long unused, the hay uncut, and as he eased the car along the overgrown track between the fields, there were moments when the clover and alfalfa obscured his view before swishing beneath the bumper. In the deep shade of the maple bush the grass was shorter but two or three times he had to stop to remove a fallen limb. Each time he stepped out of the car he left the motor running, afraid that any unguarded moment of silence might drown him. *Safe swimming.* At the edge of the swamp he stopped and threw in the axe. Here the old trail turned soft and boggy. When the wheels started to spin he slowed to a crawl and then, just to see what would happen, he tried accelerating through it. The big tires whined briefly before the car began to settle. He opened the door. The wheels were half sunk into the mud.

McKelvey grabbed the roof and hauled himself to his feet. His knee locked and he had to massage it again before he could limp around the car and assess the situation. Thirty years ago he'd dumped a few loads of sand to keep this stretch of swampy track out of the water. At the time he'd thought about solving the problem for eternity by mixing in some gravel and ditching the sides so the water could escape. But that would have been an extra week's work. Better just to use the road in late November, after the fall rains, when the frost was in the ground and a thin crust of snow lay on top. He would load up his chainsaw and drive back in the old truck with a couple of sandwiches and a thermos of coffee. A few hours later he'd have enough wood to spend the rest of the day splitting and stacking.

Now the leaves were thick and green. And even though the sky was clear and the sun high, there was a ripe marshy smell.

Mud had spattered the car's fenders and doors. McKelvey got onto a dry spot behind the trunk and opened it to search for a shovel. Not that he would have used it. "*Nyet!* Absolutely forbidden," Dr. Knight had decreed. "No physical exertion. No exercise. Nothing a pregnant woman wouldn't do." This last had mystified McKelvey since Elizabeth, when pregnant, had done all sorts of things, many impossible for him even when his knee worked, his heart hadn't needed a valve job, and that tractor tire around his gut had been just a few extra layers of muscle, beer and bumbleberry cake.

There was a loud crack. A porcupine that had hoped to scramble unseen up a young maple came crashing through the branches and landed in a juniper bush a few feet away. As it began to waddle off, McKelvey felt something release in his lungs, as if for the last eight years at the R&R, without his even knowing, his breath had been blocked. Now the swamp smell broke down into the odour of rank ferns, beaver shit, fast-growing marsh grass, spruce pitch, maple bark, decomposing bullrushes, frog breath, honeysuckle, a dozen, a hundred, a thousand different messages that crowded and fluttered through his brain like swarms of moths released from a long-closed trunk. He began to hear the peepers, the frogs, the crackling footsteps of the porcupine, the movement of bird wings through the air, the mud bubbling around the Pontiac he'd taken from Luke Richardson's lot.

He reached into his fishing vest, broke off a hunk of cheese with his fingers, wrapped it in salami. He repeated this until the supplies he'd taken from the R&R were used up and the anxious edge in his stomach had settled into a dull digestive warmth. He realized the phone had spooked him out of in-specting the rest of the house. Maybe the bedroom he'd once shared with Elizabeth now had a four-poster with a canopy. The old parlour with wallpaper that had been peeling for sixty years might be a haven warmed by a fireplace with a marble hearth. Or have, built right into the wall, one of those wood-stoves with glass doors through which you could contemplate the fire and remind yourself of the days when you were a Neanderthal roasting up a nice chunk of hairy elephant.

McKelvey found a few dead branches and pushed them into the mud under the tires for traction. He climbed back into the car. His shoes — heavy and caked with the slick clay-rich mud — attached themselves to the floormats, which he considered might be useful under the wheels if the wood didn't work. Brute force was for the young and the brainless, those whose bones were still green and pliable. Now was the age of wisdom and cunning. He switched on the motor. It gurgled enthusiastically. McKelvey pushed the accelerator to the floor.

The motor growled and roared. The wheels spun and whined. Shooting up from under the car came a powerful curtain of mud. The car sank even lower. Underneath all that mud were some rocks McKelvey remembered dumping into place on a rainy October afternoon the year his father died. McKelvey opened his door, now level with the mud, keeping the pedal to the floor.

From beneath the hood a thick black cloud of rubber-scented smoke began rising into the swamp's green canopy of leaves. The oversized muscle-bound super-tread tires clawed down to those rocks from long ago. The car jerked upward, then fell back briefly before blasting out of the mud as if kicked in the ass by a 450-horsepower hoof. Spinning and careening, it shot down the trail, mud spraying everywhere. McKelvey's door·slammed against a birch tree. When the car came to a forgotten hump, its exhaust system sheared off with a loud explosion.

McKelvey had been trying to lift his foot from the accelerator but the new-born howl of the unmuffled engine frightened him so much that his knee locked again, jamming the pedal to the floor. McKelvey could only hang on to the steering wheel while the car cleared itself a trail through the woods, picking up speed as it fought through the saplings and underbrush. When it reached the beach it shot forward with a roar, the speedometer needle swinging wildly until the car reached an unfamiliar cedar dock which moaned and splintered under the car's weight as it became the runway for McKelvey's bid for outer space.

He screamed. Unconsoled by the whipped-cream comfort of his bucket seat, he clutched the white leather steering wheel and listened to the sound of his own terrified bellow. Ahead of him were the blue sky and jagged pine horizon, beneath him a terrible series of thuds and clunks. With a splash and an ear-splitting sizzle, the white bomb hit the water. Even as it sank, it struggled to take off again, the tires churning up great sprays of water and sand. Then with a fizzle and a hiccup the engine conked out and the car came to rest — a thin film of water lapping over the hood. At some point the windshield wipers had activated themselves. They cleared away the mud and debris to offer McKelvey a view of the centre of Dead Swede Lake. A few hundred feet away a rowboat turned towards him. McKelvey waved at the familiar blocky figure, and went to work on his knee. When he got it loose he rolled down the window, then used his good leg to try to push open the door. He'd always imagined it would be impossible to open a door underwater. In movies people were always having to escape out their windows. But now, maybe because the water wasn't very deep, the door began to move. Just as well because he didn't need a ruler to figure there'd be no wriggling out through the narrow window.

By the time he'd got to shore, emptied his shoes and squeezed out his pantcuffs, the rowboat had drawn up beside the car.

"How's the fishing?" McKelvey asked.

"Slow." The occupant of the rowboat, Gerald Boyce, was short but very wide and though his hair was spun a thick and snowy white, his round baby face was smooth.

"Fucking car," McKelvey said. He stepped closer to the rowboat and peered at Gerald as though he hadn't recognized him before.

"You like a ride?"

"Wouldn't mind."

He picked up his shoes and socks and put them in his vest pockets. Then he walked his bare feet along the remains of the hot sun-warmed dock until he was positioned to step into the boat.

While Gerald was rowing towards the middle of the lake, McKelvey took a package of makings from the pocket of Gerald's workshirt and rolled himself a cigarette. He still had his own lighter at least. Dr. Knight hadn't said anything about pregnant women not being allowed to start fires.

By the time McKelvey got his smoke set and going, Gerald was near the centre of Dead Swede Lake. A stringer hung from one oarlock. McKelvey pulled it up. A few small bass wiggled enthusiastically, then started trying to swim as he lowered them into the water.

"We could go home and eat them," Gerald said. "You think you can work a fillet knife without slitting yourself?"

McKelvey undid the top buttons of his shirt to let in the sun and air. He would go back to Gerald Boyce's. They would fry the fish and sit on Gerald's broken-down front porch and look out at the orchard of hybrid trees and freak apples that surrounded Gerald's house. He would pick the bones from the charred fish flesh, smoke Gerald's cigarettes, drink his boiled coffee and listen to stories about how Gerald's dead brother Vernon, had tried to save the township from developers and cable television. Every now and then he or Gerald would go into that black hole of a kitchen, the way they used to, and kick the refrigerator to make sure the beer didn't freeze.

The sky was a deep endless blue, the kind of blue McKelvey had always loved as a boy, the kind of blue that promised to turn into a heart-grabbing purple when evening came.

"Sure," McKelvey said. "Fry those fish. Ruin that coffee."

Gerald raised his eyebrows. They were two white furry patches on his smooth and deeply tanned forehead. Beneath them, his eyes: bovine spheres of a rich chocolate brown so full of mute compassion that McKelvey felt his own eyes fill with tears at the thought of how fate had taken his life, shrunk it, dried it out, thrown it so far from its sources that until this moment — suddenly and inexplicably back in the midst of everything that nourished him — he hadn't even noticed.

At this distance the white bomb was just a curving sheet of wet white metal. It could have been anything. Moby Dick. A creamy mermaid haunch. The bulging remnant of a white kitchen fallen from the sky.

"Nice car," Gerald finally said. "Hope you didn't pay cash."

Gerald Boyce was one of three: there had been Vernon, the deceased and sainted reeve; there continued to be Vernon's twin brother, Roydon, an upright stick of a man who'd been West Gull's doctor until he migrated south to be a rich old geezer doing plastic surgery on movie stars and socialites in an Arizona clinic; finally there was Gerald, the forgettable recluse who, aside from digging the occasional winter grave with his fancy front-end loader, had squandered his share of the family money by playing mad-scientist with old television sets, breeding so-called organic fruits and vegetables and using his big cow eyes to draw various local widows and other helpless women into his dubious lair like trusting minnows to a shark's gullet.

Early on the Sunday morning he witnessed the amazing re-appearance of William McKelvey, he had been woken up by the piercing squeak of his rusted mailbox hinges. He lay still, letting his dizziness settle, then went into the kitchen and looked down to the end of his driveway. The mailbox was turned. He slid his feet into the shapeless deer moccasins Vernon's wife, MaryLou, had given him a few Christmases ago and started towards the road. At the mailbox he found a square white envelope that looked like it should be holding a Christmas card or a wedding invitation. His name was hand-printed on the outside. Inside was a single piece of paper that read:

LOOK UP AND YE SHALL SEE HIM

Gerald Boyce looked up. He saw only that the dark blue stain of dawn had yielded to a yellow shimmer announcing the sun.

"Idiot," he said.

At intervals that ranged from weeks to years and at unpredictable hours of the day and night but always when he wasn't looking, someone deposited these bizarre messages in his box, each time in a different kind of envelope, perhaps to trick him into opening it, which he always did. MY WAY IS YOURS had been the previous message. What was that supposed to mean? Was it sponsored by some kind of hitch-hikers' association? He'd put it in his truck and later, while in town, slid it under a windshield wiper at the supermarket parking lot.

He stuffed LOOK UP AND YE SHALL SEE HIM into his pocket and went back to the house for breakfast. He boiled his coffee camp-style just for the strong bitter taste of it. Walking with a slight forward bend to keep his mug from spilling, he set off on his morning rounds: first the chicken coop, the sour-smelling domicile of four sinewy hens long past stewing and a rooster whose feathers had fallen out when Gerald called it a useless tit — he later apologized but the damage was done; next the glass-and-plastic greenhouse now empty except for its raised trays of manicured earth; lastly the garden — long hummocked hay mounds divided by rows of vegetables he brought twice a week to the West Gull supermarket for their local produce section which the locals carefully avoided while tourists clustered round it like vampires at a blood bank. There had been a time when he spent whole days weeding. Now mulch, a Rototiller and laziness had made his life easier, which meant that after he had returned to the house for a second cup of coffee, he got his tackle box and headed towards the lake.

By the time he reached the shore the sun was already above the trees. Hawks squawked and thrummed. Bugs buzzed and bugged. Gerald pushed off and started rowing, the sun clanging against the metallic surface of the water, hammering at him the way it had done all summer.

He was starting to doze in the boat when he heard the sound of a car at the old McKelvey place. After it died away, he rolled himself a cigarette, stroked towards shore and began to fish. He was bringing in his fourth bass when the car started again. For the first time in more years than he could recall, he heard a motor coming from the barns towards the lake. The barely audible hum grew louder, deepened. Then there was the high whine of a stuck car trying to free itself and another silence that was broken by a new roaring — this one wild and ever louder as whatever machine it was bore through the bush towards him. Gerald remembered LOOK UP AND YE SHALL SEE HIM.

He looked up and he saw *it* — wreathed in a black shroud of smoke, accelerating along the dock until for a brief crazy moment it was airborne, a shining white wingless Armageddon beast launched to avenge the world's sins. It hung suspended while its windshield wipers suddenly went into action, the furiously blinking eyes of a demented monster, after which, with a huge slapping splash followed by a great hissing of steam and rising of vapours, it fell into the water. Gerald Boyce applauded long and loud. He was just about to call for an encore when the car door opened and a thick body pitched into the lake.

He took McKelvey into the boat and rowed him across the lake. He could hardly believe how McKelvey's face had changed: it looked like puffed pale pudding and hung off the bones as though he'd just stepped out of his own coffin — except the coffin had been one of Luke Richardson's fancy cars and was now parked up to its gills in what some incredible wit had christened Dead Swede Lake because more than a century ago, local legend had it, a landless and love-tormented Swedish labourer had swum out into the middle of the lake, yodelled out his heart-struck swan song, then drowned.

Once at the shore McKelvey, pasty face and all, showed a little of the old muscle and threw the boat halfway up the hill in his eagerness to get to the house and have a forkful of fish in one hand, a bottle of beer in the other.

Eventually the fish and the beer were all gone and McKelvey lay sleeping where he had often enough slept before: on the old couch surrounded by a couple of dozen black-and-white TV sets that Gerald had bought cheap forty years ago with the intention of fixing and re-selling them. That idea would have made a lot of money had some idiot not invented colour television just as he was getting down to work.

Gerald was out on his porch reviewing his life's lost opportunities, when Luke Richardson's sleek black Cadillac turned into the drive and came creeping towards him, pale headlights glowing like albino snake eyes. Some people you faced directly; others you just sensed until they broke through the surface like a huge boulder appearing in the middle of your best field. Luke Richardson, after the obligatory pause, got out of his car, closed the door deferentially as though Mammon himself was smoking a cigar in the back seat, and drew himself straight, patting at his trousers and shirt. He was a tall man, Luke Richardson, the kind who liked to get close and look down on you until you backed away. These days he was doing a lot of that: getting close to people, looking down on them, requesting their support for his run at the reeveship. Never said anything bad about Vernon, of course, but everyone knew how he'd tried to screw MaryLou after Vernon died. Also how MaryLou had managed to screw him in return and how Luke Richardson was now running for reeve to get back on top. Luke took off his sunglasses and carefully inserted them in the pocket of his shirt, grinning that big politician grin that made his eyes crinkle up like a shopping centre Santa Claus.

Gerald looked at Richardson's boots. They were dry and shiny, which meant that Luke hadn't yet located his stray lamb. He shook the big hand, soft and ripe, then watched how well Luke kept that smile on his face while he worked his mouth around the sad story of his missing car.

TWO

$\mathcal{T}$HE SUMMER CARL DISCOVERED THE old Motorola radio suspended beneath the dashboard of his father's truck, he would lie on his back on the bench seat, his feet hooked under the yellowish imitation-antler plastic steering wheel, and listen to country music while watching the clouds drift by the dust-spattered windshield. This strange activity made his heart pound uncomfortably; to allay the sensation he would unfold his baseball glove into a giant butterfly and place it across his chest. The glove converted the sound of his heartbeat into the slow throb of a deep bass drum which he'd join to the music, his eyebrows pinched together in concentration.

More than twenty years later, he was hearing that same deep throb and wearing that same look of pinched concentration as Chrissy — his X, as he sometimes thought of her, as in X marks the scar — told Carl of his father's latest escapade. There was a twist of amusement in her tone but for Carl, as always, news of his father came down heavy and unwanted.

"Drove it right into the lake," Chrissy said. "Gerald Boyce picked him out. They drank for six days, then Gerry wrapped him in a blanket and loaded him unconscious into the back of his tow truck. Delivered him to the R&R like that. Told them he hadn't wanted to embarrass his old friend by calling an ambulance."

"Great."

"He's back on the wagon now. Dr. Knight said he'd have a hangover for a month. That or die."

Chrissy was in the house on the Second Line Road, a few miles north of West Gull; Carl was three thousand miles west, halfway up Vancouver Island in a bunkhouse made by shoving two trailers together. But her voice was coming through so clear and perfect she could have been talking right into his ear, though he couldn't feel her breath, just remember it.

"How much was it worth?"

"Nothing now." She paused and in the silence Carl considered, as he had been ever since the beginning of their conversation, how unusual it was for Chrissy to be calling him. She sucked in her breath, the way she always did before letting out something she'd been holding on to. "If you come home, you can have half custody."

This was, Carl knew, a time to say the right thing. Or nothing at all.

"What does Lizzie want?"

"She could use a father."

"That could be me."

"You'll have to get a place."

"Thanks for telling me." Keep it light. "I was going to move in with you and Fred."

"Funny man. I meant you can't count on me to take care of you."

I never could, he almost replied. But stopped himself. The truth was that Chrissy had tried to take care of him, which was sometimes more than he had been able to do for himself.

"You still drinking?"

"Not much," Carl said.

"Fighting?"

"No."

"Well," Chrissy said. "I'll tell Lizzie you're on your way."

It came to him that the craving he had was like a wound. A line drawn by a knife through his flesh and soul. Everything had fled the sharp steel. Sometimes the yearning hunger grew more raw with every breath and if he tried to breathe deeply the knifeline opened so wide he felt dizzy.

Carl had been driving for four days, four days during which it seemed almost as many thousands of miles of highway had snaked between his eyes and coiled into his brain. He had the window open, the cab of his truck swirled with cool night air, the warm steady lick of rubber on pavement was running through him. He had his hands on the steering wheel in a way that unexpectedly reminded him of his father and he found himself recalling McKelvey in the kitchen, his hair a big unruly thatch, forehead burnt scarlet by the sun, swipes of grease on his T-shirt, wide lips wrapped around a cigarette while he looked mockingly across the table at Carl.

It was after midnight and to keep himself awake he had the radio on loud. Country music. Gospel songs. Hurting songs. Songs about men and women driving around in trucks and drinking and being sorry. All that hurting was enough to make you sad except that now it was also making him want to have a real woman in his truck, a real live voice full of smoke and fire and rough edges. Maybe it was Chrissy he wanted.

Ever since their conversation he'd been continuing it alone, picking it up and dropping it, explaining, complaining, blaming, saying goodbye a thousand different ways. Suddenly rounding a corner he was into the white glare of service-station light and he thought he saw a woman stepping out of the shadows, tall and wearing a billowy white shirt he couldn't quite see.

Carl pulled into the lot. There was no one there. Just oil-soaked air coming up from the gravel and the smell of grease from the still-open café.

Ice River, said the screen-door sign. Inside was a little of everything: fishing tackle, knives, magazines, groceries, a couple of shelves of clothes. He sat down at the counter feeling stunned. This was how it had always been when he dried out — sometimes his body would want a drink so much his circuits overloaded and he couldn't feel anything at all.

"Hungry?" asked the waitress.

Carl looked up. She had on a white apron and he realized he must have seen her outside, getting something from the trailer parked at the back of the lot. Close up she was everything but ethereal: she was wearing a hairnet over dark hair that was twisted in brightly coloured plastic curlers, and as she waited for Carl to make up his mind she started tapping her foot and twitching her mouth in time.

"Just coffee," Carl said. He'd skipped supper but couldn't interest himself in anything on the menu. Then he noticed a glass case with desserts and ordered a piece of blueberry pie with ice cream. It was years since he had seen a crust soaked through and stained purple with blueberry juice.

"Home-made," she said, bringing him what must have been a quarter of the pie. It tasted like home: sweet, sharp but no longer familiar.

On the way out he bought an Ice River T-shirt to give Lizzie and a shirt for himself so he'd have something clean. While she was entering the numbers into the cash register, the waitress asked him if he was going far.

"West Gull," Carl said, as though it was a place everyone must know.

"You want to gas up? Last chance for a hundred miles."

Hours later, still running on Ice River fuel, he was arrowing south from Northern Ontario to the rock-studded farmland that surrounds Long Gull Lake. He was back to thinking about the emptiness inside himself — the fear, the nervousness, the sometimes desperate craving that made his hands reach out for whatever could fill them. But as he got closer to home the landscape flooded into him and every moon-silhouetted tree, every silvery rock formation, every stretch of water glittering black with nightlight calmed and soothed him. He was looking at the moon, at the way it transformed the clouds into sculpted sand dunes that arched across the sky. Then there was a series of heavy thumps beneath the truck. In the red glare of his tail lights a raccoon lay motionless on the shoulder, its body torn open from neck to tail. As he pulled over and turned off the engine he was engulfed by a tidal wave of insect noise: cheeps, clicks, hums, whirrs, all supported by the slow rhythmic croaking of frogs. Carl got down on his knees and crawled under the truck. He lit a match — there was a long smear of blood along the exhaust, a patch of bloody fur on the muffler. When the match burned out Carl lay still for a moment.

In the distance he heard a car approaching. As it crested the hill its horn began to blare. For a moment the light caught his eyes and he thought the car was going to smash into the back of his truck. Its horn was still going when it passed. Carl could feel the side wind through his hair and slapping against the back of his neck.

"She asked for you," Chrissy had said. "She asks for you almost every day."

In the glove compartment was a stack of postcards from Lizzie held together by an elastic. He'd sent them to her at Christmas, stamped and addressed. For almost seven months they'd been floating back. "Love, xox, love, Lizzie." "Love from your daughter." "Goodbye for now."

The road and surrounding bush began to emerge in the dawn. Mist covered the swamps and lay in the hollows of the fields, and the pure light of morning played hide-and-seek with the hills and tall maples. When he came to the farm he stopped. The house, once fronted by a big garden that was supposed to feed them all winter, had been put into grass, spotted with baby poplars, pines and birdhouses. The house had been clad in metal siding and the Richardson Real Estate sign swung from a black post planted near the road.

Carl got out of his truck and stretched. He looked at the house where he'd been born and had lived until he and Chrissy got married and moved into their first place, the apartment above the West Gull barber shop. Away, he'd often thought that seeing the farm again would set off an explosion of anger or nostalgia. But now it just reminded him of his father lying on the kitchen floor, too drunk to move. His mother's absence. The reception after the funeral. His own child self that had gone missing from this revised and prettified landscape.

Back in the truck he zigzagged to a small road that ran beside a creek where he would be able to clean up without being seen. After he'd washed and shaved he sat looking at the moving water. On the surface were tiny rills, trails of bubbles, folds and curves that stayed constant as the water shaped itself to the rocks below. He could already feel himself coming back to West Gull the same way, fitting himself to everything that couldn't be changed.

Chrissy opened the door to him and her first thought was that he had shrunk. He was wearing jeans and a short-sleeved shirt, green and blue checks, creased across the middle and the sides as though it had just come out of the package five minutes earlier. He was standing in the doorway, frozen. She was, too. She hadn't expected it to hit her like this — just the sight of him. Then right before her eyes, in this little time bubble neither of them seemed able to break, he was growing back to normal, or was it just her heart trying to jump out of her body and into his.

Lizzie was coming down the stairs. Fred had already left for work.

"Well," Chrissy said, because she didn't want Lizzie to find them staring at each other like zombies.

"How are you?" he asked. She could see that his eyes, though apparently aimed at hers, were in fact slanting away, the way she used to see them do with strangers. Carl's eyes, when they really looked at you, were soft and unmoving — soft green-brown baby eyes that let you fall apart inside. Except when he was in fighting mode, and then they narrowed and turned grey; no person or thing wanted to be in Carl's way when he was fighting.

Carl offered her his hand.

"Good," she said. She took his hand. It was rough and sandpapery inside, the way it used to be. No special pressure, no hidden messages of love or violence. "We shook hands," she almost told Fred later but at the last minute stopped herself because she knew Fred wouldn't want to think of her touching Carl. And then she noticed his moustache; no wonder he had seemed smaller. Black and carefully trimmed, it made a precise line across the top of his mouth. She would tell Fred about the moustache. "Makes him look foolish," she would say, though in fact she was already getting used to it.

Lizzie had arrived beside her. She had Carl's eyes and they were on him now, drinking him in. He shifted his weight as though he was going to reach down to her, then changed his mind. Tiny motions Chrissy would not have noticed in anyone else, but being with Carl had tuned her to his microcosmic dances, his split-second jive steps disguised as ordinary breathing. And now, without thinking about it, she was on his wavelength again, tuned to the the exact movements of their bodies through space, suddenly uncomfortable in her clothes, wanting to brush back hairs that had strayed across her forehead, hearing and not hearing the beat Carl always lived to.

"I'm Carl. Do you remember me?"

"Sure I remember you," Lizzie said in a complicated voice Chrissy had never heard before, a voice inflected with winning and losing and ownership.

"We could go for a drive or something."

"I'd like to."

And then their backs were turned and they were walking away from her. Halfway across the grass towards the truck, Lizzie's hand came up and slid into Carl's. Chrissy was crying. She didn't know when she'd started. She was crying and for all she cared she might have been crying from the moment she opened the door to him. She wiped her eyes and by the time she looked out again Carl had his hands on Lizzie's waist and had hoisted her high in the air, lifting her while Lizzie kicked and laughed as though she were a baby and not seven years old.

"She stayed faithful," Chrissy thought. "Now she's getting her reward."

He opened the door for her and Lizzie jumped up into the seat, quickly, as though afraid to be left behind. When Carl got in his own side Lizzie had the glove compartment open and was looking through the postcards she'd sent him. Now he got his first real look at her: her hair, tied back in a ponytail — slightly frizzed the way it always got when it had just been washed — was darker than it used to be, almost black, but laced with burnished chestnut highlights from the sun. Her face had lengthened from round to oval; the tiny perfect baby teeth were now replaced in front, their new whiteness contrasting with her tanned skin. He didn't remember her long dark eyelashes being so thick, or most of all her eyes, a bright startling green he hardly recognized.

Meanwhile, not wanting her to feel stared at, he started up the truck and drove it to the turnaround at the machine shed. Where Chrissy's uncle's rusting tractor had once been parked was a new riding lawnmower. Carl resisted looking for other changes, kept his eyes resolutely forward as he glided back to the road.

"Where we going?" Lizzie asked as they turned onto the blacktop. She was leaning back now, totally at ease, her feet propped up on the dashboard, chewing a stick of gum from the package on the dash.

"See your grandfather, I guess." That had been his plan. Go into West Gull, get that part over with, his first time back after three years.

"Too early," Lizzie said. She pinched her nostrils and made a voice so like William McKelvey's that Carl had to laugh. "Never wake up before noon. Always hated breakfast."

"How about an ice cream?"

"The Dairy Queen doesn't open until ten."

"Well—"

"I want to show you my school. They got monkey bars last year. I'll teach you my tricks."

There was a new sign at the edge of town:

WEST GULL

pop. 684

Like Lizzie beside him, everything had prospered. Every house seemed to have had its trim painted, its siding replaced, its grass fertilized into a brighter more sparkling green.

He pulled to a stop in front of the West Gull Elementary. A low wide building, an oddity in town because it had been faced with yellow bricks instead of red. The old metal roof had been painted a bright blue that matched the shiny blue doors and windows; the effect was to make the whole school like an oversized plastic toy.

"Your grandmother used to teach there. Did you know that?"

"Lennie?"

"No, not your mother's mother. My mother. Elizabeth."

"Your mother," she sighed. "Were you ever in her class?"

"Once."

"Was she nice?" Lizzie's green eyes were slits in the sun.

And suddenly Carl could remember being Lizzie's age, staring at his hands on the desk, suddenly conscious of the way his nails were bitten down, inflamed. Raising his eyes to his mother and realizing she had a funny way of glancing at him every few seconds as though she thought no one else would notice. He remembered how uncomfortable it had been to have every kid in his class spend the whole day staring at his mother, how embarrassed he was if the least wisp of her hair was out of place, if her blouse was tucked in unevenly or the back of her skirt smudged with chalk. The way she stood at the blackboard, her behind swaying, the chalk squeaking. The way she had of sitting at her desk and sliding her glasses down her nose to read, as though she didn't even *care* what she looked like.

"I wouldn't want to be in my mother's class," Lizzie said. "Everyone would make fun of me."

"I know what you mean," Carl said. "No one ever lets you forget about your mother." Then Lizzie ran ahead to the play area, pulled herself up on the bars and began swinging along them, turning to him every few seconds with a proud but questioning smile.

At noon on the day Carl McKelvey came back to West Gull, Adam Goldsmith was standing in front of Richardson's New & Used. He didn't know Carl had returned, his eyes were half-closed, and he watched with his usual disinterest as Carl's truck turned in to park between a set of the newly painted yellow diagonals in front of the Timberpost Restaurant. Through the plastic windows of the truck's canopy Adam Goldsmith could see a jumble of furniture and cardboard boxes. When he was a child men would appear on the streets of West Gull, their shabby coats heavy with dirt. By nightfall they would be gone, Adam never knew where. Now it was young men in trucks packed with the remnants of their last stop, their last woman, their last job.

He had been thinking about Moses in the desert. The story told was that because he broke his magic staff, God had punished him by denying him the Promised Land. How could Moses have been so stupid? But there had been so many promises. The truth was that Moses had broken his staff on purpose. After a certain point a man wants to stay where he is. No one could say history had proven Moses wrong.

It was one of those brilliant mornings when the place a man most wants to be is outside soaking in the sun. Adam Goldsmith had made that choice. He was planted on the sidewalk letting the summer heat paralyze him, letting his mind drift from young men in trucks to the Depression to the wandering in the desert and that heavy ache in his arms and neck Moses had carrying those stone tablets down from the mountain, when the truck door opened and Carl stepped into the light. The jolt hit Adam in a single pulse which struck his chest so violently that he felt — he would have told Dr. Albert Knight except for reasons obvious and otherwise — he was going to collapse on his knees. That would have gone down in West Gull history: Adam Goldsmith, sixty-three-year-old accountant and possibly the most colourless man ever to live in West Gull, falling to his knees on the sidewalk in front of the car lot. "Did he start talking funny?" is what everyone would have asked. He could almost hear the contempt in their voices.

By the time he had consciously recognized Carl, Adam was already walking towards him. The last time Adam had seen Carl was three years ago in Kingston in a judge's chambers. Carl was sleekly obedient in the dark suit he'd bought for his mother's funeral, then worn to his wedding. His face was tense and pale, though not so pale as the white strip of skin at the bottom of his neck where his hair had been cut away in jail. Each time the judge or the prosecutor or his own lawyer spoke, Carl pursed his lips and leaned his head forward, as though to emphasize with what care and repentance he was listening. But Adam could see Carl's deference was not working in his favour. When Adam's turn came, he detailed how Richardson's New & Used would offer Carl a job and even put up a bond to guarantee his good behaviour. The judge looked unimpressed. Then the lawyer whispered to Carl and Carl offered to give up his half of Lizzie's custody and move away for what would have been the time of his probation.

You wouldn't believe this was the same boy who couldn't stay out of fights at hockey games or dances. Or the boy who had gone back to the house where he'd once lived with his lawfully wedded wife, invited her new-old boyfriend out on the lawn and tried to beat him to death with his fists. Or so Chrissy and Fred Verghoers had sworn in court. But Carl and Fred side by side made Adam think of David and Goliath, Carl being the former. Though it wasn't the first time they'd gone at it. That had been the night of the Richardsons' last New Year's party, a night that had begun full of promise, been punctuated by the fight and ended in a disaster Adam Goldsmith still shrank from thinking about.

Standing beside his truck, Carl resembled neither the biblical David nor the scared boy in the judge's office. He was too controlled, too worried, too *cured* of whatever had driven him. His moustache rode on his upper lip like something he'd bought in a store. Twenty-eight years old he would be. Trust an accountant to know the numbers. His eyes still had the same flicker as his mother's. And his cheeks had developed faint vertical seams, threatening to deepen into lines that jump from scowl to smile, also like his mother's. Or maybe they signified whatever Carl must have armed himself with in order to return.

"Good to see you."

"Well, I'm back."

Up close Carl's face took on shadows of uncertainty. "Good to see you," Adam said again. "How's your father?"

"Haven't made that visit yet. What do I owe you for hauling the car out of the lake?"

Carl's mouth twitched with a forbidden smile. Adam was tempted to tell him how Luke had screamed when he'd found out what had happened. How he'd threatened to call the police until reminded how funny the whole story would look on the television news: would-be reeve Luke Richardson is prosecuting a man for joy-riding a car into Dead Swede Lake on the very farm the would-be reeve had bought from under him. "That would be Dead Reeve Lake for you," Adam had summarized but Luke was a man who preferred his own jokes.

"Don't worry about it," Adam now said to Carl and, unable to resist, "we have Dead Reeve Lake insurance."

Carl looked startled. "Thanks, Adam."

"Luke's idea. He's glad you're back."

Carl just stood there soaking up the sun. Adam didn't mind that. Most people in West Gull were full of fake friendliness towards him because he was Luke Richardson's business manager and to cross him was to cross Luke. But behind all the oil and the devotion were the smirks: there's soft old Adam Goldsmith, the sexless eternal bachelor, Luke Richardson's court eunuch, Flora Goldsmith's boy, the boy who spoke in tongues when he was young and then, before disappearing to university, became a shy reedy teenager who walked with his head down and took to riding his bicycle around the country roads because his mother never thought to buy him a car and his father got killed in the war.

That reedy teenager had shot up to well over six feet, had developed a respectable bulge around the belly and was, as Adam Goldsmith kept telling himself, sixty-three years old. Old enough to have been part-owner and manager of the New & Used long enough to drive whatever he wanted. On the day Carl came back to West Gull, Adam was wearing the pale yellow cotton suit that was his summer uniform. With his jacket slung over his shoulder, his collar unbuttoned and his tie yanked loose, Adam Goldsmith looked like what he was: an aging member of the small and aging West Gull business community; the tall dreamy son of his own scarcely imaginable tall dreamy father; the bookish mainstay of the West Gull Memorial Library; a man as familiar to the West Gull streets as an old pair of shoes.

Now that they had run out of conversation, Carl was remembering that he used to take Adam for granted — until it struck him that Adam Goldsmith must be a homosexual, no doubt with a secret life down in the Kingston bars. What Carl couldn't understand was why Adam stayed in West Gull. "I suppose Luke put his balls somewhere for safekeeping," McKelvey had once said, and Carl had seen his mother throw his father one of those looks she gave him when he got drunk and nasty, then walk out of the room. She hadn't minded Adam. He'd often been to the school for meetings of the library committee, and Carl would come in from after-school hockey to find them cataloguing books and drinking tea and chattering away like two old ladies. After Elizabeth died, it turned out she'd made Adam her executor and left her school insurance money in trust for Carl to receive when he turned twenty-five — a little twist on the safekeeping theme McKelvey didn't appreciate. All of that money was put away for Lizzie now.

"Do you have somewhere to stay?" Adam asked. Carl had forgotten the way Adam talked to you, as though looking at an imaginary bird perched on your shoulder. Carl was free to look at Adam's eyes which weren't looking at his: they were light blue, a blue that in this intense July light was almost transparent, with pupils so narrow and densely black you had to wonder if they were the real Adam Goldsmith, tiny irreducible bits of flint usually covered by his pale bland exterior. And then before Carl could answer: "We'll go over to the real-estate office. Get Doreen to fix you up."

Carl knew he had to be back in West Gull by the way Doreen Whittier's sallow face turned to brittle porcelain as he came in the office door, as though despite the fact that he was a grown man, he must be looking for something to steal or break. She had been ahead of him in high school but he remembered seeing her hanging around the rink. Now she was wearing Ben Whittier's wedding band and was the kind of woman he used to call ma'am until Chrissy told him he sounded like a hillbilly.

As soon as Adam followed and explained what Carl was looking for, in the voice he would have used if he needed it for himself, her face snapped into a different shape. Adam had transformed him from a worthless McKelvey to visiting royalty.

"Would you be wanting it starting next month?"

"Any time," Carl said. "Tonight would be fine." She gave him a surprised look but Adam was looming over her, smiling.

"Come back after lunch and I'll have something." She turned to her papers as though he had already gone.

On the street Carl bought a newspaper and went next door to the Timberpost. He had known coming back would be difficult but he hadn't anticipated the feelings it was bringing on, this small-boy-caught-in-the-act shame combined with a distance he had never had, a second self that was calmly watching. He was grateful the waitress was someone he'd never seen. When she gave him the menu he realized he needed something more than coffee and ordered the all-day breakfast: three eggs over easy, home-fried potatoes, whole-wheat toast with strawberry jam. They arrived on a white oval platter with a maroon border, sitting in small pools of grease. Between his toast and his coffee cup he had the neatly folded Classified section of the newspaper. He began looking through the advertisements for cottages and waterfront homes. There was no doubt that for half a million dollars he could get a pretty nice place. Two or three acres on the water, big trees, a house with a stone fireplace and a family room where he and Lizzie could watch television and play computer games, or whatever people did in their family rooms. His eyes scanned further down the column and then he saw it:

Country hobby waterfront jewel. Tastefully renovated century home near tourist town offers rural playground for young family. Safe swimming in Dead Swede Lake, outbuildings that could be converted for offices or horses, drained fields, vintage maple bush.

The waitress was standing over him.

"Anything wrong?" he asked.

"I just wanted to know if you were finished."

Carl looked down. He had consumed the eggs and potatoes without noticing, even wiped the platter clean with his
toast. "I'll have the same," Carl said.

"The same?"

"The same as I had before."

The waitress took away his plate and refilled his cup. Carl
turned to the personals.

Mature anglo woman, two grown children, would welcome serious relationship with financially secure gentleman who enjoys nature. Small handicaps okay.

Fifty-six-year-old widow. Generous build. Seeking man
five-foot-eleven or taller. Any age. Must have full hair.
Willing to relocate if first meetings show possible compat-
ibility. No nudists or artists, please.

Striking woman, looks half her age, seeks vigorous male
companion. Must be gregarious and handy around the
house. Send recent colour photos and astrological chart.
If no chart, send date, hour and exact place of birth. All
nationalities welcome.

That was what he and Lizzie could do in the family room:
search the papers for a suitable companion to share their
estate. But Lizzie was probably expecting him to get back with
Chrissy. "You going to stay long?" she had asked and when
Carl had nodded and squeezed her shoulder she'd said, as
though he weren't there, "I wonder where he's going to live."

"I'll find a place," Carl supplied. "Then you can come and
stay with me whenever you want to."

"Marbles too?"

"Is that your cat?"

"Yes." So formal. So terrified of him but needing him so much. She looked like Chrissy and yet she didn't. Or maybe she looked like him. Then, as though reading his mind, she'd said, "I need you to be here."

"Good. I need you." That was after the monkey bars. They were sitting in the truck eating ice cream and holding hands. Like a first date. He was afraid to hug her, he didn't want to scare her.

She was the one who'd made all the moves. Like putting her hand to his face to touch his chin. "You cut yourself shaving. Mom sometimes cuts her legs." Which gave Carl the unsummoned memory of Chrissy in the bathtub, tan line across the tops of her small white breasts whose nipples used to aim slightly upward — anti-aircraft guns he'd call them — one long leg stretched out, with the heel on the side of the bathtub, turned out so she could get at her calf. "You look like a porno movie," he'd told her. "You wish," she'd laughed, extending her other leg and arching her back.

Lizzie had let her hand linger on his chin. She was trying things out and Carl wanted to make it easy for her. "See you tomorrow," he'd said when she finally slid across the seat and opened the door. Watching her walk so unsure and lonely across the grass, he decided that tomorrow he'd go with her right to the door.

> Mature white male, young forties. Financially secure. Seeks to retire from life's cares with beautiful, uninhibited, submissive, old-fashioned woman, age twenty to twenty-five. Education not necessary.

Retired widower with two young children is looking for
open-hearted caregiver, any weight. Serious replies only.

Carl had bought a pen with the newspaper, to mark any
real-estate or job advertisements that might be useful. Now he
found himself underlining parts of the personals. *Small handicaps okay. Any age. Education not necessary.* He lit a cigarette,
began writing in the margin.

White trash male, late twenties. Seeks understanding
woman to do all the work. Nursing experience not required
but would be helpful. Don't be afraid to apply if you're rich,
beautiful and lonely. If ex-wife, must be willing to offer
bond to guarantee good behaviour.

He was just considering what kind of bond he might have
in mind when a shadow fell across his table. As he raised his
eyes a big man slid into the booth. Luke Richardson. "Doreen
told me you're looking for a place to rent."

Carl nodded.

Luke Richardson leaned back and squinted at Carl. "Your
father used to take me hunting on the other side of the mountain. I knew the way but he knew the deer." Carl remembered
his father coming home one night and saying he'd spent half
the day dragging a deer down the mountain. The shoulders of
his jacket had been stained with blood and he'd smelled of wet
fall leaves and whiskey.

The waitress brought the bill. Luke folded it up, put it in
his pocket.

"There's a place I could show you."

"I'll pay for the eggs," Carl said.

But without answering him, Luke pushed ahead. "My treat, welcome home." He stood on the sidewalk, adjusting his tie, his jacket, hitching his belt, surveying the street up and down. "My car's over there," Luke said, pointing to the dealership garage. "Needed an oil change. Should be ready now."

Luke put his hand on Carl's shoulder and Carl had to stop himself from moving. "You know, the Richardsons and the McKelveys go back a long way." Carl, with the bigger man's hand heavy on his shoulder, felt he was now being turned into a schoolboy, someone who could be lectured in front of the whole town. He was trembling inside and as Luke kept talking he had the sudden urge to grab his shirt and push him through the plate-glass window of the Timberpost Restaurant. "It can't be easy, coming home," Luke finished, then took his hand away and started across the street.

Carl watched Luke go into one of the bays, then come out with a mechanic who led him to a big black Cadillac. Soon they were driving away from the mountain and the hilly countryside Carl knew best towards the flatter farmland to the south.

"It's out of town," Luke said, "but I figured you wouldn't mind. It's furnished and looks good outside but it needs some work on the plumbing. You could handle that, couldn't you?"

"Sure."

"You just get whatever you need at the hardware store, put it on my account. I'll give you a lease if you like it. Not for ever, but a couple of years. Give you a chance to settle in for a while."

All the sideroads had been given signs and names. There were new houses, too; big bow-windowed homes with attached double garages and landscaped grounds with rock gardens and large carefully tended lawns that looked like advertisements for riding mowers.

Luke Richardson drove slowly, like a man roaming about his own property. About five miles south of town he turned west along a paved sideroad. After a few more minutes he pulled into the drive of a green-painted clapboard house with one of his realty signs on the front lawn.

The house was smaller than it looked from the road; the downstairs had just a kitchen with an attached pantry on one side, a long narrow sitting room on the other. Cramped under sharply angled eaves were two bedrooms and a bathroom. The toilet was in the bathtub and someone had started to tear the sink out of the wall. "The plumbing froze here last winter," Luke explained. "I got the repairs started but then the guy took off. You could finish. You might need to rip out the floor, too. You up to that?"

"Depends how fancy you want it."

"Plywood, with vinyl on top. No use getting Italian tile and a Jacuzzi for this place."

"What about the heat?"

"There's a new furnace. I had it put in last spring."

Luke showed him the kitchen, then the basement. It had a fieldstone foundation and the mortar between the stones was crumbling and riddled with ant tunnels. The floor was dirt with a drainage trench down the middle. The new furnace had rust along the bottom and a big dent on one side. "Took it out of another place," said Luke. "Waste not, want not."

Outside again, Luke took down the sign, then pointed out the eavestroughs that needed reattaching, the garden with its crop of nettles and burdock, the rust-fuzzy mower in the garage that could use a new roof if he got around to it. But all the time Carl was trying to imagine himself there with Lizzie. What would they do all day? Would she follow him around the house while he soldered and hammered? Stand in the backyard and play catch with herself? Have picnics? When he got the tools for the bathroom floor, maybe he could make her a dollhouse. He'd built her one before, when she was just learning to crawl. She used to lie in front of it, peering into its empty rooms as though watching a movie of imaginary people.

When they returned to town Luke parked at the side of his car lot. "I suppose you'll be wanting a job."

"I thought I'd go back to the lumber yard. They're usually short this time of year."

"Boyce's? Vernon died, you know. Took a heart attack eating one of those Mexican-spiced veggie burgers at the Kiwanis barbecue. Terrible thing. Then MaryLou sold out to the Allnew chain. Got a new manager, too. Your old friend, Fred Verghoers."

Carl looked down at his hands. The lumber yard had been his plan. He'd always been comfortable with wood. In British Columbia he'd worked with a logging operation, piling underbrush and generally making things look pretty after the big chainsaws and tree cutters had done their damage. Cosmetic but not a bad way to get some thinking done. Over the last year he had developed a whole script for himself: back in West Gull he would start at Boyce's yard, find some sources for buying good wood; then maybe he'd go in with Ray Johnson, start up a little side business making decks and screened-in porches; eventually he'd quit the yard altogether and he and Ray would have their own company putting up cottages and retirement houses. Just to think of it brought on the fragrance of newly cut cedar.

"Fellow came to me last year and asked if he could build this little addition." Richardson pointed to a small matching extension at the end of the supermarket. Above the door was a sign: THE MOVIE BARN. "The girl who used to work the main shift just moved to Toronto. Pays almost as much as Allnew and you won't freeze your fingers off in the winter. There's a couple of high-school kids part-time. But you'll be in charge, keep things organized. And in the winter it'll be just you, except when you need help on holidays or busy weekends."

They crossed to the real-estate office where Carl signed the lease. Then, unable to put it off any longer, he turned his truck towards the West Gull R&R.

During his last year in high school, when all the senior students were doing local history projects, Carl had chosen as his subject what would eventually become the R&R but was then still the Richardson mansion. The core of the structure had been built by Caleb Richardson, a blacksmith who arrived in 1837 in what was then the mere hamlet of West Gull. Lucas Richardson, the logging baron, was Caleb's oldest son and Luke Richardson's great-great-grandfather; he had a son, Lucas Jr., who took over the house and carried on the logging tradition, making his fortune cutting primal white pine so tall and straight it was sold at the Kingston shipyards for the manufacture of masts. In 1886 Lucas Jr.'s son, Allan Caleb Richardson, started the custom of throwing his home open to half the county every New Year's Eve; the parties would be an annual event for exactly one hundred years.

Allan Caleb Richardson's years in the mansion, years when its magnificence was well known to men in top hats and ladies in layered frocks, years during which genuine European paintings in gilded frames were added to the Great Hall, the dining room furnished with a grand piano once owned by an Austrian prince, the kitchen expanded and refurbished with the latest in black cast-iron stoves, a special bread oven, sets of matching ceramic sinks half the size of bathtubs for washing the vertiginous stacks of dishes generated by lavish dinner parties, years that flowed from the dizzying heights of Queen Victoria's reign down to the rat-infested trenches of the Great War — those years were West Gull's idyll of peace and prosperity. In that golden age, logging and farming kept bellies full and money rolling in, barns and pastures thronged with sleek contented livestock almost begging to be roasted and laid out on the table, fields were green and fertile and milk foamed with butterfat. Photographs from that time still hang in the Great Hall, and the largest of all shows Allan Caleb Richardson and his wife, Eileen, in the midst of their grinning liquor-happy guests, gay and stout with the fat of the land, the muscle and sinew and blood of their hundreds of workers.

Then came the drumbeats of war. Colonel Sam Parker galloped across the country on his toy horse handing out his toy rifles, and of the 187 township men who went to war, half were sucked into the French trenches, chewed up by shrapnel and hunger, pickled in mud, shredded by bullets. The rest came home as they could. Arms or legs missing, metal plates in their heads, lungs scoured by mustard gas, the real and imaginary memories of their collective past transformed into a dark nightmare they would never stop dreaming. That, too, is recorded in the photographs: a small train at the West Gull station house disgorging groups of men in uniform. Some walked tall, others hobbled on crutches. On stretchers were two bandaged shapes who'd survived seven thousand miles of cart and sea and train in order to die at home.

From 1921 on, the photographs are organized into annual albums guarding memorable images from each year along with photos of the New Year's party itself. As the years pass, the backgrounds begin to include automobiles, radios, electric lights, once an airplane in a field — the whole glorious parade of man-made splendours. In the 1940 album Carl found a full-page portrait of William McKelvey. Sixteen years old, raw wrists protruding from a suit that fit him six inches ago, lanky face still waiting for its flesh, he is caught with his eyes open wide, a startled wild animal with his thoughts wiped clean under the pressure of this historic moment. Another picture shows him more relaxed, posing with a few other youths who'll soon step out to the stable to drink and talk about the one thing on their minds these days: this new war and whether it will end before they get sent there; this new war and whether it will be like that other one — the Great War — the war that left widows still young enough to take to the dance floor before midnight; the war that left a list of names so long it required ten minutes to be read out loud every November 11 at the Remembrance Day assemblies at their schools. They'll drink and then they'll drink some more and imagine themselves shot, gnawed and buried, nothing left but living ghosts who might come home to hear their names mispronounced by a bunch of kids who aren't theirs.

After the final New Year's bash, the Richardsons moved out of the old mansion into the new house Luke had built by the lake. Then following the instructions of his great-great-grandfather's will, Luke turned it into the West Gull R&R, a monumental sarcophagus for the living where those who once danced became paying guests, music provided by an orchestra of pocked leathery lungs wheezing towards the millennium accompanied by a chorus of drug-induced gurgles, moans and muffled cries from dreams of long-ago childhoods, memory buried deep in hairless skulls, mutating cells, dreams of nights when the forest held them and their skins were young and the cries they made were not desperate calls to a mouldy time now disintegrating in the soft cheese of their decaying brains, but cries and prayers to the gods of summer and desire.

Two of those lungs belonged to William McKelvey. Back from his big splash, the very picture of self-satisfaction and serenity, McKelvey sat on the porch of the West Gull R&R smoking a cigarette and staring into his newspaper. Everything on the street seemed frozen in place: the crystal sky, the massed leaves, the big mansions with their yellowing sheers tied open to the afternoon sun. As Carl approached, McKelvey struggled to his feet and started to speak before interrupting himself to cough. His hand rose to his mouth, the back thick with brown stains. *You are old, Father William.* "How's the boy?"

"Not bad," Carl said. "How are you?"

For an answer McKelvey spread out his arms so he could be inspected, then indicated that Carl should sit down in the chair beside him. "So. You're back."

"I'm back."

"Visit the kid?"

"Saw her this morning. She's grown. She says she comes to see you."

"Christine brings her."

Christine. Once he'd called about Lizzie and she'd had to call him back. An hour later someone had shouted out to him, "Hey Carl, there's a *Christine* on the phone for you." And his heart had started to race as though it were ten years before and

Chrissy was going to talk in that hoarse little whisper she had when they were arranging to spend the night catting.

"How long you staying?"

"For a while," Carl said. "Luke Richardson rented me the old Balfer place."

"What about the old McKelvey place?" his father said. "He's got his sign out front. Made me want to puke. They covered it in metal and now it looks like a white cookie tin waiting to be squashed."

His eyes were closed. The way they'd been the night Carl told him it was over with Chrissy. When his eyes had opened again, he'd started shouting that Carl was cursed like every McKelvey — cursed to drink and fight and lose or kill his woman and Carl should be thankful at least that he'd had a daughter and not a son.

Now William McKelvey put his newspaper down and reached into his fishing vest for a package of cigarettes. His hands were shaking.

"Liver," McKelvey said. "Liver, kidneys, pancreas, stomach, gall bladder — the whole thing." He squeezed the package open, managed to extract a cigarette and get it into his mouth. "Like it's one big septic tank in there, right? Pour shit in one end, clean water flows out the other." He reached into another of his pockets, found a Zippo, flipped it open and watched the flame dance while his hand trembled. "Then it gets plugged up, right? Doesn't work any more. Put shit in one end, shit comes out the other. Or alcohol. You're supposed to wake up the next morning sober. I wake up like this, only worse. Takes two weeks before I can walk a straight line."

"You lost the habit," Carl said. "Good thing or you'd be dead." His father's face and eyes were tinged with yellow. The way they'd been when he'd collapsed and the doctor had told him to quit drinking or he'd be dead in six months. McKelvey, being McKelvey, had circled the day on the calendar and kept on. At the end of six months, the yellow had turned orange and he was staggering around the farm like a walking cesspool. Carl had come down one morning to find his father lying on the kitchen floor, panting like a cow in labour.

"Coffee," McKelvey had commanded.

Carl had made him coffee, put it on the floor beside him. Then he'd taken down the bottle of brandy and set it beside the coffee. "Go ahead. It's fifteen minutes before I have to go to work. If you die first I can get the day off."

"Fuck you," McKelvey had said.

That was when they still had the farm. Or what was left of it. All the stock gone except for one bull and the few cows it serviced to give them some calves to sell for beef. A couple of tractors they spent most of their time repairing so they could get in enough hay to winter the cattle.

"You should have seen this place in my father's day," William McKelvey would say. At some point, Carl didn't know how or when, his father had lost it — *it* being the ability to get up every morning and make the farm a farm instead of a mass of unpredictable vegetation and broken machinery, the ability to go out there and do whatever had to be done instead of wandering about the countryside, a bottle in his pocket, or sitting at the kitchen table tied to his coffee pot and the newspaper. "I could have done it with her," McKelvey told Carl, and Carl first thought he meant if Elizabeth had lived. Then he realized that McKelvey meant not only her presence but her cooperation, he meant he could have done it if she'd stayed at home instead of going out to work — he could have done it if she had done it for him.

"You want coffee?" The door had opened and a girl was standing beside them holding a tray with two full cups, containers of sugar and milk. She was short, black-haired, almost pretty, and she was smiling down at McKelvey.

"Meet my boss," McKelvey said complacently. "Her name is Moira and I mostly do what she tells me."

"My father," Carl said, nodding at McKelvey.

"One of my favourites," Moira said. She had a quiet voice and as she set down the tray Carl could almost see her judging him, trying to make sense out of the fact that not only was William McKelvey his father, but he William McKelvey's son.

Carl McKelvey looked out at his truck. Being born William McKelvey's son was like being born with a limp or a blind eye or a birthmark on the face. "I'll be seeing you," Carl said. He stood up and started across the lawn. Now he was really back. Carl McKelvey, the McKelvey boy, another fuck-up McKelvey whose fists moved faster than his brain, always ready to lash out or wrap themselves around a nearby bottle; after everything that had happened he was back and pretty soon he'd probably either be in jail or in hospital. One certain thing: he had a long way to go before he'd be splayed out like his father on a fat wooden chair with a pretty girl to pat his head and bring him coffee.

Later that night, his first in the Balfer place — trying to drive out the ghosts with the smell of cooking, the sound of his own voice, his boots on the floor, the disorganized pile of possessions he was unloading into the centre of the living room — he wondered how it would be to have a woman here, what kind of wild echo that woman's voice might find in the empty rooms.

The truth was, thinking about women he had never met was a way of avoiding Chrissy: the way she'd looked opening the door to him, her eyes larger, more liquid than they used to be; her tawny hair cut shorter; her lips pale, full, lips he'd kissed for the first time on a New Year's Eve, kissed while he was stealing a dance with her from Fred Verghoers, kissed then kept his lips on hers through the whole song and when it was over they were sealed together, run into one another like melted candles.

More than three years had passed since, following the last and worst fight with Chrissy, he had driven to the army surplus store in Kingston, bought himself a giant cardboard suitcase, stuffed it with the contents of the bottom drawer of the big maple dresser Chrissy's uncle had given them as a wedding present. Three *long* years, he would say in those imaginary conversations he had with himself or Chrissy, rambling interviews he would conduct while driving his truck or punching holes for new trees in the grainy soil of the forest floor. Three *long* years, he would say, the *he* who believed fate, alcohol and an uncontrolled temper had set him and Chrissy on separate roads, roads that would converge as soon as his sins were atoned for, the devil bottle put aside, the temper mastered by calm reflection on the pulse of the universe, or failing that, the fact that its main victims were himself and his daughter. But no matter which of his various selves held the floor, those years *had* been long, and the more time that passed the more cut loose and adrift he felt, unable to remember being in sight of shore, unable to remember if shore existed or if its memory was merely invented to give geography to his loneliness.

After leaving Chrissy he moved into a half-finished lakeside cottage with Ray Johnson from the lumber yard. They'd played together on the West Gull Junior Hornets for a couple of years before graduating to the Hornets proper — two-thirds of a second line where he provided the speed, the determination and sometimes the craziness it took to get the puck to the net where Ray could always be found holding off the enemy with his elbows.

Chrissy had told him that she was sick of his drinking and that now he could drink all he wanted. He had wanted to drink a lot, or at least enough to make a bridge across darkness to sleep and to make him sleep deeply enough that he didn't wake up until light.

Eventually that bridge crumbled and in the middle of the night sleep would desert him. Those were the times he had gone to bed hammered but woke up even drunker. So nauseated he could no longer lie still, he would get to his feet only to lose his balance on the way to the bathroom, bouncing off the walls, grabbing furniture to keep from falling on his face. Trembling and feverish, breathing the darkness to keep himself alive, he would turn stone-cold sober while thinking that if he actually *did* manage to drink himself to death not a single person in the universe would think anything except that Carl McKelvey had got what he wanted.

"You ever hear of Socrates?" Chrissy had once shouted at him and he had immediately thought of the picture of the white-bearded man in the fat russet book she used to prop up her lamp at university. "He said all knowledge is self-knowledge. If that's true you don't know dick. Did you ever think of that?"

Chrissy had been bending over the couch, trying to change Lizzie. Carl snatched Lizzie away and yelled that Chrissy was "about as much mother as a half-ton truck." Seeing her fury, he thought he'd hit the nail on the head but afterwards, repeating it to himself, he wondered exactly what he had meant. And then for some reason he asked himself how much mother his own mother had been. All this while holding Lizzie in the crook of his arm, swaying on his heels like a boxer about to bounce off the ropes, hurtle into the centre of the ring swinging. Hurricane Carl.

Lizzie was crying.

"Give her to me."

"No."

"For Christ's sakes, listen to her cry. Can't you tell you're scaring her? Or is that how *your* father was, just scaring the piss out of you to make sure you'd end up like him?"

He was holding Lizzie, petting the side of her face, drawing his finger along the soft skin under her chin. She stopped crying, reached up with both her hands to grab at his finger.

"She's not scared of me."

Chrissy just shook her head and went into the kitchen. A few minutes later she came out and said, "Lunch," her voice high and chipper, absolutely fake. Lunch. And he'd taken Lizzie into the kitchen and sat at the table eating scrambled eggs and toast while Chrissy fed Lizzie in her rabbit-decal-covered high chair, talking to both of them in her high fake voice as though she were some weird kind of television hostess who had invited them onto her program for a meal.

When Lizzie was born, Fred was the first to send a present; most men wouldn't even *think* of such a thing, Chrissy had noted. And every time there was a dance or a party and Fred had a new girlfriend, Chrissy was the first one to get introduced. "Still burns, still yearns," Ray had said to Carl about Fred, and sometimes Carl would catch Fred giving him the look, as though taking his measure.

By the time Carl had been living at Ray's long enough to start feeling like his father, Ray told him Fred had ditched his latest cheerleader, the one he'd been parading around all summer, and had moved in with Chrissy in the house on the Second Line.

THREE

*T*HE DAY CARL MCKELVEY RETURNED was the day Ned Richardson went to pay a call at Allnew Building Supplies. He parked under the big maple and slid over to the passenger seat of his truck so he could comb his hair in the visor mirror. Part of the passenger seat was patched with strips of red plastic tape which was the final chapter of another story — the sad tale of Ned Richardson and Lu-Ann Bolger. Once romantically entangled in what he considered an almost-marriage, Ned had lost Lu-Ann over an unfortunate mistake with an axe. He'd had the axe in the truck because he'd been limbing the cedar bush that morning. When he and Lu-Ann drove to town they had such an argument about her cutting her hair that when she slammed out of the truck and marched towards the hairdresser, temper coincided with carelessness: he took the axe from behind the seat and buried it right where she'd been sitting. Even as the axe made a satisfying slice through the simpering beige leatherette, Ned regretted it.

When Lu-Ann returned she saw the stuffing oozing out of the slit like ten inches of last year's shaving cream. "You expect me to sit on that? What happened?"

"I was going to fix it after you apologized," Ned said.

"How'd you do that anyway? Take an axe to it?"

"I guess," Ned replied.

"I'll say," Lu-Ann said, slamming the door and walking away, as it turned out, for ever. Ned had waited a few seconds, for his dignity, then went over to the hardware store and bought a roll of red plastic tape — the kind you put on your bicycle or jeans to be visible in the dark. He fixed the seat, then stood in the street waiting for Lu-Ann to come back.

That had been a few weeks ago. Now the only thing he could call his own was this truck. Which wasn't much for a Richardson, Ned considered, especially given what he'd one day have. But that would be then. This was now. Now he was twenty-three years old and so broke his wallet felt thin in his back pocket. So broke that he was sitting on his taped seat, combing his hair and using his spit to wipe the dirt off his face so he could ask Fred Verghoers for a job.

"Come on, shitface," Ned encouraged himself, then slid out of his truck and marched towards Allnew. His heart was going like a machine gun. A Richardson walking into Allnew to beg for a job. If Luke could see him. Ned only had to imagine the contempt twisting his father's lips to keep on.

Fred Verghoers was on a stool behind a large counter. He was wearing the red and gold vest all the employees had, except that Fred's had a little white strip that read MANAGER sewn onto his pocket.

Fred was looking something up for a customer — Arnie Kincaid, the insurance man. Arnie was about a hundred and twenty years old.

"I wanted to talk to you," Ned announced. Arnie's big frog eyes opened up behind his glasses.

"Hello, Ned," said Arnie. "How are you doing?"

"Pretty good," Ned said.

"You doing some building out at your uncle's?"

Why did Arnie Kincaid need to be here? The last thing Ned wanted was Fred to be reminded that he already had a job. Not exactly a job, more like a sentence; because of the various ways he'd disgraced himself at home he'd been exiled to his uncle's farm to play nursemaid to old Alvin.

Fred was looking at him curiously. It was now or never.

"I came in to see if you were short someone," Ned said. "Being the summer. I wondered if you'd have room for someone to help out."

Fred rose to his feet. His big shoulders bulged out of his vest, his broad tanned arms were folded. Since he had declared for reeve, Fred talked as though someone was writing down his pronouncements.

"I don't know," Fred said, sounding surprisingly undecided. Ned's heart jumped with hope. He couldn't have believed he had that much hope inside him. "I guess not. We're okay for now."

Ned flushed. "Billy Boyce told me you were looking for someone."

Fred turned away but kept talking, his voice again amazingly uncertain. "I might have been looking for someone who could handle the work. Someone reliable."

"If I'm late, you can fire me."

Now Fred and Arnie were looking him over as though he were a piece of meat. That's what a Richardson was. A big rotting piece of meat that everyone wanted to bury. They couldn't bury Luke because of what he'd do to them if they tried, so that left him. The son. The heir. The lame-duck prince.

"Maybe I'll think about it," Fred toyed. "Why don't you come back next week?"

Ned turned and walked out. His shirt was soaked through and when he climbed into his truck, his back stuck to the seat. His knees were sore, as though he'd crawled across the asphalt. He wheeled out of the parking lot, stepped on the gas. A few miles and he was driving down the Second Line Road past Fred's place. His house looked like an advertisement for his own store. Bright new paint. Carefully trimmed shrubs and a circle of flowers. Everything but a pissing angel on the front lawn. What Fred deserved was to have a match put to the whole thing. The way Fred's eyes had stayed fixed on him while he talked, until he just turned away as though he couldn't be bothered to watch Ned embarrass himself by begging. *"Why don't you come back next week?" Why don't you go eff yourself?*

He turned off the Second Line and headed back towards town. Ten minutes later he was in the kitchen with his mother.

"I was going to come out to see you today," she chirped. Amy, everyone called her, short for Amaryllia. She'd just got her hair dyed her usual summer blonde — streaked as always — but her high-fashion hair only emphasized the weary way her skin had begun to fold around her eyes and mouth.

"I asked Fred Verghoers for a job at Allnew today."

"Your father would be very upset if you worked there."

Allnew was part of a chain owned by a Toronto consortium that MaryLou Boyce had sold to at the same time she was pretending to work out a deal with Luke. Now Allnew was West Gull's biggest landlord and biggest employer. Luke had fought against a permit for the expansion of their premises and when they succeeded he announced he was going to get himself elected reeve, just to keep them in check. That was when Fred Verghoers announced his own political intentions.

"I'm not even allowed to live in my own house," Ned said. "I don't see why Luke should be telling me where to work." Luke. That's what he called his father now, like everyone else.

"You're better off at Alvin's."

"I'd be better off with a real job and my own place. Do what I want when I want."

"What did Fred say?"

"It looks good. I'll probably start next week."

"You want brown toast or white?" The moment he'd come in Amy had led him to the kitchen, started strips of bacon in the oven for his favourite, a BLT. Now the kitchen smelled of grilled bacon, the odour so sharp it made Amy want a cup of coffee. The boy was raw, the way Luke had been when she met him. But where Luke had been looking to take on the world, this boy had something broken inside. You could see it in his every movement, hear it in his voice; that broken note had been there from the very beginning — as an infant calling for her in the night, from the moment he was born, that first cry, like one of those otherworldly wails you read about in the tabloids that make you think Martians or someone must have planted an alien in your belly except it was just Ned and his weird cracked cry wobbling through the house.

That evening Ned was the one to hear unwanted noises, the faraway rumble of motors, a mumbled conversation he knew must be the wind as it swirled around, the voices of strangers mixed with the clacking of poplar leaves, the branches of the big maple as they rubbed against each other. Even knowing the sounds were nothing but highway, trees and breeze, Ned went outside to look down the drive at his truck to see if someone had come by with a case of beer. Or the hundred dollars Billy Boyce owed him. But his truck was alone in the last shreds of twilight, slowly fading into the darkness.

Feeling restless he turned back inside and went into the kitchen. Alvin was in his room upstairs, installed in front of his television, green plaid blanket spread over his knees. Eventually he would fall asleep and when Ned crept in to turn off the television the old man would be slumped in the leather rocker, clutching his blanket. Meanwhile the night nurse would have arrived. Ned was free to read, watch the downstairs TV, drive into town and get into whatever trouble he could with an empty wallet — as long as he was back by the time his uncle called for breakfast.

Instead Ned wandered into the pantry where the broom closet had been long ago converted into a gun cabinet. The key was in the lock. Ned opened it up, tensing to the odour of powder and gun oil. At the top was a drawer with a handgun, a big German Luger, Alvin's booty from the war. Having it in his hand made Ned feel as though the gun were holding him and not vice versa, and that by picking it up he had become party to the terrible things this foreign instrument was designed to do. Carrying it with him, he went and sat on the porch while he stared through the wind and the noisy leaves towards the dark blur where the driveway disappeared into the bush.

What would Billy and the others think if they drove up and saw him like that? "Shooting bats," he'd say while they gawked at the Luger. Using both his hands he held it up in the air with his arms stiff, aiming it into the darkness like a movie detective. He imagined pulling the trigger, the loud explosion that would push him backwards, echo through the yard and the house until his uncle woke up yelling for him.

He went back into the house, locked the gun in its place, then came out, climbed into his truck and started towards town. He was twenty-three years old but somehow being forced to leave home to take care of his uncle had made him feel older. Especially when Lu-Ann moved in. It was like being married, until she left. Now he might as well be a child again: no money, no girlfriend, no nothing — just giving his uncle pills three times a day, then scaring the shit out of himself while he sat alone and listened to the wind.

Driving past the supermarket he saw the Movie Barn was still open. Before she left Lu-Ann had bought a VCR. Instead of walking around the house listening to the sounds of might-be trucks in the driveway, they would watch movies together. Even dirty movies. Sharon would tell Lu-Ann what to get; they would stand in the corner and giggle the way they used to in the halls at the high school.

After Lu-Ann left, Ned had gone in a couple of times alone. He would ask Sharon for recommendations and then she'd give him the cold "get out of here you axe-murderer" look and hand him a cartoon or a children's movie. But yesterday when he'd seen her in front of the bank, she'd told him she was going to Toronto with her boyfriend. He was taking some kind of computer course and she was going to learn to "do colours." She'd laughed and promised to do his colours when she got back. Despite what she'd said about the boyfriend, Ned could have almost thought she was coming on to him.

Remembering this conversation he parked in front of the Movie Barn. He was just climbing out of the truck when through the window he saw Carl McKelvey. His heart started flopping in his chest, the way it had five years ago when at hockey practice he'd tripped Carl and sent him flying headfirst into the boards. For a moment Carl lay on the ice, flat on his stomach, face hidden by his gloves and helmet. Ned, terrified, had inched around him, looking for signs of blood. Carl had pulled himself up, dropped his stick and gloves, started skating slowly towards him. That crazed McKelvey look. His mother had been the same. Even from Grade Three he could remember her marching down the aisle, that murdering fire in her eyes, carrying a chalk eraser like she was going to crush his face with it. When he complained to Amy she said Mrs. McKelvey was different: she was a Jew from Kingston. Then he told Amy what he'd done and she shut him up in his room for an hour.

He started the truck again and drove to the new convenience store at the strip plaza on the edge of town where he bought a carton of eggs, a paper, a bag of chips to eat on the way back, a big bottle of diet cola without caffeine. He'd told the doctor how bad he felt some nights and the doctor had said caffeine just made it worse.

"Saw Carl McKelvey," Ned said to the cashier. Her name was Ellie Dean and she was, as his father liked to say about long-standing West Gull families, "local to here."

"He's back in town," Ellie said. Ever since she'd been laid off in Kingston she'd been working the late shift at the convenience store.

Ned opened the carton and began turning over the eggs one at a time, as though one of them might be broken. "Doesn't have anywhere to stay any more," he said.

"Your father rented him the old Balfer place."

Ned now remembered that a few years ago he'd seen Ellie Dean hanging around with Carl McKelvey. Lu-Ann had once called Ellie Dean a cow because Ellie refused to let her buy on credit. But now, looking at Ellie's oval and not-cow face with its not-cow china-blue eyes and its shiny not-cow hair pulled back into a ponytail, Ned didn't care if Ellie had given Lu-Ann a rough time.

"Could have stayed away for all I care," Ned said.

"I guess so," Ellie agreed in a noncommittal voice.

Ned looked down at the egg carton. When Carl had started skating towards him, Ned backed up until he was behind the net, nowhere left to go. "It was a mistake, for Christ's sake. I wasn't trying to start a fight," he managed as Carl grabbed him by the sweater, lifted him up and slammed him against the glass. High enough that his skates were right off the ice and he was dangling like a little kid.

When he finished inspecting the eggs, he paid and took his groceries out to the truck where he laid them carefully on the front seat. The owners of the store had installed a row of super-bright sodium lamps above it and the gas pumps out front. If you looked directly at the lamps, the light was so white you couldn't see anything for a few minutes.

All the houses had their lights on, most of the driveways were crowded with cars. A little metal logo, RICHARDSON'S NEW & USED, was glued to many of their trunks. And every one of those logos had started out as a fat cheque in his father's bank account. Strange to drive around town, thinking about all that money he'd have one day. As he came to Main Street, he slowed by the bank. Even now the manager deferred to him, bobbed his head and called him mister as though he was already sitting in his father's office, dealing out wads of bills, placing his millions here and there throughout the county, playing the county the way the Richardsons always had — a big monopoly game they always won because they had all the money. Every time someone had to sell the Richardsons bought. Bought the trees to start with. Then the mill, the land and the waterfront. The hotel next. The gravel pit and the bulldozers and the road machines. The car dealership and the garage. A seat in Parliament. Seats in both churches. There was no end to what the Richardsons bought and what they got.

At one time there had been more: two mica mines at the north end of the county; a small chain of cheese factories so almost every farm in the south half of the county was bringing them their milk; a machinery dealership to sell the tractors and attachments needed to plant and harvest the fields to feed the cattle to make the milk to make the cheese to make the money to buy the cars. And if Senator Merriwell Richardson hadn't run into someone even bigger, meaner, slyer, more cunning, there'd be no saying how rich would be the Richardsons, how high the number to count their blessings.

Still, what was left was meant for him.

Thinking about the day West Gull would be a fat bulge in his back pocket, the day Fred Verghoers would wish he'd given him a job when he'd the chance, Ned parked outside the bank. He walked down past the neon-lit supermarket, the doughnut shop with its open door, the Timberpost, towards the tavern. He stopped in front of the Richardson Real Estate office. Land, buying and selling. That was finished. Everyone knew that. Except for waterfront, land wasn't worth the taxes any more, wasn't worth the spindly trees and juniper bushes growing up in the fields once dense with clover and alfalfa and corn. When Luke died Ned was going to get rid of the real-estate business and use the office for a computer store. He looked across the street to the New & Used. That, he'd keep. But he wasn't going to drive around in a Pontiac or even a Cadillac. Get a Porsche or a Ferrari and a 4 x 4 for the winter.

He turned down to the hotel. His great-great-grandfather had built the Long Gull Lake Inn. There were still pictures of the inn back then, a sprawling log building with wide verandahs looking out on the water. Now you'd hardly recognize it. The name was the same but clapboard had been nailed over the logs, the roof had sagged, the paint jobs had blistered into each other. When Alvin went bankrupt, one of the first things he'd sold was the hotel — it wasn't worth much and the restaurant was so bad it had been years since they'd gone there for a free meal.

Ned went in the side door. The low-ceilinged room was layered with smoke. Although it was a Saturday night the tavern was only half full, mostly with summer people he didn't know. Billy Boyce and the others were playing pool at the back, the way they always did. When Billy saw Ned he looked up, startled.

"Don't worry," Ned said. "I won't tell your mother on you."

Billy's thin face twitched. "You want to play?"

"Sure," Ned said, picking a cue from the rack.

"We're playing for the table," Billy said as he leaned over to break.

"I was looking for the money you owe me." Ned snapped his cue down, hard. Billy had to jump back to keep his hands from being hit.

"You crazy?"

"You're the crazy one," Ned said. The electricity was in him, his arms were hanging at his sides, loose, the pool cue dangling from his hand like a gun or a whip. People were looking at him but no one would do anything unless he went over the edge.

"I told you next week."

"Your left nut," Ned said and poked the cue towards Billy's trousers. Billy jumped back. Ned brandished the cue like a skewer looking for a chunk of meat. Billy kept dancing, as though he was already over the fire. "I warned you," Ned said to Billy, gave what he hoped was a crazy grin, threw the cue down on the table and walked out.

Outside he stood on the sidewalk for a moment, waiting to see if Billy would come out after him. Of course he wouldn't. Billy didn't come after people which was why people went after him.

He found Billy's car in the shadows of the laundromat parking lot. Ned had a small army knife attached to his key chain. He used it to take off the rear licence plate. When Billy discovered the plate missing, he wouldn't call the police — he had so many tickets outstanding he might as well just go to jail. No. He would think for a while and he would realize where it was. He'd start to ask himself what he was going to have to do to get it back. Something unexpected, Ned decided. Something to be remembered.

On his way out of town Ned stopped at the convenience store again. This time he kept his eyes on Ellie's china blues. "Forgot cigarettes," he explained and smiled quickly at the smile she gave him. In high school she'd been four years ahead — until she dropped out in her final year because she was pregnant. But even in the fluorescent glare of the convenience store she didn't look so bad. Even if she did have a kid somewhere. Lu-Ann's likely reaction to who her successor might be didn't hurt. Ned smoked a cigarette and told Ellie how he'd gone to the hotel for a beer and no one was there. So he'd decided to head down the highway to Frostie's. She smiled when he said Frostie's and he knew she'd go with him after work if he asked, but even if his gut was boiling he couldn't yet face the idea of walking into Frostie's with Ellie Dean, of all people, older than him *and* a mother.

"Gotta go," he finally said and started out the door.

"See you," she said back, her voice high and girlish, and Ned had to stop himself from screaming out his victory.

It was a flat lonely stretch of road around the Balfer place: mostly fields for the Forrest farm which was half a mile away, and a big shallow swamp that flooded every spring and grew saw-edged marsh grass for the rest of the summer. Harry Balfer had worked for the township for decades, driving the big snowplough. Then his wife inherited some money so he'd quit and they moved out west. Ned parked down the road from the house. There was a glow pulsing from one of the windows. He came up on it slowly. Carl was slouched back on the couch, a beer in his hand. A girl, just a little kid, was beside him. They had the slack-jawed look Alvin sometimes got, mesmerized by the television. Ned could even see the changing images of the movie getting flashed across their faces.

A hiss. Ned jerked around. A cat was crouched in a branch above him, ready to spring.

"Fuck off, cat," Ned whispered.

The cat hissed again.

Ned reached out to swipe it but the cat was faster: one of its paws whipped across the back of his hand. He could feel the parallel tracks opening as they started to bleed. Moving to chase it he stepped on a branch, then froze against the sound before creeping back to the truck, his hand on fire. He put his tongue on the scratches and sucked at them. But what he needed now, he realized, wasn't first aid but sympathy. He started the truck and began driving towards the store.

FOUR

*L*IZZIE WOKE TO THE FEEL OF SOME-
thing heavy on her back. "Get off, Mar-
bles," she said. She pushed at the cat to dislodge it. A blanket
shifted on her shoulder and she jerked up screaming.

Fred was standing above her in the shadows. He smelled
of stale beer. A light went on in the hallway and her mother
came in.

"She must have been dreaming," Fred said. "I was just
pulling up her covers and she woke up with the terrors." The
way Fred said it, his voice heavy and sour, he might have been
announcing that she had just wet her bed. Not that she ever
had. At least not since she was a baby and that had been
before Fred.

Chrissy, in her nightgown, came to sit beside her, stroking
her shoulder. "I was so tired. I didn't remember to check on
you until I was in bed."

"You'd think I was a monster or something," Fred muttered as he went into the hall, just loud enough to be sure
they'd hear him.

Chrissy lay beside her, stroking her hair, her back, her shoulders, petting Lizzie the way Lizzie petted Marbles. In the afternoon Marbles had been lying on Lizzie's desk and she had tried to hypnotize her by waving a piece of tinfoil in front of her eyes. The cat had finally batted it away.

"You hurt his feelings, you know."

"I didn't mean to. I was just scared."

"I asked him to come and put the blanket over you. You know me. Once I get into bed, I can't get out. Last winter it was almost always Fred who covered you up. You were asleep, you never even knew he was doing that for you."

"I'm sorry." She snuggled closer to her mother. What Chrissy said about not being able to get up after she lay down was true. Now she was lifting up the blanket, sliding in beside her. Lizzie moved over to make room. She loved the warm musty smell of her mother at night. There was always a sweetness around her neck and ears from her perfume. She put her hands on Chrissy's neck, then moved her nose up to check for that sweetness.

"You always sniff me out, like a dog or something."

Sometimes when Chrissy would come and lie on Lizzie's bed, she would let Lizzie massage her arms and back where they were sore from working in the garden. But tonight she just hugged Lizzie, then turned her on her stomach, the way Lizzie liked to sleep.

The hall light went out and the whole house was dark. Lizzie heard Fred kick off his shoes, the sound of his belt buckle hitting the floor. "Jesus Christ," he said.

"I ought to go back. You're getting too old to need to sleep with your mother."

Lizzie didn't say anything. She knew if she could stay quiet and keep her mother from talking until she counted slowly to twenty, Chrissy would fall asleep and she'd have her there, warm and safe the whole night.

By the time Lizzie got to fifteen, her mother's breathing had slipped into that other country, whatever place it was she went to when she slept. Probably somewhere far and wonderful since Lizzie had never heard of someone loving sleep the way her mother did. Every evening when Chrissy had finished the dinner dishes, she would smile, stretch and yawn, even in the summer when the sun was still in the sky. The next thing you knew she'd be in her nightgown, her hair tied in one of the special ribbons she wore for going to bed.

Lizzie turned over, backed into her mother's body. As always, her mother's arm rose, slid round her, so now Lizzie was almost entirely surrounded by the warm sweet cave of her mother. She closed her eyes. She heard the soft padding of Marbles' paws, felt the sudden weight of her across her legs. She, her mother and Marbles were on a cloud, Marbles' deep purr a motor pulling them across the sky.

FIVE

"YOU GOT SOMETHING LIKE *Star Wars?* Not that, but you know, something like it." Nancy Brookner: she came every day and when she rented a movie she printed her name in big letters. She had wavy brown hair with blonde highlights, a round face with a little too much flesh along the jaw.

Carl reached below the counter for the science fiction. She was standing near the hinge in the counter, waiting for him to come out. When he emerged he'd have to brush by her. Yesterday she'd pushed her breasts into his arm, causing a small unexpected explosion in his belly. Her neck was tanned, with narrow white creases where the flesh folded.

"You watch these at home?"

"Sometimes," Carl said.

She smiled again. Her teeth were square and so perfectly white they seemed to have been lasered clean. Carl wondered if she meant did he watch dirty movies at home. Or maybe yesterday had just been an accident and he was mistaking her friendliness for his own adult movie.

"You could give me something with animals for the kids." She was wearing too-tight jeans, a frilly-collared blouse under a loose men's sweater that she sported like a trophy. She put her purse on the counter and opened it to search for her membership card.

He came out from behind but this time she let him pass. There were a few bear movies in the children's section. He took them out and, careful to keep his distance, laid them on the counter in front of her. "My daughter liked these," Carl said.

"You afraid of me or something?"

Carl couldn't believe he'd actually heard these words.

"You're tiptoeing around like I was going to goose you."

Carl shook his head.

"Hey, I didn't mean to make you blush."

Now she was standing next to him, her hand on his bare arm. Her palm was burning. He couldn't remember the last time a woman had touched him with intent. Or maybe the last three years had activated some kind of repelling mechanism that wavered only when he was drunk.

"I was just kidding. I'm a friend of Ellie's so I feel like I know you already. I mean, I know it's not fair. My name is Nancy Brookner. I moved here three years ago, just after you left."

"Carl McKelvey," Carl said.

"Pleased to meet you. *Officially*, I mean." It was her turn to blush; her face and neck were sunburned already but now they turned an amazing, impossible dark scarlet. He wondered what it would be like to be lying on top of her, all that heat spreading under him.

"Sorry," she said. She took her hand away.

They were still standing beside the counter when Ned Richardson came in. He hesitated for a moment, stroking what might be the weedy beginnings of a goatee, then went to the rows of adult movies.

"You ever go to Frostie's on Saturdays?" Nancy asked.

Ned's snicker floated through the store. In the mirror, Carl saw him slide one of the cases under his shirt.

"*You!*" Carl took two quick steps and intercepted Ned on his way to the door. He swung the boy around. There was a big rectangular lump under his T-shirt, half-covered by his arm. "Forget something?"

"Whattya mean?" Ned said. His eyes and nose and mouth were all squinched together.

"That movie."

"What movie?" Ned asked, raising his arm and letting the plastic case drop from under his T-shirt to the floor. "I don't have any movie. Oh, look at that." He stepped back, out of Carl's range, and pointed downward. The case lay face up on the stained carpet. The title, *Tastes Delicious*, was in fiery tomato red; the movie's star had her mouth wide open.

Nancy bent down to pick it up. Ned looked over her bulging jeans and mouthed "pig" to Carl. Carl's hand shot out but Ned had danced away and was halfway out the door by the time Nancy straightened up.

"I don't know what Ellie sees in him," she said. Ned had his truck going. He turned it around in the parking lot, then gave Carl the finger as he skidded out into the street. Carl stood on the step and watched Ned's truck disappear around the corner: a black mud-spattered Chevrolet with oversized tires that must have come from his father's lot.

That evening at home Carl was putting the new bathroom sink into place when the telephone rang. An image of Nancy Brookner's scarlet face floated into his mind; as he hesitated he could feel her hand burning on his arm. Finally he went downstairs and picked up the receiver. A silence. Breathing. Carl said hello once, then hung up.

On Saturday night Lizzie went to sleep over at a friend's. Carl dropped her off, complete with everything she'd need when Chrissy picked her up the next day, then looped around to drive back by the highway so he could stop for cigarettes.

He had the window open and could hear the music from Frostie's half a mile away. Without thinking he pulled his truck into the parking lot. There was still a touch of light in the sky, enough to make out the traces of a few long submarine-shaped clouds cruising just above the horizon. The roadhouse lot was jammed: cars, trucks, vans of every description. Some seemed vaguely familiar but it was so long since he'd been a regular, he'd lost the ability to know who was inside just by surveying the vehicles in the lot. Stretching to loosen his back, Carl suddenly felt like the cast-out black sheep in some old western movie, the unjustly cast-out black sheep who is compelled to return to the place that will destroy him.

Nancy must have had a radar device trained at the door. As Carl came in, the first thing he saw was her hand waving frantically. With her was a stocky man wearing a cowboy hat and one of those western-style shirts with the pearl buttons; across the table, alone and looking at the band, was Chrissy. He could have, he realized, spent half the night in the parking lot pretending he was in a movie but he never would have thought Chrissy might be here. Wishing Nancy hadn't spotted him, Carl went over to the bar. There he bought his cigarettes and asked for what had once been his favourite foundation for a night of drinking: a double Scotch, plenty of ice cubes, no water. There was dancing at the front — the crowd was already thick and the band so loud he wouldn't have to worry about conversation. He rinsed his Scotch down with a beer, then headed towards the table. Chrissy's back was to him; she was clapping to the music. Nancy's cowboy in the pearl buttons glowered as Carl approached: his face was like a dark puffy mushroom just a rainfall away from crumbling. As Carl sat down Nancy made the introductions and pushed a glass of beer towards him. Just then Chrissy turned to face him, her knees bumping against his, her eyes suddenly lowered. She was wearing a short-sleeved black sweater and on her wrists, almost matching the shade of her tanned arms, thin gold bracelets that looked elegant or out of place he couldn't decide. Chrissy was drinking ginger ale. She had a tulip-shaped glass with a bent pink straw that could have belonged to a little girl.

It was the angle of the light. Her closed face. A sudden gap in the music. Her eyes in repose the way they used to be when she was sleeping. Right after they were married, when they lived in an apartment in town above the barber's, he would wake up to see just that: Chrissy sleeping. Chrissy's sleeping face in the street light from the window, all the daytime fierceness and want blanked out, leaving smoothness, vulnerability, absence. It was as though while she slept she put her body in his care — take this, hold it for me until I get back. So he would. Until he too fell into sleep. Though he knew that wherever she'd gone, he hadn't followed; he was locked inside his skin, ready to light up at the first sound.

When she looked to him he couldn't stay silent, as he once had, so he mumbled something about the weather.

"Dance?" Chrissy asked. She smiled and he found himself

looking at the crow's feet in the corners of her eyes. Even when they'd first gone out those crow's feet had been there, shallow then, a faint pencil sketch of the future. But there had been nothing to predict how hollow her eyes would now seem, how he would feel rediscovering those eyes, larger and darker from what he and Chrissy had done to each other.

"Welcome home," Chrissy whispered as the band started a new number. She was standing in front of him, close-dance style — one hand on each of his shoulders the way she had held him the first night they'd danced together at the Richardsons' New Year's party, when he was supposed to be with Ellie Dean and she with Fred Verghoers. By chance they had been standing alone in the hall. A song had started up and Chrissy had taken his arm, as though it were perfectly natural for someone else's date to do this, to take his arm and say, "Come on, I always dance to this, don't you know?" She'd put a hand on each of his shoulders and moved in close enough that he didn't want anyone to see them. That was the warning he should have heeded. His reaction had been all body, a lick of flame that cut his breath and sent him stumbling into full-length contact with Chrissy, who didn't speak, didn't act as though anything unusual was happening, but didn't move away until just before the song was over, saying, "I hate endings, and anyway what will people think if I steal you?" By which time his heart was pounding and he felt that he'd been thrown from ordinary life into a new furnace-world of desire.

Chrissy was holding him close now, too. She was holding him close and they were folded into each other and this was exactly how it had always been, he and Chrissy, arms wrapped around each other, bodies slowly turning like twin stars falling into each other. She had buried her head in his neck the way she used to and was softly singing along.

Then the music ended.

Carl opened his eyes.

Chrissy was standing just inches away, her head cocked quizzically to one side like a smart bitch hound waiting to find out what was next. Her eyes open and inviting.

"So, here we are," Chrissy said.

"Looks like."

The band started again. Chrissy gave a little wiggle to her shoulders, shaking them loose the way she used to a million years ago. "Looks like, all right."

Carl pushed his hair back. Reached into his pocket for his cigarettes, still wrapped in cellophane. Held the pack out to Chrissy.

"I stopped."

"Me too."

"Looks like," Chrissy said. Then she gave the little quick-silver laugh she'd always had. "Fred couldn't come tonight. He goes to meetings now." When she said Fred's name her face seemed to go blurry and out of focus. Her head was cocked, eyes seductive, but in thirty seconds or one second or one-millionth of a second everything had changed from being full and warm to a feeling of dead grey cement.

"Clunk," Carl said. He turned towards the table. Either he would have one more beer, just to even out, or he'd leave right away.

"Carl." She was so close to him he didn't know if she was talking, whispering, just sending his name right into his head.

"Yeah."

"Don't go away now."

She was holding his arm with both hands. The room was exploding with noise: the band, people shouting at each other, waiters with red- and blue-striped canvas aprons full of change, round metal trays of beer on one arm, using the other to clear a path through the crowd.

He turned back to Chrissy. There was a part of him, he guessed, that must still be in love with her. Surprise. Of course he was still in love with her. He had *expected* to be in love with her. He had *risked* being in love with her still. But now there was an unexpected change in the way he saw her. Her face had hardened and grown sharper and it made her look like someone who was doing things on purpose instead of letting them happen.

Chrissy tugged at his arm and he let her lead him back towards the table. It was empty but there were new glasses of beer in the centre, clustered together like a bouquet. Carl dragged a glass towards himself; it left a small highway of condensation as it travelled across the varnished wood.

"Hey," Chrissy said.

"What?" And then Carl put his hand up to his face and felt the wetness on his cheeks. He was crying. The tears were just leaking out of his eyes as if it was the most natural thing in the world for a man to be crying when he had a dance and a beer with a woman he used to love.

"You want to get out of here?"

The parking lot was almost as crowded as the roadhouse. Cigarette ends bobbing in the darkness. Laughter. They climbed into Carl's pick-up. Before he turned the key he heard the band start up again, double volume, and even after the engine was going and he was driving slowly away, the languid beat of country music filled the cab and he was tapping his fingers against the steering wheel.

He drove past the old Catholic graveyard near the high school, a place they used to go, then out of town, taking the loop down by the lakeshore. Luke Richardson's spotlights were shining on his house — a white-pillared, north-of-Kingston 1980s American Colonial special with a three-car garage fronted by enough black asphalt to pave a supermarket parking lot.

When the crescent rejoined the highway Carl turned around, drove through town again and this time started into a series of sideroads heading north. Also what they used to do: drive at random along the wooded sideroads until they reached an abandoned farm, a place with a driveway leading to an old barn or a burned-out house foundation.

He'd turned the heat on in the truck cab and Chrissy had pulled out a flask of peach brandy that they were passing back and forth. Driving north of town, fence posts and page wire flashed in the headlights. Country music wailed from the melon-sized speakers he'd wired into the four corners of the cab ceiling, the bass stepping up and down his spine while the electric guitar stitched its way around the voice — which he wasn't listening to though no one was talking.

All he wanted was the feeling. The Chrissy feeling. Blood full of brandy, tires humming, road blowing through the centre of his brain. Chrissy beside him. It was like sitting beside a volcano of possible explosions, love, or maybe just the pure heat he needed. Pure heat. A man could be remade in the pure heat of Chrissy, or so he'd believed. Like the night Chrissy told him she was pregnant. She was at university, living in a Kingston apartment she shared with two other girls. He was at the community college, living at home, watching over his father who was trying to drink himself to death — and doing well enough to end up at the KGH vomiting blood.

The night she told him, he'd had to leave Chrissy's apartment to go check on his father at the hospital. The idea was that when visiting hours were over he'd go back to Chrissy's and they'd celebrate. McKelvey was waiting for him, his little sad-sack canvas bag packed along with the news that he'd been released. Unwilling to share his own news immediately, Carl had allowed his father to insist that after a week of hospital food he deserved a drink. They ended up at the Royal Hotel, Carl matching his father Scotch for Scotch while McKelvey stared at the table, smoked cigarettes, talked about the old days in such apologetic tones that Carl suddenly realized his father hadn't brought him here to drink, hadn't drunk to get blasted or escape his ulcer but was in fact telling him something absolutely different from his words, was telling him that he was going to die soon. Was talking about the past not to chatter but in an awkward attempt to leave things right with Carl. Meanwhile Carl — sinking deeper with every drink into the wildly burgeoning dream of his own child yet unable to actually *say* it — was telling himself that this whole train of thought, his father's impending death, was crazy; then he'd looked up at the old man and seen him staring straight at him, face red and stricken.

"Chrissy's pregnant," Carl said.

"Good."

And, so drunk they were weaving from table to table, they'd gone to the bathroom and stood side by side, pissing into the stinking hotel urinals.

Chrissy had her hand on his knee. They always touched, driving. In town or at the mall, she would always be holding his hand or her hand would be in his pocket or sliding inside his shirt at the waist. From the time they first got together until he couldn't exactly say how long after Lizzie was born, her hands were always on him, touching, possessing, comforting, exciting, shaping the world they inhabited together until some nights, watching her sleep, her body given over to his care, his breath wouldn't come and he would get out of bed and sit in his bare feet in the living room, just smoking a cigarette and wiggling his toes and feeling the breeze on his soles and a pounding excitement with every breath.

He stretched his legs in his jeans. Chrissy's hand squeezed. Carl remembered a dirt road he must have been aiming for the whole time, and as the truck turned the lights swung from pavement and wire to a narrow vista of pocked dirt, crowded second-growth trees reaching out across the ditches.

"Here," Chrissy said, pointing to a gap between two oaks.

Carl turned in, jolted down a dirt track for a few yards, then switched off his motor and the lights.

There was just enough moon that he could see Chrissy's mouth. Lips dark in this light, parting as though she was about to say something, then closing again. She stepped out of the truck.

He hesitated for a moment before following.

From the ground came a smell he'd forgotten, the smell of winter making a brief night inspection during the height of summer. Leaves starting to compost. The soil preparing to be locked into frost. There was a cool breeze, the skin on his arms and neck contracted. He had an old plaid lumber shirt behind the truck seat. He reached for it now, offered it to Chrissy. "I'm okay," she said but moved to stand against him. "Don't worry, nothing bad can happen here." She was leaning into him the way she had on the dance floor. Then she turned, her hand cupping his jeans, her body against his. Her lips were on his neck. He slid his hand beneath her sweater at the belt. The skin of her back was softer than it used to be. She wasn't wearing a brassiere. When his thumbs came to her nipples, they were swollen with waiting. She wiggled to settle the weight of her breasts into his palms and then she moved away from him and he was left leaning over empty space, his hands closing on themselves.

"I'll take one of those cigarettes now."

When it was lit she shook her head in a way that was new and said, "Carl, I don't know what I'm doing here."

Smoking made him feel drunker, more like drinking. After drinks with his father that night he'd eaten steak and eggs, coffee, while his father had a penitent bowl of soup along a small mountain of white bread. For the first time Carl had noticed the way the old man spread his butter. He would reach out with his knife, take a glob of butter which he'd set in the middle of the slice, then methodically spread in ever-widening circles until the whole surface was yellow-white and shining.

"Lizzie's glad you're back."

"So am I."

She shook her head that new way again, not really looking at him. "I don't know what I'm doing here, Carl. I really hated you, you know?"

"I know."

"You don't know, Carl. I mean, Carl, when you messed up, I didn't have anyone to turn to. It was just Lizzie and me and all the mess you left behind you."

She was saying this in a voice that sounded the way her lips had looked in the truck, the way her nipples had felt against his hands, a dark and swollen voice that stirred him up but for which he had no answer.

"I guess you couldn't help it," Chrissy said. "Your father did it to you and then you had to pass it on to me, to Lizzie."

"He didn't mean to," Carl said. Or so it had seemed that night in the restaurant, the old man meekly spooning soup into his mouth, eating his butter-loaded white bread, drinking coffee, every now and then looking across the table to Carl. His face so white from the week in hospital, shaved raw and white and creased like sheets that had been slept on for a lifetime.

She was standing close to him again, her hand on his chest, pressing onto his heart as though she knew the exact place where the pain lodged behind his breastbone. He had his back to the truck, was leaning against the hood and she was still touching him and he thought Chrissy had all the power because in his absence she had learned to see life the way you could see any other landscape, with its unexpected trenches, its trees to be avoided, its hills that afforded the best views of the low points below; meanwhile he was still blindly stumbling about, hoping for the fog to lift. There were sounds of leaves rustling, a few bird calls, the slow plodding progress of a porcupine through the undergrowth. But through all that he could still hear, only too clearly, the echo of his own voice, the self-pity. He felt a small tearing inside his gut, a hollow space that wanted a drink. And if he drank to fill that space, he knew, soon there would be another and another and another; and if he drank to fill them all he would have to drink until he passed out and then tomorrow the tearing would start earlier, harder.

"You want a drink?"

"I'm okay," Carl said.

They were standing toe to toe, waist to waist, face to face. Their new bodies and their old seemed to be weaving in and out of each other, trying to decide if they were still the right size, if they still wanted to fit together.

"Let's say," Chrissy said, and her face was so close to his he could feel her breath spreading over his mouth and cheeks, "let's say something, okay?"

"Okay."

"Let's say we forgive each other. Or pretend to. Let's say there's a little island where we can go every year or ten."

Her hands went back to his shoulders as she pushed against him; his arms slipped around her back. They were rocking back and forth, slow dancing, saving the last dance for each other. And his blood had become so heavy it just had to slip down with her onto the soft ground. Right there in front of the truck, with the smell of the engine and the sound of the porcupine in the underbrush. Their new bodies had decided they fit after all; they were dancing the last dance and everything was as it had been except that it was better because it was slower and heavier; they were dancing the last dance and he knew that tomorrow he would wake up and the empty space would be emptier.

Ned was standing at the bar with Billy Boyce, drinking a beer and with a pocketful of change thanks to the fifty his mother had given him. Then, he couldn't believe, in came Carl McKelvey. Carl drained a quick Scotch, so nervous his hands trembled, and went to sit at Chrissy's table.

Before Carl's arrival Ned had been thinking of trying that table himself, trying to impress Chrissy with what a *reliable* person he was. Getting to Fred had become a project. Now Carl was sitting beside Chrissy and that was something Ned was sure Fred would be interested to know: that Carl McKelvey was back and was making up to Chrissy. They were practically in each other's laps right in front of everyone.

Ned ordered another beer. Billy Boyce, missing every-thing, had gone off to play video games like the little kid he was. Ned wrapped his fingers around the moisture-beaded glass. This was like being a detective in a movie; no, a *real* detective because there was *real* danger, even though he knew Carl McKelvey couldn't see him watching.

"Carl. I don't want to talk about Carl," Ellie Dean had said last night. The way she lingered on his name, the hurt in her voice like some wound he'd stumbled on from a war before his time — a war for which he'd been conscripted by coming into Ellie's bed.

"What'd he do to you?" Ned asked, an eager soldier, but she just lowered her eyes and this modest withdrawal made Ned feel important in an entirely new way. He was on the inside, he *was* inside; he was Ellie's man now, her protector, her army, her weapon against the scum on whom revenge needed to be taken, that unworthy pretender, Carl McKelvey.

The band was howling, the dance floor turning into a jostling mass — in its midst Chrissy and Carl were making a spectacle of themselves. Ned went to the pay telephone, searched through the book, called Fred's number. After two rings he lost his nerve and hung up. He went back to the bar. Now there was a slow waltz and they were dancing like they were trying to make a baby.

Billy Boyce came back from his video games. Ned pointed out Carl and Chrissy. "Christ," Billy said. Ned finished his beer and ordered another. When Carl and Chrissy left he fol-lowed them to the parking lot. From behind a van he watched them climb into Carl's truck. He went back into Frostie's to the telephone and punched the numbers so hard his fingers hurt. Fred answered right away, his voice low and threatening.

"It's Ned Richardson," Ned said.

"What can I do for you, Ned?" Just like that. No "hello" or "how are you?" All right. Let him have it.

"I was still thinking of coming to see you about that job," Ned said.

"Thanks for letting me know."

"There was something else I wanted you to know."

Silence.

"I'm at Frostie's and it's dance night. Chrissy just took off from here with Carl McKelvey."

More silence.

Ned plunged ahead. "I was going to do something about it."

"Then do it."

"I'll see you next week," Ned said. He hung up and returned to the bar. Billy was waiting for him.

"I'll buy you another beer," Ned offered.

"I already owe you."

"This one is free. Then you can start working off the other."

A plan was starting to come to him. He was thinking about a time he had watched Billy wriggle into the window of the school office.

"What have you got in mind?" Billy Boyce's voice already sounded scared. "You going to give me back my plate?"

"First we do Fred a favour."

Ned followed Billy's Pinto out to the Balfer place. He parked his truck on the road while Billy walked into the yard. The outside light was on but the house was dark. Soon Ned could see the lights going on in the house as Billy worked his way from the back to the kitchen. Then the lights went off again and Billy was out the kitchen door. He started up his Pinto, waved at Ned as he shot past. Ned waited nervously a few minutes before going through the door Billy had left open for him. He heard the faint sound of a cat meowing. He brushed the back of his hand where the cat had scratched him; the little ridges of scab had just started to peel off. The cat meowed again and it reminded him of the strangled sound that had got caught in his throat when Carl McKelvey had grabbed him. The cat was in the room with him now. Ned reached into his pocket for his switchblade.

When Carl got home he stood outside his truck for a moment, aware of the cool air touching his body in all the places Chrissy had warmed it. Even as he entered the house he noticed the smell. He resisted the urge to call out, instead turned on the light. In the kitchen the smell was dark and musky, an odour that hovered between perfume and garbage. He opened the refrigerator, expecting it to be broken, but the light went on and the beer was ice cold.

On the table was the note he'd watched Lizzie write to him:

> Daddy, Don't forget Marbles needs food, milk, love, exercise. Your daughter, Lizzie.

Lately Lizzie had taken to writing notes when Chrissy called or when she wanted to remind Carl of something. She would sign herself *your daughter* and call Chrissy *your wife*. As though if everyone could just be reminded of their official positions — husband, wife, daughter — the family would glue itself together again. Beside the note was a bowl of apples. Reading a parents' magazine at the doctor's office, he'd got the idea that the house would seem more welcoming if there was always fruit on the table. He leaned over to see if the apples had somehow gone bad without his noticing. They smelled just like apples.

The telephone started. He left the kitchen, noticing the smell again, turned on the living-room light and began crossing the floor towards the phone. Just before he would have tripped over it, he saw Lizzie's cat lying in the centre of the carpet, its throat slit and bulging, blood pooled all around.

He buried the cat in the backyard, at the corner of what had been the garden. He used a clean part of the rug to wrap its body, then rolled the rest up tightly and put it by the garage to be taken to the dump on Monday. The amazing thing was how neat they had been. They had got in through the pantry window, pushing up the screen — the only trace.

He went through the house to see if anything had been taken, got a beer, sat down in the armchair and closed his eyes.

First picture: Chrissy on top of him, her eyes filled with moons — twigs and grass digging into his back while her face slowly froze into a mask he hardly recognized.

Second picture: Ned Richardson's eyes filled with something bitter and resentful.

Third picture: Ned Richardson giving him the finger as he roared away in his truck.

Fourth picture: Ned Richardson's truck passing him as he left Frostie's, after dropping Chrissy off in the parking lot.

Ned Richardson's truck was all black, everything dented and rusting except for the right front fender which was a dark red waiting to be painted. Carl lit a cigarette. It was one of those August mornings he'd always liked. A cool hollow sky with just a few clouds strung out and bobbing on the horizon like paper boats on a pond.

The lawn was neatly mowed and a flowerbed had been recently dug around the house. Two bushes, one on each side of the front steps, still wore plastic bracelets on their branches. Carl, standing in front of the screen door, tried to imagine Ellie Dean at the kind of place where they sold bushes with plastic bracelets.

"Long time no see," Ellie said. She had come around the side of the house and Carl, turning to her, caught the sun in his eyes. "I heard you were back, living at the old Balfer place."

"You're looking good," Carl said. His eyes were still adjusting from the sudden shock of light but Ellie Dean *was* looking good: slim as ever in ironed shorts that hung above her knees and polished white sandals.

"You want to come in?"

"I was looking for Ned."

Her face contracted.

"It's okay," Carl said. "You still give out cookies with coffee or what?"

"You can have the cookies but I was thinking of getting choosy about the 'or what.'"

The house had started off as an inexpensive cottage built a couple of rows back from the lake. Most of the original cottage was taken up by the kitchen–living room, which stretched right across the front. The rest was a hall leading to an even lower structure that had been tacked on the back, a bathroom and two bedrooms.

"I don't want him slipping away on me," Carl said, looking towards the bedrooms.

"No one's going to run away from you, Carl."

He was halfway down the hall when a bedroom door opened by itself and Ned Richardson stepped out. When he saw Carl he froze.

"You shouldn't have done that," Carl said. Ned's face jumped as though he had already been hit.

"What are you talking about?"

Carl swung his forearm towards Ned, who backed into the wall. "Come on." He grabbed Ned around the bicep and marched him out of house and across the yard until they were standing beside his truck.

"What are you going to do?" Ned asked. His voice quavered. "Beat me up in front of Ellie? She'll call the cops, you know."

"Maybe I'll call the cops," Carl said. "You some kind of idiot or something? You know what you can get for break and enter?"

Ned was looking down at the ground.

"I'll make you a deal," Carl said.

"You got nothing on me."

"You want me to make that phone call now?"

"No."

"Well?"

"Billy dared me to. He said you were Ellie's old sweetheart and that I should welcome you back to town." A breeze had come up and Ned's T-shirt was flapping against his ribs.

Carl looked at the boy shivering in the morning light. He was winding up, vibrating like crystal waiting to shatter. Strange to think a boy could be that tense, that vulnerable.

"What are you going to do?"

"How about beat the shit out of you?"

"Go ahead. Kill me if you want to. I don't care." Ned was trying to look defiant but his lower lip was trembling and his eyes had filled with tears.

"Ned, do you expect me to kill you at eight o'clock in the morning?" He took his arm again, this time gently. "You come in the house with me and have some coffee. Then we'll go over to my place and see if we can't even things up."

"What do you mean?"

Carl turned Ned to face the back of his pick-up. Lying amid the rust and dried leaves was a posthole digger.

"You ever hear the saying 'Good fences make good neighbours'?"

"I hate those things."

"What things do you hate, Ned?"

"Those diggers."

"I'll get you a pair of gloves so you'll last longer. Think of yourself as being sentenced to community service. Only the good thing about this sentence is that your father doesn't know. It just stays between you and me." They were at the house now, and Carl, his arm around Ned's shoulders, was ushering him in the front door. "I hired him," Carl announced. "Slave labour."

Ellie's mouth worked uncertainly.

"I guess I'll even pay you," Carl said. "After your probation is over." He smiled at Ned, who was still shaking, then took out a cigarette and tapped it on the table — the way, he suddenly remembered, his father used to signal that one chapter was over and another beginning.

Carl reached for his coffee, pushed a cup towards Ned.

"You better eat something before we go. I'm not much of a cook."

Ned smiled weakly. Carl felt a wrench in his belly. He was still going to have to explain to Lizzie that the cat was gone. And he was still going to have to decide what he intended to do with the boy who had broken into his house and killed his daughter's cat.

He left Ned with the posthole digger and a series of marks along the back of the garden where he was to make the holes.

"You be here when I get home this afternoon," Carl said and Ned, terrified, nodded his head vigorously. "At lunch you can go in and make yourself a sandwich. I'll leave the door unlocked; it'll save you going through the window." Just before leaving, he walked along the line where the fence was to be installed and pointed to one of the places Ned was to make a hole. It was away from the house behind a big beech tree and invisible from the road. "This would be a good spot for the gate," Carl said. "You better make this hole a double one."

But when he arrived home from work, Carl saw no sign of Ned Richardson. He inspected the garden. All the holes had been made as planned. The digger was lying beside the double hole at the back. In the morning it had been covered with rust but now the rust was worn away and bits of dirt clung to the handle. Carl lowered the digger to measure the depth of the gate hole, then gave it a few extra twists. The soil was heavy with clay, hard to move. Ned would be nursing a few blisters tonight. When Carl went into the house he found him half-asleep in front of the television set, a few of Lizzie's comics spread out on the floor.

"Suppertime," Carl said from the kitchen. He opened himself a beer and started a frying pan heating for steaks. On the shelf beside the stove were two brand new cookbooks he'd bought after Lizzie moved in. If Ned hadn't killed Lizzie's cat, Carl thought, this would have been the evening to read through them, marking out recipes he could try.

He put on a pot of water for the frozen vegetables, then set the table. Next he set the steaks in the frying pan. The slabs of meat made a loud sizzle as they hit the cast iron and the kitchen filled with the smell. When Carl turned around Ned was standing in the doorway, watching him.

"I don't eat bought meat, I should've told you."

"I'll leave it on extra."

"My mother says it gives you hormones."

"You could use some hormones."

"I hope it doesn't make me throw up."

"Did you throw up when you slit that cat's throat?"

Ned hesitated at the doorway.

"Let me see those blisters." When Ned stepped forward Carl took his hands as though they were a child's and looked at them closely. His fingers were long and thin, his nails bitten down to scabs. Carl felt a flash of pity for Ned, for the man he might become. He turned the boy's hands over. Small circles of raw flesh glowed on the insides of his thumbs, along the tops of his palms. "Good thing you're planning to work with your brains instead of your hands," Carl said. He took a box of bandages from the cupboard over the stove and handed them to Ned.

By the time they were finished dinner the sun was setting and the sky had begun to turn. Carl stood up from the table and opened another beer. "Guess we'd better step outside and see what you did today." Carl picked up a spade and poked at the holes like a man kicking the tires of a used car. Beside each hole was the pile of dirt and rocks the digger had brought up. When he came to the last hole, the double one, he lowered the spade inside, knocked it from wall to wall.

"Hard to dig?"

Ned nodded.

"You need a good big hole for a gatepost. I was going to pour in concrete first, to make sure the bottom doesn't rot. You need extra space for that." He lowered the digger to the bottom of the hole. Gave it a few twists, dragged it up, emptied it, lowered it again, repeated the sequence. "A person could almost fit into that," Carl said. "If they were thin enough." He looked speculatively at Ned. "Could you fit into that?"

It had grown dark enough that a passing car had its headlights on. The beams flashed through the branches of the big beech tree. Ned looked down the hole.

"Go ahead, try it."

Ned shook his head.

"Come on. I bet you could get in. I'll give you an extra ten if it's big enough to get in. That's what my father always made me do when I was digging holes for gateposts."

Ned crouched down beside it, stuck in one foot, then sat and put both his feet in. Carl could see Ned's knees knocking together with fear. He wondered how close Ned was to exploding and if he wanted to push the boy that far. "I guess I can," Ned said, "if I point my toes." He put one hand on either side of the hole and lowered himself down. He was standing with his feet at the bottom, his arms awkwardly sticking out.

"You have to be able to put your arms in, too," Carl said. He watched as Ned raised his arms high, curled his shoulders to make himself thin, then turned and wriggled his arms into place. Now only the tops of his shoulders, his neck, and his head were sticking out.

"That's great," Carl said. "Perfect." He used the spade to pour some dirt behind Ned's back.

"What are you doing?"

"Just seeing how much room there is," Carl said. He took another spadeful, emptied it against Ned's neck.

"Hey."

"Shut up," Carl said. "Or I'll slit your throat the way you did that cat."

"What are you talking about?"

There was something about the way Ned's face was screwed up in the half-light that made Carl wish Ned was standing in front of him so he could slap him. He reached into his pocket, took out a long bone-handled knife that he opened in the twilight. He ran his finger along the blade. "Sharp," Carl said. "Don't make me use it." He kept spading the earth until Ned's shoulders and neck were covered and the dirt came right up underneath his chin. He tamped it gently into place. "Don't let me hurt you," Carl said.

"I have to go to the bathroom."

"Go ahead."

Carl sat down under the tree, lit a cigarette. Another perfect sunset, another spectacular night sky. Beyond Ned the view was of gently rolling fields going back half a mile to a jagged line of trees.

He took a pull of beer, emptying the bottle. Ned was staring at him, his face twisted and streaked with tears. "Got to get another beer," Carl said. "Promise not to go away?"

While he was in the house he heard Ned calling out but when he got back the boy had stopped and was only snivelling.

"What's wrong?"

"I can't get out."

"I know," Carl said. "That's the idea. You're lucky the bugs aren't worse; I'd have to swat your mosquitoes with a shovel."

"You're a mean fucker. Everyone always said that."

"That's true. But then I stopped fighting. Remember that? A man stops fighting and people try to take advantage of him. You know? People start to think they can get away with things. And how's a man to defend himself if he can't fight? Got to get other people to use their hands for him. Like you did this afternoon."

"My father will kill you for this."

"Shall I give him a call and tell him what you've been doing?"

Ned started to scream. Carl threw a shovelful of dirt at his face and he stopped.

"You know what they do to thieves in the desert? I read a book about it once. They dig them a hole in the desert and leave them there, just like you. No problem the first night. Nice cool breezes, winky twinkle stars. And then the next day they die of thirst. The birds come and eat their eyes. Some special kind of eye-eating bird, I guess. The idea is to die before the birds come, if you know what I mean."

Ned was crying again. "Quiet," Carl said. "Try and take this like a man. Just think, Ned, what's happened up to now is nothing compared to what you've got coming. Why don't you just think about how much fun you're having now while I decide what to do with you? Think of it this way. You're a hostage, right? Like I'm holding you because of that dead cat buried at the other end of the garden. For all we know the ghost of that dead cat is watching us, waiting to bring us bad luck. You know it's always bad luck to kill a cat."

"I'll get you another cat," Ned sobbed.

"I'll get your father another kid. Although when it comes to assholes like you I don't know how many there are."

"I'm thirsty," Ned said.

"Thinking about it just makes it worse."

"I'm going to tell the cops."

"When's that?"

"You wouldn't kill me."

"That's right. I wouldn't. But after a few days in the hole — anyway, what would you tell them? That you climbed into your own hole and couldn't get out? And then there's that little break and enter you pulled last night."

A car swept by on the road throwing off a stray bit of light that made Ned's eyes glow briefly.

"Ned, I don't want to kill you. I need you to work here with me. You, me and that posthole digger, we could really turn this country into something. The trouble is, if I let you out, I have to answer to myself about that cat. You know what I mean? Stop crying."

"I pissed myself."

"Ned, stop thinking about yourself. Don't you see we have a more important problem? Down there, at the other end of the garden, is a dead cat. That cat belonged to my daughter. It was left with me in trust. She didn't have to say to me, 'Daddy, please can my cat be alive in three days?' because she thought that with me it was safe. She trusted me with her cat. And now her cat is dead. Tomorrow my daughter is going to come home and that cat is going to be lying in the bottom of a hole with its throat slit. Don't you see what you've done to me?" He was on his feet, he was shouting, he was waving the spade. Ned's crying had grown louder, a non-stop wail that was boring into him. "Stop that noise!"

All the blood had gone into his hands. He remembered that feeling, too, what came next. He threw down the spade, stepped back. Another vehicle was approaching. It stopped in front of his house. A door slammed. Carl heard the crunch of footsteps on the drive, the knock at the door.

"Out here," Ned shouted. "Now you'll be sorry."

"Quiet," Carl said but it was too late, the footsteps had started towards him.

"Is that you?"

"It's me," Carl said.

"Heard you were back," Ray Johnson said. "Thought I'd come and see you before you got yourself into trouble."

There was something contented about Ray Johnson that always made Carl grin from the moment he heard his voice. Ray was wearing jeans, a T-shirt that stretched over his comfortable belly, a beard that was barely on the respectable side of shaggy. From his right fist a twelve-pack dangled invitingly.

He came right up to Carl, set down the beer, then made as though to embrace him but ended up just clapping his big hands on Carl's shoulders.

"Son of a bitch," Ray Johnson said. "Never wrote, never called, just came sliding back like an old lonesome wolf. Well, you picked your time." He paused. "Do I hear something funny?" He looked down at Ned who had started crying again. "Christ, Ned, is that you down there? I could hardly recognize you in the dark. Why did you have to go and bury yourself?"

"I didn't — " Ned spluttered. "He's going to *kill* me. *Please.*"

Carl watched Ray get down on his knees beside Ned. There was something about Ray that made people feel safe. At least people who never saw him after midnight. With his beard and his size he shambled around the lumber yard like a perfectly trained gentle giant, talking in a courteous stream of profanities, always shouldering the heavy end of the load. When he started to smoulder he just drank more, as though he had long ago decided that anger was something he should turn against himself instead of the outside world, as though there was no fire he couldn't put out with a bottle or a case of beer.

"How about I kill you instead?" Ray folded his muscular hands around Ned's neck. "Don't you know it's a serious crime to bury yourself in another man's garden? Used to be a hanging crime but I left my rope at home. Ned, you little sucker, your Adam's apple is making my fingers nervous. Could you try to keep from swallowing?"

Ned gulped.

"Okay," Carl said. "Why don't you finish him off? Do it so you don't leave any bruises. I'll go call his mother and tell her where to find the body." He started towards the house.

"Noooo!"

Carl turned around. Ray had let go of Ned. He had found the posthole digger and was swinging it around his head, faster and faster, as if gathering the speed it would take to drive it into Ned's head so hard the boy would be decapitated.

"No fucking bruises this way," Ray said.

"*Please!*"

"Stop whining, Ned. You think we like this? How much fun do you think we're having?"

Ned didn't answer. Ray was whirling the posthole digger and it came to Carl that they looked like they were in a scene from some high school play.

"Look, I'll tell you what. Ray and I are going to dig you up and drive you back to your truck. Then Ray and I are going to come back here and drink a few beers and I'm going to tell him a story about a certain kid and a certain cat. Your job is to decide whether you want to behave from now on or whether you're going to keep making problems. Okay?"

Ned, who had started sobbing again, managed to stop. "You didn't have to scare me so bad."

"I didn't have to," Carl said. "But I wanted to. Just like you wanted to do what you did. Or would you rather I just call your parents and the police?"

"Okay," Ned said.

"Okay what?"

"Okay, I've decided. I promise to behave."

"I don't know," Carl said. "How can I believe someone who's just a head sticking out of the ground?" As Ray, in the midst of opening himself a beer burst out laughing, Carl found himself admiring Ned — who at this point looked like little more than a talking cabbage — for having remained convinced he was still a human being who could bargain with his captor. A helpless talking cabbage — that or worse — was probably how Ned had always seemed to his father; and suddenly Carl felt sorry for the boy and started digging him out.

The next evening Carl was out back of the house again, inspecting the holes Ned had dug and wondering what after everything he was going to tell Lizzie about Marbles, when he heard a car slowing on the road and saw headlights swinging into the driveway. Ray again, he thought. The night before, they'd drunk the carton of beer and finished off a bottle of rye that Carl had driven across the country. He explained to Ray how he'd come back determined to be a sober good citizen, a responsible father to his daughter who was, after all, the only person in the world who loved him.

"Ah shit," Ray had said, "you're just fishing." The two of them had erupted into laughter the way they used to and Carl had almost told Ray about the idea he'd had of going into business together. But he hadn't and in the morning he was glad he'd held back. Because as Ray himself had said, he was an old lonesome wolf or at least a wolf that wanted to sniff a few things out before he made any big commitments.

However, he had told Ray about running into Chrissy at Frostie's and going for a drive with her after. Ray had gone silent. "You and Chrissy," he eventually sighed. They might have been back at Ray's three years ago, after Carl moved in, drinking in the darkness that was not only the absence of light but also Carl's misery, which back then had seemed to him a personal Black Sea he was doomed to drown in every night for the rest of his life.

"It's not like that any more," Carl said.

"Feeling bad about a woman is like a room," Ray said. "It's always the same, every time you're in it, but one day you learn how to stay outside and lock the door."

Carl thought about that for a moment. You never knew what Ray was going to come out with but every week or month or year he'd say something so *inside* you that you'd wonder if everything he seemed to be was just a cover-up for an entirely different person.

"Well, I guess I unlocked the door," said Carl, "but I needed to see her or it would have just hung over me until I did."

Now Carl saw it wasn't Ray's truck that had arrived but a car. Despite what he'd said to Ray he had a sudden start as a woman's silhouette detached itself and he thought he recognized Chrissy.

He walked towards her slowly.

"Mr. McKelvey?"

It was the girl from the R&R. Moira someone.

"Carl," Carl said. "You don't have to call me Mister."

"I didn't mean to get here so late. I got lost."

"Better come inside," Carl said.

He went past her and into the kitchen, flipped on the light, waited for her to follow.

"I didn't mean to intrude. I'm from the R&R. Moira Lapointe, you remember—"

Carl thought she looked almost as frightened as Ned Richardson. He moved away from her and tried to smile reassuringly.

"Hey, it's okay." Then he realized he'd been talking to her as though she were a little girl. "Do you want a coffee? A beer?"

"No thanks." She was standing near the door, poised for flight. "I just came out because your father was hoping — he didn't have your phone number or anything — that I could ask you to come visit him at the home on Sunday at lunchtime. Guests can come on Sundays. You left so quickly he didn't get a chance to tell you. And he didn't have your phone number."

"I can give it to you. I'll get something to write it down." His father had never wanted regular visits before. Was he now expected to spend every Sunday at the R&R, eating lunch and making polite conversation? What were they supposed to talk about?

There was a pad of paper in the living room, he remembered. He went in to look for it. Moira trailed him. He suddenly realized that the living-room light had popped last night and he'd forgotten to buy new bulbs. He wondered if Moira had been assigned a social-worker spy mission by his father. When he and his father were living at the farm alone, a social worker had come to visit them a few times after one of McKelvey's first trips to hospital. She would appear unannounced as though she were just dropping in to visit old friends and it was the biggest coincidence in the world that the government paid her to have tea with them.

He started to explain to Moira about the light but she had already sat down in the old armchair in the corner and was holding an unlit cigarette in her hand as if to announce that having managed to arrive, she now intended to stay.

He wondered what she'd learned about him to make her so curious. Or maybe she was just lonely like him. He wanted a beer, but if he drank a beer every time he imagined his hand curling around a bottle... He reached into his pocket for matches and walked over to light her cigarette.

"I guess you and your father are pretty close," Moira said. "He always talks about you."

It occurred to Carl that all things considered she must be joking. He tried to think of some remark to come back with. Being smart was what McKelvey used to call that kind of comeback. His mother had known how to use her tongue. "Used it like a razor," McKelvey had once complained to Carl after the accident and Carl got an unwanted picture of his father and mother kissing, of his father stepping away with blood running down his mouth and chin. These days Carl wasn't much for being smart with words. He was in too deep, too deep inside himself. In even deeper than Ned Richardson had been. Even deeper than the cat Ned Richardson had killed. He was way down deep, six feet under, down so deep he couldn't feel anything except for Lizzie.

Dark hair, a nice smile, almost pretty. Wearing some kind of polo shirt and skirt combination. Some kind of flowery scent. He lit her cigarette, accepted one for himself. He was standing across from her, his cigarette in one hand; the other was still trying to wrap itself around that phantom bottle of beer. His mouth felt dry. He took a step backwards towards the kitchen, stopped himself. He was aware of his jeans hanging awkwardly on his legs. If it hadn't been for Ned Richardson he would have soaked all his clothes in the bathtub this weekend, then hung them out to dry in the sun. He liked the way they smelled after that.

Carl sat down on the sofa, waiting for what she would say, what he would think to reply. There was a patch of light from the kitchen, the pale glow of the moon. Gradually he realized Moira had let him off the hook, she too was just sitting and breathing.

Young woman, nice smile, almost pretty. Likes to show up uninvited. Smooth breather. Answers to Moira. Likes sitting in dark. Might be social worker.

Moira finished her cigarette and sat looking at the moon. She liked Carl's face in the moonlight. His hair was combed straight back on the sides, almost to a ducktail, decades out of date. But there was something in him so fine and tightly drawn you could almost hear it — like the fine sharp twang of a banjo string. You could almost hear it — a song that keeps going in your mind after the music stops. She wished he would say or do something, or maybe his silence meant it was time for her to go. She got out of the chair and crossed the room. Carl stood up.

"Thanks," she said.

He took her hands. They were small and delicate, like a child's. When he released them, they began to slide up his arms and he drew her down to the sofa. The silky run of her arms. Legs touched with her flowery perfume, waves of muscle beneath skin that ran sweet and smooth beneath his tongue as it slid to the insides of her thighs. Her fingers digging into his hair, mapping his skull, pulling him up. Breasts wanting his mouth. Giggles as he carried her upstairs. Then her voice moaning deeply, humming, rising high, casting its spell on him.

In their new silence and the moonlight she made him lie still, first on his back and then on his belly, while she inspected him, hovered over him, cruised her snub-nosed face over his whole body, sniffing and kissing and touching and licking, massaging fingering stroking until he could no longer feel his muscles his bones the mattress the sheets the air, until he was released from everything that had weighed him down since he'd begun returning home and he was floating carefree and satisfied, safe and alive, *alive* in his own new bedroom in his own new house.

He knew he'd fallen asleep when her hands woke him. Again they glided together; this time what was torn from him came reluctantly, remnants of a bitterness hoarded too long.

And then there was the last detail he needed to take care of, the arrival that would complete his homecoming. He asked her if she would go somewhere with him. Soon they were in the truck driving through the last of the night. She was sitting beside him, her body pressed close, and as he drove she took his right hand and tucked it under her jeans and her panties, so that his hand was filled with the tangled half moon of her warmth.

By the time they got to the cemetery there was a faint blue line between the horizon and the receding dark dome of the night. They climbed over the metal fence and walked to the wide twin gravestone of his grandparents and to the matching twin gravestone with his mother's name and dates on one side, the other with his father's name already engraved but without the final date. In the light of the rising dawn the polished grey marble took on the colours of the sky.

Moira bent close to read the writing. As she ran her hands along the letters, Carl could almost feel the cut stone beneath his fingers. He went to sit on the grass. From somewhere down the road the cattle began lowing in a barn until the milkers were switched on and a low hum of machinery spread into the growing light. So strange — all these people gradually being stripped down to bone, accompanied by the twice-daily music of milk being pulsed from swollen cow teats into shining steel tanks.

Moira came and sat beside him. Carl told her how ten years ago, following the last of those New Year's Eve parties Luke Richardson threw at the mansion now known as the West Gull R&R, an all-night booze-up farewell to a century of all-night booze-up farewells, William McKelvey had got so drunk that Elizabeth had insisted Carl drive them home. About two miles from the farm, Carl had fallen asleep at the wheel and piled his car into an oak tree. "When I woke up my father was screaming from a broken knee. She was dead. I was just fine. I walked home and called the police."

They sit, silent, for a long time. "That's how close my father and I are," Carl finally says. "Just wanted to show you. Killed my own mother."

Driving home as light fills the air: trees, houses, barns, rising into the sun. Carl parks the truck, they go into the kitchen. While Carl opens the coffee tin, Moira sits at the table.

"Okay," she starts.

He's at the stove, feeling vulnerable and exposed, he knows he's shown too much. But he had needed to go there, needed someone to witness his truth. His eyes fall onto the cold world of white-enamelled metal and grease stains. "Okay," he agrees and he thinks, *Okay, so what?* He'll just make coffee and then he'll drive her back to the R&R. It's not as if he doesn't know the way. Then he remembers she came on her own. He takes the kettle to the sink. As the tap runs the sun climbs high enough to shoot its light into the streaming water. He tears his eyes away, turns off the tap.

Even at the cemetery where she watched him standing like some crazy tragicomic icon beside his mother's tombstone as the dawn came over the horizon like the yellow light of a slow-moving train, half of her was thinking: Brother, *brother*, am I supposed to believe all this or is this guy just one big good-looking slice of pure country ham. Then the train had come closer and the light began to spread along the rims of the hills and from the cemetery she could hear the noises of the farms starting and in the east see the low silhouette of the town roofs and she stopped thinking because her heart was beating so hard.

The sound of the kettle now fills the kitchen and as the water climbs towards boiling Moira decides that once Carl has poured the water into the filter he has prepared, she will stand up and go to him again.

"There are things I have to explain," Carl says.

Moira wonders what else that quiet voice of his could have to confess.

"I can't be with anyone right now," Carl says. "I mean tonight was great but that's all I'm good for."

He turns his back to her as he pours the water. She's watching her hands and she remembers what she did with his hand as they were driving to the cemetery.

"I hope you don't mind," Carl says. "For all I know you hated it but I thought you should know it's all I'm good for. I'm just too fucked up about my wife and drinking and the old shit in the R&R and the whole thing out at the cemetery and I'm going to try to be a father to my daughter and that's going to take everything I've got."

Now she's glad his back is to her. "You're more than that," she says. God.

"I'm nothing," Carl says. "I'm just an old used-up piece of shit and I know it. But I'm going to do my best for Lizzie." He turns around. "That's the way things are."

PART III

PART III

ONE

MYSTERIES BEGIN WITH THE DISCOVery of the body. Through a careful examination of the relevant details, the circumstances, facts as supplied by witnesses and other third parties, the human body no longer alive becomes the simple and inevitable conclusion to a story of tangled plots and complex motives. In the rush towards this classic finale it is easy to forget that bodies have not only endings but beginnings, beginnings surrounded by complications and entanglements, the kinds of entanglements themselves susceptible to vivid and compelling description, forensic details, even witnesses.

To the beginning in question, the catalytic event that would lead to the existence of the living body of Elizabeth McKelvey, the self-proclaimed prime witness was Flora Goldsmith. It happened late in the afternoon of December 18, 1932, in front of West Gull's historic Long Gull Lake Inn.

At noon, the day had been mild enough to set the town's icicles dripping and to melt what snow remained on its sidewalks so that a friendly almost springlike atmosphere reigned beneath the Christmas decorations that had been strung across Main Street in the hope of loosening a few tight fists. But as the sun followed its shallow arc towards the horizon all that had melted became ice once more. Flora Goldsmith, accustomed to such variations, was keeping her eyes to the pavement as she walked past the inn on her way home from a last-minute trip to the butcher. In one hand she held her shopping bag; the other she used to drag along her son, Adam, at that time a tallish three-year-old with adorable blond ringlets, a babyish way of stumbling when he walked or ran — a quiet well-behaved child who would sit placidly on his mother's knee while emitting an almost inaudible and as yet unintelligible stammer during the bible meetings she held in her kitchen.

Meanwhile, moving in the opposite direction was a Kingston couple. Louis and Lillian Glade had come north to spend a few days at Long Gull Lake Inn because Louis, a clerk at the Queen's University Medical Library, had been advised that he needed a vacation to provide relief from a puzzling series of dizzy spells. Immigrants from Galicia, the Glades made a striking couple: Louis was a tall slender man with distinguished greying temples and narrow handsome features marred only by heavy-lidded eyes; his wife, Lillian, was much shorter, almost stout, with a luxuriant mass of red hair she wore coiled and pinned to the back of her head. In her youth this hair had dazzled at piano recitals where she specialized in moody Rachmaninoff concertos. "Like a big copper snake just waiting to strike," Flora Goldsmith later complained to her son, who would have his own part to play.

Arm in arm, the Glades were also keeping their eyes to the icy sidewalk. Just before the collision, Adam Goldsmith looked up at the Glades and let out a warning shriek. The Glades, startled, lost their footing and pitched forward into Adam and Flora. All four went down, in the process jolting free the egg that must be considered the beginning's beginning. In the barrage of soothings and apologies that followed, Louis Glade insisted that the inconsolable Adam, along with Flora and her husband, Hank — the assistant manager at the local bank — join them that evening for dinner.

After the dinner the Glades retired to their room where the inadequate radiators combined with several layers of down comforters and a sagging mattress to produce an intensely romantic interlude. Nine months later the previously unimpregnable Lillian Glade, copper snake and all, gave birth to a daughter. Overwhelmed with happiness they decided their princess must be named after a real princess — Elizabeth.

Meanwhile Adam, apparently himself catalyzed by this incendiary collision, soon progressed from uncontrollable stammering to speaking in tongues. In an ecstasy of thrashing and drooling he would fall to the floor and moan wild strings of babble — possessed by the Holy Spirit, demons, or the need to show off, depending on whom you asked.

From the mouths of babes, and Adam was young.

Flora Goldsmith claimed it first happened the week after the fateful encounter with the vacationing Glades. As always Adam was sitting on her lap, relaxed and docile; she had one arm slung around his waist and stomach while her free hand held the Bible, reading to her fellow members of the Inner Circle from Paul's first epistle to the Corinthians. At that point, she said, it took him over. *It* — a thing she couldn't define but could feel inside him, a restless overexcited demon that had taken control of her son's body, twitching his muscles convulsively, expelling all manner of grunts and moans as though it were trying to burst out of Adam's skin to be born itself. It threw Adam to the floor in what she first thought was an epileptic seizure, then recognized as possession.

Adam's memories were both more vague and more general: he would be gripping his mother's thigh between his knees and rocking back and forth, pretending she was a horse which was how he passed the time when she was in her Bible-reading moments, and his tongue would suddenly fill with butterflies, fluttering spluttering butterflies. His tongue would be rocking and fluttering and spluttering and then he would start to hum, as he often did, except that on these occasions he felt something growing inside his tongue, swelling it up, and as the butterfly fluttered and spluttered, the noise got louder and the wet underside of his tongue began to bounce against his lower lip fighting and exciting him until his body would start to shake as though that imaginary horse were galloping across rough bone-rattling ground — which was where it entered next, the bones — and for the last time he would open his eyes, or sometimes he thought he was looking right through the lids, and as the sounds took him over and he fell from his mother's knee he would see Lorna Richardson or Jessica Boyce or Katherine Dean or Miranda Arnold or any of those dozen women who in varying combinations would gather in his mother's kitchen, and as he fell there was this great rush of air as though he'd been sucked down into a tunnel only to be instantly spat out, writhing on the floor among the big heavy skirts that swayed like bottomless tents, airless odiferous tents swaying in harmony to the yabbering and jabbering of his gabbly song, and as he yabbered it and jabbered it his head would open up and bits of the lives of the Ladies of the Inner Circle would present themselves, complete with coy virgin blushes stolen kisses the voices the midnight couplings the blood between the legs the trees pushing themselves up through the skulls of the dead the wild.

Afterwards Adam would be left lying empty on the floor, wet and ashamed, his bones aching; then Flora would pick him up and wrap her arms around him, rock him gently back and forth reciting: "Though I speak with the tongues of men and of angels, and have not charity, I am become as a sounding brass, or a tinkling cymbal."

Eventually the news of Adam's gift spread all the way to Toronto and an expert in such cases came to inspect. His mission was duly reported in the West Gull *Weekly Bugle*:

> The Very Reverend Samuel Everett White graced our small community today to meet our most wondrous local phenomenon, Adam Goldsmith, the West Gull child known throughout the area for speaking in tongues.
>
> After spending the afternoon with Adam and his mother, Flora, the Very Reverend White pronounced himself well satisfied with the genuine nature of the boy's "possessions."
>
> "Remember Paul," he said, "who wrote to the Corinthians: 'Concerning spiritual gifts, brethren, I would not have you ignorant.'"
>
> He further counselled those present to remember that Paul also said, "He that speaketh in an unknown tongue edifieth himself; but he that prophesieth edifieth the church." By this was meant, he explained, that personal glory, even in the religious sense, must always subordinate itself to the welfare of the religious community.

Accompanying the article was a picture of the kindly and smiling Very Reverend White seated on the living-room sofa with Adam, who looked suitably abashed and ringleted. The Very Reverend had just asked Adam what went through his mind when he "uttered." Adam, closing his eyes to conjure the moment, instead remembered that Katherine Dean's shins were covered with a strange fine fuzz similar to mouse fur.

Within a year or two Adam began to listen more closely to his mother's readings, though he heard not "charity" but "clarity," which put him in mind of the sounding brass and the tinkling cymbal. Finally when he was eight years old and entitled to his own chair, as his tongue started to flutter and slap against his lower lip and its base began its painful tumescent tremble, the words "tinkling cymbal" made him picture two large shining brass plates ready to strike against each other. This distraction was what ruined it: instead of falling on the floor and babbling he got up from his chair to look in the refrigerator.

One of the items sure to be present was a pint-sized bottle with a flower-edged label reading Adam's Deep Sleep. Adam's Deep Sleep was an anti-colic medicine his mother used to brew from local herbs and sell in fancy little bottles. Adam's Deep Sleep really worked. Or at least people thought it did because to begin with Adam's Deep Sleep had been the mixture Flora used on her son, and everyone knew how deep were *his* sleeps. Amid the flowers of the label was an only slightly idealized version of Adam's face, a little round cherub with fat blond curls and pink Cupid's lips.

The Deep Sleep was how Adam had met Luke Richardson: a baby so cranky and tormented by colic that Adam never forgot him laid out in his pram in a pink dress, face and hairless skull wrinkled blood-pitch with pain and rage, gums wide open as he howled. Flora would pick him up and give him a few mouthfuls of Adam's Deep Sleep — the pint bottle in her refrigerator was a special codeine-reinforced supply she kept for emergencies. "You're so well-behaved, such a good boy," Luke's mother would meanwhile praise Adam. "I hope Luke grows up to be like you."

Instead Luke grew into one of the tough little boys at the West Gull Elementary, booting the soccer ball about in the spring and fall, in the winter taking his lumps playing hockey with the older boys on the outdoor rink. Adam was several grades ahead and didn't pay much attention until late one winter afternoon. He was leaving the school after choir practice and a group of boys who'd been playing hockey attacked the choir with snowballs — a routine occurrence at the West Gull Elementary. This was the signal for the girls to run away so the boys could chase after and leap on top of them with much giggling and face-rubbing and sometimes kissing.

But this time Luke and two of his friends came directly after Adam. Bigger, careless, still thinking of Luke as the squalling brat in the carriage, Adam reached down to scoop up some snow. His fingers found a chunk of ice. He threw it with all his strength and it caught Luke in the face. With a roar of rage Luke leapt on Adam, fists swinging wildly. While the others gathered about, he took Adam down to the ground. As Adam raised his arms to protect himself, Luke's mittened fists crashed into his nose. There was a sharp intense pain between his eyes, he felt the blood gush out, heard his own howl of helplessness and rage. He was curled in the snow, crying, nose streaming blood while Luke, a boy four years younger, kept pounding to the cheers of his friends.

The next day at school Luke approached him in the yard. "Guh-day, *Adam*. How you doing?" He clapped Adam on the arm as though they were old cronies, equals, and stuck out his hand. Adam was twelve years old, four grades ahead of Luke and half a foot taller. As they shook hands Luke said in an unbroken boy's voice that made his words sound even more unpleasant, "Sorry about yesterday, Adam. From now on, you can count on me. Anyone gives you shit, I'll kill him."

By the next year, Adam's last at the West Gull Elementary, Luke was almost his height and his voice had turned to gravel. No one took runs at him playing hockey any more; he was growing big and strong the way Richardsons did. Just the sound of his skates carving up the ice was enough to turn the others into quickly fading ghosts.

Sometimes after choir practice Adam would pause at the rink on the way home, watching Luke and thinking that after eight years at school he had no real friends — just one enemy — and Adam would feel a stone in his heart. Sometimes Luke would see Adam, wave to him as he glided by. "Adam, how's my man?" Then Adam graduated and started taking the bus to high school. He would see Luke only occasionally on the street, and Luke would always come and greet him, shake his hand as if already campaigning to be elected.

After he was killed, a photograph of Hank Goldsmith appeared on the polished walnut corner table of the living room of the house he had bought with Flora. It showed him in his airforce uniform, tall and lanky, the handsome big-beaked face his son inherited looking at the camera as if this posing for eternity was just an elaborate hoax. A second photo in Flora's bedroom, a signed picture enclosed in a gilt-edged frame, opened up like a book and contained a message: *To Flora, from her lonely pilot, Hank.* The picture presented him in half-profile, his bony face romantically shadowed. The pictures had been sent from the Golden Memory Studios in London, England, a week before he was killed in an air raid.

"Hank liked it that way," Flora Goldsmith would say about such things as cooking the peas with the roast or mowing the lawn for the last time on Labour Day. It was Hank this and Hank that and Hank's closet full of Hank's clothes — some of them wrapped in their dry-cleaning plastic from twenty years before — waiting for Hank to come home, along with Hank's section of the bookcase and in the basement, neatly arranged, Hank's fishing tackle, Hank's golf clubs, Hank's hunting rifle and hanging from a nail, too perfect for any foot, Hank's fancy waterproof leather hunting boots, which had been Flora's last present to him, the one she bought for his homecoming. Once or twice when Adam came back from school he caught his mother in the kitchen, slightly drunk, her dead husband's boots spread out on newspapers on the table, getting a polish.

The war had left the town short of men; most who remained were quick to volunteer for double duty. And the Inner Circle was not lacking in widows who left their children at the Goldsmith house for a few days while they took a recreational trip to Ottawa or Toronto. But Flora never made such trips; no embarrassed suitors ever showed up at the door, there were never unexplained visitors or absences. There was just "Hank liked it this way" and Hank's pictures and Hank's boots and her visions that she reported to the Inner Circle of the Church of the Unique God. And of course work: she had her widow's pension and a trickle of income from Adam's Deep Sleep, but eventually Flora had to start nursing again. Often this meant she would be out all night leaving Adam to fend for himself. But his mother's calm abstinence and devotion to duty found their mirror in her studious young son. Or perhaps he'd had his orgies young — not in bed but wherever it was he lived with the voices, taken over by their rantings, their wild songs, their unending excesses as much as one person's flesh can be taken by another. Or so Adam decided. By the time the voices withdrew he had been so exhausted and humiliated by them he was relieved to be beached far from the storm, happy to stand aside while others began compulsively twitching their hormonal dances. He watched. He had girl friends but friends were all they were. His odd distance made it easy for them to confide and sometimes they used him to try their perfumes or even their wiles. But whatever he was missing he didn't miss it. When he left his mother's house to go to university in Ottawa, his aloofness gave him a new role: in the student residences he became a kind of priest — a confirmed abstainer to whom everything could be confessed.

The week after his graduation Adam flew to London in search of Golden Memory Studios. He found it in Earl's Court, a run-down shop with a dirty counter up front and in the back a little room that smelled of tobacco and stale aquarium water. The curtain was a dark moth-eaten disaster Adam recognized from his father's picture. He sat on what must have been the same stool, posed in semi-profile the same way, lit a cigarette to produce that careless swirl of smoke. Adam remembered his father as lean and tanned, the kind of outdoorsman featured on the covers of magazines. But his father's last photographs had shown a gaunt middle-aged man pale with the romantic tragedy of the forties, his thoughtful eyes filled with the horrors of war.

He was staying in a hotel near Hyde Park. He discovered that the British were an odd race: their television, their sausages, their brown sauce, their habit of looking at you as though to ask what you were doing there. Adam's only answer was that he was searching for his dead father. When he went back to Golden Memory Studios to pick up his portrait he asked the owner, a man who looked eligible to have survived all the wars since the Restoration, if he remembered Hank or Henry Goldsmith.

"Hank or Henry Goldsmith? Which was it?"

"The soldier. He had his picture taken here during the war."

"During the war?"

The next week Adam returned to Canada to take up a job at the Kingston tax department. He moved into a downtown apartment building, a one-bedroom furnished with a truckload of worn second-hand furniture he bought one Saturday morning at Turk's Antiques. The upholstery was all red-ribbed velour, popular at the time, the dining-room set was peeling oak veneer, the bedsprings were edged with rust. At his mother's insistence he bought a new mattress to avoid germs. Nights he would come home, cook himself something out of a can, read the books he spent his lunch hours borrowing from the library. Occasionally he would work up the courage to go to a movie where, standing alone in line and feeling like a freak from the psychiatric hospital, he would hide behind his newspaper until he got his ticket, then huddle into his seat grateful for the dark. After his second month he sacrificed his movie nights to begin saving in a separate account with the plan to eventually go back to London and take a graduate degree in economics.

Flora Goldsmith believed in the powers of love and coincidence: star-struck destinies, first meetings, chance encounters, fateful slips on the ice. *Testimonies*, she called these significant stories. In the Inner Circle, participants were encouraged to relate their testimonies: what they had witnessed, where they had been, how they had experienced the crucial moments of their lives.

Another coincidence: when Elizabeth gave her testimony Adam happened to be at the house. He had a day off from the tax department and was in the basement stacking lengths of maple for the big wood furnace.

Years later, Adam would ask Elizabeth, "How could you tell them all about yourself just like that? How did you have the courage? What even made you go to the meeting?"

"It was Dorothy Dean's idea. She was subbing that day and after school she invited me to go to your mother's. She made it sound like a game, not a religious ceremony. Your mother — she had such a calm face, yet you sensed that beneath the calmness was some kind of wildness, or understanding of wildness. And at the time I was feeling so … out of place here. Stranded. What was I doing living with a farmer in the middle of nowhere? Or not nowhere at all, but a very specific somewhere where everyone had known and been related to each other for a million generations. I had nothing to go back to, no way forward. When your mother asked me to talk about myself it was the first time in the five years I'd lived here that anyone showed any interest. Real interest. *Tell us about yourself.* She asked as though she really wanted to know and I thought, well, Elizabeth, here's your chance, right in front of everyone, blurt it all out; maybe it will make things easier. And once I got started I couldn't stop."

"Thank God. It was the first time I ever heard someone talk about her life as though it was something real, actually being lived every moment, and not a Sunday school lesson." At first what caught him was her voice. Between the thunking of the logs and his own panting he couldn't even hear her actual words. Until he found himself sitting on one of the stumps, mesmerized by the bittersweet honey of her voice.

"My parents had developed a fascination with British royalty, which is why they named me after a princess. Then Edward VIII abdicated to marry the Duchess of Windsor and George VI became king, putting my princess, as my parents always called her, in line to be queen.

"As I grew older I began to realize that the king was everywhere. On stamps. On money. And when I went to school I saw the king's picture in every classroom. Of course I thought he must be looking directly at me, keeping track of me just as I was keeping track of him."

She had started by explaining why her parents had named her after Princess Elizabeth and by the time Adam was really listening she was up to 1951, the year Princess Elizabeth — the British one — came to Canada. Elizabeth recounted how she and her parents gave this royal tour all the attention due a famous family member travelling through the region. Articles in the newspaper were cut out and read aloud. The best ones were scotch-taped to the kitchen wall. Sometimes certain sentences were underlined. *The Princess was in good spirits despite the fact that she has been on the train 23 consecutive days.* Or, *Elementary school students from Sudbury lined the track for two and a half miles in anticipation of the Princess's arrival.* Louis Glade, the acknowledged family master of protocol, was in charge of the underlining. He also initialled each clipping with a tiny italic flourish in the upper right-hand corner.

As the clippings took over the kitchen walls, Elizabeth's mother began to tease Louis Glade about his royal obsession. Then one Friday night when he had carved the chicken and had in front of him a crystal glass filled with the sickly sweet red wine that was dispensed once a week from a matching crystal decanter — fortunately he was no longer alive when scientists discovered that the lead contained in crystal might have brought down the Roman Empire — Louis Glade made his speech.

"If I may bring up such a subject on the Sabbath" — when about to launch an attack Louis Glade always liked to establish that he had the floor — "I understand I am being reprimanded for my overenthusiastic attitude regarding the British royal family. Am I correct?"

"The chicken is getting cold."

"Forget it," Louis Glade said and sat down. What he meant them to forget was unknown. It was October 18 — the day Princess Elizabeth had toured an egg-processing plant in Sarnia. Louis was seated behind a mound of carved chicken. In the bright light of the Sabbath candles, his cheeks looked slightly drained, his forehead clammy. He had let go of his glass. Elizabeth was still trying to decide what she was meant to forget when she realized that Louis Glade was the one doing the forgetting. Dr. Blum later told them he had probably begun to lose consciousness even while he was standing. Certainly by the time he uttered his final words he would have known he was dying. That was the way Elizabeth always remembered her father. Shirt faultlessly white, cuffs and cufflinks shot from his blue Sabbath blazer, leaning forward, his neck corded, his eyes closed, his long fingers clutching at the carved walnut arms of his dining chair.

The next year King George VI also died unexpectedly. Princess Elizabeth became Queen Elizabeth. Elizabeth Glade was by then twenty years old and in her second year at Queen's University. On the morning of the new queen's coronation address, which was scheduled to hit the Canadian airwaves at six a.m., Eastern Standard Time, Elizabeth set her alarm clock for five-thirty. Groggily she got up in the dark, wrapped herself in the pink quilted housecoat she'd received for her sixteenth birthday and set out for the kitchen to make coffee. There she found her mother, dressed in the black suit she had used for her husband's funeral, eating breakfast on her yellow rose wedding china. After the broadcast Lillian said that she had been thinking: life wasn't forever; it was time to begin finding joy in the present.

To set an example she made French toast out of white bread and poured on generous helpings of maple syrup. At seven o'clock that evening a man who radiated money showed up at the door. His name was Lionel Meyers and he told Elizabeth he was from the meat business in Chicago.

Several months after her mother's declaration Elizabeth was in a Queen's University cafeteria, drinking coffee from a cracked white porcelain mug and writing an essay on the thorny question of Henry II's contribution to the British legal system. But though she had surrounded her lined notepad with numerous reference books and had a list of quotations ready to insert at critical moments, her mind's eye was filled with pictures of Robin Hood.

Question: If England was so proud of its legal system, why was a thief, Robin Hood, its most beloved symbol of justice?

"Because Robin Hood is more interesting," said a young man who was standing opposite her.

She flushed. But if you have the tendency to speak aloud when you mean to think silently, you should expect such intercessions.

"We could go for a walk," he said.

William McKelvey was in a couple of her classes and she'd met him several times at parties, the coffeeshop where students often went in groups, even the Royal Tavern where a few fellow escapees from Early Medieval British History would occasionally pass a Friday evening. McKelvey was older: one of the "mature students" who had gone to war instead of finishing high school and ended up in university years later on a Veteran's Scholarship. Like most of the ex-soldiers he seemed surrounded by an almost visible shell, beneath which Elizabeth had always suspected there must be a tough little knot formed by various unthinkable experiences.

But where the other ex-soldiers appeared mature and certain of what they were doing, McKelvey gave off a vaguely Bohemian air. His flannels bagged at the knees, his blazer strained across his broad back, and the two strands of his tie appeared to have divorced. All winter he'd worn a shapeless navy overcoat that might as well have been made from a blanket and his blond uncut hair stuck out like so many clumps of straw from beneath his red toque. Once Elizabeth and a girlfriend had thrown snowballs at the red toque. McKelvey had laughed and the three of them had ended up drinking hot chocolate and eating fries at Morrison's, a downtown eatery that served the kind of food and clientele the Glade family had always avoided.

"When William suggested a walk I was glad to go. I wasn't looking for a husband — I had plans to be a teacher. Anyway, I'd never even had a boyfriend, unless you count Herman Bowles in Grade Seven, who wasn't exactly my boyfriend but we liked each other and everyone knew it. In Grade Eight we were both invited to Sarah Rosen's party with dancing in the basement. We were sent into the closet to kiss. He put his hand on my chest and I was so scared that I laughed. After that he was afraid of me and I didn't know what to do. In Grade

Nine we went to different schools and I haven't seen him since. But then I gave up, there was no one my father would have approved of. But I didn't mind William and I wanted to get out of that cafeteria and away from worrying about the foundations of the British legal system."

Soon they had crossed the campus and were at the lakeshore. The wind was from the south, warm, full of foreign thoughts and unknown adventures. McKelvey offered a cigarette, then lit up with the kind of sigh still permissible in those prehistoric times.

Crocuses and bluebells had already flowered in the gardens edging the lake, and from the budding branches of nearby maples the gently piercing cries of red-winged blackbirds and evening grosbeaks could be heard.

"This place drives me crazy," McKelvey said.

"We could sit somewhere else."

"This city, I mean. Sometimes I just wish I was in a car, driving."

She was at a comfortable distance from him on the bench, half turned towards him, looking at his hands; they were broad and muscular, the skin rough, the nails bitten to the quick. Bitten nails give you away, her mother had once told her.

He stood up. Elizabeth was unsure if he was stretching, getting into position for a speech or on his way back to the library. When he started walking she followed along. Without speaking they wandered along King Street, then cut across to Princess. He took her not to the Royal, where all the students went, but to a restaurant where he ordered fish and chips and half a litre of red wine.

They drank the first half-litre and ordered another. William had hardly spoken. The wine had made his lips fuller and darker and Elizabeth kept watching the way, after he put his glass down, they glistened and caught the light. She felt drunk. Maybe the wind had got hold of her after all. Waiting for the new wine she took one of his cigarettes and started talking about her father.

"You can't meet him," she began. It seemed a clever way to introduce Louis Glade's current situation — i.e., dead — but as she spoke she realized William McKelvey would think she meant he was not the right sort of person to bring home. By the time she corrected herself on this account, described the sudden circumstances of Louis Glade's passing, then moved back to recapitulate the royal tour of 1951 and her own family's peculiar and personal relationship to the British monarchy, she required a second cigarette.

The faster she talked, the dryer grew her throat and the more she had to drink; and the more she drank the more clearly she could see William McKelvey's face. Just as an hour in front of the mirror gradually draws you into the topography of your own features, so did an hour of non-stop babbling to William McKelvey draw her into his. Which was peculiar, she thought even while she went on, because although she was the one doing the talking, he was the one she was getting to know.

His dirty blond hair, a bit too long, was roughly parted on one side. A cowlick which he kept pushing back hung over his forehead and his eyes had turned a shimmering silky brown. She had developed no romantic intentions as yet but she was already thinking she had never known, or at least never noticed, anyone whose eyes shone in this particular way. With the wine, she now saw that the whole set of his mouth; the mysterious unspeakable grimness she had attributed to the war had smoothed away. Suddenly he was just like any other young man. Except for those big hands that looked like they should belong to a labourer, not a university student. The bitten nails that made her feel safe. The voice, though he hardly spoke, that lacked the supercilious tones of the other Queen's boys she'd met.

"Later I understood that what had attracted me to McKelvey was everything that was missing: the blazer-flannel uniform, the condescending voice, the calm would-be ruling-class assurance the other students exuded as though it were a perfume they showered in each morning. That perfume, that assurance, was what my father, Louis, had tried to invent for himself and his family. But what did it do for him? Turned him into a ridiculous royalty-worshipping parody of some imaginary aristocracy; just remembering him drove my mother into the arms of her Chicago meat king. What attracted me to McKelvey, I finally understood, was that he was strong enough to be nothing but himself — a man with silky eyes, a suicide tie, big comfortable hands, a way of mocking the pretensions of others that made me feel we shared something."

The bill came. McKelvey stood up and, as though he knew how dizzy and unsteady she felt, came to her side of the table and casually took her arm, helping her to her feet.

That gesture was important. She came to interpret it and its occasional successors to mean that despite everything, beneath everything, or possibly just beside everything, he was a gentleman and he understood her. Ideas like these, especially the idea that you are understood, can take years to lose. Although certain ideas, once lost, can never be regained. But in the end Elizabeth would have said being understood was never the point. What you hope for is an acceptable mix of comfort and passion. In the end Elizabeth would have also said that what you hope for is not the point. It's what you do with what you have. Unless it's throwing what you have away and not having anything.

Outside it was dark and the wind off the lake had turned cold. Adjusting her coat, Elizabeth staggered slightly and it seemed natural for her to slide her hand into the crook of William's arm.

William was lighting a new cigarette as though her hand weren't there. Again she found this infinitely tactful because she had meant only to be holding herself steady. The cloth of his navy coat was surprisingly rough. She squeezed her hand around it, running into his arm which felt thick and solid. They started walking. She kept her hand in place, letting it be pressed between his arm and his side, letting the whole length of her arm sometimes rest against his as he matched his stride to hers.

When they got back to the cafeteria it was locked. She had taken her hand away at the door, a gesture she'd been planning for a few minutes, and now they stood, separated, looking in the dark windows.

"Sorry," William McKelvey said.

"It's not your fault." She could see their reflections. They looked like a couple.

"I could walk you home," he offered.

"Eventually we're in front of my house. My mother is off in Chicago so the curtains are closed, the hall light off. I feel stunned and get ready to invite him in because the idea of him leaving makes me feel confused. But William just says 'Goodnight,' puts his hand on my shoulder, turns and strides away.

"Unlocking the door I already have a new theory: the reason William McKelvey seems so substantial is that he is alive, flesh and blood, whereas the man I'm used to, my father, is just a ghost."

She sat at the kitchen table drinking her tea. On a piece of paper listing housework to be done before her mother's return, she drew a picture of a giant bed in the shape of a sandwich. The bed was tilted forward. She gave it pillows that looked like mustard bottles. She drew the heads of her mother and Lionel Meyers on the pillows. They were smiling. They were in the kingdom of smoked meat and spiced salami; so long as their supply of cola and chips lasted, they would be happy.

The next afternoon she was back in the cafeteria, her notes recovered, working away on her essay. She had decided to be in favour of Henry II. Queen Elizabeth had her royal tours, her gold- and red-velvet wardrobe, her old masters and her hounds, but she didn't really have anything to do. Worse, her father had died of being king and her uncle had been glad to get out of it.

Henry II, on the other hand, had swashbuckled through the primeval forest, guzzling beer and decreeing decrees. A British Caesar, he had stamped the world with his mind and more than seven hundred years later, Elizabeth Glade, a second-generation Galician-Canadian Jew studying in a small city in the heartland of a continent Henry II hadn't dreamt might exist, was admiring his accomplishments.

In the millennia to come, in the library of a space-station university orbiting an as yet undiscovered planet, no one was going to read about the accomplishments of George VI. At best he would be a royal footnote to his brother's story, the story of a man who had traded an empire for his bride.

Elizabeth's mind had swerved to the Plantagenets — the royal blood, the good old sword-waving banner-crackling days when a king was a king, the days when her own ancestors were getting ready to be racked and roasted in Spain — when she felt someone standing behind her.

Before she could turn, William McKelvey had circled the table and sat down opposite. His face looked pink, as though scraped with a too-sharp razor and his dirty-blond hair was firmly slicked into place.

"How are you?"

"Okay," Elizabeth said.

He wasn't wearing a coat, just a bulky cable-knit sweater with sleeves pushed up to his elbows. His forearms were thick and sunburned. He would have a made a good knight, she thought, the kind of man a Plantagenet could use, arms strong enough for shield and sword.

"Do you want to go for a drive?"

"A drive?"

"In my car. We could—" He fell silent.

It was early afternoon. Too late for a picnic lunch, too early for a drive-in.

"Where were you thinking of going?" Elizabeth asked, afraid he might find her difficult.

"I don't know."

"Okay," she said. She began closing up her books, placing them with her notes in her father's old briefcase which, aside from his ghost, seemed to be her main inheritance. When she stood up William reached across the table and took the case.

His car was an ancient pre-war snub-nosed Ford. Dusty and bulbous, it seemed to belong to a different species than the salami king's sleek sedan. "Still runs most of the time."

The inside of the car was as newly washed and scraped as William himself. There were wipe marks on the dashboard and beneath the smell of soap were the stale odours of tobacco and oil.

She had supposed he would drive along the lake. That was what Lionel Meyers did when he took her and her mother for "a spin." They would appreciate the view of the water, drive slowly past the large gabled brick waterfront houses military money had built, maybe continue to the ferry landing and ride across to Wolfe Island where they would take tea at the General Wolfe before riding the ferry home again.

But William was heading north, away from Lake Ontario, away from historic Kingston with its historic money, its historic fort, its historic parliament that its historic city-wise legislators from Montreal and Toronto had found too historic and boring to occupy. Soon he was on a narrow paved road that wound between farms and increasingly craggy hills crowned by huge spreading maples and oaks. The landscape was a hilly explosion of mud and green swarming with life. There were cows, sheep, horses, even goats. Peeling clapboard houses with long burdened clotheslines, barns surrounded by clusters of pigs and chickens and geese and sometimes a swaggering nose-ringed bull that would turn its red eyes to them as they passed. Overhead the sky was a deep luminous blue encircled by woolly clouds that floated whitely above the horizon. The sun came in William's side. He had his window open, his left arm hanging out. The way the light came through his hair made him seem to be wearing a golden halo, and as the road wound the halo shifted but never went away.

After a while they came to a gas station beside a lake. Its windows were shuttered, waiting for tourist season but the door was open. William went inside and brought out a large man wearing overalls. While they gassed up the car, the man in overalls talked to William, his words tumbling out quickly, punctuated by toothless laughs. William seemed to understand, nodding vigorously as the man spoke and replying with a few of his own enigmatic grunts.

William and Elizabeth started off again, supplied with bottles of orange pop that William had fished out of the cooler. William was still driving north.

"Are we going anywhere special?" Elizabeth asked.

"I don't know," William said. "We have to get a bit closer, see how it feels." He looked across the seat at her, then turned back to the road.

"How I felt was nervous, afraid. I knew some kind of test was coming and I wasn't sure I wanted to pass. Suddenly I felt like my own skeptical parents, needing to know more about him. I asked his plans for after he graduated. 'We vets get offered jobs,' he told me. 'Insurance companies, government. Or I could go into some kind of engineering — I was a sapper during the war.' Then he asked me about myself and I explained that I was studying history and English, that I was planning to go into teaching.

"History and English? What was that supposed to mean to someone who specialized in blowing things up? What was I doing choosing Robin Hood over the British legal system? But I needed to be with William. Nothing fancy, just sitting in his car or standing in the middle of the street or going for a walk to nowhere, anything at all so long as I was with him, just like those women in the silly stories my mother read in the magazines she bought to amuse herself between visits with the smoked-meat king.

"On top of a hill, William pulled the car over. We were beside a cemetery. Beyond us the road curved slowly until it disappeared behind a row of trees; then it picked up again, a long black ribbon leading finally to a town flattened against the side of a lake. I asked him what the town was. West Gull, he said, on Long Gull Lake, and so there it was — so bizarre — this man had led me to the mythological place where I'd supposedly been conceived after my parents had an accident on the ice."

While Elizabeth admired the towering stone archway of the West Gull Cemetery, William undid the latched gate. Early dandelions spotted the grass as, of course, did graves. At the front there was a section marked by flat rectangular stones, hardly larger than shoebox tops, pushed so far into the earth their engraved surfaces were level with the grass. The dates there were all a hundred years old or more — this, Elizabeth saw, must have been the original settlers' cemetery, a northern boot hill placed high for the view or because of some super-stition. Beside and behind the horizontal markers rose the tombstones. Shiny, dull, large, small, expensive, modest, adorned, plain, fronted by flowers real or plastic or entirely absent — the hundreds of tombstones were a random testi-mony to lives and fortunes unpredictably gained and lost. Along a small crest stood a few trees, ancient wind-tortured maples, gnarled trunks and boughs offering their still-dense burdens of leaves to the sun. Just beyond the trees, William pointed at a double gravestone. One side read:

LORNA ARNOLD MCKELVEY
1900–1932

Carved into the other side was:

SAMUEL ARNOLD MCKELVEY
1895–

"There's my mother," William said. "My father still hasn't made it but we know where he's going."

"You must have been—"

"Twelve years old," William said. "They were some kind of cousins. When the second baby came along it was made wrong and my mother died trying to have it." While William told this his face jerked, as though he were back there watching. "Sorry," he said. "Since we were in the neighbourhood—" Elizabeth was calculating that William must be thirty-three, which was older than she had thought, and now that she could put a number to his age the confident way he had of just *doing* things without preliminaries made more sense. And then William turned, took her hands in his, looked straight into her face.

The May grass. The fragrant breeze coming across the fields. The soft sounds of leaves. His hands were squeezing hers, hard. Just as the pressure began to turn into pain, he loosened his grip. Elizabeth stepped away. The lake, the town, the farmland. The dizzy richness of the grass. The dizzy thumping of her heart in the centre of this strange universe. She had a weird presentiment that she was being introduced to the place where she would be buried. Somehow this idea seemed normal.

"Walk?" McKelvey now asked. Before Elizabeth could answer he was off again, past the gravestones and out a gate at the back of the cemetery that gave onto a path twisting down into a cedar-filled valley.

The fragrance was thick, a sweet full odour Elizabeth inhaled until she felt her lungs would burst. Further down a small creek zigzagged through a rocky descent that wound between the cedars. They sat on a large flat boulder at the water's edge. Elizabeth took in the moss, the trilliums, the ferns, the strange gradations and shadings of colour of the layered cedar bark. She picked a wild violet and as she brushed its velvety petals against her cheek a burst of blue butterflies swept by like a convoy from another world; and then mixed in with the bright rush of water she could almost hear the echoes of the voices of children come to fish or make little boats or watch birds like the small yellow-bellied canary-like creatures fluttering nearby. The children could never have guessed that one day there would be a cemetery and highway just a few steps away from their tiny paradise.

It occurred to Elizabeth that just as the children had been unable to see the future so wholly concrete to her, so was she blind to her own future. The future she and William would or wouldn't share. Perhaps one day this moment would be a remembered aberration, a fragrant unexpected digression in which she glimpsed her own beginning as a prelude to her launch into the kind of life her parents had in mind — teacher, wife of a secure professional or businessman, carrier of the Glade blood into a lakeside brick home complete with family silver and other accoutrements. That would be no place for someone like William. William was someone else, Elizabeth thought, but she was as blind to his invisible chains as he was to hers. Meanwhile William, who had taken out a penknife, was entirely concentrated on whittling a twig of cedar. He looked like a twelve-year-old in permanent hiding from being the kind of man the parental Glades wanted for their daughter. His skin was flushed with the open air and his usually angular and ironic face had gone smooth and round.

Now he raised his head, smiled at her, folded up his knife. He stood up. "Better get going." He started walking, out of the grove and towards the cemetery.

Back in the car Elizabeth felt she'd been enchanted. How was it he always knew what to do and she just ran after him? To break the spell she said, "What about your father?"

"Don't worry," William answered. "We're getting to him."

They drove into West Gull and out the other side. There was a gas station, a few stores, a church, sidestreets lined with neat frame houses each fronted by an emerald patch of May grass. Elizabeth searched in vain for a spark of recognition but it was just a small town with empty streets.

The fields on the other side of town were orderly and prosperous. The alfalfa and clover were dense and uniform, the fences solid and unbroken, the clusters of barns augmented by shining silver silos poking up like so many incongruous and boastful rockets. Between the fields and along the roads stretched long rows of elm and maple. "When men get old, they plant trees," Elizabeth remembered her father saying. If so, whoever had planted these neat lines of trees must be under the flat stones at the cemetery.

After a while the paved road turned to gravel and the car began to jostle and shake in a bone-rattling dance that set Elizabeth bouncing on the seat. She looked over to William. He was watching her, grinning. Suddenly he jerked the steering wheel so violently the car skidded around a corner and onto a narrow dirt road.

It was late in the afternoon and the light was beginning to slant through the trees. They were so far from anything

Elizabeth knew, they might as well have been on a polar expedition. Except that instead of being winter it was spring, and instead of a sky filled with a screaming blizzard they were driving beneath a bower of newly leaved maples. William turned onto a dirt path and continued until they came to a rusted mailbox.

"This is it," William announced. They were parked at the top of the drive. On one side was the letterbox on its tilted post. On the other, a rotting platform Elizabeth would learn had been used for milk in the days when William's father had set out cans for the truck going to the cheese factory.

William was still wearing his little boy's face, the face he must have worn when he walked up this drive on the way to school, a school in which he would have been taught by a woman perhaps similar to the woman Elizabeth intended to become.

"Don't worry," William said. He turned the car towards the house, a ramshackle frame structure, the remains of its white paint hanging from the siding in shreds. Behind it were two large barns. Wagons, farm implements, old tires, two cars that might have been parked for a thousand years or more, a tractor, a truck with one side of the windshield bashed in were scattered between the barns. A few pigs and cattle grazed among them, pushing at the weeds and mud.

Elizabeth stepped out of the car. The smell was strong and ripe. From the other side of the house, in the direction of one of the barns, there came a loud shout. "Jay-sus! I'm coming after you!"

Around the corner appeared a headless chicken, running at full speed and spouting an impossibly thick geyser of blood. William's father followed. He was wearing rubber boots and overalls and carrying an axe. The chicken suddenly veered towards William and Elizabeth which was when William's father looked up.

He hadn't shaved for a long time and his face had been full of anger but when he saw William and Elizabeth the scowl disappeared and his face smoothed out, the way William's had when he went down to the creek. While the chicken found a corner and sank into the mud, William's father stood in front of them, wiping his hands on his overalls. Now Elizabeth could see he had William's silky eyes. A flattened variation of the same triangular nose. The thick lips that curled a bit unevenly when he smiled. He rubbed his bloody hand across the grey stubble on his jaw as if this might make him clean-shaven for the unexpected guests.

When he took his hand away the scowl was back and his eyebrows, bushier than William's and grey instead of blond, were furrowed together.

"We were passing by," William said.

The old man nodded his head slowly up and down as if to communicate to the as yet unintroduced Elizabeth the entire injustice of the situation — the situation in which a younger version of himself was driving about the county with a beautiful girl at his side and nothing better to do than drop in on his father while he, the father, long past driving about with girls beautiful or otherwise, with nothing to look forward to except filling out the date of the tombstone that was waiting for him, was chasing headless chickens across a stinking yard.

"Pleased to meet you," he said to Elizabeth. "I guess you can see what we're having for dinner."

That night, in a field that smelled of new grass and apple blossoms, Elizabeth would take sprigs from a lilac bush and decorate William's hair and her own. Then her prince did what fairy-tale princes sometimes do: he unlocked his lady's dress, he offered her more flowers, and under a blue velvet sky with a low-hanging moon, he took her down onto the sweet cool ground and gave her little explosions and tears of pain.

"Two months later I discovered I was pregnant and that was when I knew my life as a princess was over."

And that was how the fairy tale ended the afternoon the Ladies of the Inner Circle — along with Adam in the basement — listened to the story of how the woman considered to be the most beautiful, the most mysterious, the most out-of-place in the whole township, mistook a McKelvey for her prince.

Leaving the Goldsmith house, Elizabeth was in a state of shock, hardly able to believe that she'd said so much. At the door, Dorothy hugged her tightly before moving off. Elizabeth went to the supermarket, then started home. It was snowing, one of those gritty twilight December snows where the grey sky and landscape blend together and as you drive the snow comes at you from every direction. Halfway home the feelings overcame her and she had to pull over to the side of the road to cry. Nothing to go back to, no way forward: she'd known for years but telling the story had made it real. The prospect of continuing home to McKelvey was unbearable. Yet she couldn't turn back. The school would be locked, her mother had long since moved from Kingston to Chicago, she hadn't kept in touch with a single friend from Kingston, she didn't even have enough cash to go to a hotel.

In between bouts of sobbing she looked across the road and saw a low-slung cinderblock structure with a metal roof. McKelvey had told her its inspiring story: the small building had been intended as an auto-repair shop. The day it was finished the man who built it put his own car inside, rolled down his windows and ran the motor until the gas ran out.

Elizabeth imagined herself in such a car, being found slumped over the wheel. Beside her would be her father's briefcase full of papers waiting to be marked; in the trunk her groceries would be slowly freezing. McKelvey would be the one to lift her out of the car. He would feel that was his job. She imagined him carrying her through the falling snow to his truck. The cold hitting her. Her eyes opening as she discovered that she'd failed to die. "Always figured you'd try something like this," McKelvey would say. "Can't say I blame you."

At the thought of this final injustice, Elizabeth wiped her eyes and started driving again. When she got home McKelvey would be sitting at the kitchen table methodically working his way through a crossword puzzle. Now Elizabeth remembered that one of the cattle had got pregnant out of season and might have given birth that afternoon. Jane Eyre, her name was. There were so few cows that Elizabeth had given them all names. There were the two Janes — Eyre and Austen — Anna Karenina, Natasha from *War and Peace*, Tess of the D'Urbervilles, the Brontë sisters. Nancy from *Oliver Twist* had been sold last year to pay the taxes, though Oliver himself, the orphan bull, was still in residence. Elizabeth wanted to be home when Jane Eyre's calf was born — what she most loved about the farm were the births, the blinding natal energy when the cows and ewes allowed her in the midst of their miraculous creations. Let it be tonight, she prayed, driving faster; let it be tonight, in the perfect silence of the falling snow.

But that night there was only Elizabeth, late, marking papers at the kitchen table. A kerosene lamp, just for the glow of it, flickering over the stained oak. She was looking at the flame, passing her life through it like a knife. She was in the kitchen weighing her life against the flame and she could hear her bed creaking with McKelvey's weight as he turned.

She was looking into the flame and she was watching her futures melt into each other as she invented the lives she might live. For example, only two months ago in Toronto she had gone to meet her mother and Lionel Meyers. The trip, the long weekend at the Windsor Arms, the theatre tickets and dinners were all courtesy of the smoked-meat king. One afternoon her mother had insisted on taking her shopping and bought her a long wool coat, tight leather gloves that would surely split the moment they touched a snow shovel, a pair of shoes she would seldom have occasion to wear. That evening they went to a fancy Italian restaurant near the hotel. "This is La Scala," her mother announced as they entered, "restaurant of the stars." They were seated at a table that had, following Lionel Meyers' request, an unimpeded but discreet view of the entrance. When they received the menus — embossed thick paper with elaborate calligraphy — her mother insisted on going through it from top to bottom, explaining each of the items as though Elizabeth were still eight years old. When the waiter came Elizabeth had to be presented.

"We wanted you to meet my daughter, Elizabeth."

"A pleasure, signorina."

"She is named after a very famous person, you know."

"*Si*. Elizabeth Taylor. She was here just two nights ago. What a pity you missed her. Would you like the same wine she had?"

"No thank you," Elizabeth's mother said. "What I'd like, if you could recommend, is something you personally are familiar with, something from your own village or town."

The waiter leaned closer. "Uruguay is my home. But when it comes to wine, everyone prefers Italian."

Staring at her kerosene lamp Elizabeth decided that the waiter's comment had perfectly summed up her situation: the place she was from — a strange immigrant household in back-street Kingston — was as interesting to the rest of the world as Uruguayan wine. She was going to have to cover herself with a layer of something else. The only question was what. West Gull? Toronto? Chicago? Lillian had made it clear that should she decide to "resume her studies" — a code for leaving McKelvey — she would be welcome to live at the smoked-meat king's while she attended the famed University of Chicago. Or if she wanted to go elsewhere, his pockets were both deep and willing. Lillian herself had taken on a new veneer: fancy clothes, jewellery, annual trips to Europe with stops in London for theatre, Paris for shopping, Milan for opera. Without ever saying one thing for which she might later be reproached, Lillian Meyers seemed constantly to be asking Elizabeth: Why, if this door is open, won't you walk through it?

After her first year teaching she'd had the furnace installed. For comfort of course but also to counter the guilt she felt at leaving McKelvey alone to manage while she was spending the days in town. Now the fan switched on — in a few moments the burner would light and the house would begin to vibrate as the furnace heated up. London? Paris? Milan? What would she be there? A tourist worth the exact weight of her pocket book, that item having been supplied by Lionel Meyers. As the hot air came surging out of the vents, she had a sudden image of herself on a dark London street, a lost Dickensian waif stumbling in the mist. Then it came to her that she wanted, *needed*, that mist to be there — because beneath the mist was an emptiness, the world she had failed to invent for herself.

Elizabeth packed her papers away and blew out the lamp. It was a clear night and the half moon glimmered on the snow, stretched pale broken rectangles of light across the kitchen. Inside, Elizabeth had that grinding feeling these nights sometimes gave her, a dissatisfied self-consuming void that had started after her miscarriage. Not that there was, according to Dr. Boyce, any real reason for her not to conceive again. And certainly she and McKelvey had continued to try. But as hope dried up with the years that passed, she began to feel that with her own doubts and skepticism she had brought down a curse of barrenness on herself. And the tenuous comfort of late night silence would turn to this unwanted raw edge.

It was New Year's Eve, 1958, just a few weeks after Elizabeth's testimony. Adam Goldsmith and his mother were in the great front room of the Richardson mansion. The featured theme was jazz, which meant that gold and silver cut-outs of trumpets and saxophones had been strung around the picture mouldings.

"There's the one I was telling you about," Flora Goldsmith said to her son. "Shy. Why don't you go talk to her?"

"Pleased to meet you," Elizabeth McKelvey said when Adam introduced himself. Slim, gleaming dark hair drawn back in an old-fashioned style to cover her ears, a narrow face with a thin nose arched at the bridge, lips that seemed a little too full for a schoolteacher, beautiful large hazy blue eyes like an undecided summer sky. She was standing to the side of the big hearth, a glass in hand.

"My mother says you come to the Inner Circle meetings. I only visit weekends and holidays, I guess that's why we haven't met before."

"She told me about you," Elizabeth McKelvey said. "You're the Kingston accountant. She's very proud of you."

Her lips had a way of staying parted after she spoke, as if to signal that her actual words were only the beginning of her message.

"Your suit," Elizabeth said suddenly in a strict school-mistress voice that made Adam think he must have something hideous spilled on his pants. "It's the same colour as my dress. And your eyes. They match mine, too."

At that point Luke Richardson slid smoothly between Adam and Elizabeth like a shark separating his prey from some vegetarian pretender. He was in his early twenties, full of his own gas and eager to swallow a match.

Adam was forced to listen as Luke Richardson explained to Elizabeth the histories of all the people whose photographs adorned the great hearth. But even afflicted with the first stirrings of jealousy, Adam could see Elizabeth wore the stiffly attentive expression women use when they need to endure a man's monologue. Then McKelvey appeared. Adam saw a light go on in her face and a feeling of despair swept through him so heavy and unexpected he had to remind himself Elizabeth was married. Yet as he backed away he began to convince himself that in turning towards McKelvey, Elizabeth had also turned her face towards the hearth, that the apparent glow of her response had been nothing but reflected firelight.

The next week, while trying to investigate an entirely different topic, Adam discovered an article in *The New England Journal of Medicine* that analyzed infatuation as a chemical event. It seemed that the initial sighting of the to-be-beloved causes certain chemical and hormonal reactions, creating various new substances that form what people call love; this love fluid bathes vulnerable and crucial brain cells, setting up neural pathways and synapses that repeat the process predictably each time the newly beloved reappears or is mentioned. In the absence of further love production, the original crop lasts an average of two years. Unless, of course, owing to particular and as yet imperfectly understood circumstances, obsession develops; in such cases, the troika of eminently qualified researchers cautioned, symptoms such as criminal behaviour and psychotic outbreak may occur.

TWO

ADAM GOLDSMITH AT TWENTY-SEVEN: a tall young man slightly awkward in his movements as though he hadn't yet committed himself to inhabiting his current body, always carefully dressed, sandy hair growing darker every year, thick eyebrows tipped with blond in the summer, a pale face marked by a soft mouth always ready to smile or offer a courtesy. Something childish about that mouth, the way before speaking a brief quivering of his lips telegraphs an inner hesitation. Some thought his brain must have stripped its gears in the days when he spoke in tongues. His eyes gave the same impression — they didn't so much look at things as light on them, blue butterflies poised for flight. Those pale looks, the tic that invaded every aspect of his body and speech, made people feel safe with Adam. Especially people like the Ladies of the Inner Circle. Shy but pleasant, they called him. Because with his hesitant looks, his tended clothes, his courtesy, Adam Goldsmith had always been the kind of boy who pleased. Not only elderly ladies but also higher-ups and politicians able to appreciate a man with deference, competence and unfailing modest politeness. In his few years at the Kingston tax department, he had already received three promotions and was putting aside money for his graduate degree in economics.

As might be expected Adam had a head for numbers. Take twenty-seven: $27=3\times3\times3=3$ cubed. Adam had last been a cube — $2\times2\times2$ — at eight years old. He'd next be a cube — $4\times4\times4$ — at sixty-four. After that he could anticipate being $5\times5\times5$ — 125 years old. But even the prospect of unforseen medical advances was unlikely to persuade an accountant he'd live that long. So Adam told himself life might be made up of a relatively large number of years — seventy or eighty — but all those years came down to only four cubes plus some loose change and he had just started on his fourth. Not to sound the alarm but... In addition, the fact that twenty-seven was three cubed had a special significance because three was the age when according to his mother his piercing cry had inspired the collision that had inspired the conception of Elizabeth McKelvey, whose testimony he had heard at the age of twenty-seven and whose presence at the Richardson New Year's bash had thrown him into turmoil.

After the party he returned to his routine. Kingston in January meant slogging to and from work through ever-increasing mounds of snow, occasional evenings drinking and playing bridge with other bachelors who worked for the city, endless dark hours reading the stacks of books he now found so uninteresting that he'd end up outside again, restlessly pacing Kingston's streets to exhaust himself enough for sleep.

Late one January night when Adam still felt restless despite walking Princess Street until it became Highway 2, he sat down to force himself to think through his problem. He took out a sheet of paper and printed two words:

THE MESSAGE

The problem was the message: either the message Elizabeth had actually been sending him or the message he had wanted to receive. Adam closed his eyes and ran his remembered movie of the New Year's party. He wrote:

1. Woman stands next to man.
2. Woman speaks to man.
3. Man looks at own pants.
4. Second man arrives and bores woman.
5. Husband arrives.
6. First man leaves and thinks about nothing else for several weeks.

Now that he had the list of scenes, Adam could see the drama. He even knew its title:

THE RISE AND FALL OF HOPE

Standing next to Elizabeth, listening to what he'd thought to be her words of encouragement and staring avidly at her mouth — these might have been moments from a latter-day Shakespearean romance. Even having to check his pants for spills could have been a comic Freudian sign of future intimacies. Elizabeth's wooden response to Luke had accelerated these hopes. But then there was the arrival of the husband. Adam closed his eyes, saw again McKelvey's flushed wide face, his undone jacket and sloping belly. His big hand on

Elizabeth's arm and the way Elizabeth had turned to him, her eyes filled with some kind of marital adoration or — an uncertain alternative — the reflection from the fire.

For this uncertainty, Adam now saw, he had spent hours every night ploughing through the snow and slush of Kingston. Yet having listed the scenes, he recognized the obvious: for weeks he had been concentrating on the opening and middle instead of the conclusive and penultimate scene: 5. Husband arrives.

Elizabeth McKelvey was *married.*

The next morning Adam abused his position in the city tax department to make sure the records of her marriage were in order, to check over her and her husband's tax returns, to discover that Elizabeth's maiden name was Glade and that she had been born September 12, 1933, in the maternity ward of the Kingston General Hospital. While he was being irresponsible and possibly even a criminal, Adam ascertained that William McKelvey's income-tax return — a pitiful testament to his uselessness — had been prepared by Elizabeth. He also found out some things about himself:

1. Making a list doesn't tell you everything.
2. Looking at other people's tax returns can be exciting.
3. He was obsessed with a married woman.

What Adam might have done in the absence of external events is impossible to know. Thrown off his prissy clothes and joined Kingston's small club of beatniks and naturalists? Quit his job and used his savings to take a trip around the world? Gone into therapy and ended up in Vienna training to be a Jungian analyst? Compared to his real life, each of these options had its attractions. But external events are never absent for long. One wintry Monday Luke Richardson phoned with the news that Flora Goldsmith had been found by the mailman sitting dead in her living room.

That evening Luke met Adam at the West Gull Funeral Home and helped him make the arrangements. On the morning of the funeral he showed up at Adam's to instruct the caterers. Afterwards he stayed with Adam until everyone had left, then invited him to come sleep at his house since, "after everything, you might find it hard to be alone."

"I'm fine here," Adam said. They were in the kitchen. The mourners had drawn the chairs into a circle and Luke was sitting across from Adam, twirling the ice in his glass.

"You know I've taken over the dealership," Luke said.

"I heard. Congratulations."

"You know," Luke said, "I've always admired you, Adam. I always knew you'd turn into something. And I always knew I'd stay here. And I would think Adam Goldsmith, someone like Adam Goldsmith, shouldn't end up in the city working for someone else. Adam Goldsmith shouldn't be leaving West Gull."

Ever since Luke's phone call Adam had been amazed it was Luke who was shepherding him through this situation, Luke who had been able to take charge and arrange everything, Luke Richardson who was four years younger than him and not so long ago had been sitting on top of him preparing to smash his fists into his nose.

"What I was thinking," Luke said, "was that you could do the accounts for the dealership. I'll start you at whatever you're getting in Kingston plus ten per cent of the profits. If it works out after a year, we can negotiate a raise plus I'll make you a one-third partner. Adam, I've had my eye on you for a long time. I know you don't like me much but sometimes the most important thing is to be honest. Let's face it, Adam, I've got everything you don't. And vice versa. Between us — what do you say? Take as long as you like to think it over."

At twenty-seven Adam Goldsmith had not had the opportunity to make a lot of decisions. But as Luke spoke he had been thinking about some of his colleagues in the tax office, men ten or twenty years older than him and on their way through their last cube to retirement and death, men with their stooped backs, their tax-department shuffle, their endless lunchtime games of cards, their afternoon coffee-break jelly-filled doughnuts to kill the boredom, the way they lined up at the door waiting for the hour so they could punch out with a clear conscience.

Adam Goldsmith had left West Gull as a timid young teenager mostly remembered for his fits of possession. When he returned at twenty-seven, he was suddenly a member of the town's elite — an educated businessman and homeowner with a stake in West Gull's most prominent commercial landmark: Richardson's New & Used Pontiac GM. He was also, as Luke Richardson put it, "West Gull's most eligible bachelor — the only male between twenty-five and forty who has never been married, has no bastard children and isn't on welfare." The proof: during his first month home he was twice invited to dinner by the new doctor, Albert Knight, the proud father of a certain Maureen Knight who was "taking a year off" after graduating from McGill in French. On both occasions Maureen was seated opposite Adam, smiling awkwardly, like a single mussel placed on a large platter and destined for the invited guest. From Mrs. Elspeth Knight flowed a constant stream of commentary about Maureen's amazing accomplishments in the domains of academe and housekeeping, and

despite Dr. Knight's efforts to make it appear the dinner sig-
nalled only the routine association between two West Gull
professionals, Adam felt Maureen's embarrassed silence as a
reprimand. She had mousy brown hair, small pleasant features
slightly marred by close-set eyes and an odd anxious smile.
Whenever Adam spoke to her that anxious smile came on and
she answered him in a low-pitched distant voice that sounded
as though her real brain and self were hiding behind a wall
and spying on them.

Adam knew where his duty lay. As West Gull's most and
only eligible bachelor, he would surely respond to this situation by picking up the telephone and asking Maureen to the
movies. After that would come a gradually accelerating series
of engagements leading to the much desired and inevitable
marriage of two people who were each other's only alternative.
Yet the more inevitable and transparent this future became,
the more stubbornly Adam balked.

One afternoon he was in his office when the telephone
began to ring. He had been thinking about Maureen Knight
and was sure this call would be another invitation for dinner.
He looked from his office into the showroom. The salesmen
were out, Luke was in Kingston. No one would know if he
simply let the phone ring until it stopped. As the ringing
continued he realized that never before had he had someone
in his power, someone whose heart was beating wildly at the
prospect of hearing his voice. His own heart began to race and
overwhelmed with a peculiar mixture of triumph and guilt,
Adam picked up the receiver.

"I've wanted to say how sorry I am about your mother. I
met her only a few times but she struck me as a very remark-
able woman." Eventually Adam would learn Elizabeth always
started her conversations this way, in the middle and without

warning. "How are you finding it to be back home? Do you miss Kingston?"

"Not much," Adam managed. Remembering Kingston was Elizabeth's home town, he asked her the same question. There was a silence he wondered how to interpret. Could she have guessed he had looked up her birth certificate?

"We're not exactly *Rome* here," Adam said, "but as you know my mother had a lot of books. I hope you and your husband will feel free to come and help yourselves."

"I'll tell William," she said dryly and they both laughed. "In fact, books were the other reason I was calling. The roads department is moving out of the township office; it would make a perfect place for a library. The senator is donating the money to refit the office and he's also agreed to be chairman of the library committee as long as he doesn't have to come to meetings. You'll be the treasurer, that's the hard part. Mrs. Farnham is secretary. First meeting isn't until August but I thought I'd let you know now in case you hear from the senator. Aside from him, you're the main donor."

Elizabeth's voice broke into a laugh. Adam tensed. "You're the accountant. You must know how to hide these things. I just didn't want the senator to think he was alone." She hung up — the way he would learn was also her habit — in what should have been the middle but for Elizabeth was the end. Adam stood up from his desk. On the black arm of the receiver he could see the sweat marks left by his fingers.

Adam's peculiar bachelor status had not escaped Elizabeth's notice. "They say it's marry or burn," McKelvey commented, after that first New Year's Eve when Elizabeth asked him about Adam, "but I don't see any signs of smoke damage on his pants."

At that particular moment they were sitting at the kitchen table, McKelvey with his crossword puzzle and Elizabeth with her battered copy of *Pride and Prejudice*, which she was planning to begin reading to her class.

"That's a nice way to put it," Elizabeth said. "I liked Adam Goldsmith. He's the only man in West Gull whose face isn't covered in hockey scars." She opened her novel and read aloud: "'It is a truth universally acknowledged that a single man in possession of a good fortune must be in want of a wife.'"

"Like I said," McKelvey repeated, "marry or burn."

Elizabeth looked out the window through the falling snow to the barn. A year or possibly three years ago, she would have poured herself another cup of coffee and then explained at length to McKelvey that the two sentences were entirely different. Jane Austen, she would have claimed, was proclaiming a sociological truth — though it had an individual application. McKelvey's crude but accurate expression, the opposite. In a nasty mood she might even have gone on to say — or at least to think — that marry *and* burn was more or less what had happened to them. Finally, had she been feeling positively vitriolic, she might have pointed out that in *Pride and Prejudice*, Elizabeth had gone on to marry Mr. Darcy, whereas she had married Mr. McKelvey.

Shocked at her own disloyal thoughts, Elizabeth glanced across the table. McKelvey had put down his newspaper and was looking at her. Elizabeth softened. Mr. Darcy would never have married a girl whose Galician-Jewish father had named her after a princess. Mr. Darcy would never have courted that girl he would never have married by taking her to a cemetery. Mr. Darcy would have spent his life trapped in a book, doing only predictable things that could be described in long well-formed sentences.

"You've got that killer look," McKelvey said. "Your students must have nightmares."

"Thanks."

McKelvey leaned back in his chair, his eyes still on hers and Elizabeth knew he was thinking, as was she, that if there was a child things would be different.

"I was going back to the maple bush to check the rabbit snares before lunch," McKelvey said. He got up, moved heavily towards the door where his coat was hanging.

"I'll make pancakes," Elizabeth said, knowing he would like that. "I'm in the pancake mood."

When she called Adam about the library she thought how peculiar it was that he should seem so nervous about the senator. A couple of months later she was given the duty of organizing West Gull Elementary's annual careers day. The participants were almost always distinguished former students who had gone on to successful careers in nearby cities, and of course the star of these occasions was invariably Senator Merriwell Richardson.

"Now here's your chance to meet the senator," she began. Adam coughed and Elizabeth found herself wondering what it was about this Adam Goldsmith — an accountant and a car salesman, after all, not a piano tuner or a harpsichordist — that made him so decorous and hesitant that his nervous system stammered.

"The senator, the library," she reminded him.

It was an April Saturday morning and she was calling from her kitchen. The snow had finally melted and her lawn was a sodden brown, sloping down to the muddy driveway. McKelvey was over at Gerald Boyce's helping out on some project that would require coming home at suppertime with a case of beer in his belly and another cradled in his arms.

"Yes, the library, an excellent project," Adam said.

"This is a different favour," Elizabeth said, "I wanted to ask you for careers day at the elementary. We've never had an accountant."

It occurred to Elizabeth she shouldn't be telephoning Adam. The other men she'd asked had simply checked their schedules and given her a quick answer. Perhaps Adam, with his mother's death and this move back to West Gull, was having a nervous breakdown.

"It must be hard," she said. "I know I was very upset after my father died. Losing a parent is always a shock."

"To tell the truth, I think I was relieved. In her quiet way my mother was very overpowering."

On the far side of the driveway outside the barn, Anna Karenina and Jane Eyre were standing head to head, as though having their own bizarre conversation. By the time Elizabeth had finished fixing the date with Adam, the cows had gone back to chewing away at the new grass. She couldn't imagine why Adam had found his mother overpowering. Perhaps she'd had secret vices. She could just imagine how he'd be in her class. A quiet boy always staring out the window. Never having any particular problems or showing any particular intelligence. A carefully cultivated blank waiting to be discovered but afraid to put himself forward.

When careers day arrived and the participants were gathered in the staff room, it seemed to Adam that they all felt — as did he — that their younger selves had been summoned for an unwanted interview with the principal. Aside from Adam there was Senator Merriwell Richardson, a sleekly silver-haired mountain in his late seventies; his son Alvin, a pig and chicken farmer; Hugh Greenley, the furniture store owner;

Arnie Kincaid, the insurance man; Peter Farnham, the publisher of the weekly and owner of the local printing shop; and of course Dr. Knight, who immediately approached Adam and began talking to him about the possibility of buying a small used car for Maureen. By the time the speeches began, Adam had agreed to meet Maureen at the lot on the weekend and let her test drive two or three possibilities.

After each of them had given his brief talk, the senator was summoned to the stage. Having announced that the title of his "short speech" was to be "Virtue Is Its Own Reward," he offered twenty minutes on "The Need for Capital Punishment to Keep Canada Safe from Murderers and Rapists," then an hour on "The Sacrifices Demanded by Public Life," for which the only compensation, despite the ill-informed comments of journalists who should know better, was The Affection and Respect of His Own Community as demonstrated on Occasions Like This One.

Afterwards came tea and cookies. Tea from a giant metal urn in which tepid water had been assaulted by enough tea bags to stain it the colour of crankcase oil. Shortbread cookies baked by the home economics class and topped by fossilized maraschino cherries. Adam was trying to pry one of those carbonized pebbles out of a back molar when the senator singled him out, shook his hand enthusiastically while congratulating him on working for Luke, and announced he'd known Hank Goldsmith back in Ottawa. All this while keeping his back to Peter Farnham, who had recently devoted the front page of the *Weekly Bugle* to publicizing the senator's good fortune in being a member of the board of directors of a company that had just landed a lucrative contract selling attack helicopters to South Africa. "West Gull's Treasure," the article had been headlined, and ever since Luke had been muttering phrases like "in the hands of lawyers." Eventually the senator interrupted himself to look at his watch and remember an appointment. By the time Adam had returned from seeing the senator to his car, Elizabeth McKelvey had gone home.

Just before the August library meeting Adam received a request from the senator, passed through Luke, to drive him from his cottage to a committee hearing in Ottawa. "I hear you're in pretty thick with him," Luke grinned. "Guess he wants to see what you're made of."

Adam arrived at the senator's cottage early in the afternoon of the appointed day. His son Alvin struggled out to meet the car, his weekend stubble splotched with fried egg, tobacco stains, the stigma of being the only Richardson unable to find a way to fleece people, then pound them to a pulp. His "daddy," as he called him, was ready to go: shaved and powdered, resplendent in white gabardine, he was carrying two black attaché cases with multiple locks that he stowed carefully in the trunk of the Cadillac Luke had insisted Adam use for this errand. Adam expected a continuation of the capital punishment talkathon but shortly after they reached the highway, the senator fell asleep, snoring in a smooth and unwavering tenor vibrato. As they entered Ottawa he woke up and gave Adam directions to his apartment building. After unloading his cases he pressed a hundred-dollar bill on him — which Adam reluctantly accepted — then disappeared into his apartment.

It was a beautiful July day. Adam, six years away from the city, decided to park his car near the canal and take a walk.

When he saw Elizabeth she was standing in the dappled shadow of an old maple, leaning against the rail overlooking the canal, gazing out over the rippling surface of the water. She wore a yellow-orange flowered dress and carried a white straw hat. Her hair, highlighted by the sun, was drawn back and gathered loosely at her neck. Her eyes seemed to be following a group of sculls. Her face was so composed and still, so perfectly concentrated, she might have been posing for a portrait.

He stopped, unsure of whether to speak. Suddenly she turned towards him, catching him in the act of spying.

"You," she said. She laughed. "I didn't expect to see you here...."

Adam started to explain about the senator, but Elizabeth just shook her head.

"Never mind. It's too nice a day. Isn't the water just lovely with the shadows?"

Adam stood beside her looking into the rippling surface. The reflections of the trees, the long railing, even their own silhouettes magically shimmered and merged on the slowly moving water. This, he thought, watching as the water put them together then drew them apart, was as close as he was going to get to Elizabeth.

"I could stand here for ever," Elizabeth said.

"I'll bring you a coat when it starts to snow."

"Don't say snow." The light from the water had filled her eyes. Adam was transfixed. "I have to catch my bus," she said.

"Bus?" he managed.

"I came here for a one-day conference. I skipped out on the last session but I have to get back to the hotel and catch the bus for Kingston. William's going to meet me there."

"But I could drive you. I have Luke Richardson's car. His very best Cadillac with air conditioning and four speakers."

"Four speakers," Elizabeth said gravely and Adam felt foolish.

"I think so."

"I'll go back and phone William. He'll be glad to avoid the drive. If you don't mind dropping me at the house..."

They drove to Bank Street and Adam sat in the car watching Elizabeth call her husband. From the way his heart was beating it seemed clear this must be the climax of his life so far: twitching anxiously behind the wheel of Luke Richardson's black Cadillac while a married woman, almost a stranger, stood in a dusty phone booth speaking words he couldn't hear. A few moments later she came back and joined him in the car. "Thank you," she said.

As Adam drove out of Ottawa he pointed to various places he had gone as a student until, afraid he was playing the tourist guide without having been asked, he suddenly stopped talking. At first the silence was almost unbearable but then he began to see the comic side of things. The prospect of being alone with Elizabeth might have been the climax of his life but the reality was just a heightened version of the torture he had experienced in the Knight living room or listening to Luke boast about his various plans. What was needed, as always in those situations, was a distraction: he asked her about the library, she responded in kind, and soon the emptiness was filled.

As they drove he began to feel more sure of himself. Being with Elizabeth required only the same routine as being with one of the Inner Circle ladies or even his mother: undemanding conversation, a casual tone of voice, the pursuit of minor forbidden pleasures. At a gas station they bought two chocolate cones and a huge chunk of cheddar that Elizabeth convinced him could be frozen. For years the yellow wedge stayed in Adam's freezer. Bit by bit frost grew out of its centre and broke through its surface. There was a decade in which he watched the last vestiges of yellow disappearing beneath the encroaching white fur, until one day he had a vaguely triangular snowball. Still he kept it, hoping that one day Elizabeth would come to his house and he could show her this amazing memento. Finally, two years after she was killed — in one of those moments when he felt he ought to purge himself of her — he threw it in the garbage.

But back on the day when the cheese was merely "medium aged," when Adam still had the taste of chocolate in his mouth, he decided that things were going so well he would do what he would have done had he been on a chocolate-ice-cream-eating excursion with his mother: he would tell an amusing anecdote, something light and lacy that would spin out the time and leave the listener filled with admiration. It was the story of what he thought to be his very humorous attempt to step out from the accounting office and actually sell a car. Not to Maureen. That had been too easy. In the chosen episode, exaggerated for effect, Adam tried to convince a local farmer who didn't want to pay the price for one of Luke's trademark boat-sized Pontiacs that a compact car, only slightly used and an unfortunate shade of piggy pink, would in fact be a bargain, especially since — this was a trick he had heard the other salesmen use — he could probably exert his influence to get him a five per cent rebate.

"That thing!" the farmer exploded. "That's the kind of car a *fairy* would go for." And then he'd stalked off.

But instead of laughing Elizabeth gave Adam a close look. "It can't be easy for you here," she said. He started to reply — then realized what she meant.

"I'm not—" He stopped. His eyes flicked to the mirror and he saw the way his mouth had twisted in surprise. What wasn't he? What was he? He could feel his face burning.

"I didn't mean to embarrass you," Elizabeth said. She reached out and touched his arm.

"It's all right. It's just—"

"Please. I'm not one of those narrow-minded...." Then she herself began to stammer with embarrassment.

That night Adam did penance for falling into the river of Elizabeth McKelvey's eyes and asking her to drive home with him, by getting down on his knees on the kitchen floor and scrubbing the star-patterned linoleum on which he used to writhe through his trances of babble and jabber. By the time he was finished cleaning the kitchen it was one in the morning. He poured himself a Scotch — a habit, Flora assured him, that Hank Goldsmith had indulged "every night of his life" — and cleared a seat in an armchair in the living room. "Wouldn't it be interesting," Adam suddenly said aloud, "if I was in love with Elizabeth McKelvey? If this isn't a game but real? Wouldn't that be something?" For a long time he considered what his voice had proposed to the empty room, then he began to feel weighed down, as though he had just heard a judge pronounce his life sentence.

Senator Merriwell Richardson had been appointed to office after the war as a reward for decades of fruitless service organizing the fortunes of the governing Liberal party in the infertile regions of Eastern Ontario. "Good thing he didn't have to get elected" was the local verdict. When his son Alvin faltered, Luke was chosen to carry the flag. His first test was to get himself elected to the township council.

Following the senator's instructions, 144 large cardboard signs announcing LUKE RICHARDSON FOR COUNCILLOR were made up by a printer in Kingston and delivered to the dealership at closing time on a Friday. Adam stayed late that night, helping nail the lawn signs onto the wooden stakes Luke had bought. Afterwards, the back seat of his car loaded with signs for distribution in the morning, Adam followed Luke back to his place for a barbecue — steaks with Luke and Amaryllia had become a Friday night ritual.

In those days Luke's father still lived in the mansion. Luke had bought the land he'd eventually build on but meanwhile he and Amaryllia were "camped" in a small cottage a few miles south of town on one of the long shallow fingers of Long Gull Lake.

After dinner, while Adam watched the last of the light emptying from the water, Luke sipped at a cognac, puffed a cigar and mused about his prospects. Suddenly he leaned towards Adam, put his hand on Adam's shoulder and confided that being town councillor was only the first step to living in the prime minister's residence on Sussex Drive. "So," Luke said, as satisfied as if he were already in the PM's study treating Adam to a snifter of Sir John A.'s best Confederation single malt, "what do you think of that?"

When Adam got home, Luke's *What do you think of that?* was still ringing in his ears.

He made himself a pot of tea, got out his mother's old typewriter and a stack of paper. On each of almost a hundred sheets he typed, in capital letters, BEWARE THE LESSER EVIL. Then he folded and stuffed the sheets into one of the batches of envelopes he occasionally picked up in Kingston, and with the helpful inspiration of the telephone book, addressed them.

Writing and distributing these messages — the kind of homilies his mother used to propose as subjects for meditation — had become an occasional hobby since his return to West Gull. One Valentine's Day he had gone out at three in

the morning with several dozen letters proclaiming REMEM-
BER THAT LOVE IS ALL and the newspaper had written a column about "our local anonymous Cupid." On that same
Valentine's Day he had left one of the envelopes, addressed to
"Elizabeth and William McKelvey," in the McKelvey mailbox, thinking with great satisfaction as he drove away that
this message would surely cause a painful examination of her
heart, but if it did she never mentioned it.

The morning after Luke's declaration, before dawn, the
signs still piled in his truck and back seat, Adam seeded West
Gull's mailboxes with BEWARE THE LESSER EVIL. After a
return home for coffee and toast he set out to search for abandoned fields in which to plant his signs. When he came to
Gerald Boyce's, Gerald was standing in the middle of the
road, waving. Adam stopped and got out.

"Look at this crap! Did you put this in my box?"

Adam took the piece of paper. BEWARE THE LESSER EVIL
had been stained with butter and jam. He showed Gerald the
signs in the back of his car. "Want one?"

"I'll tell you what. Let's drive around the back and we can
burn the lot of them. I won't tell if you don't." He closed his
hand on Adam's arm. His palm scraped against Adam's skin
like the gritty lichen-covered granite that is West Gull township's best crop. "Just joking. But I could help you with a couple of those signs."

Half an hour later they were out on the water of Dead
Swede Lake. Gerald had Adam rowing. It was his first time in
a boat since the days when he used to fish with his father.
Compared to his child's memory, the oars were surprisingly
thin and light; a few hard pulls and the old boat was skimming through the water.

Gerald's plan was to hug the shore until they reached the

point that jutted towards the lake's centre — a long treed finger with a giant willow at the tip — then continue on to the McKelvey dock. There they would plant two LUKE RICHARDSON FOR COUNCILLOR signs, one facing up to the house and one facing the water. "The one thing I can't promise," Gerald pointed out, "is that William is actually going to *vote* for your man. But at least he'll have the choice. And that's the democratic way."

Adam knew McKelvey and Richardson were barely on speaking terms. At the last West Gull Hornets' Christmas fundraiser, Luke had dumped McKelvey to the ice when he wasn't expecting it. But McKelvey had done his drinking before instead of after the game. The next time Richardson came down the ice McKelvey dropped his stick and gloves, grabbed Luke by the shoulders, whirled him around and threw him over the boards. The next week's front page of the *Weekly Bugle* was taken up by three pictures: the first showed Luke Richardson sprawled in the front-row seats; the second had McKelvey lying flat on his back on the ice, his hand over his mouth; the third showed the two men shaking hands.

To sweeten his proposition Gerald Boyce offered to help Adam get rid of two more signs, which he would use to plug a hole in the barn and remind the animals what kind of a country they were lucky to be alive in.

Adam had been rowing for only a few minutes when Gerald Boyce put a finger across his lips for silence, then grabbed the oars. They were just emerging from behind the willow when Adam saw the McKelvey dock. Someone had come out from the woods and was walking towards it. Elizabeth. Now Gerald Boyce was soundlessly pushing them out of sight under the huge willow into branches that curled and drooped down to the water. The long thin leaves brushed

Adam's face and he was enveloped in their dry lemony smell. Through the leaves he could still see the dock. Grey weathered boards creaked dangerously as Elizabeth, apparently oblivious, walked to the edge then stood stretching in the sun. She stripped off her sweater, slid her feet out of her shoes. Slowly rocking, she balanced on the dock. Adam was concentrating so intently he could feel the planks flexing beneath his own feet. Elizabeth removed her T-shirt, her pants, her underwear. From this distance her nipples were tiny pink blurs at the tips of her breasts. She was looking straight towards them but they were the sun, the blinding light off the water, a cascade of lime green leaves. She took a quick run. For a moment she was suspended in the air, her dark hair flowing back like the feathers of some mythological bird. Adam went to push the boat further out of sight but Gerald Boyce grabbed his arm again. His brow was trenched, his mouth half-open.

Elizabeth was swimming. She had a smooth strong stroke, the lake was not large, soon she would be able to see them. "We could look the other way," Adam whispered to Gerald.

"*You* look the other way."

Elizabeth broke the surface. In a few seconds her eyes would be locked onto Adam's. Then came a loud bellow from the woods behind the dock. McKelvey appeared wearing overalls and a flannel shirt, a towel over his shoulder. Elizabeth turned and swam towards him; when she got to the dock he reached down and pulled her out of the water. Elizabeth's wet hair fell halfway down her back; she shook it and McKelvey barked with pleasure and surprise as the spray whipped across his face.

"Jay-sus," Gerald Boyce whispered. He gave a long depressed sigh. McKelvey put his arms around Elizabeth, who pressed herself against him, overalls and all, and it appeared certain that the McKelveys were going to lie down on the dock and devour each other with Adam Goldsmith and Gerald Boyce crouched in their boat behind the willow tree, going insane with jealousy. But McKelvey just wrapped Elizabeth in the towel. He gathered her clothes in his arms as they started away from the lake. For a moment their voices were inaudible, then Elizabeth gave a laugh that faded as she raced to the house, McKelvey calling as he followed.

Luke Richardson was voted to the town council the same week John F. Kennedy was elected president of the United States. Luke didn't hesitate to identify with the glitter and excitement of the Kennedy accession. The Kennedys were glamorous, surrounded by the famous and the prestigious; their parties and their cheerleaders and America's love affair with them filled the newspapers and the television screens. Luke would put his hand on Adam's shoulder and confide that when he saw Kennedy on television, he *knew* he was seeing his own future.

One Friday afternoon in early September Luke stopped by Adam's office at closing time to ask him to telephone Amy, tell her he wouldn't be home until midnight or morning because he had an emergency committee meeting in Cobourg. It was six o'clock and the sun was already low enough in the sky that Adam could see its reflection off the big plate-glass window of the Timberpost. When he called Amy, knowing Luke had put him up to this to avoid her anger, she thanked him coldly and hung up abruptly. A few minutes later she called back and asked Adam to join her for dinner since she had already marinated the steaks.

Adam paused. He'd been having barbecues with the Richardsons all summer and the prospect of being released for one night was not unpleasant. His dining-room table was still piled with papers from his mother's estate and he'd begun renovations on the second floor — finally giving away his parents' clothes and redoing their room with the intention of turning the house from a mausoleum dedicated to his youth to a place he could either make his own or sell.

"We'll have a good time," Amy said, her voice pleading. Adam gave in. On the way to the cottage he found himself dreading the evening alone with her, the inevitable confession of unhappiness. But he arrived to find she'd made a giant pitcher of martinis she seemed already to have sampled. Martinis! The Infant Voice of the Inner Circle of the Church of the Unique God had never allowed such a vile concoction to touch his holy tongue. By sunset Adam was lying face down on the living-room couch, looking out on the dark mirror that was Long Gull Lake while Amy massaged scented oil into his back.

Then it was Adam's turn to do Amy. She was wearing tight white pants and a brassiere he couldn't unhook. "If you don't know how, you'd better learn" was the only help she'd offer. When he finally got the brassiere open, its two narrow wings lay limply by her sides like a fallen bird of modesty. This was definitely not a Ladies of the Inner Circle situation.

"What next?" Adam asked.

"Now you put on the oil." She handed him the bottle. The massage oil was a dark amber fluid with a sharp minty odour. He poured a small quantity into his palm, tipped the oil from his hand onto the centre of Amy's back. "You have to rub it in," she said. West Gull's most eligible bachelor had never touched the naked back of a woman other than his mother. He found Amy's skin was soft, if vaguely rubbery. As Adam pushed down she gave out a little sigh and the sound startled him because a few evenings ago, at the Knight house, Maureen had also sighed, and in that sigh Adam had heard a loneliness even more lonely than the time she'd been the single mussel on the guest platter. "Both hands," Amy instructed. Adam pushed and pulled. The room filled with the scent of mint mixed with Amy's sweat. After he'd rubbed in several palms full of oil, carefully working his way from the small floating shoulder blades he was beginning to see as the lost islands of her innocence down to the thickly muscled small of her back, Amy asked him to put on the kettle. Drinking his coffee in the darkness, watching the stars grow denser as night fell, Adam could feel — even more than during the actual event — Amy's touch on his back. Her hands had been small and delicate and as they rubbed the oil into Adam's skin he'd felt his muscles bunch up in resistance, first twisting away from the unprecedented touching, then giving in to the invasion of a peculiar floating warmth — something dangerously close to gratitude. Amy sat silent, entirely calm and self-possessed, as though in Luke's absence people were always coming over from the New & Used to exchange a backrub or two.

By the time Adam got home the martinis were starting to wear off. He made some more coffee and switched on the television news. One segment was a special look at the incoming presidential couple. The camera zoomed in on Jackie's face: her eyes softly luminous, her bones perfectly honed, her cheeks hollow with unknown sorrows, her wide eager mouth flashing its brilliant smile to all in need of her light. That must be, Adam thought, what Luke wanted from Amy: poor Amy who walked around town in her bulging white sweaters and overtight pants looking as though she was about to burst into tears.

The camera went to John F. Kennedy, the legend himself, the war hero, the carnal embodiment of the American Empire.

Empire, yes, if ever there had been Empire, this was surely Empire itself, the most powerful the world had ever known, and when Kennedy raised his hand in what seemed to be a wave to the crowd but was in fact an effortlessly graceful salute directed to the entire population of the entire planet, Adam could almost hear the electronic roar sweeping through the skies: Caesar! Caesar! Caesar!

Suddenly Adam felt an unexpected tender stab for Amy; somehow — despite his half-contempt for her because she, like him, was under Luke's dominion — she had effortlessly seen his invisible chains, undone them with a lot less fuss than he'd made over her brassiere, yet known where to stop so there would be no hangover of guilt. Why, Adam suddenly asked himself, could he not in the same spirit supply Maureen with what she needed, yet do so in a way that left them free of obligation? After all, what did Maureen want? Just a bit of company and some face-saving ritual.

Elizabeth thought about him sometimes. Dorothy Dean, her friend from the Inner Circle who credited prayer for taking her from subbing to full-time Grade Three, told her that he was being set up with Maureen Knight, the doctor's daughter. Maureen came to the school three afternoons a week to teach the senior classes French. Elizabeth found her stilted and artificial, as though she was keeping her real self back — a real self that judged them all provincial and wanting. "I don't know if I can see them together," Elizabeth said, immediately ashamed of herself. "Two old maids," Dorothy shrugged. "They'll be slow but sure, believe me."

That September Elizabeth discovered she was pregnant again. She treasured every minute of it and she was so desperately happy that she almost had to laugh at the way she kept checking her panties for stains. One night she woke up, her stomach convulsed with cramps, the sheets soaked in blood.

"Bad luck," Dr. Knight said, "but at least we know you're still fertile." He admitted her to hospital to have her womb scraped in case some irregularity was preventing a secure implantation. Elizabeth took a month's sick leave, got a book on nutrition and much to McKelvey's disgust began eating yoghurt and wheatgerm. But aside from a false alarm, which made her realize she wanted a baby so much she was afraid to get pregnant for fear of another miscarriage, nothing happened.

Adam didn't see Elizabeth again until the next New Year's party. He was looking out on the township's celebrants from his usual station at the mantlepiece when Elizabeth and William McKelvey came into view. She was wearing a long navy gown that fell elegantly from her hips and made everyone else look as though they'd forgotten to dress for the occasion. But before Adam could greet them the McKelveys moved off. Adam, determined to make it through the party, braced himself. Having learned to live without so much else, he could surely survive his feelings for Elizabeth.

He had joined another conversation when there was a hand on his elbow, a touch so light he wondered if he'd really felt it.

"Look, I'm really sorry about what I said last summer. It just—"

"Don't worry about it. Anyway I'm not what you thought."

"You don't have to say that."

"I know. But I am. Because I'm not."

"I'm glad. I mean — I'm glad you told me. Would you accept my apologies?"

Her voice was back to its usual intimacy and Adam's face was as flushed as when he'd spied on her across the lake. "Why don't we just forget it?" he said.

"I felt so terrible when you stopped coming to the library committee. I was afraid I'd offended you."

"No. Really. I was just busy helping Luke get elected."

Whenever a tray came by she would change their empty glasses for full. Gradually the room shrank and nothing was left but Elizabeth's voice, Elizabeth's face looking up to his. By midnight he had drunk so many glasses of wine that most of his weight was on the mantlepiece. The orchestra was playing, Elizabeth had folded herself into McKelvey, and the whole room, except Adam, was joined in a circle singing "Auld Lang Syne." Amy finally dragged him into the circle, inserting him between herself and Luke, and as the voices raised in a chorus Adam joined in, his own voice loud and grateful to have been rescued from a moment he was still shaking free of, like a saved swimmer who'd already given himself up to the despair of loneliness. That was when he looked across the room and saw Maureen Knight, bracketed between her parents, her eyes reproachfully on his.

That January Adam started going to the movies with Maureen. Once a month plus occasional holidays or special features, he'd call on her and they'd drive into Kingston. First it would be dinner at one of the hotels accompanied by a half-bottle of wine. During dinner Maureen would talk about her father's various cases, the adventures of her two cats, the birds they did or didn't kill. After a post-dinner cup of tea which Maureen always took with lemon and a trip to the washroom, they would go to see whatever was showing at the university film club. Often it would be a European movie and when there was subtitled dialogue Maureen liked to whisper her own translation. Then it was time to drive back to West Gull. Near the beginning there were some uncomfortable pauses when they arrived at Maureen's door. Should he progress from the customary handshake to a chaste kiss? Delay the decision by going inside? Somehow without discussing it they settled on a peculiarly vigorous method of shaking hands, a rough dance that involved all four hands jumping up and down followed by Maureen saying, "See you soon." Adam felt proud of himself, a virtuous Samaritan who'd offered a bandage to a wounded fellow-traveller.

With Elizabeth his role was less clear. Sometimes she would meet him at the office and they'd commiserate about library problems over lunch at the Timberpost: the heating, the volunteer staffing, the fact that more people used the library to dispose of old books than to take books out. Every week or two it would be Elizabeth on the phone about something or other. "Adam," she would start. *Adam.* That was how he knew he was alive, hearing Elizabeth say his name. Or so he thought.

Between his dates with Maureen and his vaguely illicit conversations with Elizabeth, Adam began to see his passage from the traumatic moment of being three cubed to that of his comfortable early thirties as the triumphant story of an emotionally crippled youth who had somehow thrown off his shackles and become a charming sophisticated ladies' man, secretly in love with one woman while doing his duty with another. Certain mornings while knotting his tie in front of the mirror, he would even catch himself whistling and winking at his own image as he prepared for another day of flattery and deception.

But one Sunday in December 1965, one of those Sundays after a Saturday when he had taken Maureen to the movies, the accountant took over. The accountant had had enough. The accountant started talking numbers and the first number was zero. Zero was what Adam's idea of being a ladies' man added up to. Zero was the amount of romance in his life. Zero was the number that best corresponded to his sexual activities. Zero, zero, zero, the accountant decreed. For his next number the accountant took out Adam's agendas for the past several years and calculated that between Saturdays, holidays and special features, he had just gone to the movies with Maureen for the sixty-fourth time. 4x4x4. The fateful end of the fateful cube. In their journey through those cubes their partings had not increased in passion. Although now he sometimes came into the house with her where they would sit in the Knight living room — always alone as the parents, Albert and Elspeth, would have discreetly ascended — and in the hinting rosy glow of the tiffany lamps Adam would feel for Maureen something approaching a very strong fondness.

He had discovered she was not unamusing. On the contrary. As they'd got to know each other and as she got to know West Gull, it seemed to Adam that much like him she was an independent and detached observer of the town's affairs. Instead of haltingly making their way through dinner and a half-bottle of wine, they doubled their alcohol dosage and often got so involved in gossiping that they risked missing their movie.

Sixty-four. Adam wrote the number in large figures on a pad in front of him. Sixty-four = 4x4x4. That was a lot of dinners, a lot of Saturdays and holidays and special-feature nights. At the rate he was going he would be sixty-four years old, moving from his very last complete cube into the unpredictable loose change and still wondering when it was that slow-maturing Goldsmith gene was going to drag itself over the finish line. And he remembered something peculiar about the sixty-fourth Saturday night. While trying to put his coat on in the Knight hallway, his arm had caught in his sports jacket and Maureen had moved close to help him. There was absolutely nothing sexual in her gesture, just an assumed familiarity that had left them standing face to face touching each other with no need or desire to move away. Adam thought about this moment, the microscopic micro-moment buried within it like a speck-sized mussel on a gigantic platter, a microscopic micro-moment he had perhaps tried to hide from himself. Within that tiny irreducible moment in time, he now remembered he had come very close to creating yet another irreducible moment by putting his arms around Maureen Knight. A sudden flare had filled his belly; an inner voice had commanded him to wrench his hands apart, spread them wide, then rejoin them behind Maureen's back. Adam Goldsmith had been on the very verge of this action, his arms had even begun a slow surround, when a noise from upstairs had frozen him. At the memory Adam's heart thumped so loudly he thought someone must be knocking at his door. No one's there, the accountant said. Zero is the number of people coming to your door. And that was when Adam Goldsmith resolved that in a week and a half, at the Richardson New Year's party, he was going to ask Maureen Knight to be his wife.

He spent the whole day cleaning his house and feeling quite pleased with himself. It was only in the evening, standing in front of his stove stirring a can of soup and preparing the exact words of his proposal — *Before I begin let me assure you that even the most negative, hostile or shocked reaction to these words will in no way decrease my esteem for you or my desire that our friendship continue* — that he found himself envisioning

Elizabeth in the place of Maureen. A warm melting glow suffused him and into his mind came the blurred image of Elizabeth he couldn't let go of — Elizabeth, hair streaming like a goddess, diving white and naked into Dead Swede Lake.

By the evening of the party Adam had refined his plan. Early on he would ask Maureen Knight if he might walk her home after midnight. On this walk, fortified by a few drinks and the fact that he'd already prepared the way by requesting this extraordinary interview, he would pop the question.

To bolster his courage Adam decided to buy a new suit, hand-tailored from a shop Albert Knight had once mentioned at dinner. In front of the full-length mirrors for the final fitting, Adam hardly recognized himself. In his perfectly tailored suit, his hair that with the years had become a dark chocolate brown — except for his sideburns which were now a snowy white — he no longer resembled the old pictures of the bony-faced Hank Goldsmith. Now he had the sleek look of the sort of man he would expect to see in a movie about an expensive ocean liner. "You've got the figure for clothes," the tailor said in a contented voice and Adam decided this was where he would buy his wedding tuxedo.

At nine o'clock on New Year's Eve he was at the Richardson mantelpiece, wondering if anyone would notice his finery, when the Knights arrived. Maureen, too, was in costume: she was wearing a low-cut black dress with a layer of lace netting stretched modestly over her décolletage and her hair was swept up in a way Adam had never seen, leaving her ears and neck exposed. It unnerved him, the way her thin naked arched neck seemed to be offering itself to some invisible guillotine, and he thought he might lose his courage. But strolling with Maureen towards the dining room, which had been transformed for this year's party into a casino palace complete with velvet-covered

gaming tables ruled over by girls of the graduating class cos-
tumed as croupiers, Adam stopped and took hold of Maureen's
elbow. He could feel the flesh giving under his fingers and he
almost let go for fear he was hurting her. "I was thinking," he
said, "I might walk you home after midnight." Before he could
retract this outrageous statement Maureen gave her anxious
smile, inclined her head and said, "Of course," as though she'd
expected exactly this, and moved on.

He was back at the hearth wondering what his mother
would think of his marrying Maureen, when he heard his
name. "Adam."

"Elizabeth." If there was one person in whom he could
confide his happiness, it was surely Elizabeth.

"Adam, this isn't white wine, it's a martini. Why are we
drinking martinis?"

He explained to her that the gaming tables and martinis
were a celebration of Luke's new passion: money. He had
decided to leave politics — "a loser's game," Luke had confided — to make his fortune in real estate. Just as Adam was
about to change topics and tell her about Maureen, Elizabeth
began talking about the problems she was having with a
mother who was convinced the school was plotting against
her child, and another who was incensed Elizabeth was reading *Pride and Prejudice* to her Grade Six class — "You can tell
by the title it isn't suitable" — and then they were on their
third martini and discussing a censorship movement in another school district; meanwhile the band was playing and
they were on their fourth martini and Elizabeth was telling
Adam about the time her father had insisted they celebrate
New Year's at the Holiday Inn but walked out before midnight because he didn't like the way the bandleader looked at
her mother. "Adam, Adam, I'm drunk."

Adam looked at his watch. It was only an hour until midnight, his last bachelor's New Year's Eve midnight. "There's something I must tell you," he said, because while listening to Elizabeth's accelerating chatter and keeping pace on the martini front, he had become ever more determined to divulge his secret.

"I *must* tell you something," he repeated.

"I know, Adam, I *know*. And I *must* tell you ... my story ... Adam, I've hardly started but I'm so drunk I need to go home. Adam, show me where the coats are."

"You'll drive yourself into a ditch," Adam said, twice, but Elizabeth kept shaking her head and insisting. "*Adam, I know what I'm doing.*" He decided he would humour her, then tell McKelvey Elizabeth was sick and needed to be taken home.

They went upstairs to the guest room where Elizabeth knelt on the bed and began sorting through the mound of ladies' coats. Finally she dragged hers out. It was a cast-off from her mother that looked, as she'd said to Adam a couple of weeks before, as though it had been made from underprivileged raccoons. She struggled into it, straightened up and suddenly her face was so stricken Adam was sure she was about to be sick.

"Kiss me, Adam," Elizabeth said. Her voice was dry. Adam bent down and gave her a peck on the cheek.

"Come on, Adam, I want your best. Give me your number one."

This time he pecked her on the lips. Elizabeth wrinkled her nose and sighed with disappointment, the way she sometimes did after ordering dessert at the Timberpost.

"Let's go, Adam." She got off the bed, took his hand and led him out of the bedroom. But instead of heading downstairs she continued towards the back of the house. She pulled him into an empty room, locked the door and gave him her number one. Adam stood there, stunned. It was as though another universe had wrapped itself around his face, the universe of Elizabeth's lips, her eyelashes, her breath. She's drunk, he suddenly thought, but even drunk she's going to realize — hey, God, I'm kissing old *Adam*, how embarrassing. Instead she unbuttoned her blouse and put his hands where his hands had never been. They lay down on the carpet in the dark and soon his whole body was surrounded by what he had once mistaken for a blurry white mermaid.

At first he came to consciousness thinking he must have dreamed the whole thing. He was lying on the bed alone, his pants in humid disarray, his shirt unbuttoned, and with his eyes closed he could still feel Elizabeth's body on his, his on Elizabeth's everything. He stood up and reassembled himself. "Wait a few minutes" had been her last words. He patted his shirt smooth, tried to slap the wrinkles from his new tailored trousers. The strains of "Auld Lang Syne" were beginning to rise from the hall. He pushed at his hair — luckily his hair had always been easy to smooth into place — and opened the door. When he got downstairs the music was over. Elizabeth and McKelvey were chatting with the Boyces, Maureen was standing slightly apart from her parents, her white neck gleaming sacrificially beneath the chandelier.

It was early May when Elizabeth told Adam she was pregnant. "It happened at New Year's. Can you imagine? Bill got too drunk, the way he always does at the Richardsons' and when we got home — well..." She said all this while looking Adam straight in the eye. They were at the Timberpost. Since January Elizabeth had been stopping by for lunches as though nothing had transpired. No coy hand-holding, no whispers or winks. Nothing at all to relieve the terrible secret Adam felt weighing on him the whole time, a secret so literally, *physically* heavy, he felt, especially when he saw Elizabeth, that it could send him crashing through the earth.

He had thought of that secret as an actual stone expanding inside him; when Elizabeth told him about the baby his first impulse was to point out this comical connection. And yet there was that other smaller lighter secret, the one he had already tried to tell Elizabeth; in fact, the coincidence was that Adam had been planning — that very same lunch — to let Elizabeth know of his engagement to Maureen Knight. For months he and Maureen had been keeping it "to enjoy it for ourselves," as Maureen had put it but now that they were about to tell Albert and Elspeth, Adam had decided he must first inform Elizabeth. But with her eyes on him — daring him to contradict? begging him not to? — he felt his tongue begin to tremble with the words he couldn't find. Tremble, then tingle and swell. That old feeling had come over him, his face was layered with sweat and he was gripping the table, terrified by what was coming. Elizabeth started again: "When I got pregnant with McKelvey the first time, I changed my whole life, which turned out to be a mistake. So this time I'm not changing anything. I'm just going to go on as I am and hope the baby gets born alive. That's what I want and I want it very much."

Adam could feel the sweat pooling in the hollow of his collarbone and armpits. Elizabeth pushed her glass of water to him. Eventually he was able to let go of the table and take a sip. "I... I..." he started but had to wait until his tongue was almost normal. "I wish you every happiness."

That night Adam sat in his kitchen drinking Scotch and asking himself what it would be like to be married to Maureen while watching the baby he might or might not have given

Elizabeth become a man or a woman. That would be a secret big enough to fill a whole house. Then Adam asked another question: what might Maureen think of being married to a man who'd made another woman pregnant on the night of their engagement? Of course there was no need for Maureen to know. But if he told her it would be her secret, too. They'd both have their guts filled with it. Until it killed them or dissolved or wore away or turned them into something else — whatever it was such secrets did.

When Carl was old enough to start school Elizabeth started teaching again. In the meantime Adam saw her only at the New Year's parties; as always Elizabeth and he would lean against the mantlepiece and drink, though the martini experiment was never repeated since half the township had ended up in ditches. The first year she was back teaching, on October 1, Carl's birthday, Elizabeth called Adam to suggest lunch. He hadn't expected it and had to break an appointment which of course he did. As always they went to the Timberpost. It was strange to sit across the table from her again. Over the years her face had grown narrower, her eyes brighter. Although she'd had and nurtured the child she wanted so much, it was easy to imagine that whatever had been driving her before was now beginning to consume her. There was a new way she had of folding and unfolding her hands, as though they didn't quite know what to do with themselves. But meanwhile she talked easily, as she always had, this time about the changes that had transpired at the school and in West Gull since she'd last been teaching.

"Walk me back to the school," she asked on the way out. And then, a block away from the restaurant, she said in a low voice, "You might as well know he's yours."

Adam kept walking.

"Did you hear me?"

"I hope so."

"Well?"

Adam turned. Elizabeth was smiling wistfully. She was someone out of a life he could never have imagined. "I'm very happy," he said.

Mysteries begin with the body but sometimes the mystery is not death but love. There is so much to love. Cats. Bits of dust caught in the light. Colours. Unexpected waterfalls. And of course: the body. Warm skin on cool sheets. The blood's night hum. Summer heat seeping through damp moss. The raw smell of an oak tree opened in winter. A long-missed voice over the telephone. So much to love that life should be made out of loving, so many ways of loving that all stories should be love stories. This one is about a man and a woman. Adam and Elizabeth. They're on a library committee and on their way to buy cut-rate cookies for a fundraising tea. It's the winter after she told him about Carl.

The car is dark green, freshly waxed and polished to a gleam that sends the slate grey February sky flickering back into itself as the car pulls off the highway and into the shopping centre parking lot.

"You know," Elizabeth says, "I have a crazy idea."

This is a long time ago. It is 1972. Elizabeth is in her late thirties. Creamy skin with a slight cast, high cheekbones, a thick fall of chestnut hair that curves suggestively over the shoulders of her black wool coat, hazy blue eyes she turns inquiringly towards Adam. A beautiful woman: almost elegant and almost exotic, a woman difficult to place. A woman from somewhere else who is beautiful and used to being thought beautiful but who finds the question of her physical appearance, all things considered, uninteresting.

Adam takes the key out of the ignition and slowly strips off his gloves. He has big hands that go with his height, long white fingers, soft.

"Did you hear me?"

"Yes. You said you had a crazy idea. What is it?"

"I thought that instead of buying cookies we could go to a motel."

Adam looks down at his gloves, his hands, the key. He sets the gloves on the seat between himself and Elizabeth, slides the key into the ignition. Very slowly, very carefully, he backs the car out of its parking place, drives out of the lot and eases onto the highway.

"We don't have to if you don't want to," Elizabeth says. Though of course she knows he wants to, she has only to look at his face, normally as pale, as cool, as transparent as his eyes. Her own skin is also flushed. She can feel her earlobes tingling, the corners of her mouth.

They pass two sets of traffic lights and come to the first cluster of motels at the edge of town. "We'd better keep going for a while," Adam says, "if keeping things secret is part of it."

Then he does something exceptional in the extreme: he lifts his right hand from the wheel and puts it on Elizabeth's sleeve. She undoes her seatbelt, moves closer to him, takes his hand, slides it under her black wool coat, squeezes her thighs together until he can feel her nylons digging into his skin.

"Don't wait too long," she says and settles down to watch the road.

About a month later she called him at night.

"Take Anna Karenina," she said.

"Who?"

"Used to be my favourite cow. Before she ruined her life over a man who wasn't worth it. Some people would say that's a mistake. What do you think?"

Adam was at home. He had never read *Anna Karenina* but knew his mother had. The book was in the walnut case upstairs, the one with the glass doors, beside *War and Peace*. They were in matching leatherbound editions, thin paper with gilt edges. He could picture the faded chocolate-pebbled leather, the raised ridges across the spine.

"You wouldn't want to ruin your life," Adam said. Nor he supposed would he have wanted to ruin his. Although it was a dilemma — him ruining his own or others' lives — that had occupied him for the past several years. Without conclusion.

"You disappoint me," Elizabeth said. He strained to understand.

"You mean she wanted to ruin her life and ruining it over a man was the only available way?"

"Almost but not really," she said. "Because a man was the only available way, ruining her life was all she could do. There was nothing else."

In the middle of the night Adam woke up. Or realized that he hadn't yet slept. He put on his dressing gown, a threadbare once-turquoise satin fantasy with a tasselled belt that had belonged to his father and went to the bookcase to find *Anna Karenina*. It was so many decades since anyone had taken it off the shelf that it had stuck to *War and Peace*. They came apart with a sad dry popping sound. He brought *Anna Karenina* down to the kitchen and set it on the old pine breakfast table he always ate on — the dining-room table and most of the chairs were permanently mounded with papers and bills — and heated himself a pot of milk. He mixed his chocolate the old-fashioned way: two teaspoons stirred into a few drops of cold water to make a smooth paste, adding the hot milk just after it began to bubble at the edges. As he poured, it scalded on the lip of the pot and the familiar smell soothed him right away.

Adam opened the book to the first page. "All happy families resemble each other, but each unhappy family is unhappy in its own way...." And suddenly he could hear Flora reading those words to him. He was back on the gold-brocaded couch, long gone, wedged into the corner formed by the arm with the woollen doily and the back cushion that bulged, his feet tangled with his mother's. She was lying down, her head on the other arm, and after she read those words she repeated them. She continued: "Everything was upset in the Oblonsky house." Unlike their own where nothing was ever upset. Now, after a gap of merely thirty years, he understood what she was trying to tell him. "Each unhappy family is unhappy in its own way." In the Oblonsky house "everything was upset." But his mother's unhappiness, an issue he had never previously considered, expressed itself by being covered over. By the smooth seamless surface of the everyday. Unexpected: to be sitting in your kitchen in the middle of the night when you are thirty-nine years old and what you are thinking about is whether or not your mother was unhappy.

But of course she had been unhappy. Her husband at war, no job, only a few friends and a bizarre child that tied her to this life of waiting. He was sitting there, sipping his hot chocolate and feeling guilty about having been that bizarre child that tied his mother to her unhappy life when a completely different question, equally obvious, arrived: all those happy families that "resemble each other" — what are they like? But of course he knew: they are like something seen from outside — a light-strung Christmas tree glimpsed through a curtained window; a bicycle carelessly abandoned on a lawn; a group standing around a barbecue, sunburned, beers in hand, children tugging at them. The happy families are always seen from a distance because when you get close the illusion melts.

Then Adam thought about his own family, himself and his secrets, those huge rocks that the passage of time and a certain amount of Scotch had worn down to something smooth and almost bearable. There was Carl — now six — who at various moments he was able to believe might be his. There was Maureen whom, in the end, he couldn't decide to sacrifice. There was Elizabeth for whom he was the sacrifice, constantly offered. Or then again, perhaps he had no family at all, just a few people he wished he could call his own.

The next afternoon Elizabeth telephoned again. "You wouldn't happen to be free...," she began. He looked out his office door to the showroom, pale blue eyes locked as he calculated how many minutes it would take to make a necessary deposit at the bank. He had no idea what Elizabeth had in mind: some library emergency he supposed, or perhaps something about Carl. "It would be better if we went in separate cars this time. You could meet me at the shopping centre where we went before, pick me up in the parking lot," she suggested.

It was four weeks since that first trip to the motel and they hadn't spoken of it since. Like that first New Year's Eve it simply stood as an event, completely unique, beyond anything else he'd ever known, impossible to judge or evaluate. They'd gone, they'd done, they'd bought cookies. Afterwards they'd driven home, hardly touching but for their hands, which stayed locked together the whole time, fingers constantly stroking, caressing, turning on each other in a last continuing echo. He'd brought her to the school where her car was parked and after slowly drawing her hand from his, she'd got out. She hadn't offered a kiss, a goodbye. She'd just climbed out of his car and walked away, her shoulders ever-so-slightly hunched with shame or regret — or was he only imagining that, the way he might have imagined her eyes burning for McKelvey? He'd waited for a moment to make sure her car started before driving back to his house, free to think whatever he wanted. The possibly imagined set of her shoulders had discouraged him from the idea that it might happen a second time. Now his face glowed its lighthouse red. He stood up and closed his office door, returned to the phone.

"I have to go to the bank," he said. "I could meet you in an hour."

"Don't sound so enthusiastic." She had a teasing note in her voice that he was coming to recognize. How it could have taken him so long, he didn't know. All he knew was that he felt *eager*. To please, to be pleased. That was a novelty he suddenly knew he could count on: being pleased by Elizabeth.

"I am very enthusiastic," he said. "My enthusiasm is without limit."

"That's better."

At the bank he stood in line twitching nervously, hardly able to speak even about the weather. His business accomplished, he drove too fast, worrying the whole way that she would crash or change her mind or get a flat tire. The sky was brilliantly clear, the sun a shivering yellow splash on his shining roof. He stopped at the liquor store to buy a bottle of white wine and a corkscrew but still arrived at the shopping centre fifteen minutes early. He got out of his car, paced around nervously thinking she might be parked in a different section. In this unimpeded sunlight his hands looked whiter than usual. And even though he'd done nothing but replay in his mind the two hours of that first forbidden afternoon, he now remembered something different: the sight of his long white hand on her ribs, the way with the heel of his hand resting against her hip bone, the tips of his fingers landed just beneath her breast. How bizarre it had seemed that so many diverse and various landscapes of her kingdom — hip, belly, ribs, breast — could be encompassed by something so insignificant as his hand. To satisfy himself this memory was real he twisted to place the heel of his hand on his own hip, just to see how far his fingers would stretch. He was doubled over sideways, trying to estimate the exact necessary compensation for the fact that she was much shorter than him, when a car pulled up.

Two women got out, looked at him oddly, started off towards the supermarket.

It was another half-hour before Elizabeth arrived. By this time he was back in his car, drenched with sweat, reading a newspaper he'd bought from the coin box. She came towards him, running, her coat open, purse slung over her shoulder, a blue and red kerchief knotted around her neck; and he thought nothing in the world could be more desirable than her throat.

Later, her head thrust back, that throat flushed and corded, arched up to his waiting mouth. He slid his quivering tongue along the swollen arteries that ran up from her collarbone to beneath her ears, surrounded a throbbing blue vein with his teeth. Squeezed to feel the thick blood resisting.

"Go ahead, vampire," she whispered.

A sudden image of his teeth slicing in, the blood showering as it pumped from the heart now covered with his hand.

He shifted downwards, put his mouth over her heart. Then further down until his lips touched her salt, until his mouth filled with her moist heat his tongue began to tremble and swell and her thighs closed about his ears his skull filled with the numb hot buzz of his own breathing the silent cry of the voices once again released.

Elizabeth was sitting cross-legged on the bed, her nightgown tucked beneath her knees. If there was one person in the world to whom she felt loyal, aside from Carl, it was Adam. Somehow, without meaning to, she'd taken up his cause, become his flag-bearer, got into his corner. She believed in him in a way she had never believed in McKelvey, was cheering for him the way she cheered for Carl. She wanted Adam to get what he wanted — but what he wanted was her.

Earlier that evening she had been reading Carl a story while he sat on her lap. He had one arm around her neck and his head pressed against her chin. "I want to stay here for ever," Carl said as he often did. And she replied, this was always her line, "Good, because you *are* staying here for ever; I'm never going to let you go so you'd better arrange to have your meals delivered." Then she wrapped her arms around him and locked her hands while he wriggled and squirmed and pried at her fingers. Eventually, and as he always did, he broke her grip — which was her cue to say, "Lucky you," after which he came back to her lap and she continued the story.

Later on, looking into his room as he slept, she knew nothing that happened to her body — no pleasure, no pain, no danger — could possibly affect her compared with the possibility of Carl's world being endangered. Yet nothing could be more dangerous to Carl than her desire to be with Adam.

"Adam," she was going to have to say, "life is too small."

———

The very last time Adam Goldsmith saw Elizabeth was also a New Year's party. That was 1986, the last Richardson bash. When he was ready to go he said goodbye — nothing inspired — and then went home. He stayed up drinking coffee, packing his suitcases, writing the necessary letters. It was almost seven in the morning when the telephone rang. "I'm sorry to have this news for you, Adam," Luke began and Adam knew it was going to be bad but of course he had no idea. None. He just hung on to the telephone while Luke gave the details. "I know this has to be hard for you, Adam," Luke ended up. "You come over today whenever you want to. We're hoping to see you."

My Elizabeth, Adam said to himself, over and over. He thought he must have gone crazy because inside there was nothing but a storm battering to get out. He finished his coffee, went upstairs and changed. Then he drove to see for himself: huge raw splinters had been torn from the tree when the right front fender, Elizabeth's side, smashed into the oak. Gerald Boyce was out there with a tow truck, surveying the mess. There was blood all over the car, the hood, the snow. The whole front of the car was twisted to one side, the right headlight pushed halfway back to where the windshield gaped open, shattered as though Elizabeth had shot straight out to heaven, leaving nothing behind but the hole in the windshield, the blood and a piece of her scarf which had caught on the glass. Adam put the scrap in his pocket, then stood looking at her blood on the snow. She hadn't gone to heaven after all. At least not her body. There remained the outline of her legs, one arm and the stained dent left by her skull.

"Pretty awful," Gerald Boyce said. They were standing in the snow. Twenty-five years had turned them from whatever they'd been that day in the rowboat into two almost-old men bundled up so heavily they could hardly move. They'd never spoken of that time on the lake but now they moved close and gave each other little taps on the shoulder.

Adam was helping Gerald get a hook under the rear bumper when Arnie Kincaid arrived to check things out for the insurance. Another car stopped. Soon the whole township would be gathered around, shaking their heads over another drunken crash.

Adam went home. He tried doing various consoling things like reading *Anna Karenina* or remembering their motel visits but in the end all he could do was lie on the floor, clutching his belly and moaning. It wasn't until he read the paper the next day that he learned Carl had been driving.

The funeral was two days later. A raw January day at the West Gull Cemetery with cars stretched down the hill from the graveyard towards town. After all these years Elizabeth, who had started out so different and apart, had touched hundreds of lives: through her years in the school, on the library committees, as the one with the courage to telephone people about such bizarre issues as nuclear warheads or dumpsites or to help raise money for an extension to the school. Maureen was there and also her father; it was he who offered the eulogy. But what he said Adam couldn't hear because of the wind and the hat he'd yanked down to avoid the looks Maureen kept throwing him.

After the funeral Adam went to the McKelvey place to pay his respects. Again there were a lot of cars; Adam had to park a long way from the house. The wind had picked up and by the time he got inside his eyes were red and tearing. He thought back to his mother's small wake. She hadn't lived to a very old age but nonetheless her life had seemed, from the outside, complete, and her ending peaceful. With Elizabeth there was no such consolation. *My Elizabeth*. The lives the two of them might have lived. Now that she was gone it was as though he had never been alive.

Carl was in the living room, sitting on a small couch in the corner. His face was puffed with crying and drink. Chrissy was sitting beside him, rubbing his hand. McKelvey was on crutches, his leg swollen with bandages. He looked awful. Partly because his face had been bruised in the accident but it was more than that. Elizabeth had been his light, his true crutch, his everything. Adam closed his eyes to keep from crying. What he saw was himself, a dark blank ghost standing in the midst of the living.

PART III

ONE

BY AUGUST THE LIGHT IS A DUSTY BLUE-
gold and every morning it seems a little
more green has bled away during the night. No one can remember the day it last rained. In the afternoons the fields
shimmer under the sun and as evening deepens, the haze rises
and deepens with it, turning the sunset into a long Techni-
color symphony until the moon, tinted yellow and orange,
floats high in the sky to preside over summer's waning.

In the hollows by the Second Line the morning breeze
rises from the clover, dry and sweet. Floats into a bedroom
where a man, almost naked, is carefully adjusting a camera on
a tripod, bending his wide back and peering through the eye-
piece to focus the lens on a sleeping woman. To centre the
frame, the frame that includes most of the bed, most of her
body, he chooses her face, homing in on her eyes, the dense
curved resting lashes. A button is pressed, the motor activated,
the camera begins a soft whirr that could almost be mistaken

for the hum of summer insects. The man pulls off his underwear and slides under the covers. The woman adjusts her body to his, there is a moment of repose, then the sheet begins to ripple as his hand strokes her thigh. She sighs and moves away. He follows. At the centre of the frame is the moving shape of his hand sliding down her belly. The sheet goes slack as the target is found, then comes a first sharp cry as he draws the woman onto him, a second when she opens her eyes and sees she is looking into the camera.

Mid-August and Carl was lying in bed thinking he could feel the exact measure of drought by the scratch at the back of his throat. Drought was what people were starting to call it now. In the north, the radio was reporting new fires sparked by lightning every day. Around West Gull the farmers were complaining about withered corn crops and wells running dry. Not that he had been so dry himself. Last night, just as he and Lizzie were about to watch a movie, Ray Johnson had dropped over with a case of beer and a soccer ball. Instead of turning on the VCR the three of them had gone outside and ran around like little kids in the last of the light, using fenceposts for goals, Ray taking on Lizzie and Carl until it got so dark that not even the moon could find the gleaming white ball.

Lizzie, tousled and sweaty, had collapsed into bed. After he had kissed her goodnight, Carl had gone down to the kitchen where he and Ray started to work on the beer. Now, wide awake, he could see the moon through the bedroom window; the pollen had given it halos and in the halos were the dark spots his father had always called moondogs. "See those dogs," McKelvey would say, "and you know they're coming after you. Werewolves is what they should be called. You can almost hear them howling."

Carl couldn't hear them howling. It was a more a feeling of lying there and being gnawed from the inside. Chrissy of course. That night with Chrissy. These days — these nights — when he'd had a few drinks he just had to close his eyes to be back in the truck with Chrissy. That Chrissy feeling blowing through him except now the Chrissy feeling was empty and gnawing and like the moment that began with his hands under her sweater and ended with his hands empty and her walking away. He had come home to start something new but he was sinking into everything that was old, sinking into it so deep he might as well be climbing into his mother's grave. Or his own. That was a thought he also had these nights — not so much when Lizzie was there but when he was alone. How much easier it might be for everyone if he put an end to things. Drew a line through his name. Erased it altogether. Evaporated.

He was taking Lizzie home the next morning when he saw Moira Lapointe and, he thought later, he must have unknowingly had her on his mind because he recognized her right away. She was half-hidden by the hood of her car, which was up like a distress flag at the side of the road barely outside of town. This Moira was a dilapidated version of her R&R self, baggy T-shirt flying up in the wind to show strips of her waist, chewed-up straw hat, butterfly-frame sunglasses. As Carl slowed he could see her radiator fluid spreading in a dark pool beneath her car.

"You think we should stop?"

"It's Moira," Lizzie said. "Of course we have to stop. She always brings me cookies when I go to visit."

Since the night he'd spent with her, he'd seen her at the R&R a few times, but though she'd spoken to him when he was with McKelvey there'd been nothing more than those few words of greeting. It was as though she was telling him that however indifferent he was to her, she felt the same way. There was something forced and brisk in her manner; it made him glad things had stopped when they did.

After he showed her where the radiator had burst, Moira got in the truck, Lizzie between them, and soon she and Lizzie were talking about one of those summer movies that make a hundred million dollars in the first weekend, then end up at the Movie Barn six months later. The artificial tone was gone from her voice and Carl found himself remembering the weight of her body. It occurred to Carl that the three of them could go to a drive-in movie. Lizzie would sit between, they'd eat popcorn and drink Cokes. Just to think about it was a vacation. Lizzie and Moira would chatter away, always rushing off for more food while he slumped behind the wheel, smoked cigarettes and didn't worry about anything.

He pulled up in front of the garage at the New & Used but when he offered to go in and explain the problem with her car, Moira looked over Lizzie's head, gave her nice smile and said she could handle it, but thanks.

Friday night Carl was at the Movie Barn, dealing out the weekend's entertainment. So much of West Gull would spend the night goggle-eyed in front of their TVs watching what he'd given them that his hand was cramped from entering film titles in the register. When there was a momentary lull and he was about to step outside to stretch, the telephone rang and it was Chrissy calling to ask him to pick up Lizzie an hour late in the morning. In their conversations since the night at the tavern her voice had been measured and cold, as though they were supposed to be in some kind of purgatory for taking a drive into the past with a bottle of peach brandy.

The morning after, he had called to tell her that Marbles had "run away" — the lie he'd decided on until he could think of something better. Her initial reaction had been, "So you've spent the day worrying about a cat." But now her voice struck a curious new note.

"I hear you did something to Ned Richardson."

"Where'd you hear that from?"

"Ellie Dean. She just found out. You'd better expect her."

"Thanks for the warning," Carl said.

"You used to go out with her, didn't you?"

Chrissy's voice had a little buzz-saw edge Carl hadn't heard for a while and still didn't know what to do with. "This some kind of memory test?"

"Just that I was thinking the other day that you'd probably be getting a new girlfriend."

The truth was, that stupid idea of taking Moira and Lizzie to a drive-in had come back to him a couple of times but he hadn't figured out how he would ask her or how he would manoeuvre things afterwards. It was irreconcilable that a man could first lie in bed contemplating his own suicide, then plan to get another person to lie beside him, or maybe even on top of him or beneath him.

"I guess I'd be jealous if you started up with someone else," Chrissy said.

"For Christ's sake, you're living with Fred. Might as well be married."

"How much do you like that?"

Out the window of the shop he could see car headlights flashing by on Main Street.

"You're the one who's with him," Carl said. "You're the one who has to like it."

"Fred wasn't too happy the way I was when I came home."

Carl got a picture of Fred standing at the door of the Second Line farmhouse, wearing his lumber-yard vest with the little tag saying MANAGER sewn over the pocket where he kept his cigarillos.

"How were you?"

"I tried not to be anything."

A car had stopped in front of the store and Carl recognized Adam Goldsmith approaching. "I better go," Carl said. "Anyway, it's all over now."

"Baby Blue," Chrissy said softly, hanging up. That was what they used to call each other back before they called each other names, Baby Blue. Then, like now, being with Chrissy had been a state of its own, a state he still didn't know how he was going to live without.

"Hi there," Adam said as he came in. "Thought I might as well start giving you my business." He stood motionless for a second so awkward and bewildered that Carl wondered how difficult it had been for Adam to leave his house and come here. "Felt a few drops on my way over," Adam said. "Almost needed my umbrella." Again he hesitated and Carl smiled and gave a little snicker so Adam would know he was appreciated. Nine-thirty on a Saturday night. Weekend evenings the Movie Barn was like an open house for every lonely person in town. Often they made excuses for themselves: just picking up something for the children or grandchildren, just dropping something off. After his first week Carl had borrowed an old coffee maker from the R&R and set it at the end of the counter. People who wanted to helped themselves, then put some change in the styrofoam cup beside the machine. When Luke Richardson had seen the coffee maker, he raised his eyebrows and asked Carl if he'd been taking community-care courses while he was away. He'd poured himself a cup of coffee, gulped it down and left a bill in the styrofoam cup, just so Carl would know who was the big man.

"All this dry weather," Adam said. "They say dry weather brings on the fall."

"I guess."

"Just get used to summer and the snow comes."

Adam had taken half a cup of coffee and was adding his second plastic container of cream when Ellie Dean came bursting through the door.

"Jesus!" Then she saw Adam. "Good evening, Mr. Goldsmith. Excuse my French."

"What's up?" Carl asked.

"So the birds are going to eat his eyes out, are they? God, you're one to talk."

"That's all ancient history," Carl said.

"*I* just found out. Fred Verghoers got it out of him. You scared him so bad he was afraid to tell me."

"Did he tell you what *he* did?"

"I don't care what he did. You're just a bully."

"Calm down," Carl said. "Have a coffee."

"How long have you been back anyway, Carl McKelvey? A month? You're already in more trouble than when you left."

So it seemed. Ned Richardson had slit the throat of his daughter's cat but somehow he was the one being blamed. He looked down at the floor. Ellie was wearing those same shiny white sandals she'd had on when he'd come to get Ned that morning. But that morning, not so long ago, she'd been all legs above the sandals. Now she was in a carefully tapered and pressed pair of jeans. Adam Goldsmith was right: despite the dry weather, fall was on its way. Soon they'd all be wearing boots and ski parkas and clapping their hands together while they talked about how cold it was and how if it didn't stop snowing soon old so-and-so would take a heart attack shovelling himself out of his driveway for his daily trip to the liquor store.

"What are you looking at me that way for? Carl! Do you even know why I came here?"

"Not exactly," Carl admitted. More headlights were drawing up to the store. "I suppose you were upset about Ned."

"I'm upset about *you*, Carl McKelvey. I don't like what you did to Ned and I don't like what you're going to get done to yourself. I used to know you pretty well before the accident, Carl. Remember that? And Carl, an accident is what it was. You don't have to destroy yourself and everyone around you for the rest of your life. If you don't know your own daughter is more important than a cat then you don't know anything. Isn't that right, Mr. Goldsmith?" Then Ellie left the store as a new wave of customers came in, a young couple holding hands with their sunburned children, and a group of teenagers wearing LONG GULL LAKE CAMP T-shirts.

Carl looked down at his hands. Always rock steady, they were trembling now, an uncontrollable high-frequency shudder that he couldn't will to stop. He forced himself behind the counter, gripped his pen tightly, numbly registered the videos and took the money. Adam Goldsmith was still standing at the Academy Awards shelves. Carl could see him out of the corner of his eye; he was planted in the aisle, reading and playing with his coffee. From the moment Carl had told Chrissy he was coming home he had known this was the bargain, the price he'd have to pay to be in his own place with his own daughter: getting the accident thrown in his face whenever he was least ready. And it would never end. For the rest of his life he would be Carl McKelvey, the boy who drove his mother into a tree.

The customers kept coming until after eleven. It got so busy he didn't see Adam leave, nor did he notice Arnie Kincaid arrive — he just came upon him standing at the end of the counter with his usual cup of coffee, a pile of videos ready to check out, while he leafed through the magazine of future releases. When Carl started cleaning the store Arnie hung in for a second cup of coffee and Carl had to lend him the key for the supermarket washroom. Finally it was closing time. Carl locked up, then went outside to his truck and stood for a moment in the darkness.

The town had slowed down to a few clusters of voices, music coming from an open window. An almost peaceful feeling though Ellie's visit had left him anything but. He got into his truck and drove slowly past Adam's.

The modest two-storey brick house with its sharply peaked gable would have looked like a small face with a big nose had it not been for the tall pine tree that blurred the effect and scattered the light glowing from the living-room window. Beside the house was a garage with a covered walkway connecting it to the side door and in front of the garage — no one in West Gull seemed to use their garage for its intended purpose — was parked Adam's car, a dark forest green that matched his tree.

From Adam's house he continued down to the lake and around the crescents of the old section of West Gull until he reached the R&R. He glided to a stop beneath a big oak that sheltered his truck from the street lamp. In the R&R's bedroom wings all the windows were dark. McKelvey would be in his bed, the way he'd seen him often enough at the farm, splayed out and snoring, dreaming whatever old man's dreams he had left. Last Sunday Carl had brought Lizzie to visit and the three of them had sat on the porch having what Lizzie had decided was a little tea party. She was always offering McKelvey something, passing more cookies and sugar and buttering slices of bread for him. When he took out a package of cigarettes Lizzie looked so disapproving you would have thought his clothes had flown off. She took the pack right out of his hand and asked him in a very serious voice if he had considered the health consequences of smoking.

"The health consequences of smoking," McKelvey had repeated. "Where did you learn words like that?"

"In school this week," Lizzie said primly, "and I know what's good for you. My mother and father have both pledged to stop smoking and you can, too."

"I have," McKelvey said. "Dozens of times."

"That's not funny to your loved ones," said Lizzie, then she had raised her rear end and sat on his pack.

When Moira came by Lizzie gave her the crushed remains of McKelvey's vice and asked her to throw them in the garbage. Carl, sitting on the steps, found himself watching Moira's calves as she walked away.

In the converted barns where some of the staff lived and in the kitchen and great hall of the R&R itself, the lights were still on. Moira lived in, Carl knew. McKelvey had told him she was a lawyer's daughter from upstate New York. The family had vacationed in the area. She could well be in the kitchen having a last cup of coffee. Years ago, after Lizzie was born and things had started to unravel with Chrissy, he'd had a habit of getting in his truck and driving around, looking for something. Late at night you could believe almost any lit doorway or window was an invitation waiting to be accepted.

Carl started up his truck again, went back to Main Street, past the Long Gull Lake Inn and headed out to the highway. On nights he worked the late shift and didn't have Lizzie he would either go home or visit Ray Johnson. He'd never spoken to him about the business he'd imagined because Ray had told him he was saving to start a family. Who with, Carl didn't know but he always called before he dropped by, though Ray was always free. They'd sit on Ray's new screen porch and drink and watch the water. Sometimes they would gossip. Ray could do a good imitation of Fred squirting overly hot coffee from his mouth, even if it was a waste of good beer. And Carl could work up a hoarse whisper that sounded a lot like Nancy Brookner asking him if he had any sex films suitable for kids. Eventually Ray would pick up his old gut-string guitar and pluck away at some song while Carl moaned along on the harmonica. At the senior high-school concert they'd brought down the house pretending to be Bruce Springsteen drunk and crying on the streets of West Gull. When Ray had collapsed onto the stage he'd fallen so hard Carl had to drag him off.

It was before midnight but Carl didn't feel like seeing Ray. His blood was still crawling with what Ellie had said. Even though he was halfway home he turned around and headed back into West Gull, and when he got to Ellie's house and saw that the lights were on but she had no company he switched off his headlamps and parked beside her car.

He got out of his truck the way he used to, wondering if he would be hating himself when he got back, closed the door softly. Her curtains were drawn but there was a small gap and he was just looking through it, thinking she must have gone to bed and left the lights on, when she appeared, her blonde hair wet from the shower and hanging close to her skull the way it did after swimming, a towel wrapped around her waist.

Carl backed away so quickly he tripped on a shrub and fell to the ground with a thud he imagined loud enough to wake the whole town. But as he scrambled to his feet nothing happened. No dogs barked, no sirens wailed, no Ellie Dean came to the door.

He'd closed that door behind him more than once but now he went back to his truck, eased out of her driveway and glided slowly down her road towards the highway and the Balfer place. There was no one he was planning to tell but the news was that Ellie Dean was looking pretty good. Narrow waist, not a hint of a fold in her belly, full pale breasts with a crescent of suntan extending down from her throat the way it always had. Come to think of it, there was a whole world of women out there — an extremely small world — women he'd wanted and held and known, women with whom he'd groaned and moaned. If his ad-hoc survey was any indication, every one of them was probably looking as good as ever, every one of them was more grown up than she used to be and every one of them knew he was only the fucked-up drunken teenager he'd always been who'd got older but not much else. Yet, if Chrissy, Ellie and Moira were any examples, every one of them was one way or another on the loose, so desperate that even he was an attraction. But here he was driving home alone. Tonight, seeing Ellie in a towel had been enough to settle him down. Maybe he would tell Ray Johnson about this after all, this late-night non-knightly non-tryst, this aborted late-night lonesome wolf howl, where if Ellie Dean had walked into her own living room dressed in the jeans and sweatshirt she'd been wearing earlier that evening, he might have knocked at her door. Instead, seeing her undressed — but no more undressed than they would both have ended up — he had for some peculiar reason lost interest and driven home, happily ensconced in the nothing that had happened, so content that the only drink he needed was a half a glass of cold water, which was strong enough to send him straight to bed and to nine of hours of sleep that ended only when Lizzie telephoned to tell him he was four minutes late.

Sunday nights were the slowest. At the Movie Barn, the end of the weekend was a low tide that deposited a few returned movies and a lot of empty time before retreating completely. A beach littered with garbage. That's how Ellie Dean had left him feeling the other night. He poured himself a coffee from the machine, always a sign of boredom, and as penance paid the styrofoam cup two loonies.

Ellie Dean: he should have known it would be her. In high school she'd been the cheerleader type, always behind the bench at hockey games or hanging around with girls who bantered with boys like him, boys who were better at sports than studying. She was blonde, petite, not exactly pretty but there was something eager about her that made her easy to talk to so when she asked him for a drive home he thought nothing of it. Back then she lived right in West Gull; her father had taken off for Toronto, her older sister had gone to the Maritimes and her mother was working the long shift four days a week at the Zellers.

The first time she had invited him in was to help him with geometry. Walking into her house with her he felt as though his body might fall apart from all the electricity jumping around and when she turned to close the door such a jolt went through him he couldn't move. But she was just fixing the lock. After that she led him into the kitchen where they spread their books on the table and she made them a snack of grilled cheese sandwiches in the frying pan.

He'd never actually been in a bed with someone. She was shy, made him close his eyes while she undressed and insisted on pulling the sheet over their heads. In their pale illuminated tent filled with the fragrance of her milky skin and the sweetly sour remnants of her perfume, he lay on top of her the way she wanted him to, unmoving, waiting, her chin dug into his shoulder and her arms wrapped tightly around his back while he stared down into the pillow. "Don't move until I tell you," she instructed. Her hands slid down his back and then her fingers hooked into his buttocks, locking him into position from both ends. Every time a car went by he thought it was her mother home from Zellers and that he'd have to jump up and hide in her closet until morning. "Are you hating this?" she asked him. "No, no, it's great." Her stomach muscles were banded against his, he raised his head and looked down at her face. Her eyes were squeezed tight, tears trickled down her cheeks. He kissed her tears, her eyelids, ran his tongue along the narrow ridge of her nose. "This is crazy, isn't it?" she said. He pushed up to look down at the V where their bodies joined. In the light that strained through the sheet her pubic hair was a delicate damp pale gold. Lying in Ellie Dean's bed, covered by a sheet and wedged between her teddy bears, as well as being inside that place surrounded by those beautiful golden curls, Carl was again gripped by the same overexcited electric buzz that had hit him as they walked in the door. "You're trembling," Ellie said. She had gone from leaking tears to weeping and Carl was just about to offer to withdraw, electricity and all, when whatever it was inside her unlocked and she began a long liquid shudder that made Carl close his eyes again as they clung together like two sailors trying to survive an unexpected storm.

Two minutes later they were back at the kitchen table for another round of grilled cheese sandwiches and apple juice. "These theorems are incredibly easy," Ellie said, a bit of beard burn on the left side of her chin and jaw but otherwise entirely restored and ready to face the news from Zellers. "All you have to do is concentrate on the first few, make sure you really understand them, then the rest will make sense on their own." *Concentrate.* There was something about the way she said "concentrate" that reminded Carl of his mother looking over his shoulder as he worked at the kitchen table.

In the end what he liked best with Ellie was lying under her tent, those few times they felt free to, looking at her naked body in the filtered light. Just being there with that cool skin, the spun gold hair that surrounded everything nervous and needing about Ellie, breathing easy after the frantic locking together, then pushing back the sheet and feeling the air dry the moisture on his belly and thighs.

The only time she truly relaxed with him was talking. Sometimes they would walk out from school to go sit by the lake and she'd chatter on about the different families in West Gull. For two years after her father left, her mother had made ends meet by cleaning houses. For every household with enough money to afford to pay someone else to do the dirty work, Mrs. Dean had apparently found more than enough dirt, which was why as soon as Ellie was old enough to come home alone, she had grabbed the sales job in Kingston.

Perhaps Chrissy "stole" Carl, as Ellie later put it, though if there was an actual moment when he decided to switch, Carl had missed it. He knew only that he'd gone to that last New Year's dating Ellie, then danced with Chrissy and had to fight Fred. The next day, after the accident, it was Chrissy at the house, Chrissy by his side, Chrissy somehow having taken possession of him when he didn't know he was available to be owned. Even at the funeral Chrissy clung to his arm as if the grief was equally hers, while all he could remember of Ellie was looking up once and seeing her in the crowd. Her eyes had been on him and they didn't move away but the drawn accusing face hadn't even flickered in recognition. At that moment it seemed to Carl whatever he was in with Chrissy, this life-and-death drama, was a planet away from those baby steps he and Ellie had taken together. By the time a week or two had passed and he'd seen Chrissy every day, the event he hadn't noticed was over: he'd become Chrissy's and Chrissy was his. Losing themselves in each other's bodies had become what they did all night and all previous ties had burned away.

Eventually he started to see Ellie Dean again: when losing himself in Chrissy had gradually been replaced by losing himself in drink; Ellie had been through a quick marriage and divorce, and her mother's sharp tongue had become her own, turned with a bitterness that Carl found satisfying. It was as though because just a few years ago they'd shared the innocent protective cocoon of Ellie's sheet, they could now find comfort with each other in this new place — not a tent filled with pale golden light but a purgatory of self-hate and uncertainty where the only sure thing was that another few drinks and another few cigarettes would use up some of those empty hours after midnight. Sometimes they would go to bed together but with Ellie, by this time, Carl felt old — not just older than they'd been in high school but *old*, old like an apple with thickening skin and a rotting core, old in a way he didn't want to feel with Ellie or even expose her to; surely she'd had enough poison from him the first time around. By the time he moved in with Ray Johnson she was just an occasional stop on a desperate night, a place he'd cruise by once in a long while and if he saw her light on he'd park the truck quietly and look through her window to make sure she was alone before knocking.

He was just picturing how he used to find Ellie those nights — lying on her back on her couch, holding a book stiff-armed above her eyes because she'd been told this position was

good for her posture and would ward off dowager's hump —
when Nancy Brookner came in. Her hair was windblown, her
face puffy as though she'd been drinking.

"Isn't that a scandal about the new dump site? You'd think
the township would be smart enough not to get held up on
something like that. Bob says they were looking for a place
twenty years ago."

Carl nodded.

Nancy set her return movies on the counter. Two martial-
arts ball-breakers — "for the kids," she had explained — and
an old Barbara Stanwyck black-and-white for herself because
Bob had spent the evening at old-timers' hockey practice.

"How's business?" Whenever she asked a question she
raised her eyebrows. "Did it rain over by your place the other
night? The way everyone's talking drought you'd think the
whole town was going to blow away like a pile of sticks."

"You'd think," Carl said. Though those storm clouds that
never stormed had been coming and going all day and when
Nancy opened the door he had smelled rain in the wind.

"What are you so happy about anyway? Out dancing last
night?"

The fact that she had seen him leaving the dance with
Chrissy was something Nancy referred to whenever she got the
chance. "I just drove her home," Carl had told her the first
time, repeating it twice more before giving up. If Nancy
Brookner wanted to think he was the town stud, why not? She
rented three movies a day and lately that made up a big part of
his business.

"People ever ask your advice on sexy movies?" Nancy now
asked.

"Like man, give me something with some action?"

"Yeah."

"No."

"Just wondering." She was moving along the aisles. "I think it's wrong that people take pictures of each other doing those things. Maybe I'm just old-fashioned but I like strangers better with their clothes on."

Carl had no idea what to say. He tried, "Takes all kinds."

"What's that mean, takes all kinds? I wish there weren't all kinds. I wish there were just people like ... you know what I mean."

"I guess," Carl said.

Now Nancy had made her selection and he was writing it down in the log.

"They should get you a computer for this."

"I don't mind."

"I would have thought this would be the most boring job in the world. You don't even watch movies any more. When I first started coming in, you always had something on at least. You reading books now? Or does that newspaper last you all day?"

Carl kept writing. He didn't know what it was about Nancy Brookner. One morning he had been sitting at the kitchen table eating his toast and doing a crossword, and it had come into his mind that he could dial Nancy's number and she would most likely be at home eating her own breakfast, nothing better to do than wait for him to open the shop so she could come and ask questions. Or look at him and wonder whatever it was she wondered about him. He could just call her up and say he was home alone for another couple of hours. He'd even taken out the telephone book and found her number. Now she was leaning over the counter, so close to him he could see the fluorescent lights reflected in her eyes.

Grey eyes, a dark bitter grey that made him feel the way he had when he'd been leafing through the phone book.

"That's a 'G' there," she said, pointing down at his list.

"I know."

"Sorry. I thought it looked like a '6'."

"Luke hire you to check my spelling?"

She backed off, blushing so fast and deep that Carl wanted to apologize but couldn't find the words. "Hey," he finally said. And when she looked up, still scarlet, he winked at her the way he had seen Moira wink at his father.

When Nancy had gone he went back to the paper. He had bought it for the crossword but now he opened it to the help-wanted section. There was nothing except jobs like the one he already had and "business opportunities" for people to buy franchises. Maybe he and Lizzie should be opening some kind of Lonesome Dad Fried Chicken Palace. Lizzie would like that. She liked fried chicken, fries, anything with grease. They would have chicken-emblazoned aprons and chicken-feather hats to keep their hair out of the food. In thirty years they would be rich enough to go to Florida for a month every winter.

Arnie Kincaid came in and somehow Carl didn't look up until Arnie was close enough to see him circling the franchise offers with a red ballpoint pen.

"Thinking of moving on?"

"Not really," Carl said.

"Good. I like the way you keep this place." Then Carl realized Arnie had only been talking about a change of job but that in truth he *was* — or some part of him was — getting ready to leave. It was as though whatever Ellie had dealt him had defeated his whole plan. She was right: the accident might have been bad luck but ever since he'd been compelled to try to destroy everything around him. Sooner or later he'd be taking it out on Lizzie. The truth was, they'd be better off without him.

Kincaid moved over to the coffee machine. "Running a restaurant isn't such a bad idea."

"Can't cook," Carl said.

"Most can't." Then Arnie Kincaid laughed. Carl made himself smile. Every time Arnie came into the shop he made little jokes. By the time he had finished his two cups of coffee, told his funny stories and left, Carl was exhausted.

At eleven Carl emptied out the coffee maker and started sweeping the floor with the big push broom. It was amazing how many candy wrappers and cigarette butts could accumulate during one boring shift. He took the heaped-up dustpan to the bathroom and emptied it into the garbage bag. Then he washed his hands and splashed some water on his face. When he came back into the store Fred Verghoers was standing at the counter, big arms folded across his chest.

Carl hesitated for a moment, looked around the store. Just the sight of Fred made him feel as though he was just stepping out of his truck, his face still damp with Chrissy's kisses.

"I was driving by," Fred said. "Thought I'd stop to say hello. I'm always missing you at the house." He stuck out a big hand.

Carl moved forward slowly. Everything had gone into slow motion, the way it used to before a fight. His eyes flicked around the room. Fred's face had thickened in the three years since he'd last seen him. In another few years, just looking at Fred was going to be enough to make a man run. Fred's mangy blue-brown eyes were squinting into an imaginary sun. Carl felt so tight he could hardly move. Fred was a bit taller and had about thirty pounds on him but whatever Fred did to him he could return in kind because, as he had once explained to Chrissy about his fighting, he was faster and mainly he was crazier.

"Afraid to shake?" Fred asked.

Carl took Fred's hand. Fred squeezed hard. "Just thought I'd come and welcome you back in person," Fred said, still squeezing. "Seems like you've seen just about everyone else." Fred had his hand locked into place but there was something spongy about his palm, as though he was spending too many hours in his office. "Guess you look about the same," Fred said. "Maybe a bit smaller." His grip loosened and Carl could feel Fred's body approaching the edge.

"Hear they made you manager over at the yard," Carl said. "Congratulations."

Fred let go of Carl's hand and stepped back. "That's right."

"Hear you're going into politics, too."

"Trying to," Fred said. "If your boss lets me."

They were a couple of feet apart now, still within reach. A set of headlights swept in towards the store. A car door slammed. Arnie Kincaid came back in the door, a video cassette in his hand. "Didn't mean to interrupt. I forgot to leave this."

"We were just getting acquainted again," Fred said. Carl wondered if he'd find the words to tell Ray just how strange a smile Fred then gave, a twisty little smile that showed bits of his teeth, like the big bad wolf's when he was talking to Little Red Riding Hood.

Arnie put the cassette down on the counter. "See you."

"Me too," Fred said. "It's getting late." Carl waited. His chest was on fire with adrenaline, his arms half-cocked. But he wasn't going to move unless Fred moved first. Fred's face was smooth, unworried. He rubbed his hands together, pushed back his big ring. Then as Arnie went out the door, Fred stepped away from Carl. "Guess I should ask you if you're going to behave yourself," Fred said.

"You a cop now?"

"I asked you a question," Fred said. "What's your answer?"

Driving east Carl had known this moment would arrive: he and Fred standing toe to toe, ready to start swinging, winner take all. What *all?* another part of him would ask. That's ridiculous, you're twenty-eight years old and what you want is to be a father to your daughter, not to play the teenage idiot. The idiot you were. When the time comes, just turn around and walk away.

"I don't have any answers," Carl said. "I just rent movies."

"If that's the way you want it," Fred said. He gave his twisty smile again and left the store.

Carl stood flexing his back and neck, trying to relax as he watched Fred get into his car. He made a couple of false starts backing up, trying to let Arnie go first, then drove off down the road towards town.

Carl filed away Arnie's cassette, marked it in the register. Then he picked up the broom and continued sweeping until exactly midnight when he turned off the lights and stepped outside. The clouds had mostly cleared but even as he stood on the step a pale fork of lightning glowed briefly in the sky. His truck was at the front of the gravel parking lot, the mirrors and windshield gave off glimmers of light from the moon. As he went down the steps he noticed there was a car still parked in the shadow of the supermarket. He heard a noise behind him. Then, just as the adrenaline began to surge, his head was hammered from behind. He felt himself falling, slowly, as though the air had turned liquid and was trying to support him, and all the while he was trying to curl up and move his arms to protect his face from the gravel. When he hit the ground a boot drove into his ribs once, twice, three times — then into his head where it had been hit. He blacked out until he heard Fred's voice grating in his ear, "Next time it's your nuts." Then the sound of a car spitting gravel as it skidded out of the parking lot and onto the highway.

TWO

*W*HEN CARL CAME TO HE WAS LYING face down in the gravel. His ribs were the first thing he noticed because it hurt to breathe. Then there was the back of his head which he finally gathered the courage to touch; his hand returned sticky with blood. When he tried to stand pain exploded along his side. He fell back to the ground, which sent something through his head like a crowbar clawing at his skull.

He dug his fingers into the gravel. It was clammy and it stank of oil. He dragged himself towards the steps. His idea was to get the key in the lock, pull himself across the floor and to the telephone. He lifted his face onto the wooden steps. His skull was pounding and the back of his neck was warm with blood. He imagined himself in a Movie Barn summerheat special, prostrate in the buzzing darkness while Lizzie, watching from wherever she was, cheered him on: "Don't die, Daddy, don't *die.*" But he wasn't dying, he was just emptying out. Cars flashed back and forth but none seemed to notice him and he hadn't the strength to shout or wave. He wondered what it would take to get himself to the door. If he could rise to his knees, he realized, he would be able to unlock the door then crawl across the floor and call Ray. But as he tried to lift himself that old movie buzzing darkness buzzed even louder and put him back to sleep.

For the first time in years, Adam's voices had come back. When he was a child they had possessed him, taken hold of his tongue, grabbed his body from the inside, thrown him to the floor in a frenzy of jabber and drool. When his love for Elizabeth broke open they shot through the gap and joined in, frisky young animals happy to tumble with their master. Now he was too old to be taken thrashing to the floor, far past rolling about on a motel bed or bracketing his head in a loved one's thighs. Now the numbers were running out and all that remained was the stately march to his dignified and inevitable end, a pre-purchased funeral that foresaw the mourners' needs in everything from vegetarian spring rolls to single malt Scotch, as well as his own destination in a modestly classic maple casket that would be lowered into its preordained slot in the West Gull Cemetery. On his occasional visits to Elizabeth's grave he had experimented standing on the ground that would one day hold him. It was beside his mother, where else, and only a stone's throw from Elizabeth. The idea that the three of them, along with everyone else in West Gull, would be snoozing through eternity together was both a consolation and its opposite. Nonetheless he was on his way and the voices had reassembled, like wolves was how he pictured them, darting in and out of sight, constantly testing his defences. Asleep he would dream he was being attacked by them at the office. That suddenly while talking to Luke or a customer he would be filled by a hot liquid chaos dissolving his bones and his will until he'd end up lying on his back, looking up at Luke's grinning mug. One afternoon while visiting at the R&R, he had gone into the big hall to talk to Moira about McKelvey. She had been in the corner cleaning and as he waited at the hearth with his coffee, he had the memory of standing in that exact space at one of the New Year parties, as though his old body had invaded his present one, forcing two or maybe a dozen selves into the same electric configuration; then the wires crossed and he was leisurely chatting to Elizabeth as though they had all the time in the world. But suddenly Moira was in front of him and he didn't know whether to apologize for talking to himself or if he was only imagining the echo of his own voice. "Daydreaming," he'd muttered to cover all possibilities, and suddenly wondered what it would be like to tell Moira everything. There had been Elizabeth who knew her half — her more-than-half — of the story. There'd been Maureen who'd known her part but guessed more, though not about Carl who knew nothing at all. Finally there was himself and his voices, looking from the outside in like one man with one body and one life but with a whole crowd of imposters pushing and shoving and ordering each other to keep quiet.

In books, secret sinners always go crazy in the end. For almost thirty years — it was that long since his first night with Elizabeth — he'd held everything in check, divided himself into as many people as necessary, each locked away from the other. Now the mind-control muscles were gone. He'd worn them out or forgotten how to use them.

Nights he couldn't sleep any more. He'd lie in bed until two or three in the morning, then get up and drive by the old Balfer place just to see how Carl was doing. Once or twice the lights were on and he'd wanted to stop and knock at his door.

Back in West Gull he'd snake guiltily into his own driveway, feeling like a Dr. Jekyll who'd been out playing Mr. Hyde. Finally, afraid of where this might be leading, he bought a do-it-yourself book, ordered in a load of building supplies, and began putting new gyprock on the walls of the upstairs bedroom that he'd slept in as a child but used as storage ever since he'd moved back to town.

It took him weeks to empty the room of its furniture, carefully remove the wooden mouldings and the window framing, put up the panels, tape, plaster, sand and paint. Although it had to be admitted he spent most of the time re-reading the instructions or admiring each tiny increment of his accomplishment. As he stood, paint-spattered in his childhood room, listening to the baseball game with paintbrush in hand, he convinced himself that once his bedroom was finished he'd remodel the entire house. The incredible prospect of becoming a virtuous handyman who actually increased the value of his residence rather than coaxing it from crisis to crisis became immensely comforting.

But one night when he was standing on the stepladder, his knees began to tremble, his tongue to flutter, and the pure current of the voices shot through him with such force that he fell down in the newspapers that were covering the floor and began to beg for mercy. But who was he begging? he'd asked himself afterwards, although when it came to mercy he was prepared to accept it from whoever or Whoever wanted to give.

In mid-August the junk he'd moved from the room was still piled, sheet-covered, in the hall and the ladder was still poised beneath the naked light bulb. To keep himself from driving around the township in the middle of the night, Adam now returned to an old remedy for sleeplessness — night walking. Maybe it was the low dollar or the exceptionally dry weather, but even late at night this summer there were always a few tourists roving and the Main Street convenience store was often open. What Adam most enjoyed was staking out the Movie Barn. From where he stood, which was under an old tree fronting the dress shop, he had a view of Carl through the window and could see customers coming and going. It was strange to think of Carl being observed without knowing — in fact it was strange to be always thinking about Carl but Adam couldn't stop. Carl's return to West Gull, his life with Lizzie, even his job at the Movie Barn, obsessed Adam day and night. When Luke brought up Carl's name, it was all Adam could do to keep his face straight and murmur in agreement. Sometimes he would imagine Carl sitting in his kitchen drinking a cup of coffee, or Carl driving around in his truck, and he had to ask himself why whether Carl threw his coffee in the sink or turned his truck at this or that corner could be so important, while what he himself was doing had become so dull he could hardly stand to be in the same room with himself.

Friday, to break the spell, he'd actually taken a step he'd fantasized about in his car: he'd walked into the Movie Barn and stood face to face with Carl, daring his voices to take him over and spill the secret. Then Ellie Dean had swept in, furious about Ned, she claimed, but that was just an excuse to start in about the accident as though it was something that had happened to *her*. "I could tell *you* something about the accident," Adam had screamed. "What would you think if you knew this boy who killed his mother was my son, that when he killed his mother my own son was killing the only life I ever had? Was what she and I did so bad we had to be punished like that? Did you ever hear of the sins of the fathers being passed down to their children and then their grandchildren? You're standing there with your hands on your hips like a bad joke blaming Carl and he doesn't even know that he's cursed, or why he's cursed, or that his whole life and his children's lives and who knows how many generations will be lived out under the shadow of this curse he can never be told about...." But as always the scream had been silent, just something that boiled through Adam's bones until it drove him back into the street.

Sunday night he decided to return. It was well after midnight. The rain had started with a loud crack of thunder that split the sky like a celestial earthquake. Pellets of hail came pounding down, then a harsh downpour that overflowed the eavestroughs and covered his windows in thick sheets of rain that suddenly thinned, then disappeared, leaving him so agitated that he threw on his jaket and started searching for his mother's umbrella, a heavy red monster forgotten in a cupboard for years.

By the time he got outside the noise of the rain on his umbrella was only an intermittent tapping, even though his feet got soaked in the puddles. His plan was the only one left to him: like a retired general with a phantom army planning a war that would never happen, he would map out this final campaign in front of the empty store in order to better imagine exactly what he would say to Carl if ever he summoned the courage to say anything at all.

The lights were off, Main Street washed clean and silent. As his shoes crunched into the gravel of the parking lot, Adam felt a wave of confidence that everything would work out — the same feeling he'd had after asking Maureen if he could escort her home. He remembered he had come down the stairs from the dark bedroom where he had been with Elizabeth and Maureen had been standing beneath the chandelier waiting for him, her eyes turning to him as he nervously checked and straightened his clothes in the contrasting brightness. With the taste of Elizabeth still in his mouth he inquired if she was ready to leave. In return Maureen had offered her usual anxious smile, tinged with what might have been meant as encouragement. Outside, she hooked her hand into his arm and as soon as they were out of sight of the house, Adam, still dizzy with Elizabeth, dropped to one knee in the snow, closed his eyes to avoid seeing her face, and proposed. "I'll think about it," Maureen had replied. And he'd been so confused he'd left her there, halfway home, retreating to his own house and into his pyjamas, Elizabeth still caked to his skin, and drunk himself to sleep.

As always, the Movie Barn's windows had posters of the latest video releases. Avoiding the puddles Adam stepped closer to read them, and that was when he became aware of someone breathing — a tiny shallow breath that was hardly a breath at all — and his first thought was that the whispery sound must be running water. Then he caught the glow of a cigarette in the dark and came closer. A rain-drenched Carl was sitting in the gravel propped against the steps with his eyes raised to the sky and, as he told Adam later, "smoking my last cigarette."

As Adam realized Carl was hurt his throat filled with a thick choking pain. He knelt beside him and following Carl's mumbled instructions, checked his ribs, his head, his neck. He took Carl's keys and opened the store, called an ambulance, then Luke. "Now I'm going to help you up," he said to Carl. "I'm not going to let them find you like this." He bent over the boy, hooked his arms under Carl's while Carl looped an arm around his neck. For a moment Adam strained and it seemed that he would drop him. But then his back straightened and he walked Carl up the steps into the store, eased him into the chair beside the counter. Fifteen minutes later the Movie Barn was swarming.

Early the next morning, by the time Moira came into the main kitchen, McKelvey was sitting at the table, doing one of his ever-present crossword puzzles and laughing about something with Kate Rawlins, the cook.

"Look at him turn red," Kate said to Moira. "I was just reminding him he had the wife everyone else wanted to dance with."

"Never would," McKelvey said. "Except for old Adam. Old Adam was what she called him, like some kind of whisky. Guess that's what he is, some kind of whisky that stayed in the bottle."

"Adam Goldsmith?" Moira asked. "The man from the dealership?"

"Also the chairman of our very own board of directors," Kate said. "That's why he's always dropping by. He's always been old Adam, though I never thought of the whisky angle. I think they said old Adam because he would never actually do anything with Maureen Knight, the doctor's daughter. That was the one he was engaged to — she was the French teacher at the elementary and everyone always joked she was waiting for old Adam to get off the mark. My father used to say they were engaged so long they should have had an anniversary. There was a rumour once that they had run off and got married. It was an Easter holiday when I was still at the elementary, and after the holiday everyone was making jokes about it but it turned out they weren't even living in the same house. I heard she left town a few years ago."

They started talking about something else but Moira was thrown into thinking of Carl and the time he'd taken her to the cemetery. Ever since, watching Carl with his father, with Lizzie, she had been sure she could see his mother's absence in every gesture, every shadow. But she'd never before considered who that mother might have been, the family they must have made. And Adam Goldsmith dancing! That must have been something. She was trying to imagine exactly how Adam would dance when he came through the door.

"Look like you've been up all night," McKelvey said.

Adam was pale and unshaven, his eyes rimmed with red. While he told McKelvey what had happened to Carl, McKelvey just sat there, not looking up, pushing his pencil into the newspaper until the lead snapped.

"Fucking idiot," McKelvey finally said.

Kate handed Adam a cup of coffee.

"He didn't start it," Adam said. "Someone hit him from behind."

"Anyone hits him any other way they're dead."

"It's nothing to be proud of," Adam said.

"Boys," Kate said. She leaned into McKelvey. She wasn't as tall as him but she was wider, and as she squeezed McKelvey's shoulders his face loosened a little.

"I'm not going down there to see him," McKelvey said. "Unless he asks me I'm not going. Anyway, my car's in the lake."

Even Adam laughed. Moira waited for Kate or Adam to volunteer to drive McKelvey but neither of them spoke.

"I could take you down there," Moira said.

"He that sick?"

"Be out tomorrow," Adam said.

McKelvey looked questioningly at Moira. "Maybe you'll be driving by. You could take him something for me. Chocolates or flowers or something."

By the time she got to the hospital he'd already been released. Later Carl would tell her Ray Johnson had driven him home. She wouldn't have gone at all except that she had found out the real reason McKelvey didn't want to go: one that Carl hardly ever visited, he said there was one time he'd got drunk that he shouldn't have. Moira had realized he blamed himself for his wife's death, blamed himself for having made Carl the instrument of the tragedy. Too bad she couldn't give them therapy. Too bad she wasn't really a psychologist-in-training as her job application claimed. Too bad she was just the twenty-three-year-old daughter of a rich lawyer who'd found a few plastic baggies in her dresser drawer and threatened to report her if she didn't get away from her friends and do something useful for a year, like going to Africa or working at that old folks' home in the town where they spent their summers.

When she got to Carl's place she brought in the chocolates she'd bought at the hospital gift shop before discovering he wasn't there. To make things easier, she kept her sunglasses on and held the chocolates in front of her like a shield as she knocked on the kitchen door. He called out to come in; she found him on the sofa, sitting with his bandaged head resting on a towel to protect the upholstery. He hadn't shaved. One cheek was bruised and rising to a shiner and he seemed to be holding the ribs Adam had said were cracked. In front of the sofa on the coffee table was a hospital pamphlet about concussions along with a couple of bottles of pills. She set down the chocolates. "From your dad," she said, thankful for her sunglasses. "He sent me to deliver them." She immediately thought she should have at least asked how he was feeling.

"And so here you are," Carl said. "Angel of death or angel of mercy?"

"No angel at all." She crossed the room and sat down in the same chair as the last time. "You want me to get you some coffee or something? Some water for your pills?" She reached to take off her sunglasses, then kept them on.

"I shouldn't have said what I did that time," Carl said. "Not that way. I didn't mean to be nasty. But as you can see, I'm not my own man."

Moira looked down at her purse and took out her cigarettes, held out the pack.

"Quit," Carl said. "Decided to get clubbed to death instead."

"How was it?"

"You're supposed to feel sorry for me."

"I tried that."

"And how was it?"

Carl was leaning back on the sofa, his feet up on the coffee table. He looked pitiful or arrogant, depending on your slant. And, thought Moira, he was either someone she could like very much or someone she could easily learn to hate. "You tell me," Moira said. "How was it for you?"

She could see Carl's lips opening and she had the feeling that what he said would cut deep and she would be sorry she had left herself open.

"It was perfect. It was great. It was so good I was going to ask you to a drive-in with me and Lizzie. I was afraid you'd say no."

She wondered how her face seemed to Carl: two green discs, a nose, a mouth. She wasn't sure if she was liking him or hating him, if he was playing with her or trying to apologize. And if he was apologizing, was he saying they should just be pals or was he saying he wanted to pick up with her again? And if that's what he wanted, what did she want?

"How was it for you?" Carl asked.

"You're supposed to be taking fluids. How about some tea?"

"You have time?"

"They gave me a few hours. I was sent to visit you in hospital so I can tell them you're still alive. Your father really cares about you, you know."

"Thanks."

"Look." Moira was suddenly so sure of herself she took off her sunglasses. "I'm just a college kid who got busted by her own father. But I can tell you for certain that you have no idea about anything. If it makes you feel any better."

"Yeah. I guess it does. Okay, I'll have some tea. Please. And after, if you really do have time, I'm supposed to see Lizzie today but I don't think I can drive. If you could pick her up for me. She knows you so it won't be too weird. And I'll explain what happened on the phone so she doesn't freak out when she gets here."

"No problem," Moira said. "I'll make the tea first." She went into the kitchen to put on the kettle. It was odd the way you got into things with people. Like the time she had gone to visit her friend Lucy in New York and they dropped into a Spanish bar that Lucy said was cool. It was a tiny little tavern down in a basement with a black-moustached red-nosed waiter who sweated wine and brandy, turned the music loud enough that Moira could hear the paper speaker cones trying to tear themselves free, and she and Lucy had ended up dancing around the bar stools with two men in top hats and capes, one with a silver-tipped cane. "I'm sure that's Truman Capote," Lucy had whispered into Moira's ear, and the next day Moira had gone out for lunch in another dim bar with this man who might be Truman Capote, of course she was too cool to ask, and the man who might have been Truman Capote leaned forward and told her wicked gossip about everyone else in the restaurant and by three o'clock in the afternoon she'd had so much brandy her bones were like hollow varnished antlers nailed to the middle of outer space. On the way to the bathroom she had to catch the wall to keep from falling. Didn't dare look in the mirror. Fell out of her chair when she was trying to fall back in. Found herself lying on her back on the cigarette-pebbled floor of a dark hallway and looking up at a ceiling that was the colour of a dark tobacco sea when the man with the silver-tipped cane who might have been Truman Capote reached down and undid her top button.

When she'd got herself back in her chair he leaned forward and asked if she and her girlfriend would like to come to his hotel room and let him tie them to the bedposts. "I don't think so," Moira had said. Afterwards Lucy had told her she wasn't any fun and she should have pretended to go along, so they could have at least found out who he really was. "A pervert," Moira said.

"Spoilsport," Lucy objected. "That was just his way of coming on. What was he supposed to say? 'Honey, without you my life will end'?"

THREE

ARNIE OPENED THE DOOR. THE RAIN had stopped but the roofs and trees were still dripping, his front walk and the road spotted with puddles. All day people would be talking about how the rain had finally come, hard and strong. They would complain it hadn't lasted long enough to soak through the caked ground, or that it had soaked through too much, drowning the roots of their tomatoes and that special bush they'd bought at the Kingston nursery. At least he'd never sold crop insurance. You had to be the government to afford that.

"Kerry Bates," the policeman said, showing his badge. He was hatless but in uniform, his cheeks and forehead burned pink, his light brown hair cut close and neatly parted at the side. A bit overweight, was Arnie's first thought; better watch those fatty foods. "I was told you were at the Movie Barn last night. May I?"

Arnie motioned him in. "Was there some kind of fire?" Years ago, before his wife, Evelyn, had died, he'd covered the insurance for the supermarket but then it had gone to a big

Kingston broker who offered a better discount. Which is fine if you're trying to get new business but if your customers live next door to each other, they all have to be treated the same.

"Not a fire. An attempted robbery. The fellow who works there was assaulted as he left the store."

They had been standing in the hall but now Arnie started towards the kitchen. "Carl McKelvey. Was he hurt?"

"Saw him at the hospital just an hour ago. He seems okay. They say he has some kind of concussion."

"Concussion..." Arnie sat down at the table. There was that hockey player he'd been reading about in the paper. *Coma* was the word they started using after he wouldn't come round.

"He's in no danger. Concussion and broken ribs. He said you were one of the last customers."

"Who did it?"

"That's why I'm here. Seems they came at him from behind."

Talking to the policeman, Arnie thought how strange it was that on a Sunday evening the place would be so empty. The Movie Barn not only had a door opening outside, but also one into the supermarket — that was for fire regulations — making it possible for a gang, if there was one, to have been hiding in there at the time.

He told the policeman, to whom he was sympathetic because of his own profession, that he was an insurance adjuster and had therefore driven all around the township and been in and out of a lot of homes, including where Carl grew up. Had known him since he was born, along with his parents. He'd been the one to assess the accident — terrible thing — another of those late-night tragedies. If you were in his business, to tell the truth, you'd be afraid to give your son the keys to your car until he was fifty years old and had sworn off drinking. Elizabeth McKelvey was another story. He had been on the library committee with her for two years. She spoke like a man, which was probably normal for a teacher, and there was something wild about her that made you think one night she was just going to give out a big loud whoop, let down her hair and start dancing on the table. Though she never did.

On the kitchen table, between him and Kerry Bates, who was asking the questions and writing down his answers in a lined spiral notepad, there was a Bible. Not that he was born again, the way some people claimed to be, just that the Bible had turned out to be his favourite book so he had copies here and there in the house. That way they'd be easy to pick up wherever he was sitting instead of him having to search one out from wherever he'd left it. He would often open it at random, the way he used to with whatever magazines were lying around. "I've never seen someone like you for always having to be reading," Evelyn had once said. But even she would have been surprised to find him with all these Bibles.

In his opinion, but he didn't bother explaining this to Kerry Bates because he suspected that just catching sight of the Bible was enough to make him devalue anything he said, you didn't have to be born again. He'd been born once and that was enough. But lately things were just seeping into him. It was like walking up a big wide set of steps in the sunlight. He knew he was climbing, he was going somewhere, but he wasn't sure what he'd find at the top of the steps. Maybe a fancy paradisal cathedral or maybe, after all that effort, he would reach the top only to fall off the other side.

His fall might be triggered by something as ordinary as a pill, a needle in the arm. The pill would come first thing in the morning, just to calm him down. "A happy pill," his daughter called it. Arnie had insisted they name her Marilyn, as close as possible to Evelyn's name, and in the end Evelyn hadn't minded. After the happy pill would come the needle to put him out. Then the mask over his face and all the fancy equipment. A triple bypass was what they had planned for him. If he could watch himself go out in a moment of glory, hooked up to all those contraptions, he might have been more tempted. But to be put to sleep like a dog: a happy pill, a needle in the arm, one last breath and suddenly they've blown out your brain, a dead candle when the party's over.

That night at the Movie Barn, the first thing Alvin had noticed was that one of the fluorescent lights was flickering. Carl was sitting on a stool behind the counter and watching the monitor. Sharon, the girl who'd worked there before Carl, had been nice but with Carl it was different. He smiled and was polite but it was a guarded kind of thing. When you took your movie to the desk and Sharon was there, she sometimes kept looking at her own video while she talked to you, chatting away as though you were her best friend. Carl always switched his off as if he didn't want you to know what he was watching because that might give you a way into him. And then there was that tattoo on his left forearm, a butterfly whose red wings fluttered every time his muscles moved.

But last night Carl hadn't been watching anything. He'd been looking at the restaurant franchise ads.

"I thought he must be planning to buy into one," Arnie said, "but no, he claimed he can't cook. Like most men, I suppose. Though since Evelyn died you'd be surprised. The other night I made myself spaghetti with vegetables. Used to eat steak every night." The policeman had his pen politely suspended above the page.

Because of the light it had taken him longer than usual to select his movie. Hard to concentrate. A couple of times he had found himself shaking his head, as though the faulty electrics were in his eyes. So he just told himself to choose something, anything. Then Carl had offered him a cup of coffee and he'd kept Carl company until almost eleven. After he paid for his movies, Carl said, "Hope you enjoy them," in that way he always did, a grain of something in his voice as though in fact you might get home, put a cassette in the TV, and suddenly find your grandchildren watching a naked sex party. But of course he didn't say that to the policeman. Just told him that outside he'd looked up at the sky because there'd been rumblings of thunder all evening but it was a nice night and aside from a couple of cottagers who'd also been in the store, he hadn't seen anyone.

"Then I came back home and I was cleaning up the kitchen when I saw, under a newspaper right on this table, an overdue video from last week. *Sleepless in Seattle*. It reminded me of my daughter, I don't know why, she's never even been to the States. I didn't want to owe another day's fine so I drove back to the store and when I went inside Carl was talking to Fred Verghoers."

"You remember the time?" the policeman asked. He printed Fred's name on the pad.

"Kerry Bates," Arnie said. "Now I remember you. From the Hornets. Used to play goal. I didn't recognize you at first."

"It's the mask," Bates said. "You were telling me, Fred and Carl were talking."

"Shaking hands," Arnie said. "Fred was giving him the welcome back to town — probably trying to round up his vote."

"Well," Bates said, "he's got mine. Not that I minded Vernon Boyce but with everything that's changed here, someone like Fred might have something to contribute. Anyway, I'll go over and talk to him. Thanks for your time."

Arnie stood at his living-room bay window, watching Kerry Bates as he got into his cruiser and slowly drove away. Bates's father — Lawrence was his name — he was in a Kingston old-age home. Winnifred had been his wife, Winny Bates, the one with diabetes. She'd even been in Evelyn's bridge group for a while. He had done their house and car insurance; once they'd had to replace the chimney for their wood stove to satisfy new company regulations. He didn't do Kerry's but that was no reason to forget he existed.

Reflecting on his memory, or lack of it, Arnie got so gloomy he decided to cheer himself up by driving to the property to see if the rain had done anything. When he'd bought it, the place was so far out of town the value looked like it could never climb — which was how he and Evelyn had been able to afford it after all the money they'd sunk into the house. Now West Gull was creeping closer and the nearby road had become a small highway. But the entrance was still unmarked and he slowed down carefully before easing off the road onto a dirt track that led through a small meadow to a parking place, just the right distance from the house he'd never built. After he switched off the motor he sat for a moment looking at his hands on the steering wheel. He was breathing hard, as though he had just stopped running. Or maybe it was only that lately he was always listening to himself breathe, checking his pulse. "You're alive," he reassured himself. In fact these days he felt more alive than ever. Some outer skin that used to keep everything at a comfortable distance had peeled off; time had slowed down and was rubbing his face in it — *it*, everything from the way clothes itched against his skin to the colour of the air which, suddenly, he could see so clearly he had started to wonder how anyone could ever look at anything else.

He took a package of cigarettes from the glove compartment and stepped outside. It was about fifty more paces to the line of maples that edged the ridge overlooking the lake. A few of the leaves were starting to turn but the green was still dense and massive against the blue sky. In the winter you could see through the bare branches and down to Long Gull Lake. More than a few years ago he had spent twenty thousand dollars buying the field and all the hope its purchase implied: a retirement home at the edge of town with a view of the lake on one side and on the other of the town nestled in the small valley.

In those days West Gull had been what the real-estate brochures called picturesque: stone buildings more than a century old, a few tree-lined streets that ended at the lake, two churches, a tavern made of big pine logs from the time when a white pine only seventy feet high wasn't yet worth cutting.

Once he had imagined the dirt track where he was now parked would in his lifetime be transformed into the start of a circular drive leading to a white frame house. That was before a certain series of events. Events that had led — or perhaps they had been only a coincidence — to Evelyn's death. So instead of having a fine retirement home he still had a field with a view.

Meanwhile West Gull, the picturesque farming village bent around Long Gull Lake's curve, had stretched into a tourist centre, a little kernel of past surrounded by a shell of convenience stores, strip plazas, used-car lots and the expanded lumber yard. Now Arnie's field was only a few minutes' walk from a strip mall with a small supermarket, an all-night doughnut shop and a dry-cleaning outlet. Arnie looked down at his hand again, the package of cigarettes; he took one out and lit it. The matches were from Chez Piggy's, one of those trendy whole-grain health-food restaurants Marilyn always chose for their lunches. *Chez Piggy*. It looked like a barn. And despite the whole-grain menu the men at the bar looked ready to fall on their faces. Of course he hadn't smoked during lunch. A man going into hospital for a triple bypass doesn't smoke in front of his daughter, especially if she works at the hospital. Nor did she know he'd been sneaking cigarettes for eleven years, ever since they first tried to talk him into the operation. No way he would have had that operation then. In those old picturesque days, he had imagined the hospital as a medieval torture chamber and the doctors as dim-witted incompetents who opened people up just to find out what they had inside. But you had to hand it to them now. Miracles were routine. Also back then, with Evelyn just a year dead, he didn't know if he wanted to survive. But the children had still been his responsibility, not like now when the balance was shifted and he found himself pretending his life for their benefit, offering them the lies they seemed to require just the way they must have pretended to him and he had pretended to his own parents.

He walked from the car towards the line of maples. When Evelyn was still alive and they still believed in the future, he used to sketch out plans on graph paper. In the plans there was always a carefully drawn outdoor stone fireplace near the maples. That would be for summer barbecues with the grandchildren. Up on the ridge above the lake they'd have the view and the breeze off the water. And there he'd perch like an old fart telling them stories while the coals turned white.

One of the maples arched over a big slab of rock. That was where he liked to sit when he came to smoke a couple of illegal cigarettes and worry his way through whatever problem was currently tying his gut in a knot. But now, as he stepped towards the rock, he saw others had been there first. There was a small circle of stones around the remains of a fire. Off to the side was a cardboard beer container sodden from the rain. The bottles it should have held were smashed to pieces at the edge of the rock.

At first he had no reaction at all. "It was like if I kept looking it would just go away," he told Marilyn later. Then before he could move, anger began spreading through him. His heart tripped. "I wouldn't give them the satisfaction," he said aloud, as though they might be hiding in the bushes and waiting for him to drop dead.

He turned and starting walking back towards the car. He was standing beside it, unsure where to go or what to do when Luke Richardson's black Cadillac pulled off the highway and onto the shoulder. It was the middle of the day and Luke had taken off his suit jacket. His tie was loosened and his pants were creased from driving in the heat.

"Terrible thing that happened to Carl last night," Luke said.

"Police were over this morning."

"And?"

"Nothing much. Thought I'd come over here and look around."

"Surveying the property?" Luke asked.

Arnie's throat was filled with bile and he felt his stomach was about to turn. Luke stepped closer, took his arm, peered into his face. "Something wrong?"

"Ah, those bastards, they left broken beer bottles on my rock." As soon as he said these words he regretted them. What did his crazy selfish dream matter compared to Carl getting his head bashed in.

"What rock?"

Arnie was amazed to hear this. What rock? Didn't Luke Richardson, the real-estate millionaire who owned a condominium in Florida, for God's sake, know every square inch for fifty miles around? Hadn't he offered to buy this place a dozen times? "Name your price," he would say, as though challenging Arnie to recognize that in the modern world, the world of strip plazas and convenience stores, the world he had effortlessly turned to profit and an endless stream of new black Cadillacs, there was nothing that couldn't be given a number.

"We could get some lunch," Luke now said. "Why don't you come to the hotel with me for a bite?"

Arnie looked up. There was a look of concern on Luke's face that made him worried about himself. "I don't know."

"Come on. They have a new chef there. Someone they got from Ottawa for the tourists. He wears a little hat and comes out in his apron to ask how you liked the food."

"Well—"

"We'll go in my car. I have to drive back this way afterwards, anyway."

And before he knew it Arnie was in the passenger seat of Luke Richardson's air-conditioned Cadillac, looking at Luke's big hands folded comfortably over the wheel. It was years since he had been in the passenger seat of a car, not since he tore the ligaments in his ankle stepping out of a rowboat and Evelyn had to drive him around for three weeks. Somehow Luke Richardson in his big hearselike Caddy seemed to have mastered time; sure, he was overweight and thinning and the backs of his hands were dotted with liver spots but as he steered through town, it was as though it was *his* town, as though he had welcomed the changes that had happened over time, had grown and prospered with them, swallowed them up like food for body and soul.

At lunch, watching Luke eat, Arnie found himself admiring how the big hands handled the knife and fork, the unselfconscious way he cleaned his plate, leaned back, patted his stomach like a favourite old dog assured of being coddled through the afternoon. When he told Luke about the bypass, Luke looked at him hard and long. Arnie felt that if he wanted he could have cried, complained, said he was afraid of dying. He didn't want this but knowing he could made him feel he had somehow gone into debt to Luke. Even when Luke told him, after they'd talked about Carl, how he was taking blood-pressure pills and had had his gall bladder out last year, it didn't make things even.

FOUR

ADAM HAD DRIVEN BEHIND THE AMBU-
lance to the hospital and two days later
he went to visit Carl at home. The impossible had become the
normal. Adam had telephoned Carl first and following instructions, he let himself in.

The door was next to the kitchen counter. There was a
case of empty beer bottles. And on the table a mug half-filled
with black coffee sat beside a foolscap pad with a list of necessary groceries and hardware.

Adam wished he'd thought of bringing something, flowers or a treat from the bakery.

"Up here," Carl called.

Adam mounted the stairs, guiltily aware of the rolls of
dust in the corners, the house's musty smell. Wearing Lizzie's
Ice River souvenir T-shirt, Carl was sitting on his bed, which
was only a mattress on top of a braided carpet on the floor,
his back propped up by pillows. At the hospital his skull had
been swathed in bandages; now there was just a wide strip of

adhesive across the back. His face was patched with bruises and scrapes stained with yellow disinfectant.

"Thanks for coming. And thanks for finding me the other night."

Adam, shocked by Carl's face, just shook his head.

"You going to throw up? The bathroom's down the hall."

Beside the bed Carl had his cigarettes, along with an ashtray, two half-empty coffee cups, and a folded down paperback novel.

"Sorry," Adam said. "How are the ribs? And your head, have you been dizzy?"

"I'm okay. Maybe I had it coming but I'm just a little pissed."

"You could always change your mind. Tell the police who did it."

"And go to court? Carl McKelvey's word against Fred Verghoers'? I don't think so, Adam. It's my problem and I'll fix it."

Carl's voice sounded strong and now that Adam was getting used to it, his face wasn't so bad.

"The doctor told me you were very lucky. Said you must have a very hard skull."

"Always have."

"Don't worry about your job or the rent. Whenever you're ready to go back to work is fine with Luke."

"I'll be back this week. I'd rather be there, doing something, than just sitting around."

Adam saw Carl had shaved off his moustache. There was a scar on his upper lip from the fight he'd had with Fred after Chrissy had kicked him out and Carl had come back to find Fred living there. Adam remembered that in the judge's chambers that scar had been a bright red gash and then, looking at

Fred's big hands, Adam had seen the fat ring that had made it. *It's my problem. I'll fix it.* Not if I can stop you, Adam thought.

"Not an easy way to come home," Adam now said.

Carl looked directly at him. He had hooded eyes. Maybe that was one of the things the girls liked about him, Adam thought. He remembered that, too, thinking bitterly how obscene it was that this drunken young id with hooded eyes and half the girls in the township crazy about him had strutted and danced on his skinny little legs, poured the booze back into his flat little belly, then drove his mother into the oak tree just down from the Fennerty place.

"Not easy. I was almost ready to give up but now I'm going to stay."

Carl's eyes stayed on Adam, and Adam couldn't help thinking that Carl looked as though he himself had been slammed headfirst into a tree. Though he had survived. Maybe, after everything, fate had published its judgement on that night in the Richardson back bedroom: Elizabeth would be killed, Adam would grow old alone, Carl would be released after a ten-year sentence and a crack on the skull to create his own destiny.

When Chrissy got pregnant Carl had come to Adam's office to tell him, like a child reporting what might be a disaster to a trusted uncle. He explained that their plan was to get married and move into the farmhouse where Carl was watching William McKelvey try to drink himself to death. The prospect of Carl and Chrissy reliving what Elizabeth had gone through was too much; Adam invited them out to dinner and told them that there was a provision in Elizabeth's will which would allow Carl to receive his full inheritance when he got married, if that was before he turned twenty-five. The two of them, lost little waifs, Adam thought, sat bewildered while Adam suggested there might be enough for a small house in Kingston. In fact, most of the money would have been Adam's, but nothing could have suited him better than this chance to give Elizabeth's eventual grandchild a passport out of West Gull.

Over the following weeks Adam had spent hours on the telephone and inspecting possible houses. In each of them he imagined Carl and Chrissy safely ensconced, taking turns learning useful skills while their child went to a series of private nursery schools, kindergartens, etc., which would culminate in a brilliant academic career. Instead Chrissy's uncle died and she inherited the old farmhouse on the Second Line Road.

"You know," Carl said, "Lizzie aside — and all the bullshit — it's great to be back. This place ... I don't think I could live anywhere else without feeling I'd left the best part of myself behind. I know, I sound like a bad song. Millions of people leave home."

"Not everyone," Adam said. "I ended up coming back." The bedroom's one chair was piled with clothes and Adam was still standing in the doorway. The important thing was to remain composed and remember who he was — Adam Goldsmith, West Gull businessman, face like a slab of rock. "I was working in Kingston but then my mother died and Luke Richardson offered me a job. I thought it was just for a while. Until I got my balance. Then I was going to sell the house and go back to university."

"Balance," Carl said. In the changed angle of the light the colours of his face took on depth and Adam could see the bruises flowering through the pale flesh. "What stopped you?"

Adam got a sudden image of himself sitting on a hunk of firewood in his basement, listening to Elizabeth tell her story.

It had always been so easy to make Elizabeth his explanation. "I guess it turned out I'm the staying kind."

Carl laughed, that short laugh that could sound so much like his mother's, and Adam wondered how much more of Elizabeth was hiding in Carl. Carl was silent a moment but Adam could see his jaw working, as though he was struggling to say something or keep something back. Adam had broken into a sweat, a grainy and uncomfortable slick covering his chest and back. Maybe it was because Carl was on the bed and having to look up towards Adam in the doorway but suddenly Carl looked like a child and Adam realized that for a long time, a time so long it might have begun Carl's whole life ago, he'd been afraid of Carl and hated him for it. "You remember the accident?" Carl asked. "That time—" He stopped.

Adam waited. Then: "Of course I remember."

"I just wish it hadn't happened. It and everything that went with it."

"Me too," Adam finally said. After a minute or two of standing in the doorway, all the time so silent inside himself, he turned and made his way down the stairs.

Moira knew Carl needed her. Although she was no psychologist-in-training, at least the R&R had taught her something about taking care of sick people. She came back a second time and that afternoon convinced Carl to let her help him take a bath. It would get rid of the hospital smell so he could officially start getting better — also, as she later wrote to Lucy, after what had happened she wanted to see his body again. She had thought of him as infinitely strong and powerful, but seated precariously in the water, his bruised ribs purple and yellow while his bandaged head wavered above like Humpty Dumpty trying not to fall, Carl looked so pitiful that, ashamed at having exposed him in such a cruel way, she knelt down beside him. He was still in the bath when someone started pounding on the door.

It was a woman who'd come bearing a huge casserole full of vegetable macaroni — you would have thought he was dying or something — and announced herself as "Nancy Brookner, one of Carl's very best customers. And who are you? They send you from the hospital?"

"Moira," Moira said. "I'm from the retirement home."

"I guess you nurses get around," Nancy Brookner said. She proceeded to put the kettle on the stove herself and before it had finished boiling she told Moira that a few weeks ago Carl had gone to a dance and driven away with his ex, Chrissy, while half the township watched.

"Just so you know," Nancy said. "I don't think Carl and Fred are the best of friends."

After Lizzie fell asleep, Carl started to tell Moira about how Adam used speak in tongues. But that was another local legend Moira had already heard at the R&R — from Kate Rawlins, who had called it uttering. Her mother, according to Kate, had actually witnessed the child Adam "down on the floor like a baby goat bleating and mewling and no one knew if he was possessed or just epileptic, but Flora was so proud that everyone pretended to believe God was talking right out of his little mouth. Though why God's mouth would choose to work for Luke Richardson all these years is a question."

"They say he made a fool of himself," Carl said, "rolling around on the floor. No one ever thought too much of him for that."

Poor Adam, Moira thought. So meticulous. So clean. So proper. He must have been ashamed to find himself down among the feet of the West Gull matriarchy. Ashamed to grow up with everyone knowing. She squeezed Carl's hand. She liked the way their arms ran together. No one else's arm had even tried to fit against hers this way. "We rolled around the floor," she said. "Made some pretty weird noises, too. There's probably a lot of others out there doing more or less the same."

That night Moira dreamed she was with Adam Goldsmith in the Garden of Eden. They were dressed in big green plant leaves, hers was too stiff to be comfortable, and they were in a junglelike setting with thick entangling vines that needed constant brushing away. Adam was explaining that he truly loved Maureen and was still hoping she would forgive him. "I thought you might know her," Adam said. "Your name is a bit the same." He told her that Maureen had recently gone missing and he couldn't find her despite the fact that he spent most of his time trying to track her through the jungle. "I thought it was Elizabeth you danced with," Moira said and then Adam turned in the vine-mottled light and gave Moira a peculiar and intense look exactly like Carl's the last time she had said Chrissy's name. At that point in her dream Moira realized Carl and Adam had identical faces. But when she woke up, the dream still vivid, she remembered Adam's face the way it really was: white hair carefully parted, steel-rimmed spectacles perched precariously on his nose, timid transparent eyes — and wondered how such a man could have so many rumours attached to him or be so transformed by her dream.

On the way to the bathroom in the morning, she saw the source of at least one dream element: the hall wallpaper was a tangled mass of vines and leaves. But the dream stayed with her and standing in the shower she found herself wondering what really had happened between Adam Goldsmith and Maureen

Knight. Would he have told her he loved her? Cried after she left? There was something so *reposed* about his face that made it impossible to imagine Adam in pain, Adam in despair, Adam on fire. But of course he must have been, once, like everyone else. Like Carl whose every cell twitched and quivered with every second of pain and passion he'd ever known.

That was what she should have said to Lucy: that Carl's attractiveness to her was that he was so vulnerable and maybe that meant she was some kind of tourist, a high-nose upstate girl who had come to Canada and was inscribing herself on Carl like a sightseer leaving footprints on a freshly poured piece of sidewalk. But no, that wasn't it; you don't roll around on the floor making weird noises with a piece of sidewalk. And you don't expect the sidewalk to tell you when it's time to move on.

She woke up in Carl's bed. At first she had to remind herself it was her day off and that Carl had told her he was going in to work the short shift at the Movie Barn. Just to get started back. As she dressed, Moira could hear Lizzie padding back and forth in the hall. Moira wondered what Lizzie would think of suddenly being taken care of by the person who was supposed to be taking care of her grandfather. Now Lizzie stood frowning in the doorway. Moira felt herself being inspected in light of her new location. Lizzie hesitated, then took a step inside. Moira stayed sitting on the bed. She was holding one of her sandals and as she waited for Lizzie to speak she fiddled with the straps. That was something else she could have mentioned to Lucy — that one of the reasons Carl had come back to sink into the past was his desire to be Lizzie's father. Unlike her own, who had leaked in and out of her life until all that was left was the stain.

Lizzie came closer. She still had a child's face, oval with dark eyes and long wavy hair, but you could see the bones were going to be strong and there'd be a time, after puberty, when she'd look almost mannish. Not the soft snub-nosed blonde look Moira had at that age. Lizzie would be harder for boys to imagine as a date. Less fresh sidewalk, more herself.

Lizzie sat beside her on the bed. At the R&R they sometimes played cards while talking to McKelvey. Now Moira, suddenly embarrassed to be seen in this new way, reached out for Lizzie's hands. Lizzie didn't resist, didn't speak.

"You hungry?"

"I guess."

"We could have pancakes."

"Pancakes," Lizzie said, sounding disappointed.

Moira turned Lizzie's hands over, took the right one and traced the lifeline with her fingernail. Lizzie giggled and tensed. "I used to read palms," Moira said. "Did anyone ever tell you you're going to live to be a hundred and eighty-four years old? And look at this line. It means you're smart but that what you think and what you want aren't always the same. This mark here is very rare. I bet you have dreams. I wouldn't be surprised if you dreamed Carl was coming to see you. Am I right?" Lizzie's hand had loosened and her face relaxed. "It says here you're going to take a lot of trips. You'd better get a suitcase for your next birthday. And this means you know how to tell people what you really feel."

She was holding Lizzie's hand and talking and everything else had dropped away except the satiny feel of Lizzie's skin and the beat of her pulse in her wrist, and as she kept going and felt Lizzie growing into her, she was thinking how strange it was women could come together this way, even if only for a second or a minute.

"I guess I would take some pancakes," Lizzie said warily, sounding so like her father accepting tea that Moira laughed. "I'll break the eggs," Lizzie ventured, "you do the dishes."

When Carl returned he set out to drive Lizzie home. Moira had meant to leave at the same time but, still cleaning up after pancakes and — she had to admit to herself — curious to be there alone, she was standing at the kitchen window and humming a tune that had been doodling in her throat all morning when Luke Richardson's Cadillac pulled into the driveway and parked beside her battered Tercel. He didn't get out right away. Instead he sat and honked his horn as if Moira had the choice of pretending he wasn't there.

Luke Richardson at the kitchen table. There was something about his head, about the way his black hair that came to a sharp triangle in front was combed straight back, making his eyes look wider apart, something about the way his whole head was balanced on his long neck and shoulders, swaying above his coffee cup, weaving and leaning in towards her, that made her think of a big old adder snake getting ready to strike. Even as he was saying how glad he was that she was "giving Carl a hand" and how everyone told him she was brightening the R&R, Moira was waiting for a chance to say she was on her way into town.

"I have to check the furnace," Luke Richardson suddenly announced. Reluctant to leave him in the house, she trailed him down the old rough-sawn stairs into the cobwebby basement with its dirt floor and beams that were axe-squared timbers set into little puddles of cement. "A lot of people leave their thermostats on all year," Luke said, as though she'd asked him for a course in furnace repair. "Then late August or early September, one night the temperature drops and the dang

thing switches on before you've had time to check it out."
While Luke Richardson sniffed around she stayed at the base
of the stairs. Back in the kitchen he sat down again and said he
was the kind of person people were either for or against, and
he wasn't talking about the fact that he wanted to follow
Vernon Boyce as reeve, Fred was welcome to it, he meant "the
real Luke Richardson everyone knows." He looked at her
across the table, talking slowly as though she were a moron,
and explained that he'd taken a chance on Carl, done something for him because he'd hunted with his old man and knew
how hard Carl had been hit by the accident. "Takes a lot of
drink to break up a marriage," Luke said, a sanctimonious
tone in his voice. Then: "Look, Moira, I've known you for a
long time and I've known your dad longer. If you ask me,
you're old enough to know you're not Carl's kind of girl. You
slumming or what?"

Moira stood up. "I have to go to work. If you'll excuse me."

Richardson played with his coffee cup. "Don't take me
wrong. I just think Carl's got a few problems. Look, Moira,
everyone knows that he almost drank himself to death after
that accident with his mother. And it wasn't his first accident.
Or the first time he almost drank someone into the grave. Did
you know that?"

"Thanks for the warning, Mr. Richardson."

"I just don't want Carl getting mixed up in things. He can
live here, work at the store. Stay as long as he likes, leave whenever he wants. A few more months, if Carl can straighten out,
I want to get him involved in the business. Half the farmland
in this township is for sale. I could use someone like Carl who
knows his away around when he's outside. You know what I
mean?"

"Maybe," Moira said. "And maybe he doesn't want to be used."

"My family and his go back," Richardson said. "Way back. Carl's ancestors came over with the Hudson's Bay Company. The old fur traders who crossed the country in canoes. My grandfather used to go hunting with Carl's grandfather. Used to say he must have got some Indian blood in him. Those traders often had second wives, out in the west, then they'd bring home their children and try to mix them in. People don't talk that way these days, but they did. Carl's grandfather used to be able to find his way around anywhere. And my uncle, you know he was made a senator, and Carl's grandfather would take him and his government friends fishing up north, back when there were lakes no one had ever seen. They would fly bush planes in. That was just after the war. I've got pictures of them at the house. I'll show them to you one day. And then my father used to get Carl's father to do guiding for the Kingston Kiwanis, up north. You wouldn't believe it to look at him now but old William, once he got on the trail of something, he was like a hound. I always said those McKelveys weren't meant for farming; they're hunter throwbacks to the days of cavemen and hairy elephants. So that's a long time I've been worrying about Carl and his family. Think about it. Maybe you won't look at me that way the next time I come around."

His big fingers unwrapped themselves from the empty coffee cup, like a team of pythons unwinding from the neck of their prey.

"I don't have to explain the rules of the game to you," he said. "With Carl, you're coming from the same place I am." He got up and Moira thought she had never liked big men who stood too close. They were making some kind of statement about being a man, being big, like their shadow was enough to swallow you up.

"Don't take this the wrong way. You and I both know what Carl did was wrong. He just got what was coming to him. But I'm going to close my eyes this one last time because I know what Carl's been through. With his mother and his father and Chrissy and Lizzie. You know, I admire Carl. That stunt with Ned — well, maybe the boy got what he deserved. Though I wish I didn't have to say so. Peck his eyes out. The man's got a sense of humour. He should be *making* movies, not renting them. But you know, a loose cannon like Carl, someone's got to keep an eye on him, make sure where he points himself."

In a movement so fast she didn't even see him start, he was on his feet and his hands were on her shoulders. It was as though he'd somehow hypnotized her with his rich voice and those eyes that bored in on you, moving around as his head bobbed and roved in that snaky way. He was touching her, his jaw had dropped either to speak, or worse, in some sort of prelude to a kiss, his face close enough that she could smell his aftershave. Then he was out the door, waving from the yard as though he was just the big friendly shambling uncle he played when her father was around.

He knows I won't tell Carl, was all Moira could think, and then she started wondering how long she'd been standing rigid in the same place Richardson had left her, her shoulders locked into position, paralysed by his poisonous concoction of fear and hate. Then she added doubt; because as his car swung out of the drive, his big hand flapping in a last avuncular wave, she had to admit to herself that she didn't really understand why Carl had mixed in so thick with Luke Richardson. Maybe that was just the way the men around here acted, needing to rub up against each other to remind themselves they were still alive, still men. Recreational violence, Kate Rawlins called it. Barnyard blow-offs. Better than just going out and having sex, she had said, and Moira hadn't dared ask why.

Early evening and Ned Richardson is pulling into the Verghoers driveway on the Second Line Road. It is Labour Day Saturday. At the West Gull Boyce Memorial Park the annual softball tournament is well underway. Ned looks at the house, pats the red tape on the seat beside him — a habit he's started lately to remind himself to think before he acts — then takes a plastic grocery bag from his glove compartment before getting out to stand on the grass.

It's a perfect evening for a visit but Ned already knows Fred and Chrissy aren't home. They're over at the ball diamond under the lights with their swirling crowds of moths. Fred is suited up in his catcher's outfit; in his heavy old-fashioned brown leather pads he looks like a huge bald bear daring the world to try to shoot him. In the stands, wearing her West Gull Merchants T-shirt, Chrissy is still finishing off the ice-cream cone Ned saw her buying as he left the parking lot.

"When are you going to learn there's a time to ask for favours?" were Fred's last words to him. *Why don't you just fuck off and disappear*, he might as well have said — that's what it sounded like to Ned Richardson who'd already tried to see him twice at the lumber yard and had spent two days working up the courage to confront him at the ball game.

"Favours" was the word Fred had used. He seemed to have forgotten that Ned had been buried up to his neck and had practically got his eyes eaten out on Fred's behalf. And now Fred is talking about favours. Ned knocks at the door, waits for a moment as though he is being watched, as though someone might answer, then walks in. Everyone in West Gull is always boasting about not needing to lock their doors.

He goes right upstairs and finds the room where Fred and Chrissy sleep. The plan is simple enough. He is going to steal some of Chrissy's underwear, then plant it someplace to convince Fred she is sleeping around. That seems to be the only thing that gets under his skin, and that's where, after what Fred has done to him, Ned wants to be.

They have matching dressers. Ned opens one, Chrissy's right away. You would think she would keep her underwear in her top drawer — his mother does and so did Lu-Ann when she was with him — but Chrissy's top drawer is full of jewellery on one side, T-shirts on the other. The next drawer is jeans, then come sweatshirts. He doesn't find the underwear until the bottom drawer. She's got mounds of it, stacks of underpants sorted by colour, two rows of brassieres neatly laid out on top of each other as though on display. Confronted with all this care, his resolve wavers. Meanwhile a car passes on the highway and his panic level, already at what he thought must be the maximum, shoots up. He grabs some panties and bras — one from each pile so they won't be noticed — and stuffs them into his grocery bag. The car passes, Ned's nerves subside. Looking around the room he sees the tripod with the video camera mounted on it. It's pointed out the window and Ned tries to imagine Fred as an amateur bird watcher. He briefly considers stealing the camera, but decides it would only get him into trouble.

He's on his way out, then wheels to peek into Fred's dresser. Its top drawer *is* underwear and he's about to push it closed when he sees the dull metal glint of a gold bracelet — Fred's watch, the one that's always bulging on his wrist while he stands impassively in front of Ned telling him to come back in two weeks or six months or never. Ned reaches for it, then his hand hits something else. A cassette which along with the watch, he adds to the underwear in his grocery bag. Thirty seconds later he's in his truck again, backing out of the driveway, the bag stowed safely under his seat. Nothing more natural than for him to be here, dropping in for a visit, too bad they weren't home but he'd forgotten about the baseball game, see you later.

And, in fact, Ned Richardson *did* see Fred later, twice. Once at the ball diamond where he scooted back to catch the rest of the game. Only an inning missed; if anyone had noticed his answer was that he'd gone to get cigarettes. And then a second time, unexpectedly, at about one in the morning. Normally at that time, Ned would have been at Ellie's but this was the nurse's night off and he had to watch Alvin.

By the time he got the old man to bed and all the soiled sheets and towels in the washer in the kitchen, it was after midnight. He took a beer from the refrigerator and watched Letterman for an hour, wondering what it must be like to be in the band and have to blow your guts out every time the man gave his stupid grin and waved his arms as if shooing geese. Then he brought in his spoils from the truck, spread them out on the couch.

Fred's heavy gold watch hung loosely from his wrist so he pushed it up his arm and onto his bicep where it squeezed into place like one of those old-fashioned expansion bands pool sharks wear around their sleeves in movies. Chrissy's underwear was another question. There were two pairs of white panties, both cotton with pictures of hearts around the crotch, and one delicately stitched pink mesh pair that must have been satin or silk. The brassieres — one white, one black —

were also mesh, and each had a small satin bow sewn to the low point of the cleavage. He had never before taken the time to examine a woman's underwear, not his mother's nor Lu-Ann's nor Ellie's. Now that he did, he was amazed at how white the white was, how pink the pink. No wonder they had all those detergent advertisements on television. There was a whole world of women out there worrying about how to keep their underwear pure. And those little satin bows! No guy would walk around with little bows or butterflies sewn to his jockeys. Or hearts next to his thing. Ned held the bra to his chest. Chrissy must be as thin as a little kid. He put a fist in one of the cups. Lu-Ann's boobs had been big, too full for his hands to cover and even the cups of her brassiere had seemed enormous. Chrissy's were smaller, like Ellie's he supposed, though in trying to imagine Chrissy's brassiere on Ellie's chest, all he could get was a vision of Ellie asking him what the hell he was doing playing with Chrissy McKelvey's underwear. Feeling guilty, he shoved it back in the bag, although he did have an answer: it had been a revenge against Fred. But now that he had the underwear he couldn't think how to use it. Mail it back a piece at a time with Carl's return address on the envelope? Tie a bra to his truck aerial? Put an ad in the Kingston Shoppers' Lost & Found? Like most of his schemes, this under-wear idea had been a waste of time. He took the bag to his bedroom and was hiding it under the mattress when he realized the cassette would make a lump.

He took the tape out and popped it into Lu-Ann's VCR which he still had though her parents had called to ask him to return it, and suddenly there was Fred. Fred without his clothes, looking more like Fred-the-old-bald-bear in his catching outfit than any other Fred. Fred in what Fred must think to be Fred in all his glory. Then Fred and Chrissy. It wasn't exactly a movie, even a dirty movie. Just a bunch of screw scenes strung together. Sometimes it seemed Fred was handling the camera, other times the camera must have been set on the tripod. Every scene had the same basic plot line though with certain very unexpected variations including some with a very unhappy Chrissy. There was no doubt that living with Fred was even worse than having to chase him around asking for a job.

Ned watched the whole video, every frame, though there were at least a dozen times he paused it, checked on his uncle to make sure he hadn't miraculously risen from his drugged sleep, and looked outside in case a posse of vengeful Freds was descending to rip away from him this unexpected item which he was very sure Fred Verghoers, would-be reeve, Allnew manager and midnight cowboy, would definitely prefer had not fallen into Ned Richardson's hands.

FIVE

Twenty-nine. It was six a.m. on the first of October so he had been twenty-nine years old for exactly six hours, the "exactly" because, as his parents had often told him, after a long procrastination, much of it on the kitchen table, he'd popped out just after the cuckoo clock Elizabeth's mother had given them for a wedding present began to signal midnight. He has always liked the timing of his birthday: "The way sunset is to the day, October is to the year," his mother had told him once. "October is the magic month." He had enjoyed that, the idea that his month was the magic one. The month with the dying light, Indian summer, heat in the afternoon, turning leaves, the increasingly heavy frosts, the first snow, even Hallowe'en, the party at the end.

October 1, six in the morning and still pitch black. Carl made coffee then started on the waffles. As a birthday treat from the birthday boy he had promised Lizzie that they could go to the beaver pond with the camcorder he'd started bringing home weekends so that when he started renting it out from the store he'd be able to tell the customers how to use it. This new item was Luke's idea of a way to perk up business: "We'll have the whole township needing one every time there's a birthday party."

Two hours later Carl and Lizzie were lying on a soft fragrant mound of rust-coloured needles beneath the huge pine at the southern edge of the pond. As the mist came off the water's surface Carl scanned the lake with the camera. Lizzie was curled into his side, asleep, her legs drawn up to her belly and her hands tucked between her knees. Carl aimed the camera for the beaver den, turned the zoom control on to bring it closer. The dark slick crown of a beaver's head broke the surface; the water rippled as the beaver crossed the pond in their direction. Carl switched on the power and the camera emitted a high-pitched grating noise. Up came the beaver's ears. Angry red triangles. Carl had them in the centre of his focus. Lizzie stirred against him. The beaver's head rotated. Dark eyes glittered. Hoarse scare-the-enemy breathing rasped across the water. Then the beaver's body convoluted, snapped forward; Carl had to jerk the camera to keep the creature in the field of vision as the broad tail slapped the water and the beaver submerged. "Got it," Carl said but just as he spoke there was a crash in the underbrush, only twenty yards away, and before he could swing the camera around a summer-fattened buck leaped into the air, twisting, disappearing into the trees.

When they got home Lizzie took the cartridge out of its plastic case and loaded it into the VCR while Carl made hot chocolate to drink in front of the TV set. The tape began with images from the night before. Lizzie, familiar with a camcorder because Fred had one, had taken the camera on a tour of the outside of the house, starting with the front door, which had been nailed shut in some previous era and had no steps, then walking around the back, the landscape bouncing as the camera jiggled in her hand. The camera climbed the back wall of the house, then whizzed up to Lizzie's bedroom window. That was where she had tried to use the zoom feature. There was a good shot of white paint peeling away from the wood siding and of the geranium on Lizzie's window ledge. Down the siding again, across the lawn to the garden. A brief duty tour of the small vegetable patch, most of it already levelled by the first frosts, then on to the real attraction for Lizzie: the wooden cross she'd spent hours making, then hammered into the earth over Marbles' grave after Carl had finally decided it was better to inform her Marbles had been killed — in his story by a car — than to have her spend the whole summer searching. All this time the only sound had been that of her feet in the grass, a passing car, a few giggles. Now she spoke, her voice tinny and faltering: "Here lies the noble cat, run over by a brutal stranger. In this ground I sank this cross. But, brutal stranger, I would have driven a stake into your heart until your blood came out all over you. Yuck. Well, something anyway, I don't know." Meanwhile the camera lens had dropped so that the image was of Lizzie's feet, shifting uncomfortably as she spoke, her shoes coming together as her voice trailed away. "I'm going to shut this thing off until I can find Ashes. He better not be dead."

The tape started again in the kitchen. Carl was holding Ashes up to the camera. "I'm Carl," Carl said. "This is Ashes. We're in the kitchen here and we're hungry. As soon as the oven gets hot we're going to put the chocolate brownies in." Carl's face got bigger as he walked towards the camera. "Move it over there, honey. Let me hold it while you pour the brownie mix in the pan."

"What if I spill it?"

"You won't. But if you do, I can make a movie of you cleaning it up." Suddenly Ashes' head filled the whole frame so that it went dark briefly, followed by an image of the table with a big blur in the centre.

"She licked it," Lizzie said

First thing in the morning Carl had taken the camera to Lizzie's room. Lizzie had her pillow locked in a bearhug. Ashes was curled up and lying on her back. Lizzie made Carl rerun the footage of the cat. She said, "Well, I love him, but not as much as Marbles. Marbles will always be my favourite cat."

"Good thing Ashes doesn't understand you," Carl said.

"He knows about Marbles. But I promised to love him a lot, just the same."

By the time they'd finished watching the video it was lunchtime. Carl went into the kitchen to make a salad to accompany the French toast Lizzie insisted on for her Sunday lunches, and when he went back into the living room she was sleeping, her face smooth and opaque. As he put a quilt over her she murmured, "Rub my back." Ever since she was an infant he'd put her to sleep that way, rubbing her back in slow circles. His hand had covered her whole back and he'd barely touched it as he circled. Now her shoulder blades, once like stunted chicken wings, were sheathed and surrounded by the wiry muscles that propelled her along the monkey bars or sent her sprinting so fast that Carl had to strain to keep up. "More," Lizzie said, and then started mumbling as she often did as she fell asleep, words from her dreamworld language, then she was gone.

That night Carl woke up. Or maybe he hadn't yet slept. These days it was hard to tell. For a moment he lay still listening for Lizzie's breathing. For the last week she'd had a cold and Carl found himself checking her all through the night, the way he used to when she was a baby.

His bedroom was directly above the kitchen. He was still listening to Lizzie when the refrigerator went on. At first a smooth hum, then a gradual rocking that evolved into an insistent humping rhythm. The other night Ray had come to visit and they were playing cards in the kitchen when the refrigerator got so excited it actually started to travel across the floor. "Got the devil in it," Ray had croaked. "One of these nights it's going to get all worked up and blow its own motor." "Me too," Carl had said, and Ray had wheezed, "Me too too" as they started to laugh at the absurd spectacle of themselves, two aging West Gull boys whose big night out was playing cards and drinking beer in the kitchen of the old Balfer place.

Carl was lying on his back and slowly became aware that his skull was throbbing, a deep painful pulse that with every heartbeat pulled at his wound. He swung out of bed, gathered his clothes from the chair and went downstairs to the kitchen. Once on his feet, the pain drained away. He made himself coffee, had a piece of bread with jam which he ate standing up. Soon it would be time to wake Lizzie to get ready for school but right now the sky was still dark and through the kitchen window the only sign of the morning to come was a yellow October dawn that lay weakly across the horizon.

Dressed, Carl put on a pair of heavy socks and his boots. Then he took his hunting jacket from the hook beside the door and went outside.

The wooden steps creaked with frost as he stepped down to the driveway, but though the sky was clouded over, no snow had fallen overnight, and the ground and road were bare. Carl crossed the driveway to his truck. He had only intended to take his gloves from the front seat but now, opening the door and seeing his keys in the ignition, he climbed in and sat behind the steering wheel. He turned on the motor and eased out of the driveway onto the blacktop.

Down the road a couple of miles there was a swamp. If the swamp froze hard before the snow, Carl was intending to take Lizzie there on weekends to teach her how to skate. Past the swamp he followed the sideroad that curved back towards the highway. Where the road climbed there was a sweep of sloped land facing southwest. Light shone from the barns of the fortunate farmers who worked these sun-powered fields; they had already started their milking and as the sun rose it turned their corn silos into giant silver obelisks. "All that money," Carl said aloud. "Luke Richardson will find a way to screw you." And as though at this iconic time of day it was necessary that every sentence uttered be a prophecy, Carl noticed as he came to the highway in front of the biggest and richest farm — one with three silos all to itself and a brick house adjoined by the ultimate local sign of wealth, a fence of green pressure-treated lumber surrounding an in-ground swimming pool — one of Luke Richardson's election signs was hammered into the centre of the expanse of lawn.

He turned onto the highway, possessed by a sudden unwanted vision of the sun coming up to greet Luke Richardsons stepping out of every single house in the township, all at once, big grins on their faces, hands outstretched and waving.

When Carl got home he woke up Lizzie. She had her arm around Ashes and when she sat up the kitten leapt to his shoulder and started licking at his face with his sharp sandpapery tongue. He made Lizzie's lunch while she ate breakfast. Then he drove her into West Gull. When she got out of the truck and started walking towards the school, with her colourful little yellow-and-blue plastic lunch pail matching the yellow-and-blue school, something in Carl's stomach gave way. He started the truck up again and drove slowly through West Gull, tapping his fingers on the steering wheel. That black and unpredictable feeling in his gut had grown to fill his whole body.

A few minutes later he was sitting in Fred Verghoers' office at Allnew. Fred was leaning back in his swivel chair behind his desk, at one hand a computer with a screensaver of a rabbit running across a field, at the other a telephone console with a panel of lights that were busily blinking.

"So here you are," Fred said. "Come to pay a return visit? Should I get Anne-Marie to bring you a coffee?"

"Gave it up," Carl said, "ever since I went into training to beat up the shitface who knocked me on the head a few weeks ago."

"What were you planning to do to him?"

"Well, I don't really have a plan. Just thought I might drive over to his office, ask him to step outside, see what happened."

"Maybe he doesn't step outside any more. Maybe he's getting a bit old for that."

"I was wondering about that, too," Carl said. "But most likely he still thinks he's a pretty big boy. Though he does prefer to work in the dark and from behind. But I don't think he'd like to say that to my face."

"Well," said Fred, "there's a lot of different things people could say to each other's faces. And there's a lot of different things people could do to each other or with each other behind each other's backs."

"I was wondering about that, too," Carl said. "I figured he might think I owed him one."

"What are you doing here, Carl? Why did you come back? You still trying to get yourself killed?"

"Is that a threat?"

"I'm not threatening you, Carl. See my little tag here? See my election signs all over the township? I'm building a life, Carl, and it's going to work. What are you getting done? You going to spend the rest of your life down at the Movie Barn, renting out jerk-off kung fu movies? You're just asking for it, Carl. You always have been. You figure you're such a fighter and maybe you are. You can scare a little kid like Ned Richardson. But steal other men's women and take them out for a quick screw, is that what a big man does? Fuck you, Carl, we're even."

Following Carl's birthday there were a few nights of sharp frost that cut down the remaining garden and left clouded skins of ice on his windshield. Then came a week of cold rain. The evening it stopped the sky was blue-black with an angry red edging in the west. Carl left the Balfer place about seven. He was dressed in a pair of grey slacks he'd bought at the shopping centre and under his ski jacket he wore the new blue shirt Lizzie had given him for his birthday. For the occasion he'd even got rid of his bandage, and with artful combing the remaining swellings and scabbed dots left by his seventeen stitches were almost invisible.

When he arrived, shrub-surrounded spotlights were shining on the huge white house. Tonight it looked like the unsuccessful bastard offspring of a colonial movie-set mansion and the Acropolis.

Carl had just stepped out of his truck and was patting the wrinkles out of his pants when Moira arrived. Except for awkward moments at the R&R, it was the first time he'd seen her since the night they'd spent together after he got back from the hospital.

"My turn to say I just can't do it," she'd told him over the phone.

"Your choice."

"I just can't be casual about this kind of thing. I'm not the come-and-go type."

"No need to explain. You've been great."

"I guess I should wish you a good life or something."

"Don't have to," Carl had said. "See you around."

And now here she was, dressed like some kind of university girl, dark wool coat, dark dress, stockings and high heels. Her nice smile, her almost pretty face that wasn't quite turned towards him, so he couldn't tell if she'd been expecting him.

"Hey," Carl said. "Nice surprise."

At the R&R she had that brisk way of talking fast but friendly that was meant, he supposed, to combine professionalism with letting him know her heart was protected by chain mail. The last time, left alone with him for a moment, she'd asked him first about the Movie Barn, then Chrissy's health. Before he could answer McKelvey had returned and Moira drifted off leaving Carl saying to himself that, all things considered, both times Moira had come to his house it had been on her own initiative and without an invitation.

Moira glanced at him appraisingly. "Surprise for me, too. Look at you. Dressed like a real blade."

"Blade? Never heard that one."

"Everyone says it. Means kind of a sharp guy but I wouldn't ask you to carry my wallet."

The front door was a massive wooden slab with a slit window that would have been the perfect place to conceal a machine gun. Beneath was a wide brass nameplate:

LUCAS & AMARYLLIA
RICHARDSON

The doorbell, a dark green glass button illuminated from the inside, set off a two-toned chime. "You'd be doing me a favour," Luke had said to Moira about the dinner, as if he was planning to call her father if she refused. Carl was standing passively, his mouth turned and thoughtful. Maybe Luke had got the wrong impression at Carl's place, and now had brought them together to deliver some unwanted advice. When Luke opened the door, his eyes went to Carl first, and he smiled, a big relaxed smile that made his face crinkle into a friendly cartoon. He turned to Moira, cartoon smile stretching wider, eyes flicking nervously away from her in that way some men have of pretending you aren't there because they know they aren't allowed what they'd like: to swallow you right up.

"Evening, Moira." His arm curved around her, barely touching, and he ushered them in. "Italian marble," he said as she wiped her feet. "You ever get a windfall, all you have to do is ask Madame Amaryllia to redo your front hall."

The Richardson living room was all soft pastels and looked to Moira as though it must have come out of one of those decorating magazines at the R&R: peach wall-to-wall broadloom, white laminate endtables, a pink marble fireplace with a neat pile of birch logs stacked beside it waiting to join those already crackling away inside. Luke led them to a battleship-sized sofa covered in apricot-rose leatherette with tasselled cushions in the corners. A Gordon Lightfoot song filtered discreetly through hidden speakers. Luke stood in front of them asking what they would like to drink, his fancy black Italian loafers winking from the peach shag like kinetic amphetamine eyes.

A few minutes later, Amy appeared. Moira had met her a few times with her parents but they had never really spoken. Amy was squeezed uncomfortably into a red-sashed satin dress that made her look like an overcooked sausage left on a barbecue so long that its skin was about to split. Beneath her lacquered hair, her face was swollen and inflamed and with each step she seemed about to collapse. Moira struggled to rise from her oversized cushion.

"Please," Amaryllia said. She pushed Moira back with a tiny touch of her thick hand. Moira fell into place. The woman had little concrete blocks for fingers. "Did you get something to drink?"

Moira nodded towards her glass. The sherry she had asked for, hoping to impress Luke with her ladylike choice, was making her tongue feel as though it had been coated with cough syrup. She turned to Carl. This had to be the strangest way to see him again. She had helped Lizzie select the shirt at the SuperWay. Thick blue cotton, meant to go with jeans, it was wrong with those slacks. He obviously wasn't back with Chrissy. No woman would have let him out of the house like that. She tried to imagine describing this scene to Lucy: three fat fruity leather cushions away from a man she'd slept with, a man who might or might not be getting back with his wife, a man she might or might not like, and all she could think about was whether his shirt went with his pants. Also, to tell the whole truth, when she'd helped choose the shirt she'd wondered if she'd ever be unbuttoning it.

While they worked their way through their drinks Luke told them about the various places they'd had to search out to buy their furniture and carpet. When they sat down at the table, Luke explained that the made-to-order chandelier was of such splendour and weight that in anticipation of its arrival a special steel beam had been put in the ceiling during construction of the house.

From the moment they entered the dining room Carl had been eyeing that chandelier. Seven separate circles of lights, tiny pointed Christmas-tree-style bulbs shining on what must have been hundreds of pounds of crystal and silver. So bright you could hardly keep your eyes open. In fact, the whole room was done up like some sort of fake castle. The ceiling was at least sixteen feet high and aside from the chandelier and the gigantic feast-sized table with its high-backed chairs done in throne-red plush, was the extraordinary panelling on the walls, brilliantly varnished cherrywood with a bright flaming grain. Luke caught Carl running his fingers along it as they came into the room. "Full-inch tongue-and-groove," he confided. While Amy lowered her head to recite grace, Carl calculated. The panelling was just above his eyes, say six feet, and the room was so large there'd have to be at least seventy running feet of panelled wall. Which made, Carl figured while eating shrimp on crushed ice with what seemed to be red hot-dog relish, somewhere between twenty and thirty thousand dollars' worth of cherrywood.

After the shrimp Luke carved the roast. It reminded Carl of a hunk of meat at a restaurant buffet, grilled and channelled on the outside, the insides glistening with blood. Luke was standing over it, sizing it up as he went along, using a cordless electric carving knife that gave off a high buzz as he shaved slices onto the platter. Meanwhile, Amy carried the conversation; whenever she slowed down Moira would dutifully chip in with a question. Carl had been concentrating so intently on the price of the panelling that he half-missed Amy describing her brother's farm, where their beef came from, but he did hear her say that some cows were so valuable people were offering to pay him five thousand dollars for just one of their eggs.

"Sight unseen," Luke Richardson put in. "If I could sell real estate that way I'd be rich." Then he was doling out slices of Amy's brother's five-thousand-an-egg beef onto the plates and passing them around.

There was wine, too. French from France, Luke explained, and then Moira cut in to say she'd been to France on a tour. The only images Carl had of France were the Paris he'd seen in movies, especially the Eiffel tower, and the wine bottle on the table which showed a château fronted by a row of trees.

"With your parents?" Luke asked.

"Other kids," Moira said, and Carl found himself grinning at Luke's discomfort at the unthinkable thought of ball-cap-wearing gum-chewing teenagers spending their parents' money roaming around some foreign country where they didn't even speak the language.

"You ever go to France?" Moira asked Carl. She was right across the table from him. Luke and Amy were at the ends. The whole thing was out of a bad television show. "Did you?" she asked again. As he was trying to decide what to reply he felt the pointed toe of her shoe against his shin.

"My brother went to France about the cows," Amaryllia said. "He was on a tour, too: cheese and beef. There was a whole group of farmers and they all came home pretty happy and twice as big as when they left."

Luke Richardson was looking at Carl, eyes open wide, as though challenging Carl to match that. "My mother went to Rome and saw the Pope," Carl said. "She asked for a special prayer to stop my father's drinking." There was a silence during which Luke Richardson laughed without making any sound and Moira looked down at her plate. Carl remembered there had been a big silver crucifix in the front hall.

"Just kidding," Carl said. There had been a first weak Scotch and water, then Luke Richardson had refilled his glass, just as tall but without the water. He wanted to go outside, get some fresh air. Amy started talking again, this time about how she had travelled to Toronto and stayed in a hotel while she was choosing fabric for the curtains. With her brother's wife. They even took her sister-in-law's dog, a pedigreed Irish setter that knew how to use kitty litter. She shopped in Toronto all the time. She was Greek. She had some sort of passport problem and couldn't shop in New York. Her brother didn't like her going to Montreal because of the French thing. Which was okay in France but not at home.

"I went to France with my high-school choir," Moira said. "We spent two years having raffles and selling cookies, then we went to this little town where they had choirs from all over the world." She looked at Carl and added, "But I've never been to the West Coast."

Luke started serving out the beef and Amy went to the kitchen because she'd forgotten the horseradish. For the first time since coming into the house Carl looked directly at Moira. "Help," she mouthed.

"I wanted to show you this one." The moose head, so big the rest of the body must have been attached on the other side of the wall, was stuffed and mounted on a giant heart-shaped plaque. Moira stood and stroked its nose as though she were about to feed it a lump of sugar.

"I tell him this whole place is a zoo," Amy said. They were in another oversized room, this one windowless with mahogany panelling that rose to within a couple of feet of the ceiling, where it was topped by a trophy shelf. "My den," Luke had announced. After admiring the moose, Carl and Moira sat down on a black leather sofa — across from them, on its twin, were Luke and Amaryllia. From side by side on the big living-room sofa to sitting opposite in the dining room to side by side again in Luke's den: it seemed to Carl this dinner was an agonizingly slow dance designed to turn him and Moira into a couple. Or maybe they were to be the victims in some weird fairy tale Luke had concocted, one of those grim Grimm fairy tales where the children get eaten or turned into repulsive animals. If so they were in the right place. Except for a wall given over to gun racks, they were more or less surrounded by a taxidermist's paradise. Beside Luke, a stuffed dog lay with its head in its paws, its mournful brown eyes permanently tilted towards his master. On the desk, on the arm of another chair, on the tops of two of the gun racks were stuffed squirrels and chipmunks, raccoons, rabbits, even a skunk. From the trophy shelf hung wood-backed antlered buck trophies; the moose head above the fireplace, the one Luke had pointed out, had a huge spread of antlers that seemed ready to turn into wings and carry the moose crashing to freedom.

"There I am with it." Richardson pointed to a picture of himself standing beside the fallen moose. He was holding his rifle by the barrel, its butt on the ground, and in his fringed leather jacket and wide hat he seemed to think he was some kind of old-time buffalo-hunting pioneer instead of a small-town businessman who'd hired a booze-soaked farmer to lead him through some second growth to an animal all past and no future. "And there's the butcher at work." A picture of William McKelvey kneeling beside the moose with his knife buried in its guts, grinning to the camera with that after-killing look he often used to get, his mouth stretched wide and his eyes calm, as though for a few pacifying moments the life he'd just taken filled some gap in his own.

"Looks just like you," Moira said. "I didn't know he used to look like *that*."

"Thanks."

"Just his eyes."

Since dinner Carl had been drinking bourbon, trying to go slow but pushed along by Luke, who kept refilling the heavy cut-glass tumbler that fit so comfortably in the palm of his hand. Luke began to recount hunting trips with William McKelvey, different times Carl's father had driven game towards him, the stag he'd missed because he'd fallen asleep waiting and woke up only when it crashed by, sporting a rack of antlers that would fill the back of a truck.

Suddenly Luke stopped. Carl was beginning to have the feeling he'd promised himself to avoid for ever, the thick dulled feeling he got when he'd had too much to drink. Luke Richardson was peering in at him, as though he knew how uncomfortable Carl was. Carl's wound was pulsing.

"Hell of a thing at the store," Luke said, his voice sympathetic, the same voice he'd had that first day when he came into the restaurant where Carl was eating his eggs.

Friend wanted. Someone to trust. Someone to take this drink from my hand. Someone to take this body from this house.

Now Carl remembered Chrissy telling him Luke was seeing Doreen Whittier on the side. "He takes her to the Fireside Motel in Kingston every Thursday for lunch. They get a room in a corner at the back, overlooking the squash court. Ellie

Dean told me; her cousin works there. Sometimes they go to the lounge after to drink cocktails. Ellie went to check up one time and Luke spotted her at the door, made her come in and have a drink with him and Doreen. Said they'd just been doing the banking. Ellie made up some story about how she always stopped there to give herself a treat on the way home from the shopping centre."

Carl pushed his hair back. He wanted to be sober, to be sharp, to see into the centre of Luke's game.

"I was glad you could come tonight," Luke said. "You know, your father meant a lot to me. I always felt bad that things went down for him. And by the time it came to me I should be doing something for him it was too late, he wouldn't accept anything from anyone."

His own man, his father always said about people he respected. Not Luke Richardson. He was just another of the geeks he took hunting. "What were they like?" Carl had once asked about two men his father had taken on a canoe trip. "Like the rest of them. Blind, deaf and stupid."

Luke continued, "I was fond of your mother, too. A fine woman."

On the one hand Carl was sober again. Luke's concern had taken care of that. On the other his thoughts were still somewhere else, in that familiar place his mind had gone in those alcohol-soaked months after his break-up with Chrissy. He remembered living in an underground universe, a blurred rubbery world where everyone had mysterious subterranean tunnels connecting their minds together, so that while on the surface everyone appeared to behave with so much calculation and propriety, underneath they were really just moles stumbling about, butting and clutching at one another. He wasn't that drunk now. Only drunk enough to remember. Only drunk enough to wonder what exactly was going on with Luke, who was now telling him about a time he'd met Carl's mother in a Kingston men's store, trying to choose a present for William McKelvey.

The idea of Luke Richardson and his mother doing something ten or twenty thousand years ago laid siege to his mind again. But whatever his mother had wanted, even blind and at the bottom of a dark tunnel, it couldn't have been Luke Richardson, so he turned back to the conversation; Luke was saying how he'd told Elizabeth that what every man really wanted was a sweater so warm he could have coffee in the morning before making a fire.

"A sweater. I've got a dozen sweaters like that. Amy says I have so many luxuries I don't even know how to appreciate them any more." Between the leather sofas was a coffee table spread with hunting magazines along with a silver tray of liqueurs Luke had brought out. Amaryllia had taken possession of a snifter filled with a thick yellow fluid which she kept replenishing; yet with every sip her mouth pursed and she recoiled slightly, looking down at her glass as though it had just dealt her a nasty surprise. That would be, Carl couldn't help thinking, how she looked when she kissed Luke.

"It must be fun to be so rich," Moira said. "I wouldn't mind being rich, so long as I didn't have to work too hard."

"You've got it, Moira. That's the important thing. You can't ruin your life over money. Your dad knows that." Luke lifted his glass. "I have a little money, it's true, but the thing that makes me different — you know what it is? Not hard work. This township is filled with people sweating their guts out and getting nowhere. They'd be better off sweating less and thinking more. But they don't. And I do. Because what I've got is *savvy*. You ever hear of that word? You must know that word, Moira, you went to France. It comes from the French *savez*. You knew that, right?"

"We just went there to sing," Moira said. "I didn't actually take language lessons."

"Neither did I. But I got the savvy thing. Having savvy is knowing what's going on, and what's going on is what I like to know. What do you think about that, Carl?"

Luke's big head had been pointed towards Moira for a long time. Carl had been admiring Moira, the way she seemed to be able to face it down without either striking out or retreating. Maybe it was the navy dress. If she'd arrived at the Balfer place wearing that navy dress, he wouldn't have known what to think.

"Sounds good to me," Carl said. Though it didn't. Everyone knew Luke Richardson had money not because of some French word but because he was born with it, and that he'd used what he'd been born with to screw people out of whatever they had.

"What would you do if you were in my position and you had all my money?" Luke's eyes were on him now. It reminded him of something McKelvey liked to say: "Every now and then you get a chance to shoot."

"I'd do something about Fred," Carl said.

Luke looked into his bourbon. "I guess you would."

"He's running against you for reeve, isn't he?"

"That was his plan," Luke said softly.

"Fred's the problem."

"Carl. I've heard that tone of voice from you and from your dad. You touch Fred and you're in jail for ten years. Do you believe me?"

"*I* believe you," Moira said.

"I know *you* believe me, honey. It's your friend who has me worried."

Carl pushed himself up from the sofa. In the corner was a big pile of LUKE RICHARDSON FOR REEVE signs, just like the ones already scattered through the township. "What did you mean when you said 'that *was* his plan'? Is something supposed to happen to Fred?"

"That would be ugly," Luke said. "You know, Carl, you can't see this because of where you're sitting, but Fred's a pretty interesting human being. Probably a lot more complicated than you give him credit for. In fact, Fred's the big winner. Though he doesn't know it, Fred Verghoers is going to be the next reeve. I've decided to withdraw from the race. I'm going to go down to Kingston and call a press conference. Pulling out because of health reasons is what I'll say. Amy will be right beside me, a tear in her eye. Then I'll announce that Fred has my full support. Hand on my heart."

Now Luke had his big smile. Somehow, without seeming to, he'd managed to gobble everything down.

"You see, Carl, it's better not to fight. If I let Fred beat me, then it's not going to look so good on me, is it? And if I beat Fred, which I could and I would, well, everyone's going to think it's the senator's nephew whipping the young lad and trying to grab everything for himself, and no one likes that. What's more I'm going to have Fred against me — and you know better than me how unpleasant that is. So I'm going to use my savvy. I'm going to step aside to let Fred win. And Fred's going to be my man."

"How's that? He might have beaten you anyway."

Luke wagged his finger. "Nope. He wouldn't have. Because, like I said, Fred has his complications though he likes to keep them to himself. But I've got something on Fred. Something no one knows. And when I say I'm going down to Kingston to be on television, our little Freddy will be so scared of my going public he'll be the one having the heart attack. That's why, when I withdraw instead, Fred Verghoers is going to *love* me."

There was something about Luke Richardson's voice, its smooth deep purr. That's how he'd be with Fred. He'd tell him he was letting him win, then Fred would owe him.

"You know what I've got on Fred?"

"You tell us." Amy had woken up.

"Something very interesting. Very unusual. Something our Fred has been trying very hard to keep secret. Something that must never leave this room."

"Spill it," Amy said. You wouldn't believe the way she talked to Luke Richardson, Carl thought. She had a voice like an outboard motor. But Luke just smiled and put a big paw on her shoulder.

"Steady now, girl. Here it comes: Fred beats up on Chrissy. Sent her to the hospital over a month ago. Three broken ribs. Got copies of the X-rays in the office safe."

Carl started up, as though he himself had just been hit. He saw Chrissy's face at the dance, heard her saying "Not so good," remembered the way she'd sometimes insisted Lizzie be back by dark. "Jesus," Carl said.

"What I've got on him," Luke said, "is that if he steps out of line I'll let you at him. You can bury him alive. Let the birds eat out his eyes. Whatever you want. But not until I say so. Because like I told you before, you touch Fred without my permission, you're in jail for a long time. And Lizzie's not going to like that, is she?"

"I'd better go," Carl said. "If you haven't fired me yet, I have the morning shift."

Luke's big hand came up. "You will get fired if you leave before we talk about deer-hunting season. I don't suppose your father ever took you hunting?"

Carl could only half hear Luke. He was picturing Fred in his swivel chair, comfortably leaning back behind his desk, his voice full of contempt. *Fuck you, Carl, we're even.*

"He must have taken you a few times."

"A few times."

"I'll tell you one thing. He never came back empty-handed. He must have known where those deer hung out."

"He never told us where he went."

There was a brief silence and now Carl was remembering how when his father was away on hunting trips, he would often come home to an empty house, because during the hunting trips his mother would go directly to Kingston from the school to do her errands. He'd get off the school bus and the house would be waiting like some kind of abandoned museum. In the centre of the kitchen table would be a plate with cookies or a slice of cake covered in plastic wrap. He'd let the dog inside for company, feed it some refrigerator scraps while he made himself hot chocolate. When his mother returned she'd be laden down with bags and smelling of perfume and wine. Eventually Carl had wondered if she had some kind of special friend.

"I was thinking maybe you'd come hunting with me," Luke Richardson said. "Your father must have taught you something."

"I don't even know when the deer season starts."

"Not here. I've got a hunting camp in the north end of the county. We could go up for a couple of nights in the fall. Get away from things."

I don't want to get away, I'm still trying to get back, Carl thought of saying. And why was Luke Richardson talking to him this way? As if they were friends. As if they knew each other.

"So that's great," Luke said. "We'll go after the first snow. Looking forward to it. Right?"

"Sure," Carl said. "Not on a weekend, though. I have Lizzie then. And I should go for only a couple of days. Gotta pay the rent."

"Don't worry about that. You're my guide, right? I'll give you the regular rate. Like with your father. Okay?"

"Sure."

"Just one more thing about Fred," Luke said. "When we go hunting, we're going to take him." He smiled up at Carl. "Right after the election. It'll be like a celebration. It'll give us a chance to get to know each other a bit. The three of us. And don't get any crazy ideas about having an accident. In fact, you're going to be so nice to Fred he won't have a single idea in his head except what a great pal you are now that he's on his way to the big time. Because if you *do* something to him, well, he's got to do something to you. Like before. And then you'll have to get him back. The way you want to now. And so on until one of you gets killed. Which isn't the way the Richardsons do things, Carl. It's the way you do things. Or used to. That's why your head's stitched up and why both you and Fred will be worse off a week or a month from now — unless you learn to do it my way. So I'm going to try to teach you, Carl, because I've been watching you since you came back and despite the stupid things you've done, I really believe you're ready to learn. Which means we're still going to do things to Fred, Carl, oh yes, we're going to get right into his mind and do things he doesn't even know we're doing. And pretty soon he'll be doing just what we want him to be doing. Isn't that right, Moira?"

"Just the way you do with me," said Amy, and then she started to laugh but as she laughed her outboard-motor cough spluttered and threatened to choke her until Luke stood her up, held her against his shoulder like a baby, and gave her a whack on the back that was followed by a loud burp.

"Excuse me," Amy said. "My gas goes down the wrong way."

Outside Carl waited until Amy and Luke had closed the door, then asked Moira if she wanted to come back with him. "You could follow me in the car or I could come with you to the R&R and drive you."

"Just like that," she said, as though all the little signals he'd thought she was sending him were now supposed to be forgotten.

"Don't worry about it." He turned back to his truck, wishing he hadn't said anything. "Nice to see you, anyway." He got inside, started the engine, waited for her to leave first. Winter manners. Can't leave a woman alone in a car when the temperature is below freezing. Even if you wouldn't mind her digging a hole and disappearing into it.

She pulled out ahead of him, then stopped, blocking his car, and came back. "I want to come with you. Still okay?" The exhaust was clouding around her and she looked almost frightened.

"Very okay."

"I'll leave my car in town. This time you can drive me."

Just in case Luke was watching, Carl turned the opposite way from Moira, circled around and picked her up at the R&R. She got into his truck, shivering, and slid across the seat to press against him.

"I'm glad we're doing this," she said. And rushing on, as

though it was a speech she'd prepared, "Let's just be ourselves, no big deals, no lectures about why we can't get married. We'll just do this now. Deal?"

"Deal," Carl said. He liked the way she felt against him, the way her eyes and her voice were filled with the moon's sharp light and he felt eager to get home. He put his hand on her knee, pulled out of town onto the highway. But everything Luke had said started swirling through his mind and there was something about the snow on the edge of the road that reminded him of another time, this kind of night when the snow was scattered thin, the night when — Chrissy pregnant with Lizzie — Carl had the crazy idea that this budding new life might expiate his mother's death. When he told this to Chrissy she'd suggested they drive out to the cemetery and stand beside his mother's grave so that she or her spirit or whatever was left of her would somehow know her son's seed had been planted in the small white welcoming belly of the girl on the other side of the ground, that there was to be new life where before there had been none. That was coming up on three years after Elizabeth's death.

As Carl had stood above the grave trying to get himself in the mood for this solemn communication with the possibly-still-extant soul of his dead mother, Chrissy, leaning close to him, had murmured, "You know, graveyards are so romantic. If it wasn't so cold like this, Carl..." That had been Chrissy when she was pregnant, so sexy, all body. And then he saw himself and Chrissy in the graveyard again but this time she was lying on the ground, wearing the big nightgown she'd always had, cold and stiff. And he, in his suit, hands folded devoutly in front, was standing in front of her, looking down.

"What are you thinking?" Moira asked.

Her voice surprised him. He had almost forgotten she was

there. "I don't know. I was thinking about Chrissy, the graveyard. I was standing in the graveyard with Chrissy and suddenly she was lying on the ground dead."

"We could call the police about Fred."

"Don't make me laugh."

"Luke could have been lying."

"I don't think so. She's always wanting Lizzie home before dark. Like it's for protection. And one time I picked Lizzie up and Chrissy had a big bruise on the side of her face. She said she'd tripped going to the bathroom in the middle of the night and that's what she got for drinking too much beer."

"You think?"

"Yeah. Chrissy doesn't drink beer." Because now he was thinking of that night at Frostie's and he could see Chrissy's green ginger-ale glass with its lipstick-tinged straw. *How are things going with Fred?* Chrissy's stare. *I was just asking.* Chrissy nodding. *Not bad. Not so good. You know. We'll work it out. Fighting?* he had asked. *A kind of fighting. Not like we used to. Fred's kind.*

"Why don't you talk to Fred?"

"Before I left here, after Chrissy started with Fred again — I went a bit crazy one time. With Fred. I guess that was one of the things he was paying me back for."

Moira took his hand from her knee, raised it to her mouth. Kissed his fingers. "You still feel the same way about Chrissy. The way you always did."

Moira's lips on his fingers brought him back.

He stopped the truck. The wine in her breath was mixed with her flowery scent and he was suddenly so thirsty for her he wanted to drink her all down, right there on the highway with the snow in the headlights like a white curtain falling over them.

PART IV

PART IV

ONE

*D*URING THE FIRST THIRTY YEARS OF their marriage, Elizabeth and William McKelvey attended every one of the Richardson New Year's Eve celebrations.

But at the beginning of December 1984, Elizabeth received a letter from her mother informing her that since Lionel Meyers the salami king had, at the age of eighty-four, retired to a nursing home for the duration, she had decided to pay her daughter a winter visit. At that time Elizabeth McKelvey was forty-nine years old. Her husband, William — a decorated war veteran, unsuccessful farmer, sometime hunting and fishing guide, uxorious husband and dedicated alcoholic — was sixty-two. Their son, Carl, who looked like one grandfather but was apparently intent on acting like the other, was seventeen. They were, in sum, a family with a couple of ribbons and more than 130 years of life experience between them. Surely that century plus of intelligence and resourcefulness should have enabled them to deal with the visit of a close and semi-bereaved relative for a few days. Or is any family ever in such a state? William, who was unrelated and thus apparently unconcerned, said, "We'll just fix up the back bedroom for her. Paint the floor, buy a new bedspread and wash the curtains. She can have Christmas with us and then we'll take her to the Richardson New Year thing. It'll give her something to complain about."

Her mother at the Richardsons'! Elizabeth could just imagine it. William, his shirt stained from the Richardson annual chili, his gut bulging over the trousers of the wedding suit he still wore, though buttoning his jacket had retreated from a possibility to a joke to a dream, would be in the kitchen socking back the rye and planning hunting trips. Meanwhile Carl and his high-school buddies would be dancing wildly, pulling moronic practical jokes on each other, behaving, in brief, like all those hysterical teenagers the parental Glades had always disapproved of. She and her mother would be in the Great Hall with Adam, standing at the mantlepiece as they always did. She would be holding the glass Adam always kept full. And Adam, tall and pearishly elegant, his round baby face peering down at her, would be emptying and filling his own glass; until gradually that round baby face grew dark and angular, and the Adam-in-the-Adam appeared, the unexpected genie popping out of the unremarkable pale bottle. What was it about Adam? There had been that one martini-soaked night that led to Carl. Then, much later, the year they spent their dozen afternoons sneaking off to motels. Now Adam was once more the pearish gentleman of elegant and distant refinements. William was the primitive, the caveman, the unremitting pulse of whatever kept the creatures of the planet reproducing. Even his fifty extra pounds and thirty extra years hadn't changed that, just made him bigger and heavier and furrier and more intermittent; but when he bore down on her in the night, whatever it was that opened up in her had nothing to do with the little princess her father had wanted to be raising.

Adam's appeal was in being William's opposite. He was another case of the accidental king. The dutiful but noble brother following in the footsteps of the primitive rule-breaking cad. She'd stopped their motel afternoons because she didn't want to get caught. Not that way. Either they would make themselves a life or they wouldn't. In the meantime they would have lunch at the Timberpost. When she told Adam she was shocked by his nonchalance. There were no declarations of love, no pleas, no tears, no bursts of rage. He just nodded, then drove her back to her car which she had diplomatically parked a dozen miles away at the shopping centre. Two weeks later, when they met for their usual lunch, it was as though the clock had been rolled back. There were no cow-eyes, no double-edged reproaches, nothing but a normal lunch between a schoolteacher and the manager of the car dealership who were both on the local library committee.

This year she and Adam and her mother would stand in front of the fire and politely sip at their drinks. The problem: she'd finally made up her mind. She had decided that since Carl was now seventeen he could fend for himself. Meanwhile she couldn't. Fend for herself. She had decided to tell Adam that if he was still willing, she was too. All she asked was that they get into a train or a car or an airplane and head off to some place thousands of miles away. England or Australia or Vancouver or wherever — she didn't care so long as it was far. She was feeling the call, the call her mother had felt with the salami king, the call the Duke of Windsor had heard from his sexy divorcée; she was hearing the call and she wanted to answer it. Just as her father, at the moment of his greatest clarity, had decided to make an announcement, she too had an announcement to make: *Family, I'm gone.* But she wasn't going to tell them in words, just disappear.

A week before her mother's visit, when Elizabeth in preparation for her departure had already moved her savings into an account at a Kingston trust company, William got kidney stones and needed an operation. The visit was cancelled. They missed the New Year's Eve party and Elizabeth didn't have a chance to get drunk enough to tell Adam she had decided to run away with him.

She took a month off school to nurse William. The next time she met Adam for lunch it was mid-February. Her money was still in Kingston, burning to elope. Adam looked pale and exhausted, as old and worn out as her own husband. He had taken to wearing his spectacles in public, thick lenses encased in steel frames that made him look like someone's grandfather. Not that she'd ever wanted Adam for his *youth* of all things, but a blizzardy February day seemed a strange time to declare what she had planned to tell him weeks before. At the end of the lunch she walked away glad she'd kept her mouth closed. At least William had his drinking, his hunting, his ever-mounting rages against his dead father and the fact that he had wasted his life running down the already run-down farm that his father had managed to graft onto him. Adam — crazy Adam who'd been brought up as the mouth of the Church of the Unique God — seemed to have simply worn himself out. The slim transparent moonlit pear was now only transparent. Empty. It was as though he had disappeared in front of her eyes.

The next New Year's Eve she couldn't bear to drink with Adam again and she found an excuse for them not to go. Then Luke Richardson built a new house and announced the coming New Year's celebration would be the last. That was December 1986. Elizabeth went out and found a new dress. The following week she took William and Carl into Iron Mike's at the shopping centre and made them buy suits.

At seven o'clock New Year's Eve, 1986, she called her men downstairs to be photographed in their new suits. That was when William surprised her. Over the years William had been turning into the nightmarish figure she'd seen chasing a headless chicken the first time he brought her to the farm. Like his father he now drank too much, ate too much, complained too much. No one could have been less suited to farming. Every decision he made was the wrong one. When the milk marketing board had told the McKelveys they'd have to renovate their operation or give up their licence, William sold his quota to go into cheese instead. When shortly after the local cheese factory was put out of business by the American conglomerate that had bought all the township's factories only to close them down, he went into beef. Now, his "farming" like his father's, consisted of chasing a few chickens around the yard, harvesting ever-shrinking crops of hay for his ever-shrinking beef herd and sneaking off to hunt at every opportunity.

But suddenly, that New Year's Eve, he appeared in the kitchen of his own house wearing a suit that transformed him from a shambling wreck into a large Dickensian patriarch. His white shirt covered his sloping belly like a richly textured tablecloth and the dark luxurious blue of his suit enveloped the shirt, the swollen body, the six decades of physical abuse and decline, and re-presented them as a large and undeniably impressive gentleman. His ruddy cheeks shaved close, his bushy white eyebrows matched by the dazzle of his shirt, his usually unkempt thatch of hair carefully brushed, William McKelvey had suddenly emerged as the man Elizabeth, when she married him, knew he could become. And Carl, Carl *gleamed*. His hollow cheeks, his slicked-back hair black with moisture, his narrow waist cinched tight in a black belt that glowed against his grey suit and the fitted blue shirt that made him look like some sort of television muscle-boy. He had always seemed so small beside William but in the photograph she took of them that night, he was, as McKelvey later said, a tall narrow pencil beside a fat crayon. Elizabeth, framing them for this last picture she would ever take, felt absurdly moved to see the man she'd chosen and the man she'd begotten standing side by side this way, worthy of a princess she might have said, at least until after the photo was taken when William McKelvey cracked open a bottle of rye to christen his new suit.

"Just a moment," Carl said. He picked up the camera and made his parents stand together.

In the photograph William McKelvey is leaning against the refrigerator. In one hand he has his bottle of rye. The other is on his wife's shoulder. Steady and relaxed, the same hand Elizabeth had watched with such fascination thirty-odd years before as he drove her towards this same place, an as yet non-existent point on the map of a future that was opening up so quickly she was only just beginning to see the contours of its landscape. On William McKelvey's face plays a full contented smile, in part the smile of a man holding a bottle full of New Year's promise but mostly in celebration of his great triumph, his most enduring victory over the meanness of life and fate: Elizabeth herself, the wife, as he called her, that coolly beautiful and enigmatic female upon whom his hand had somehow settled, with her unpredictable seasons of fire and ice, her strange idea that she had arrived in this bizarre landscape of rock and wood as a privileged visitor from some other cosmos. Fine-featured still, chestnut hair carefully waved around her ears and falling to just above her shoulders, narrow lips unusually tinted with a dark red lipstick that contrasted with the severe blue of the dress and jacket she'd chosen for this occasion, icy blue regal eyes that too often blinked in school-mistresslike disapproval but in this photograph turned up in mock submission to William's victorious smile. It would be months before Carl realized, looking at the camera he had so carelessly shoved onto the pile of magazines that topped the refrigerator, that inside might be this unprecedented image of togetherness. And after it was developed and he showed it to his father, William McKelvey shook his head and muttered something about knowing he shouldn't have wasted good money on that suit, though he supposed they could use it to bury him in if the moths didn't get it first.

They climbed into the car. The three of them shoulder to shoulder in the front. "We should have a picture of this," Elizabeth said, and sitting between her two men slid her hands beneath their arms. In the old days the drive to the Richardson New Year's party had so often been through bad weather that Elizabeth couldn't imagine a New Year's Eve without thinking of gusts of snow beating against the windshield, the tension of driving while only half-seeing the road. But this night was warmer. The large melting flakes were mixed with rain and on the paved road strips of bare pavement emerged between long mounds of messy slush.

By the time they arrived at the Richardsons', the sleet had thickened and the windshield wipers of William McKelvey's ancient Pontiac were moaning under their burdens of half-frozen snow. But the giant house beckoned to them. Its roofs and gables were strung with rows of Christmas lights and over-seeing everything was an illuminated Santa Claus standing on the back of his gift-laden sled and whipping the dozen reindeer strung out on the long ridge that stretched between the chimneys at either end.

As always they parked on the street, the car faced towards home. McKelvey had even thought to bring a piece of cardboard to place on the windshield beneath the wipers so they wouldn't emerge from the party to be confronted by a thick crust of ice.

Luke and Amy were at the door. Luke, big and patrician, leering happily at them as he grasped their hands, "Glad you could come for the last one, folks. Let's make the last the best." He leaned to make his annual attempt to kiss Elizabeth, which she ignored, hugging Amy instead. Tonight Amy had her hair dyed a flaming brassy blond that could have crowned an Amazon on a holy crusade.

"Ah, beautiful as always," Amy sighed, looking at Elizabeth's new outfit, which Elizabeth suddenly realized was more suited to the township library board than this party.

"You too," said Elizabeth. "I can't believe your dress." Amy had on one of her customary shimmering white satin creations — a mass of unyielding polyester cloth that stuck out at all angles like a bow tied by a ten-thumbed giant. As Amy had once explained to Elizabeth: "When you're with someone like Luke you're always having to dress up. So I decided early on to choose my colours, white and gold, like my face and my hair."

In the Great Hall the boys from the hockey team were doing their pre-midnight waiter stint, circulating in white linen jackets with trays of drinks and hors d'oeuvres. Mid-season tourneys had supplied a fresh crop of stitches, and some smiles were already in need of post-season dental work. At one time or another most of the players had been Elizabeth's students at the elementary, so there was much "Would you have a glass of champagne, Mrs. McKelvey?" and "Oh my God, Robert, you look like you ran into a truck!" as she moved amidst the throng.

At the far end of the room in front of the huge stone fireplace, Adam had already taken up his position and was apparently deep in conversation with Albert Knight. It was two months since she'd last had lunch with Adam. He'd called her up saying he had something special to ask her. When he leaned towards her over the table at the Timberpost, Elizabeth had thought that for once he was going to break out of the mould he had assumed, the mouldy mould he'd climbed into the day she told him they had to stop sleeping together. But when he explained what he wanted, her heart had truly turned grey: was being together on the board of a retirement home supposed to be a substitute for making a new life? How could she have given herself to this man? Where *was* the man she had clutched at that long ago New Year's Eve, those motel afternoons? She seemed to have a talent for turning men into idiots by sleeping with them.

She headed for the kitchen to refill her glass. McKelvey was sitting at the big table, his jacket off, one shirt-tail dangling. Since his ideal pre-party moment he had regressed to an overgrown and hairy eight-year-old, face scarlet with rye — and he was laughing at some foolish joke with an equally foolish grin on his face. On her way out she bumped into Amy.

"You look furious," Amy said. "Who crossed you?"

"I crossed me," Elizabeth said. "Me and all the stupid things I've done."

"Join the crowd." And as Amy spoke Elizabeth looked out at the room. Every single face was familiar to her. Not only did she know every person in the room but she also knew their parents, their children if they had any, their secrets, their victories and humiliations, often even the comments their teachers had written on their Grade Three report cards. Drinking, dancing, chattering away in front of her was a massive interconnected tangle she had spent her whole adult life sinking into, and now more than anything else she wanted to shake herself free from it.

Adam was waiting for her. His poised transparent self. And perhaps because she had once hoped Adam would be her means of escape, she finally saw the Adam-in-the-Adam again: his disappearance, his transformation into the man who'd asked her to be on the retirement villa board was just something he had contrived for her; his invisibility was only a costume he'd taken on so that she needn't know how much she'd hurt him.

Adam's face was suddenly threatening to turn into that of George VI, his eyes fixed on her as though to confirm, "Yes, out of duty and devotion this is what I've done."

"You're looking very regal tonight," Elizabeth said.

"Winter was always my time."

Their very first motel afternoon together, after they had made love and she was in the bathroom, he had carefully piled the pillows behind his back so that she emerged to find him sitting up straight, his eyebrows drawn to a single line as he read the newspaper. She had said, "You're looking very regal," and he had replied, "Winter was always my time."

Well, I'm drunk again, Elizabeth thought. Winter is my time for getting drunk and now I'm *so* drunk I've fallen into my running-away-with-Adam mood. And instead of worrying about it she decided to give in to the idea. Why not, speaking of drunk, which was McKelvey's preferred state, and Carl would soon be leaving home, so why not run away with

Adam? Maybe he'd even let her call him King George — it was her destiny — after all. And as she drank and nestled into him and the band started to play it was like twenty years ago when she didn't know any better and a dark burrow with Adam was the only place she could imagine wanting to be.

The music changed to suitably royal waltzes. She danced with Adam. He held her gently, then gently and close, as they floated slowly around the room.

Elizabeth moved her lips to his ear. "I've got a plan."

"A plan?"

"Tomorrow, New Year's Day, I bring my car into town to pick something up at the milk store."

"It's a good one," Adam said.

"Shut up. Then I come to your house and we leave."

"Where for?"

"Far. We disappear. Like that. No one ever knows. Okay?"

"Okay," Adam said.

"I'm serious."

"Are you?"

"Yes," Elizabeth whispered, and then, so the accountant-in-the-Adam would wake up, "I've had my money in a Kingston trust account for two years, waiting for this." She moved in so close that Adam would have to know, close enough to wake the Adam-in-the-Adam and feel him press against her. She had her eyes shut, she was already gone, they would be on an airplane or a ship or a dining room atop a sky-scraper. When she looked up again William McKelvey, who had at least managed to tuck in his shirt before emerging from the kitchen, waved them over. "You know," he said, "you two can really dance." He gave Adam a look full of speculation. "I suppose everyone asks you why you never got married? Or are you in love with my wife like everyone else?"

The music started again and William swept her out onto the floor. Where Adam's arm around her waist had been light and suggestive, William's was heavy and possessing. He held her against his belly and she was aware of his belt buckle as it pressed through her dress. "Well, how's this?"

"You're pretty good," Elizabeth said. "Amazing." Which was true — William, who was emitting more fumes than a distillery, *was* amazing her by being able to stay on his feet, let alone dance. But then William stopped in the middle of the dance floor.

"If Adam wasn't who he was, I'd say he was sweet on you."

"You just did. And anyway, he *is* who he is. And so am I." Now Elizabeth realized she really *was* going to go away with Adam. She was who she was. Why hadn't she known that before? Because she'd wanted to be someone else. She'd wanted to be a romantic and carefree young girl who could survive running off with the first man who made her belly jump. Well, she'd done it and she'd survived, but she'd also wasted most of her life. Might as well make use of what was left. Adam might or might not make her belly jump, but they would go places and see things and he would look like a somewhat pearlike George VI and she would play the faded library-committee princess and when they went out they wouldn't have to put cardboard on their windshield.

"Well, I am who I am," William McKelvey said, "so I think I'll go into the kitchen and have another few drinks while you and Mr. Goldsmith solve the problems of the world. When you're done we can go home."

"Why don't we go now?"

"Now?"

"You've had enough to drink. And so have I."

"Speak for yourself. I'll see you in an hour."

She was about to go back to Adam when Carl asked her to dance. She hadn't danced with Carl since he was twelve years old and she was teaching him the box step. Now he fairly glided about the room, still gleaming as he had earlier in the evening but before she could tell him how handsome he was, how dangerous he looked, how well he danced, one of the boys from the hockey team had taken over and was swirling and twirling her as the music picked up.

"Your mother can really dance." Carl turned. Chrissy had appeared beside him, her cheeks flushed, eyes sparking. "You?"

"Sure," Carl said. She stepped towards him. Into him. Put her hands on the back of his neck, pressed her breasts into his shirt. They were dancing, turning, Carl had drunk too much, he felt like a merry-go-round that couldn't stop. He closed his eyes but it didn't help, his body was trying to get out of his skin and into Chrissy's.

"You like this?"

He opened his eyes. "It's crazy," he said, his head bent down to her, his mouth so close to hers that their lips brushed as he talked. "What's—" And then they were in the hall, still standing mouth to mouth, not talking or kissing or anything at all except feeling their bodies go wild. Until a hand fell on Carl's shoulder and Carl turned to see Fred Verghoers, Chrissy's boyfriend, squinting into his face as though Carl were a bucket of beans, a bucket of beans he was about to pour into the garbage.

They were surrounded, separated, pushed outside. Standing in the thick drifting snow, light clinging to the moist flakes. Drunk, he had been drunk and then his blood ran hot for Chrissy and now Fred's fist was coming at him like a fat bulldozer and before he could move it ploughed through the centre of his face. All he could feel were his nose and cheeks going numb and his arse banging into the snow so hard he bounced up again, arms and fists churning, until it was him looking down at Fred writhing in the snow while his own knuckles burned and burned. Chrissy kneeling over her man, others pulling Fred up, leading Fred and Chrissy away while he was taken to one of the stables, surrounded, fed brandy and cigarettes.

It was five in the morning when they came out to take the cardboard off the windshield. The sleet had stopped, the sky was clear, a brisk north wind was blowing in their faces. "You're too drunk to drive," Elizabeth told McKelvey. "Give me the keys."

McKelvey, pale and exhausted, brought his keys out of his pocket, then looked searchingly at Elizabeth. "If I'm too drunk, so are you. Carl can drive." As he handed the keys to Carl he slipped on the ice and Elizabeth and Carl had to catch him. They packed him into the back seat. Then Elizabeth got into the front.

"You can drive if you want to," Carl said. "Dad's asleep."

"Go ahead."

They started off, rolling slowly out of town towards their farm. The blacktop that had been partly clear on the way in now had a thin layer of ice but at least it had been sanded.

As Carl drove, Elizabeth hummed. She liked having Carl drive. She felt safe with him, the way she once had with McKelvey. When she closed her eyes and started dreaming, the afternoons in the motels came back — the starched smell of motel sheets, the way one time she and Adam had drunk a bottle of wine and watched soap operas — and as the car began to fishtail she dreamed they were on an ocean liner, she and Adam, he was holding her in his arms, and as the floor tilted they were waltzing — she didn't wake up until the car left the road. Carl's face was twisted in fear and panic; she wanted to reach out to reassure him but there was no time, the car was already folding into the tree, her head smashing into the windshield. And as she began floating out of her body she promised herself that she would hover over Carl, stay with him always, keep him safe. But her whole body was still in motion; the car had stopped, she was hurtling through the windshield, her skull had broken open and the last thing she saw was the snow alive with starlight.

PART V

ONE

*F*OR THANKSGIVING, ARNIE WENT down to visit Marilyn and the children in Kingston. The bypass had been postponed until February because hospital budget cuts had taken two nurses off the heart unit. "You'd think they wouldn't want people dropping dead in the street just to save a few dollars," Arnie Kincaid said. This was after the meal was finished and the children were out playing in the last of the sun. Following the sharp frosts and the rains, the warmth had suddenly returned and the smell of gold and scarlet leaves was enough to make you cry — if you were the kind to cry about the weather or to think this Thanksgiving might be your last.

"You're not going to drop dead in the street or anywhere else," Marilyn said. "You're too important to too many people."

"One person thinks I'm pretty important. Fred Verghoers. Remember him? He's running for reeve now and he came by. First to fire up his policy — you wouldn't believe how much that man thinks he's worth — then to ask me to go on the radio to support him. Imagine! On the radio! Big-time politician, he's putting together some kind of advertising campaign. They've even done a television special on him. It's going to be broadcast tonight. Can you believe it? Fred Verghoers on television? He told me he's part of a whole new wave of independent politicians who are going to save the country."

"Fred Verghoers?"

"Him."

"Lives with Chrissy McKelvey? The girl who used to be with Carl?"

"That's the one."

"You like him?"

"Fred? Not much."

"What did you tell him?"

"Well, I told him I'd think about it. Luke Richardson is running against him and I guess the Richardsons already have enough."

Marilyn looked out the window towards the children, the way she always did when she was about to say something important and Arnie had the horrible feeling she was going to tell him she had some kind of disease. Trust Marilyn to wait until lunch was over and the children outside.

"Chrissy was in the emergency a few weeks ago. She thought she was having a heart attack. Twenty-nine years old. Then they found out the real problem was she had three broken ribs."

"How do you know?"

"I've been filing in the X-ray department this month. I recognized the name so I looked. Don't tell anyone."

"Is this is a big secret?"

"I didn't think it was. How secret is a broken rib? But I told Doreen and Doreen said Fred must be beating up on her. She used to be in the book club and twice she had bruises on her arms. When Doreen asked her about them, Chrissy stopped coming. Anyway, how else could you have broken ribs and not even know? Or want to say?"

That night Arnie switched on the television to watch the clip on Freddy. The Allnew people must have somehow arranged it, Arnie figured. There was a long advertisement for nursing homes that started him thinking he should make some sort of arrangement for himself, then without warning came a big picture of the sign outside town:

WEST GULL

pop. 684

On TV Fred came across as forceful and surprisingly artic-ulate. He stood in front of the lumber-yard office, arms folded across his manager's vest, and looked straight into the camera while he spoke about "folks having to pull their weight" and the need for "responsible people in the countryside to rebuild from the ground up while we look to the future and respect the past." There was something appealingly direct in the way he talked and that same straightforward quality came out in a clip of him playing hockey with the West Gull Hornets. A strong-skating defenceman, nothing fancy or dipsy-doodle, he was shown scoring on a lucky slapshot, then getting knocked over. As he stood up grinning for the camera and wiping his hands, he wore the same smile he had after he scored. Here was a solid team player, a man who knew how to dish it out and how to take it. Another segment showed him going to church with his "life partner" and her child. A believer but not a conformist, a businessman but not wealthy. The kind of per-son you feel you know because you've seen his face close up and it's a face that isn't trying to hide anything.

———

The next morning Arnie went into Allnew, as he'd promised, to talk to Fred. His broadcast must have been an instant success: there was a television crew from Kingston in the store, the floor was a tangle of wires and a battery of cameras and lights were being focused on the counter behind which Fred usually stood making up the orders.

"I never knew it would be like this," Fred said. He took Arnie's arm, led him towards his office at the side. "It must be costing them a fortune. Look at all these people, all this stuff."

Arnie closed the office door behind him. Fred was shaven clean as marble and he wore a fancy striped shirt beneath his vest.

"Well?"

"I have to tell you something," Arnie Kincaid said.

"Shoot."

"My daughter works at the KGH."

"I support the KGH, Arnie, you know that. There's people all through the township depend on that hospital."

"She says Chrissy came in there a few weeks ago with three broken ribs." Arnie hadn't planned these exact words; they just popped out. Fred's eyes stayed on Arnie's as though they were engaged in a staring contest. His arms were folded across his chest.

"She fell on the old outside stairs to the basement. The concrete must have caught her. It took me days to talk her into getting an X-ray."

The door opened. But it was too late to stop now. "I don't believe you. Touch her again and I'm calling the police."

"You're confused, old man." Fred turned to the open doorway. Ned Richardson was standing there. He was carrying a plastic bag, as though he had brought his lunch.

"They told me you were in here," the boy stammered. "I was coming by to ask about that job."

A television crewman appeared beside Ned. "We're ready if you are. Come over here and we'll give you some make-up. Otherwise everyone's going to think you're a ghost."

Fred's face cleared. He moved towards the door. "Just a bit of business to finish," he said. He closed the door. The room was too small for the three of them. Fred folded his arms again and Arnie could feel his anger surging out, a tidal wave of rage. This must be how it was for Chrissy, helplessly waiting for Fred to explode. Fred stepped close to Arnie and Arnie's heart felt like an old blood-filled sock, leaking and oozing into his chest. He reached into his pocket for one of the emergency pills the doctor had given him.

Fred Verghoers turned to Ned. The boy was pale but strangely defiant. "You came at the wrong time," Fred said putting his left hand on Ned's shoulder.

Fred's move was too much for Ned, who clutched his bag to his belly, gave a little cry and looked as though he was about to evaporate from terror. "Don't panic, boys," Arnie said, in control again. "I guess we found out what we need to know." He pushed past Fred and sat down in his chair. "Ned, you go out and get me a glass of water so I can swallow this pill. Fred, go powder your nose. We can continue this meeting later."

By the time Ned got back with the water, Fred was getting his instructions in front of the cameras. Arnie sat in the empty office awhile, reading the newspaper. After a time his heart felt normal again. The old sock might be oozing but it wasn't quite ready to split. He walked out the back way and into the sunlight. Just like that. He leaned on the car and let the heat reflect into his face. Alive! Every now and then came a slight understanding of how temporary and unlikely that was.

Ned was on the highway again, goosing the pedal to the floor, filling his head with the sound of the engine. At the Second Line Road he wheeled to the right, a skidding turn that sent out a fan of flying gravel behind him. Lu-Ann had called him the other night, half-drunk, sounded like she had a roadhouse behind her. Started crying about how much she missed him but she hung up without saying where she was, just when he was going to tell her how he had been dumped by Ellie. Left him standing there, holding the phone, all charged up. The last time he'd driven by Fred's house he was afraid to slow down. Now he had what he had and he turned in, suddenly feeling calm.

He honked the horn, then sat in the driveway for a moment. Chrissy was at the kitchen window looking at him. He walked across the lawn. Chrissy opened the door before he could knock.

"Just driving by," he said. "Thought I'd drop in."

She started towards the kitchen and he followed her. She was wearing tight faded jeans, a sweatshirt, old running shoes. After that video it was weird to see her in clothes and he wondered how she would react to knowing he had examined every detail of her body. Or that one night he had taken her two brassieres and three pairs of underpants out to the manure pile behind the pig barn and dug them in there with the rest of the compost. She seemed to Ned to be small and tight, a wound-up little package. Something electric in the way she moved. Nothing like Lu-Ann; Lu-Ann was a *girl*. But still. He'd figured out what he was doing. He sat down at the kitchen table.

"So?"

"I was over at Allnew. Fred has been telling me a job might open up."

"Okay."

"Well, it didn't. Not yet. Anyway he was busy with the television. I was hoping you could put in a word for me." She had a sharp little face. Probably a sharp tongue, too. Being with her this way — in the kitchen, Chrissy in her clothes — he was starting to forget what she looked like on the tape. Of course he'd heard what Arnie Kincaid said. So now everyone in town knew what was going on. He always left her face clear so you couldn't easily tell. But you can't go to hospital and keep things a secret.

"Sure, I'll tell him you came," Chrissy said.

"I did the swimming once at Point Gull. In the mornings. You used to bring Lizzie."

"I remember. Okay. I'll tell him."

Ned wondered what his father would think if he knew he was here in Chrissy's kitchen. "You remember Carl," Ned said.

"Yeah. What are you doing here anyway? I'm going to have to ask you to leave. If you don't, I'll call the police."

"Don't call the police," Ned said and saw her face jump.

"Yes, I will." And suddenly she had one of those cordless phones in her hand and was punching in numbers.

Ned moved back towards the door. "Wait. I just wanted to warn you—"

When Ned jumped out of the truck he had stood there in the drive, bobbing and twitching like some kind of nut. Then, when he'd come in, she had noticed the streaks at the corners of his eyes from crying. She had thought at first that Fred must have hit him. A little surprise attack when it wasn't expected, that was his specialty. Except that after the first one you were always expecting it, always afraid, always ready to believe he would go the next step, which in her case would mean Lizzie.

When Marbles had disappeared she'd been sure Fred was responsible. Even after Carl called to say he'd found the body and buried it — which at least made Lizzie feel better — she thought Fred was behind the whole thing, just raising the stakes the way he liked to when he played poker. Poker was how she'd met him again. She'd just dropped in for something at Doreen and Ben's, and while they were trading gossip over coffee she'd somehow ended up standing behind Fred. There was something so confident about the way he played his cards, so *solid*, that she fell back into being with him almost before they'd said hello.

Ned Richardson was still a boy. Skin like boiled marrow, pale pebbled eyes. He was trying to scare her but he was just scaring himself.

"It's time for you to go," Chrissy said. She held up the phone. Her father had given it to her after that night Fred had totally lost control, when she'd come back from being with Carl. Well, she'd brought that one on herself but at least she got something for it. She'd told her parents she'd fallen while feeding the chickens and her father had given her the phone so she could carry it around with her in case she did something incredibly stupid again, fell down the well or something. Then at least she could call. She'd wondered if he suspected. Not that it mattered. Whatever he knew he couldn't know the whole thing. The way she'd made it part of her life.

The Allnew number was coded in but she wanted to see what Ned would do. She was surprised how quickly he'd jumped, how fast he got to the door. Then he started again about what Fred was going to do to Carl.

Carl's number was also coded in. That was for Lizzie. When he answered, his voice rough with sleep, she said, "It's

Chrissy here, Ned Richardson is standing in my kitchen, telling me something you should know. I'm going to give him the phone."

"Sure."

"I don't want to talk to him," Ned said.

"Now he doesn't want to talk to you."

"Something going on?" Carl asked. "You want me to come over?" His voice had cleared. Suddenly Chrissy had a huge lump in her throat and was on the verge of bursting into tears.

"I'll come to you," Chrissy said. And then, looking straight at Ned, "Ned Richardson's in my kitchen. He's bothering me. If I'm not there in twenty minutes I'd like you to find Ned."

"You can tell him I'm looking for him already. I'll look a bit harder."

"I will. Twenty minutes. Set your watch." She hung up.

Ned was standing at the door, rigid, as though he was wrapped in some kind of invisible ice. Chrissy put the phone down. "Carl says he's looking for you already. I think you've been pretty foolish, Ned. No matter who your father is, you shouldn't come around threatening people. Now what you'd better do is go home, talk to your mom and dad, get things worked out and keep it quiet for a while. Do you understand me, Ned?"

"Yes'm."

"I'm telling you the truth, Ned. Now why don't you just get going?"

He was still hesitating at the door. His lips were parted and he was starting to pant. The smell of sweat filled the room. For the first time it occurred to Chrissy that she might have pushed too hard.

"I got something in the truck," Ned said.

Chrissy tapped her watch. "Go home, Ned."

"I know something," Ned said, "but I'm going to leave. I never wanted to hurt or threaten you. I was just trying to warn you. Next time I won't do you the favour."

He swung out the door and slammed it behind him, then started towards his truck.

"You smoking again?"

"I guess so," Chrissy said. Except for when they were exchanging Lizzie, this was the first time she'd seen him since the dance. He looked good. Less hollow in the cheeks and under the eyes and more solid than when he'd arrived. Better without that moustache, though there was still a small ridged scar from Fred's ring. "Things going well for you?"

"Not so bad," Carl said. "It's good to be seeing Lizzie. Good for both of us."

"And living here, living here alone, is that good too?"

"It's better than what I had."

"It's all right. I don't mind. I was the one who threw you out, remember? We were like one of those hurting songs. That's all we could do, hurt each other."

She wasn't really looking at him but she caught that little flicker. So. Carl had heard about Fred, too. That's how she thought about it — something about Freddy. She knew it was going to start getting around after she went to hospital. She truly hadn't realized her ribs were broken. She just thought he'd given her some kind of heart attack. Fred had sure chosen his time to run for reeve. Even the way everyone hated Luke Richardson.

"What about you and Fred?" They were sitting at Carl's kitchen table, across from each other. They each had their mug and there was the coffee pot between them. The way they used to sit at home just after they married and before Lizzie was born. Carl had quit drinking to keep her company and they would spend the evenings across from each other like this, Carl smoking cigarettes and doing crosswords while she knitted all those crazy little pink clothes she'd started on when they were told it was going to be a girl.

"We hurt each other, too," she finally said. She was looking down at her hands. It was strange how small they still were. Carl's hands, Fred's hands, even Ned's hands were big and meaty with nasty swollen knuckles. Men's hands. Her own were just her old little girl's hands, stubby and rough despite the dozens of tubs of skin cream they'd absorbed. "We do it in different ways. Same idea though. But he takes care of me, too. Pays the bills. Always comes home. Doesn't screw around."

Pays the bills. Always comes home. Doesn't screw around. Three points about which Carl couldn't have boasted.

"I've heard it's pretty bad."

"Ned Richardson's talking it up because Fred won't give him a job at the lumber yard."

"Seems to me Fred's getting a bit carried away."

"I heard what happened to you." Now she was looking straight at him. He was so vulnerable still. "I'm really sorry. It was my fault."

Carl stood up and took the coffee pot to the stove. "All over now. We're the best of friends. Luke is getting me to take them both hunting after the election, haven't you heard?"

"Yeah. It made me laugh. I figure you'll be crawling around trying to shoot each other." She liked the feeling of his kitchen. Warm and cozy. And it was important for Lizzie to live here part of the time. Not always. Lizzie needed her mother. You just had to know Carl to see what could happen without one.

"So what are you going to do? You going to wait until he kills you?"

"Maybe I still love him. It's not so bad. He's not going to kill me. It's just that he's always been crazy jealous of you. Because of Lizzie. We tried to have another baby but he can't. So it's like you got something he didn't. Then you came back and you got what he has."

"You making excuses for him?"

"Maybe for myself." She was looking at her hands again and her throat was choking up. Couldn't Carl figure out that if she phoned the police Fred would do something to Lizzie? Did he think she was some kind of saint or punching bag or that her father had pulled her pants down when she was a little girl?

"I don't like it," Carl said.

"Neither do I."

She folded up her cigarettes. "I better get going. I'm supposed to be throwing a tea party this afternoon for all of Fred's lady canvassers. You wouldn't believe what you have to go through to get elected reeve these days. And then there's this television stuff—" She stopped. She couldn't believe the sound of her own voice, how she was boasting about Fred like a mother boasting about her favourite son.

"Probably going to win," Carl said. "They'll put you on a throne or something. You can slip me a fiver for a bowl of soup." They were both standing up and now, Chrissy thought, it was as though they hardly knew each other. As though she had only been here canvassing for Fred, just another cup of coffee, another vote to mark down on the chart.

She moved towards the door, Carl lagging at a good distance. "We'll see you later," he said. Then he winked.

That stopped her. "I never saw you wink before."

He grinned. "Got a few new tricks."

They were standing outside now and the gold late-morning light was shining straight into Carl's face, making the silver hairs in his stubble glitter like bits of foil from a Christmas tree. She stood on her tiptoes, the way she used to, and kissed him, just once, just quickly, just enough to touch the strong coffee taste of his lips.

She saw him at the door watching as she drove away. Maybe she hadn't told him what he hadn't already heard but it was the first time she'd said anything at all to anyone. The weird thing was that even right now, even with the taste of Carl's kiss on her mouth, she didn't want to leave Fred. She had wanted to hurt him but she didn't want to leave him. The night with Carl had been — well, it had to happen once.

Driving home she found herself counting campaign signs, the way she always did these days. The truth was, things were changing fast. Fred was gaining; sometimes, if you took the right roads, you'd hardly see a Luke Richardson sign, it was Freddy all the way.

TWO

You got something he didn't. Then you came back and you also got what he has. When she'd said this, Chrissy had been looking down at her fingers as they fooled around with a cigarette. But Carl had known what she meant; and he knew how having and not having Lizzie had eaten away at him for three years. How there was nothing that being cut off from Lizzie couldn't make hollow and worthless.

It was three weeks since the signs had gone up. Meanwhile the rains had stopped and West Gull had settled into Indian summer. Carl, driving along, tried to imagine himself as Fred seeing a big blue VERGHOERS FOR REEVE sign floating across a field. Luke and Fred and their little games, tossing him back and forth between them like two dogs worrying a rabid fox, each hoping the other would get bitten.

Carl looked at his watch. One-fifteen. At noon the air in town had been smoky with October heat. Now the sky was already emptying out, leaving a gold-blue bruise at the horizon. From behind the seat he pulled out the shotgun Luke Richardson had brought to the store. "I use it for deer," he had said, pushing it across the counter.

Carl had set it down on the floor, out of sight. He'd almost had to laugh, as if where Luke wanted him to aim it was supposed to be a big mystery. "The weather's so good," Luke had said, "I thought you might like the day off. You could run up to the conservation area. See if you could scare something up."

The campgrounds had been closed since Labour Day, the gate left open for the winter. Carl drove down the dirt road, then across the small field to the dam before he stopped the truck and got out.

Now he leaned against the fender, popped open a can of diet cola. Across from the dam was a ridge he'd once climbed with Chrissy. It was this time of year, October, during another Indian summer, the fallen leaves thick in the hollows between the roots. He'd buried Chrissy in maple leaves, just her nose, her toes, her nipples sticking out, then burrowed under to be with her. A cold earthy smell on her skin and breath. Wanting him over and over until they were both exhausted and crawled down to the lake, covered in leaves and bits of grass and sticks, two grubby earth animals emerging after a hibernation of sex, cigarettes, grunts and groans, a new way her face turned up and away from his as though he was in so deep her brain was burning up from it. And swimming he had been surprised to find himself wishing he knew what it was like to be a woman and feel things so deeply his brain burned up from all that feeling.

He walked slowly along that same ridge, his legs and back slowly relaxing. When he flushed a pair of grouse from beneath some junipers he didn't even think of shooting. As their wings beat against the ground his heart hammered along. Then they emerged, great brown stonebirds rising slowly into the air, gathering speed as they crashed their way clear to open space.

"Carl McKelvey without a gun," Luke had said, shaking his head. It now seemed to Carl that Luke had been trying to get into his mind and possess it from the moment he walked into the Timberpost Restaurant his first day back.

"What else is new," Carl said to himself. Then stopped. *This* was new. Having a man like Luke Richardson trying to do something to him was new. He thought again about Luke coming into the Timberpost, how Luke had stood over him as he ate, sizing him up. But if Luke Richardson was doing him, he wasn't the only one getting done. When he said the words "Mr. Richardson" in the supermarket next door, no one flinched or giggled. Everyone walked around the name of Luke Richardson: Luke Richardson, the black Cadillac of Luke Richardson, even the thought of Luke Richardson was a big hole to be avoided. Luke Richardson and Fred might be toying with him together, but Luke, Luke with his "savvy" would figure he had both of them outmanoeuvred.

The sun angled through the trees. Ping ping ping. Little bursts of yellow-gold light, ripples of warm air, the slush-slushing of leaves underfoot. After he had circled the lake and started moving north along the old hydro slash, he took out his cigarette package and found the joint of homegrown Ray Johnson had given him the other night.

Hearing the sound of an airplane he moved from the open into the woods. By the time the airplane, a single-prop, was overhead, Carl was under the canopy of a large oak. As a child on the farm his favourite game had been to imagine that while he was asleep a war had started and everyone he knew had been captured or killed. The War Game, he called it. His job was to hide until he had a chance to rescue his mother. So he had taught himself to move out of sight at the sound of motors, to always leave gaps in his conversation and even his thinking so he could hear everything around himself before he was heard.

Now he was hidden where neither Luke nor Fred could see him. One way of assessing his position: he was comfortably crouched in the centre of a sun-dappled thicket smoking marijuana, absolutely invulnerable to the Richardson-Verghoers single-prop spy network. Victory! Second assessment: Luke and Fred had succeeded in driving him to ground. He was hidden from them but they were likewise hidden from him. When he emerged — from these shadows, from this afternoon, from behind some tree he hadn't yet seen or some door he hadn't yet opened — Luke or Fred or both of them would finish him off. The way Fred had jumped him that night when he came out of the Movie Barn. The way he'd jumped Chrissy when she came home from the bar.

Carl was sweating. He made himself breathe out all the air in his lungs. Without his willing it a new map had grown into his mind. It was a rectangle of trees criss-crossed by old logging trails and hydro slashes. In one corner was a lake, in another a picture of a compass pointing north. In the centre of the map, surrounded by bush, was an X. X as in X marks the spot, X marks the scar, X marks Carl McKelvey, stoned and sun-dazed, just waking up to what was really going on. His only weapon was the shotgun Luke had given him, a small box of cartridges he'd bought at the hardware store. His only supplies: half a pack of cigarettes and some sugarless cinnamon gum that Lizzie had put in his pocket the day they took the video camera out.

Above him in the plane, or waiting out of sight near the truck or somewhere in the woods, was Luke Richardson. Carl pushed back at his hair. This was crazy. He got a picture of himself pushing back at his hair in the centre of Luke Richardson's scope. The ultimate mindfuck: a bullet passing through his brain. He stripped the tinfoil off a stick of his gum and began to chew. The cinnamon reminded him of the smell of Saturday night toast the way his mother used to make it: butter, brown sugar, fresh-ground cinnamon. He could feel his brain pulsing in his skull, twitching like an overheated muscle.

He opened the shotgun, let the shells fall to the ground. Immediately he felt better. He lit a cigarette. Luke Richardson, he advised himself — if you can't handle the Luke Richardsons of this world, you're in trouble. He was sitting cross-legged on the ground, his back against a thick beech, the collar of his denim jacket bunched around his neck.

The sun was starting to angle and the long grass of the hydro slash danced with its own shadows. He got to his knees, looked slowly around. He stood up. Walking slowly, silent as night, he edged back towards the lake. The woods. The ground. The ruts of glaciated earth. If he moved slowly now, the way his father had taught him, the way he'd always known, no one, not even Luke Richardson, would see him until he wanted to be seen. The War Game. It was the game he always won. Until, of course, instead of saving his mother he had killed her. What do you think of that? Carl asked himself. How long do you think it will be before, when you finally go calm inside yourself, your first thought isn't that you killed your mother? For ever? So far it was ten years going on eleven. At least in that time it had become a thought he could allow himself to think without immediately needing to drown it. That was progress. And more: sometimes he could propose to himself that the accident had actually *been* an accident, not a manifestation of his personal evil but something that had happened by chance. *Chance.* As if anyone could believe there was such a thing as a random throw of the dice.

A small scraggly V of geese honked their way through the pale blue air. Travelling refugees. The other night he'd brought *Star Wars* home from the shop and watched it with Lizzie. Played with the idea that he, Lizzie and a few others scattered across the face of the planet were the rebel army. The only ones left who knew how to say no. Everyone else was part of the Empire; whether they knew it or not they were conscript soldiers, life-crushers, mindfucked robots blindly tramping over other life-crushed, mindfucked lives. Not McKelvey. He'd lived on the edge of the whole thing, watched it crumble around him. But Luke Richardson, all Luke Richardson needed was an officer's uniform and leather boots. Luke was one of those officers who thought he was smarter than the system, was convinced he could play it both ways. In movies, men like Luke Richardson scared you at the beginning, then got finished off by someone bigger, stronger, smarter. Someone like Fred. Despite all his plans, his "savvy," his toy castle.

By the time Carl had circled the lake and regained the beech tree, two hours had passed. He sat down in a pile of leaves to smoke a cigarette and watch the fading play of light across the dark mirror of the water. He had forgotten about Fred, Luke, anything that wasn't air, water, earth, the long clouds parked above the horizon, the violet merchant ships of night bringing their cargoes of darkness.

On the way back from the campgrounds he kept taking little sideroads, making excuses to stretch out the drive. It was that lazy late afternoon feeling. You could drive for ever with the windows open, taking in the sharp snap of the leaves, the way the slanted light ran between the trees. The October after the accident, when the weather turned irresistibly golden, he and Chrissy had played hooky for a week, slipping out every afternoon to drive around in the sun, find somewhere to park the truck, walk through the bush until they found a little sunlit meadow, a warm patch of moss, a pine tree waiting for two people exactly like them to whip off their clothes and roll around in its soft blanket of needles.

Without meaning to he realized he'd worked his way close to the farmhouse on the Second Line Road. There was a back concession no one used any more with a dilapidated barn beside a creek. After they moved into the farmhouse from the barber-shop apartment, Chrissy so pregnant he'd groaned carrying her over the doorsill, he would walk from the farmhouse back to the barn and daydream that when he'd saved some money he would turn it into a carpenter's workshop. There would be the stream, the trees, some chipmunks he always saw when he went there — Lizzie would come and sit by the water, have her own daydreams while he worked away inside. Of course he knew it was foolish. Furniture was made in factories now. No one was going to search out a fixed-up barn on a dirt road off the Second Line just so some guy who should be working in a milk store could watch his daughter playing with chipmunks beside some stream. Still.

He parked the truck behind the old barn. Then he walked out to the dirt road and kicked leaves over the tire tracks. Since the last time he'd visited another of the barn's corners had given way. Now the barn was toppling forward in slow motion like a giant beast whose front legs had collapsed.

He'd left because he had to, left Lizzie without wanting to, but also left everything that could remind him of Chrissy: the places they'd made love, the smell of her skin, the way they'd burned together. Burning and intensity: that was what he'd liked, Carl knew. They'd burned down all the barriers and then Lizzie had been born and Chrissy had turned away from him and so, eventually, he also had turned. First to drinking, then to someone warmer to fill his hands when he ran out of bottles. Now that he was back, it was as though he was inside where they'd been all the time. The sky. The quick little licks of breeze. The flutter of poplar leaves against the barn's torn tin roof. That morning she'd come for coffee, whatever separated present from past had momentarily disappeared. He could have reached across the table to her. It wouldn't have been like that night they'd met at Frostie's, a memory desperate to be rekindled. A kiss he had almost forgotten. Almost lost the taste for. Until the second, the third, the tenth. But he still felt he owed her something, something to be delivered to Fred.

For a long moment he looked at Luke's shotgun on the truck floor. He opened the door, took it out, carefully wiped his fingerprints before hiding it under a nearby juniper bush. Then he locked the truck and set off on the old cowpath that would eventually lead him to the hills behind Chrissy and Fred's house, the house where he'd once lived with Chrissy.

The trail skirted the edge of a cedar swamp and climbed into a maple bush that Chrissy's uncle had still been tapping when he died. The barn, the swamp, the bush, all the fields and pasture that had gone with the old farm had been sold off to the neighbour. Now the bush was littered with deadfall and thick piles of maple leaves that swirled around his ankles with every step.

When he came up to the big field on the other side of the swamp he could see that the neighbour had converted the hay into corn. The dark rich soil was littered with fragments of stalks and corn silk. The field joined the neighbour's land and in the distance freshly painted barns and silos rose like a mirage of a city.

It was twilight by the time he had worked his way to the small hill overlooking the house. He drew his jacket close and lay on the ground. Now he was perfectly positioned to worm his way to the hill's crest and look down at the house. From the house itself he would be totally invisible. A perfect hiding place for a war game, when you wanted to watch as the enemy soldiers came and searched for you. He had always meant to introduce Lizzie to the game, show her this perfect place but for now it was his secret, and after the sun set only he could find his way through the dark to the old barn where he'd hidden the truck. Even Chrissy had never made the walk with him — just he and the cattle knew the way through the cedar swamp that separated the two.

He moved forward and peered over the hill. A cluster of cars and trucks were parked near the road and a dozen people were standing on the front lawn, silent and waiting. White screens, light umbrellas, two long foam covered sound booms had turned the lawn into a mini-Hollywood. Spotlights began to glow and gradually worked themselves to a dazzling brilliance that bathed the front of the house, the driveway, the entire movie set full of technicians and equipment in a glaring white light.

Carl now remembered that Nancy Brookner had told him they were doing television shows about Fred. He had thought that meant Fred standing in front of Allnew, giving some kind of speech to be played on the Kingston television news. This was more like *Gone with the Wind*. Customers would probably be clamouring to rent it at the store.

He began to retreat but found himself too curious to leave. Chrissy emerged from the house, accompanied by a woman with a clipboard giving her instructions. They went back in. The lights dimmed for a moment and Carl saw a car sweeping down the Second Line towards the house. Up came the lights again, full force. This was *light!* The spots on Luke Richardson's house were dim toys in comparison. There was a red glow from the camera following Fred's car into the driveway. As he stepped out, another camera had the same red glow — this one was pointed to the door of the house and was focused on Chrissy as she came out to meet him.

Strange to think that movies were made this way: giant concentrations of lights, screens, cameras and technicians all focused on a couple of tiny figures playing out their parts. Too bad the cameras hadn't been in position a few weeks ago when Fred had broken Chrissy's ribs. A little punch-up was always popular. Or in his kitchen that morning to get Chrissy's version of Fred. Or maybe the fact that Fred beat the shit out of Chrissy *wasn't* the big story. After all, *this* was the Fred Verghoers people would play on their video clips, show to their grandchildren. Even Lizzie would look at it over and over again, the way she'd watched that silly scene Carl had taken of her waking up. To Lizzie, the movies of herself were more real than the Lizzie who was watching. Like actors who drank, fought, screwed around, needed operations to fix their livers and their bellies and their faces. Everyone knew but no one cared. They were hungry for that moment on the screen, that moment when the bright lights closed in on the smooth shining skin, just the way the bright lights were now closing in on Chrissy's face. All that glare must be killing her eyes, Carl thought, but her eyes were wide open and she was floating towards the man of her dreams — *Maybe I still love him. It's not so bad* — as he smiled and waited.

Passing cars stopped to watch. From one of them came a shout. The lights were so bright Carl couldn't see through to the disturbance. Meanwhile Chrissy and Fred were replaying the heartwarming moment where she wafted dreamily towards Fred while Fred, smiling, moved up to her and gave her a kiss. Nothing too sexy. Just a little smooch to show how loving this loving couple was. Then Lizzie appeared, walking towards Fred and Chrissy as though joining this celebration of love was the high point of all her afternoons. Of course they would need that. The token child. Maybe they'd hired a few dogs to jump up and lick at Fred's face.

The shouting had started again; "He's a fucking fraud" ripped through the dark autumn air. Ned Richardson burst into the circle of light. He had a plastic bag and was waving it accusingly at Fred. "Do you want me to show them what's here? Do you want me to—" A technician grabbed at him but Ned pushed him off. He plunged his hand inside the bag as Fred started towards him.

"Everyone stand back," Fred said. It was amazing how cool he sounded, the dry authority of his voice cracking through the night, the lights, the cameras.

"I told you to get out!" Chrissy shouted.

Ned was still advancing. "I warned you. Now everyone's going to know."

Lizzie was standing at the edge of the light, her mouth opening in a scream as Ned's hand emerged from the bag. Fred jumped, his arms and legs spread wide as he came crashing down on Ned, taking him to the ground.

Culture and intelligence can recognize each other — or so the intelligent and cultured like to believe. They know each other's ways, each other's books, each other's costumes and disguises. "O what a tangled web we weave." And reducing such a web to a single filament leading from beginning to end makes excellent grist for detective novels, even for actual detectives if they recognize in the tangled motives and deliberately blurred trails minds like their own.

But before the master detective must come the mastermind, the master criminal. That would be me, Adam decided when Carl, lying half-dead in front of the shop, told him Fred was responsible. In his first moments of rage Adam wanted to chase Fred down and shoot him. But Adam, being himself, had neither a gun nor the know-how to use one. After his visit with Carl, he joined the Napanee Target Shooting Club but one night of blasting out his eardrums told him not even rage could transform the court eunuch into the mad gunfighter. One advantage of reading Shakespeare — or even Tolstoy — is that you learn every player is doomed to stay in character.

Stay in character. Accept and understand the situation fate had dealt him. That was what he would have to do. Fate had first given him love, then a son. But the love had been taken away and he had been walled off from the son by secrecy. Now, after almost thirty years of keeping that secret, the wall had started to come down: fate was offering him the chance to save his son's life. The first instalment had already arrived. He'd been the one to find Carl. Now he had the opportunity to secure Carl's future.

Adam needed time to think, yet he also needed to be sure Carl would do nothing precipitous. That was why he had suggested Luke take Fred and Carl hunting. Luke caught on right away, slapping Adam on the shoulder, grinning until his face threatened to break with the cunning hilarity of it all. The idea that three would go and only two would come back was something Adam didn't have to say. Afterwards Luke would explain it was an accident or a camp-fire brawl and then he'd have Carl so deep in his pocket that Carl would never crawl out.

So. Perfect. Perfect for Luke. And perfect for Adam because Carl, believing his revenge was coming, would hold back until the hunting trip, which would be the second week in November, a week after the election and the beginning of the north country deer season. That gave Adam almost a month to come up with a plan.

Bits of dust caught in the light. Colours. Unexpected waterfalls. And of course the body. Warm skin on cool sheets. The blood's night hum. Summer heat seeping through damp moss. The raw smell of an oak tree opened in winter. So much to love that life should be made out of loving, so many ways of loving that all stories should be love stories.

The day Carl walked to the house on the Second Line after hiding his truck near the collapsing barn that had once held so many of his dreams was one of those mythic late October days — a sunset day in a sunset month when the gold and scarlet autumn leaves shine as though shining from inside, when every hill, every tree, every rock and blade of grass is etched in the perfect light.

That same October day Adam Goldsmith was also caught up in the magic of burnished sun, burnished memories, collapsed dreams. He left work in the late afternoon to walk the road from town to the West Gull Cemetery. A tall man who had begun to take on weight over the years, washed-out blue eyes hardly visible behind the thick lenses of his steel-rimmed glasses, Adam Goldsmith seemed to be floating about in even more of a trance than was his habit. So serene, so ethereal were his movements that as he opened the gate and let himself into the cemetery he might have been a ghost returning to his grave after a hard day of haunting. But even inside the cemetery Adam Goldsmith kept moving: from his mother's grave to what would one day be his own, pausing only briefly to consider the grass that would form his ceiling and roof; to Elizabeth's grave where he stood for a long time; lastly to the cemetery's western edge where he watched the beginnings of the sunset and thought about what he had to do. By the time he started back towards West Gull, the cemetery was in shadows and as he walked down the hill darkness folded over the lake.

When he got home, Adam took out his mother's typewriter and began pounding out the message of the graveyard:

THE LION SHALL LIE DOWN WITH THE LAMB

Hope, yes. The mastermind had been at work but aside from fate and what fate had willed him to do, there was also hope. Hope in the purest sense. His desperate and unfounded hope that Fred, Carl and Luke might suddenly resolve their differences, open their hearts, submit to the harmonies of peace and love. A hope unsupported by reason, reality or even faith. Faith! "I hope I've taught you faith," his mother had said to him when he left West Gull for university, and ever since Adam had been puzzling over her meaning. Belief in the scriptures? In God? In the triumph of good over evil? At the time he had wondered how anyone of any education or experience could possibly have faith in such things. But when he began distributing his messages, he thought his mother would approve of his efforts in discipleship. And now the triumph of good over evil had become his sole and overwhelming task. Justice was his to render. Justice! He sat at the typewriter euphorically pounding out his optimistic prophecy at the same time that he was perfecting the last details of the most masterly of his master plans.

One night when Lizzie was in Carl's care, Adam would park the car on the road outside Chrissy's. From there — this he had already checked — he would be able to see Chrissy and Fred eating dinner, framed by the light, their heads bobbing up and down from their plates like birds at a birdbath. They always sat down at exactly seven o'clock, half an hour after Fred got home. Using his cellphone Adam would telephone Chrissy. She would go into the kitchen to take the call. Beneath the kitchen, another detail he had verified, there was no basement because it had been a late addition. The basement was beneath the dining and living rooms, the oil tank exactly under the table where they ate. When he saw Chrissy rise from her place at the table and come into the kitchen, Adam would know it was safe to press the button that would set off the explosion in the oil tank. Oh yes, he had worked the whole thing out: the location of the tank; where he could buy the remote-controlled detonator; how he could set it in place while Chrissy was in town and Fred at work. Baroque but simple: like all complex problems its solution was just a question of understanding and acceptance. He had understood the opportunity fate had offered to save his son and he had accepted the challenge. It required only patience, careful planning and deception, surely his strongest qualities. Let someone try to unravel that. On the appointed night, just to make sure Carl was beyond any suspicion, he and Lizzie would be at a play in Kingston, thanks to the tickets Adam had already bought.

When he had finished typing Adam brought his stack of paper into the living room so he could work on the envelopes while watching the news. Then he took out a bottle of single malt Scotch, which he sometimes treated himself to, poured himself a drink. All this masterminding took him back to the times he'd connived with Elizabeth, and remembering their delight in their childish deceptions, he raised his glass to that vague spot in the heavens, a little west of the North Pole where he liked to think she lived.

When Adam turned on the television, the national news was over and they were just announcing that following a few messages, there would be a local news special on Fred Verghoers — "a man who was making waves in his bid to become reeve of a small township in the north country." Fred's sudden emergence as a public figure had taken everyone by surprise. In the interviews following his first television appearance, he took such a strong stand against "government pampering" and "hotel prisons" that a syndicated newspaper columnist in Ottawa hailed him as one of the "rising breed of young merchant princes eager to transform the Canadian federation from a navel-gazing former British colony to a full participant in the American reality," and he had been profiled in newspapers across the province.

The local news began with two columnists — one from Kingston and the other from Toronto — discussing what was now apparently called the Fred Verghoers phenomenon. Since that first documentary letters of support had come in from across the province. Here was a new clip of Fred. He was shown at Allnew again explaining that he saw himself as nothing special, just an honest man looking to serve his community as best he could.

"But why do you think you've drawn so much attention to yourself? What makes you so different?"

The camera zoomed in. Fred's face was clear and squarish, his brown hair neatly combed. He was wearing his Allnew vest. He smiled and exposed his strong even teeth, the same "I'm ready for anything" grin he'd worn as he got up from the ice. "To tell you the truth," he began — and the viewer had only to look at those round open eyes, that boyish grin, those solid arms, that modest yet assured set of his mouth to know that he or she could count on this stranger, that he would never tell anything but the truth because truth was all he could know — "to tell you the truth, ma'am, I don't really understand the fuss myself."

"Tonight," the presenter explained, "we were going to try to crack the Fred Verghoers mystery. We were going to spend a quiet evening at his home where he lives with his partner, Christine, and her daughter, Lizzie. That was our plan. A nice domestic profile. Instead I think you'll agree that what you're about to see is one of the most amazing demonstrations of grace under fire you're ever likely to witness."

Onto the screen came Chrissy in her kitchen, whipping up cookie batter in a big bowl just as though it were half a century ago. And beside her, wearing a flowered apron, was Lizzie.

Adam had not yet stuffed even the first of his THE LION SHALL LIE DOWN WITH THE LAMB flyers. He started folding while Chrissy explained that Fred was a man who liked his cookies but that she had almost killed him the first time he came to dinner; he had a near-fatal allergy to chocolate and she'd had to rush him to hospital after dessert. Hearing this information the master criminal with the mastermind, the very one who had realized he could fulfil his fate only by staying in character, began weaving a back-up plan that involved him inviting Chrissy and Fred for dinner, then serving a strongly flavoured stew heavily laced with unsweetened cocoa.

On television Chrissy — who in life seemed so unpredictably explosive — looked pert, blonde, vivacious but not entirely sure of herself. Lizzie was the perfect touch. She appeared to be entirely unconscious of the cameras, gave them endearing gap-toothed smiles while rolling out the dough and cutting the cookies into animal shapes while her mother watched proudly and explained that Lizzie liked animals so much she hoped to be a veterinarian when she grew up.

Then the scene switched to the front lawn. It was dark outside; Fred was coming home and Chrissy and Lizzie were going out to meet him. The camera showed Fred opening the car door and emerging into the bright television lights, his eyes blinking. "There's been a huge reaction to your statements on abortion today," an interviewer began. "Can you tell us what you mean by the township withdrawing funds from the local hospital?"

Just as Fred was about to answer, shouts of "Fraud! You bastard! Tell the truth!" came from the edge of the light. The camera swung along an unplanned path past a group of technicians until it stopped at Ned Richardson. He was holding up a plastic bag. "Do you want me to show them what's here? Do you want me to—," he shouted and suddenly started to pull something from the bag.

Later Adam would find out that black something was not a gun, as it first appeared, but a video cassette. But at the time it seemed that Ned Richardson was pulling a gun on Fred and that Fred, a true frontier sheriff-in-the-making, had thrown himself on the boy to disarm him and protect his family and the onlookers. There was a wild scramble, the camera veered as though someone had been shot, then Fred's rugged and determined face came into focus. He had Ned Richardson on the ground with his arm twisted behind his back.

"Well," said the presenter, "a day in the life of Fred Verghoers, family man, lumber-yard manager, would-be reeve and apparently bulletproof hero. I have a feeling we're going to be seeing a lot more of Fred Verghoers." He paused, looking at a sheet of paper he had just been handed, while the background screen showed images of police cruisers arriving at Fred Verghoers' place and Ned Richardson being led away in handcuffs.

"This just in," the presenter now continued. "The name of the young man subdued by Fred Verghoers is Ned Richardson, the son of Luke Richardson, Mr. Verghoers' opponent in the race for reeve of West Gull township. In a very magnanimous gesture, Fred Verghoers has stated that he will not be pressing charges against Ned Richardson, whom he says must have been carried away by family feelings in the fervour of a heated campaign. Mr. Richardson, who has now been released from custody, can consider himself a very lucky young man. We also have, also just in, a statement from Luke Richardson, Ned's father. I'll read it in its entirety. 'I wish to announce at this time, following the regrettable incidents of this evening, that I am withdrawing my name and will no longer be standing for the West Gull reeveship. On behalf of my son, myself and my wife, I wish to extend our deepest apologies to Fred Verghoers for this uncalled-for incident. We all would also like to wish Mr. Verghoers the best of luck in his political career. Mr. Verghoers has all the qualities required to lead our township into the future and he may count upon my support in the months and years to come.'"

Adam poured himself more Scotch. A STAR IS BORN was the message he should have been printing.

The sweetness of October. The first frost on the window. The crisp smell of autumn nights. The scent of burning maple hanging over the villages.

It had taken him all summer to get used to the water.

Make the oars of his rowboat so they wouldn't wiggle and slip. Get his sunglasses right so he didn't come back with light trapped in his brain, hammering all night to get out. Sleep deeply for a few hours then wake up early enough to catch a string of fish. Find whatever it was, that feeling that the clock was ticking *inside* of him, ticking to his own pulse. Getting old, yes, he was getting old. Dying even, soon. But he wanted to die easy and smooth, slide into it prow first, a graceful glide, not be knocked off the cliff backwards, arms and legs and brain flailing like some crazy fool. Die on an evening like this when he was sitting calm and peaceful smoking a cigarette and looking out at Dead Swede Lake. The way Dead Swede Lake looked on this particular October evening. Dark and purply, full of the coming winter, little black-purple wavelets rippling with the cold whippy breeze, the sky a big goose highway south.

Finally he walked up to the house. These days it seemed to Gerald Boyce that dense shadows had taken over the planet which, like a top that has been spinning too long, had suddenly started to wobble. "Earth Falls Flat on Its Face," they'd soon be saying on the news, followed by one of those hot-shot politicians who sound so dumb you'd think they must have flunked out of kindergarten.

When the news was over Gerald Boyce turned off his television set and went to sit outside. Fall nights. Put on a thick coat and a wool cap and you could sit outside all night so long as you had a bottle of brandy in your hand. Watch the constellations rising as the sky turns black. Smell the crisp sweet maple smoke.

He rolled himself a cigarette. Despite the television, nights could be lonely. Having McKelvey visit had settled on him. He had even considered going to the R&R and asking

McKelvey if he wanted to move in with him for a few months. But he couldn't face the prospect of always being aware of that big body, all that snoring and coughing and worrying about how many cups of coffee he drank in the morning. He had thought of asking him to come fishing but he hadn't got around to that either. Maybe in the winter. There was nothing like winter fishing when Dead Swede Lake was a refrigerator waiting to be raided. While Vernon was alive, as soon as the ice was thick enough, always by New Year, they would drag out the fishing hut, bore a hole in the ice, start pulling in the pike. A lot of times McKelvey had snowshoed across the lake to join them. Before he went to war. He could still see him the day he came round to say goodbye. Big raw-boned William McKelvey looking almost like a grown-up man in his khakis except for the foolish grin on his face that said, "Look what I got myself into." Even fishing he'd always been a bit off-balance. As though he couldn't quite stand whatever was already boiling away inside. Never able to sit still for more than a few minutes. Never able to settle into himself.

Gerald stood up, stretched his back, walked slowly towards the road. A truck approached and he waved at the headlights. When it stopped Carl McKelvey got out.

"Speak of the devil."

"Thought I'd say hello," Carl said, "since you were standing there, trying to get run over."

Gerald looked down. The truth was, he *had* been standing in the middle of the road without quite knowing it.

"I was thinking about your father," Gerald Boyce said.

"Me too," said Carl. It had taken him only a few minutes to get away from the television lights and the voices. By the time he reached the cornfield he could have been anyone,

anywhere — himself a hundred years ago, a hunter from another planet, a strange creature drifting through fields thick
with the smell of raw earth and rotting corn. These fields.
This earth. This sweet sour smell of decay. And he'd dropped
to his knees just to feel the earth soaking into his pants, pushed
his hands into the damp ground, spread it on his face. He
wanted to howl, to cry, to fill the sky with his gratitude, his
happiness at having been finally released from Chrissy. That
was when his mind had gone to his father, the way after
Elizabeth died, he'd sometimes disappear on foot during the
morning and not show up again until hours after dark.

Carl spent hours wandering through the cedar and the
maple, filling his lungs, rubbing his face and his body against
the bark, bending to drink at every little stream and pond.
Until finally he got to the old collapsed barn he'd dreamed of
so often and so deeply for so many years. *Chrissy loves Fred,* he
said to himself. *Chrissy loves Fred.* He took out his hunting
knife and carved a big heart into one of the splintered posts.
In the centre of the heart he carved an F and then a C and
then he gashed a big arrow through them. *Chrissy loves Fred.*
Whatever that meant, it was true.

He stood up and took a few steps. His feet flowed into the
ground. This was him, what he'd once had, what he'd been
born to, and he felt the edges of his body dissolving in the fading light, his centre of gravity dropping into the wet ground,
into the deep place in this earth which was the only place that
knew him. Then he took the shotgun from its hiding place
under the juniper bush, stowed it behind the seat and drove
until he came on Gerald Boyce standing in the middle of the
road with his arms up in the air like a confused old soldier
looking for someone to surrender to.

———

After sitting on Gerald Boyce's porch and drinking two brandy-laced coffees, Carl got back into his truck. It was past midnight. As he drove by the darkened houses, he had an overwhelming feeling of having been shut out: from those curtained bedroom windows he was passing, from Chrissy, from whatever world she and Fred were smooching their way into. War Games. Maybe he was destined to spend his whole life alone like this, the old lonesome wolf, stalking his imaginary trails, hiding from imaginary hunters.

"At least Chrissy's gone," he reminded himself but it only made him feel that much more the outsider, unable to make any kind of promise to anyone. When he got to his place and saw a glow from the kitchen window, he had a wave of hope that Moira was there waiting until he remembered he himself had left the lights on.

Taped to the door was a big brown envelope and he thought of Moira again. The envelope held a video cassette, unlabelled. After he set it on the counter he started towards the refrigerator for a beer, then changed his mind. He seemed to have gone completely herky-jerky: every few seconds he was off in a different direction — reaching for a drink, putting some plates with toast crumbs in the dishpan, wheeling and pacing from kitchen to living room. He took out his wallet, held a piece of paper with Moira's number to the light. She made elegant oval letters and numbers that reminded him of the way she had dressed for the Richardson dinner. He walked into the living room to the telephone, picked up the receiver. Then he saw that Lizzie had left some school books spread out on the couch. Around the room were scattered various sweatshirts, a pair of overalls, some Archie comics. He put down the phone, gathered Lizzie's things and took them up to her room.

The lamp beside her bed had a shade she'd decorated with animal decals. When Carl turned it on, shadows of teddy bears and squirrels were thrown onto the wall. He lay down on her bed. Her ceiling was wallpaper that he'd painted white and he could see that some of the seams were starting to peel. On one wall was a Superwoman poster, on another a rainforest poster she'd won at school for hard work on a project. The wall beside her bed was decorated with cat pictures she'd cut out from magazines. Quite a little kingdom she'd arranged. While her mother was getting beat up by her stepfather who was running for reeve, and while her real father was driving around worrying about shooting or getting shot, Lizzie had her official universe of innocence. Easy to think that one day she'd remember her childhood in a much more sinister way; but for right now, Carl considered, Lizzie's world was a pretty good place to be.

He started to doze but decided to turn off the downstairs lights and go to his own bedroom. In the kitchen he saw the blank cassette which he'd forgotten about. He popped it into the VCR.

Later he would re-examine the envelope, see what he'd missed the first time, the lightly pencilled message: "To Carl, from your pal, Ned." But for now what he saw was a room in bright sunlight, a bed, a woman's face, Chrissy's, jumping into focus, her mouth opening in surprise, then a stifled cry of protest as one large hand covers her mouth and the other jerks away the sheet.

THREE

THE FIRST SNOW CAME AT THE BEGIN-ning of November before the ground was frozen hard. Using a sledgehammer, Carl was able to loosen the posts of Luke Richardson's election signs. There were sixty-six in all, enough to make a big mound in the back of the truck that he had to tie down so they wouldn't blow free while he was driving them to the dump. Even so, they clattered and banged the whole way, a weird raucous chorus, Carl thought, to the sound of Luke's voice when he'd called to ask him to gather the signs and added that the hunting trip had better be put off. "Or maybe we'll just go alone," Luke had finally said. "You and me and a couple of bottles of something." After unloading the signs, tactfully placed between a truckload of green garbage bags and a rusted woodstove, Carl went and opened the Movie Barn. While he was still making the coffee, Arnie Kincaid appeared in a brightly coloured parka with fur trim around the hood that reminded Carl of Christmas.

"They say the first cup is the best," Arnie offered, watching the coffee drip into the pot.

"You shovel your way out?"

"The lad next door does my driveway with a snowblower. Guess he's going to have a pretty good year." Arnie set a heavy briefcase on the counter. He unfastened it and withdrew a thick file.

"You ever see anything like this?" Arnie opened the folder. On top was an insurance policy.

"I never took out insurance," Carl said. "You think I should be getting some for the Balfer place? I thought Luke took care of that."

"This is life insurance." Arnie leafed through it. Then he went to the next policy. "This is house insurance." He quickly flipped through the other files. "Automobile, theft, disability, furniture and contents, animal — there must be fifty kinds of insurance I deal in and maybe another hundred in the city."

"That's something," Carl said, pouring two cups of coffee. His hands were still cold from working out the election signs. "But I'm not in the market that I know of."

"I thought you might like to read them over just the same. Something to do."

Carl looked down. He thought he would have to be stuck at the Movie Barn for a very long time before he started reading insurance policies. "Sure. Let me just put them under the counter. I'm getting sick of crosswords."

"I was thinking," Arnie said, "I could use some kind of assistant. Someone who could eventually take over the business. Unless you're planning to spend the rest of your life renting videos to horny housewives and old geezers like myself. What do you think of that idea?"

Arnie Kincaid's face: grey, a bit loose under the ears, his eyes slanted down towards the policies. Carl was conscious of a desire not to hurt Arnie. "I don't know," Carl said. "I've never really thought—"

"You keep this place pretty organized," Arnie said. "You're good with figures. And the customers — well — just like here, it's a bit of everyone. You seem to be able to handle that."

Now Carl's hands were on the policies. Touching them made Arnie's offer more real.

"I know you didn't grow up hoping you'd be an insurance agent. But it's a good living. Reliable. It paid my mortgage and put my daughters through school. You'd have to take a course. Maybe two. Why don't you think about it? We can talk again in a few days."

Mid-November the snow melted, then the cold returned, hard, and the ground was like one huge slippery rock. Carl called Moira. That night he hovered over her and the icy light turned her skin to white glass.

Again and again he emptied himself into her. "Wouldn't have thought I had that much juice," he said afterwards, embarrassed. Moira curled around him until sun-up when he came into her one last time, at first stiff and sore, then moaning and groaning along with Moira until it turned into a song, the howling music he'd needed during all those long lonely drives in the truck, except that he wasn't in the truck, he was in Moira and was naked and new and sweaty and for at least a few seconds nothing meant anything.

Later in the month the sky softened and it snowed again. One evening he and Lizzie made a giant snowman in the backyard. That Sunday Carl went with Lizzie to the West Gull

R&R and brought his father back for lunch. With the help of a recipe book, Lizzie baked a meatloaf that came complete with ketchup on top. "Like icing on a cake," Lizzie explained. McKelvey ate three helpings. Sitting at the same table with his father for the first time in years and watching him as he methodically spooned up his food, Carl felt unsettled. Something about the way the old man's head dipped submissively towards the plate with each mouthful. Lizzie, meanwhile, chattered on as though McKelvey being there was entirely normal. As soon as he had finished the meatloaf she rushed to the freezer and presented him with a giant bowl of chocolate ice cream decorated with two circles of chopped nuts.

After they drove him back to the R&R, Lizzie told Carl she was going to make his father a scarf just like the one she'd made for the snowman. Carl thought she seemed to take particular delight in saying "your father" to him. The knitting took Lizzie well into December and she was so pleased with the result she decided to make a toque as well. For hours every evening Lizzie worked at her grandfather's Christmas presents. It was as though she was knitting McKelvey into their life. And on Christmas Day when he put on his new hat and draped the scarf around his neck, he announced that he was warm for the first time in ten years.

On Boxing Day, McKelvey, Gerald and Carl were sitting in the middle of Dead Swede Lake. They were surrounded by the fishing shack Carl had constructed out of lengths of two-by-four covered by double-sheeted plastic. A wavering grey-white light filtered through the plastic, which was so fogged up all they could see was the altered colour of snow and the vague silhouettes of the pine and willow trees at the edge of the lake.

For warmth, aside from Gerald Boyce's five-star brandy, they had a kerosene heater going, and there was even a fishing line dropped through the hole in the ice.

William McKelvey had given up shaving. With his grizzled hair and beard he had the look of an old lion patiently waiting to die. Even walking the few hundred feet out across the lake had made the pain in his left knee spread all through his leg and hip.

"You know," McKelvey said, "it's pretty strange to be sitting here in the middle of Dead Swede Lake absolutely blind."

"We got nothing but window," Carl said, gesturing to the plastic around him. "If everyone wasn't breathing so hard, we could see out."

McKelvey looked at his son. He hadn't believed Gerald when he'd called to say that Carl had made a shack on Dead Swede Lake and they were going fishing. "Impossible." Meaning, first, impossible that Carl could find a way to drag out the ton of materials that went into an old-style fishing shack; and second, impossible that Carl would ever do something so … something so much for him. Like the crazy hope he used to have that Carl would grow up, marry, have a herd of grandchildren and transform the farm into a little heaven of carefully planted gardens, groves, a Noah's ark of animals. He, the proud granddad, would walk through this miraculous paradise, grandchildren scampering about him like so many friendly little puppies.

"You shouldn't complain," Gerald said. "You probably can't see that well anyway."

"I *have* seen," William said. "I have seen so much I don't need to see much more." Then he reached into his coat and pulled out a dark cardboard cylinder, opened it up to reveal a green smoked-glass bottle. With a penknife he slit the seal. He read out the label before handing the bottle to Gerald. "You remember the bottle I brought back after the war?"

"Yeah," Gerald said.

McKelvey had been twenty-three years old when he came home. Travelled down from Ottawa on the train, still wearing his uniform. It was September 1945. His father was away on a fishing trip when he arrived. Some neighbours took him back to the house. Like an overflowing privy was how his father had left it. McKelvey'd dumped his bag on the porch, then driven the tractor over to the Boyce house.

Gerald and Vernon had been standing in their yard. "When I came to your house you were trying to make a car go. The two of you. You were wearing matching pairs of suspenders. You remember those suspenders? I never saw anyone look so foolish in suspenders as you used to."

They'd drunk the bottle, then McKelvey had driven his tractor home, thinking the whole time that if there was one thing he was not going to do, it was to sink back into this pile of mud and spend the rest of his life rotting away like the Boyce brothers.

"You see some foolish things around here," Gerald said. "I've even seen people try to drive across this lake."

McKelvey looked at his son. Carl was inspecting the label and had his eyebrows raised in admiration.

"Things aren't so bad," McKelvey said. "If you'll excuse me for a moment." He stood up and pushed open the blanket that was the door and went out onto the ice. There was a north wind that had given the snow a hard crackling crust and was so cold he could feel it biting through his beard. Those first winters back, before he got the money to go to Queen's, he'd spent enough winter days out on the ice of Dead Swede Lake with the Boyce brothers, drinking, fishing, trying to invent a future.

But he'd always held back. Always known he was different, that having got away once he would get away again. Even that day he'd brought Elizabeth to meet his father, it had been just a visit to a country he'd escaped for ever. And yet here he was. His whole lifetime later. Standing with his back to the wind pissing out his brandy the way he'd pissed out his whole life.

He turned towards what had once been his dock, his shore, his road up to his house. Five years ago, even one year ago, he couldn't have come back to Dead Swede Lake this way, practically a tourist, and stood looking at what had once been his and before that his father's without feeling loss twisting through his gut like a knife. The only way he could have returned was the way he had: in Luke Richardson's white bomb, with his foot on the floor.

But now, with Carl back, it was almost beautiful — the snow-covered frozen lake ringed by leafless trees, the blue-grey dome of the sky, even Carl's fishing shack. That had to be the most unlikely building, or unbuilding, that he'd ever seen. Strange, the way the sun shimmered and rolled in all that curvy plastic, and just as Carl had appreciatively raised his eyebrows looking at the label of his single malt Scotch, McKelvey had to admire this bizarre construction of his son's. That was the thing about Carl. You just never knew where he was going next. All the way to the Pacific Ocean or straight into an oak tree.

For New Year's Eve, Luke Richardson gave the R&R money to throw a special New Year's bash. The occasion was the senator's one-hundredth birthday. Two hours before midnight he arrived in his van, got wheeled in, a fur rug draped over his knees, and Reeve Fred Verghoers presented him with a big old skeleton key he said was the key to West Gull. The senator drooled just a bit, a few whispered jokes were made about what graveyard or coffin the key might or might not be intended to open, the senator had a glass of champagne and was wheeled out again.

Adam Goldsmith saw it all. Positioned at the mantelpiece like a ship berthed in a familiar port, Adam stood tall and pearish, radiating his usual deferential courtesy. Tonight his attentions were concentrated on Dr. Albert Knight. Since his daughter's departure, Dr. Knight and Adam had rekindled their old friendship. "You'll forgive an elderly man for speaking his mind," he'd said to Adam on the evening he came over to mend fences, the "elderly" adding that touch of ironic exaggeration Adam was known to appreciate. On this occasion, suitably unsuited in shapeless grey flannel and a hairy tweed jacket, Dr. Knight puffed at his pipe and amused Adam so well with his comments on the passing crowd that Adam almost forgot to spend the evening bemoaning his lack of Elizabeth.

But when he got home it struck him in a way he hadn't experienced for years. Even walking through the snow, his left side was burning and tense and by the time he got his coat and boots off and had collapsed in an armchair, his chest was so tight he was certain he was having some kind of heart attack. That's how it had been after Elizabeth was killed: attacks of the heart, where it cramped and constricted, as though unable to stop clutching its emptiness in search of what used to be there. The first few times he believed he was having some sort of cardiac emergency, even if grief was what had brought it on. He would be curled up on the floor with pain, pounding his ribs to release the cramp in his heart while waiting for death to take him. Not that, *in extremis,* such a wait was obligatory: Albert Knight had long ago provided

him with a means of escape should his situation become in-
tolerable.

Once, a much more ideal departure had almost been assured
— that last night, exactly eleven years ago, when Elizabeth told
him she was going to leave with him New Year's morning.
"Adam, Adam, you must believe me." And he had, or almost
had, or had at least been willing to pretend.

What a New Year's that had been. Barely able to keep from
howling his good fortune to the sky, Adam had rushed home
from the party, his heart cavorting like a moronic puppy, and
run up and down the stairs to prepare his suitcases, too excited
to sleep but making himself stretch out in the easy chair with
his feet up on the same hassock his mother used for propping
up her swollen feet in the heavy heat of summer. With his
head back and plans whirling through his mind like clouds of
asteroid dust, he'd been able to taste the taste of Elizabeth on
his lips, hear the cosy sound of her voice, sink into the coming
luxury of a life spent with her. The future: a carefully planned
and furbished treasure chest of bank accounts and hidden
investments that Adam had spent twenty years waiting to open
and enjoy. That night in the half-darkness, nursing a drink in
his easy chair, Adam imagined himself somehow communing
with his mother. Triumphantly broadcasting that after everything, he had finally ended up with the Glade daughter, the
daughter Flora claimed he had inspired into existence.
Although she would not have approved of him stealing her
from another man. Adultery, deceptions, such sins had not
been her stock in trade.

When the pains in his chest eased, Adam took up paper and
pen to indulge in his annual New Year's ritual, his substitute
for their evenings of gossip by the hearth: writing a letter to

Elizabeth recounting the year's events. This year's letter was longer than usual. Carl's return to West Gull, the state of his relationships with Lizzie and Chrissy, the events with Fred, all required long explanations. Then there was the video. It was hard to know whether minor-key porno deserved a place in an essentially dignified medium — a letter to a dead person — but in the end, because Carl had given him the video for safekeeping and its presence in his house was an endless irritation, he divulged. Adam described how their world had become an absurd parody, how an event that between them had been so romantic and so satisfying had been transformed by Chrissy and Fred into a series of celluloid impressions depicting various unimaginative acts, carried out by two near-animals apparently equally hungry for pleasure and pain.

When he finished it was almost morning, almost the time of night eleven years ago when he had started wondering if he should begin to expect Elizabeth or prepare to be disappointed, almost the time when Luke Richardson had called to tell him about the accident. He made himself a hot chocolate to wash down his sleeping pill, watched the letter burn in his woodstove, went to bed.

In the beginning were the voices. Adam was a child then, with the innocence of a child. The innocence, the craft, the cunning. At night he would awake crying out in unknown tongues, nightmare legions flaming across his walls and ceilings, and his mother would carry him to her bed and fold him into the hot flannel of her nightdress until finally the voices stilled and Adam was asleep again, asleep among the marching legions of old empires. And then the dream would start again and in the dream Adam was a child of those legions, a soldier's child was the child he was, and one night his father took him in his arms and told him that the empire had called, that the empire had need of his legion, that he would be marching on to other countries, other wars, and then in the dream it was dawn and Adam was alone on a cold hill watching the legions as they disappeared in the direction of the rising light, and only he was left behind to remember, to preserve, to await the return.

In the beginning were the voices and Adam was nothing until the voices filled him and when they woke him in the night he screamed out their scrambled message while his mother held him close and tight because Adam had become his father his father's father his father's father before him. Adam was the father of all fathers the voice the sun the son the tongue of the Church of the Unique God and then the voices left and Adam was nothing again, just emptiness waiting for a memory he could no longer speak until Elizabeth came and spoke his name and hers was the voice Adam heard and then she was gone and Adam was empty again.

In the end it was easy. Adam called Fred at work and said Luke had something for him that he'd asked him to arrange.

"I don't know what you're talking about," Fred said, his voice full of suspicion.

It was a few days into January and the serious cold had begun. There was a familiar minus-thirty-degree crackle on the line. "Something he got from his son," Adam explained. "A copy. You have the original."

Fred hung up. The next day he called back. "You want to explain yourself?"

"I think I did," Adam said. "We're all just looking to do the right thing here. I want you to be in possession of this item."

"You can bring it by the office."

"I wouldn't be comfortable doing that," Adam said. "I don't even have it with me. It's hidden in one of Luke's houses. We'll go get it, then you'll have it."

The next day Fred came to the dealership a few minutes after closing time. Adam was waiting for him. He extended his hand. Fred shook it. In the months since becoming reeve he'd developed a new ingratiating way of slanting his head and smiling. "What now?"

"It's out at the old Fennerty place. We'll go in my car."

"I don't mind driving."

"Mine needs a run. Gets all gummed up just going back and forth from the house to the office."

When they went outside it was after six. The Timberpost was still open, and security lights were glowing in the real-estate office and the supermarket. It was clear and cold. Adam was wearing fur-trimmed gloves but he still had to clap his hands together. January weather: there were always a few weeks like this, minus thirty at night, block-heater weather.

They drove out of town past the West Gull Elementary. Despite the cold the spots illuminating the outdoor rink were on and the sound of frozen pucks deflecting off the boards banged angrily through the darkness.

"Still play?" Adam asked.

"Just old-timer hockey now," Fred said. "Too busy for the real thing."

As they left town Adam was still hesitating. The previous week, in preparation, he had put the video cassette under a kitchen floorboard at the Fennerty place, which Luke Richardson had bought and was now selling, but except for the first fuzzy images of Chrissy in bed, the tape was now erased.

The Pontiac warmed quickly but Adam kept his gloves on. Somehow that was reassuring, as though leather might be capable of more than skin. On the way he asked Fred about his plans for the township and just before the high beams picked up the old oak tree, he asked Fred if after a term or two as reeve he was planning a move to the national political stage. Fred took off his hat and looked into it, as though it might hold the answer. The sides of the road were banked with snow but where the road jogged at the oak tree, the wind always kept the shoulder bare and icy.

"I don't suppose they've already been calling you," Adam said, his voice purring with the hum of his tires on snow, purring with the sly tone widely known for sixty years as Adam Goldsmith's way of starting one of his inoffensive jokes.

"Just once or twice," Fred replied, smiling, and as he did Adam pushed the accelerator to the floor, "goosed her" as Luke would say, put so much gas to his V-8 special that his very new and very expensive French snow tires skidded for a frightening fraction of a second, just enough to start a high whine that ended as they clawed and gripped the snow, slamming Adam and Fred back into their seats as the car exploded forward shot along the icy road Adam's gloves locked to the steering wheel and holding firm even as Fred's elbow hammered into his face tore through the pagewire fence and into the oak tree where in a still more frightening fraction of a second it stopped.

The coroner's report noted the multiple fractures to the passenger's skull, lacerations on the arm thrown up in self-protection, internal injuries unenumerated since an autopsy was not deemed necessary, and other outrages to what had been a healthy living body before it took an unplanned trip through a suddenly stationary windshield attached to a car that had accordioned into a large oak tree.

The driver had also died, though he had been retained by the steering wheel, a padded collapsible model intended to prevent impalation. The report also noted that the alcohol content in the driver's blood was high enough to cause the loss of a Province of Ontario driver's licence; had they also tested for drugs they would have discovered that the driver had ingested a lethal dose of sleeping pills. As it was, Adam's death was ascribed to cardiac failure caused by the shock of the impact, an analysis strengthened by the fact that his physician, Dr. Albert Knight, stated that he had twice treated Adam for minor heart attacks. The report also noted that Adam sustained a fractured nose, though it remained silent about the curious fact that blood from this fracture was present on the passenger's coat, leading others to speculate that the accident had been caused by a struggle between driver and passenger.

When Albert Knight checked Adam's medical records he found that Adam had been killed on the eve of his sixty-fourth birthday. Those who remembered such things also noted the fact that Adam Goldsmith and Fred Verghoers were killed on the same corner, against the same tree, as had Elizabeth McKelvey eleven years before. The centre of impact was halfway between the driver and the passenger side. Both airbags had been disabled and neither passenger had been wearing his seatbelt.

The anniversary was not exact: Elizabeth was killed early New Year's Day, Adam Goldsmith's car lost control the night of January 11. Because Fred was a newly elected politician, someone who had made a certain public splash, the tragedy of his sudden death received wide coverage. There was even a wire-service story that showed Chrissy standing over the wrecked car, wiping her eyes.

———

Carl is driving from the Balfer place across the flatlands towards West Gull. Lizzie has her hand in his pocket for warmth and her head on his shoulder, the way she's taken to doing these winter mornings. He has Lizzie all the time now except every second weekend and holidays. Chrissy has moved to Toronto to live with an aunt and take courses at a business school. Midweek she calls Lizzie. When Carl answers he talks to her for a few moments. Her voice has new layers of fatigue and distance. "I'm starting again," she's said to Carl, twice, and he understands what she's doing: she's trying to make herself small, small enough to slide backwards in time to that Richardson New Year's Eve party when she first asked him to dance. He can't tell her it's a place he's also tried to get to, or that he used to tell himself that had he turned away from Chrissy he wouldn't have fought with Fred, wouldn't have guzzled half a bottle of brandy to kill the pain, wouldn't have driven his mother into a tree. Over Long Gull Lake the sun is coming up grey-gold and along the concession roads small clusters of children are waiting for the school buses. A few other vehicles, like his own, are homing in on West Gull. In a few minutes the school will be open, the supermarket working its way to daytime temperature levels, the bank computers processing the night's numbers. Richardson's New & Used will have unlocked its doors. Adam's office, a corner cubicle off the showroom, will be lit and waiting for Carl who ever since the reading of the will has been cleaning and organizing Adam's files.

When he gets to the New & Used, Carl parks at the back of the lot and buys a coffee from the Timberpost before going into Adam's office. He closes the door with its frosted-glass window, puts his jacket on the hook, opens the top drawer. Every day for a week, he's looked at the wax-sealed envelope with his name on the outside. He takes the lid off his coffee, brings the steaming surface to his lips. He opens the letter Adam has written him. For the next two days his tongue will be scalded and he'll always associate what he reads in the letter with the overheated bitter Timberpost coffee.

It was the beginning of September, the first week of school, and the warmth and humidity of a late-August heat wave still blanketed the township. With a cup of coffee in her hand, Elizabeth stood at her kitchen window, soaking up the morning light and wondering if her geraniums would last out the month.

Carl and McKelvey came down for breakfast radiating a great mute wooden wall of hungry maleness. In their collective silence they ate, they drank, they piled the dishes, after which McKelvey went out to the barns while Elizabeth prepared to take Carl to school.

On the highway she said to him, for no reason at all except that it had come into her mind, "If there was one thing you could have different, what would it be?"

Carl was twelve that year. He had developed a transparent fringe of fuzz on his upper lip and his sideburns were growing wispy extensions. He sat silently for a while and Elizabeth thought about how essentially reserved Carl was, how he always seemed to be holding something back, as though he'd divided himself off to keep from finding out the secret that he'd never be told. "Be someone else, I guess," Carl said.

Elizabeth was stunned. Finally she asked, "Who?"

"You, maybe."

That night Carl came into the kitchen while Elizabeth was doing dishes. "If you were me you'd be washing these," Elizabeth said.

Carl sat down. "I was just kidding. Giving the teacher the smart answer."

In the middle of the night Elizabeth woke up, uncomfortably warm. McKelvey lay beside her, his usual night mountain, breath rising and falling in that noisy chorus that grew louder every year. She got out of bed, put on her slippers and a robe, went downstairs and outside.

The sky had a thin veil of clouds and the moon, tinted orange by the pollen held in the mist, hung ripe and heavy over the barn. "You, maybe," Carl had said in that flat, diffident way he had when something truly mattered. She should have stopped the car and hugged him. She should have crowed in triumph or gratefully wept at having mothered this child she had touched just as he'd touched her.

A breeze came up and she found herself surrounded by the familiar rustle of leaves. Tomorrow she was seeing Adam for lunch at the Timberpost. Not a word would be said about Carl. They would chatter about the library, his work at the New & Used, her new class. Maureen Knight had returned to town; according to Dorothy Dean she was thought to have Parkinson's and Adam was spending a lot of time with her. He should have married Maureen Knight, Elizabeth knew. And her telling Adam that Carl was his son was what likely prevented him. And yet, just as she had been helpless to resist the strange passion for him that had overcome her for so many years, so had she been unable to let him go. Of course she had stopped their afternoons. And at first, afterwards, she could hardly bear to see him. Later it was as though they were fellow survivors of a brushfire that had burned everything around them. She could even look at his hands without blushing or melting, walk by his side without wishing they were back in the make-believe motel world, a world she could only truly remember on

New Year's Eves when she'd had too much to drink and Adam waltzed her slowly around the Great Hall.

"If there was one thing you could have different...?" she'd asked Carl. And what about herself? The wind had got under her robe and nightgown; her skin contracted with cold. And suddenly from the barn, like an echo of her dream, came the questioning moo duet of Jane Eyre and Anna Karenina. Had she, like Anna Karenina, ruined her life over a man? Or was it that she had been too frightened to ruin her life and wished she had? The cattle, sensing her presence, had put their heads out the barn door and were staring at her as if to say they wouldn't be able to sleep until she solved the riddle of her life. "Maybe what I'd like," Elizabeth said to them, "is to have it both ways, the way you do: my rear end in the barn, my front end free to admire the beauties of nature, speculate on the foolishness of others and have a few snacks." Anna Karenina and Jane Eyre, unmoved, continued chewing their cud, jaws slowly grinding in harmony with Elizabeth's slowly grinding thoughts. Her skin was tight, painful with desire and the need to be released. She walked to the fence and leaned against it, trembling. The cows took a step closer. The pain that had started in her skin, her breasts, was now radiating out from her groin, a screaming reproach to everything she had denied in herself. Just as she opened her mouth to scream back, the pain faded and she was left clinging to the cedar rail, soaked in sweat and wondering if it was pain that she'd felt or something else, some excess of unlived life demanding to be born. "You tell me," she said to her cows. They nodded their heads slowly, either in sympathy or confusion, then backed into the barn as Elizabeth went towards the house to make tea.

When she had the cup in her hands, steaming and aromatic, a candle lit to keep her company, she stood at the window looking out at the barn. She saw the yellow flame reflected in the mirror of the glass, the blurred image of her own face, the night-black lawn sloping down to the driveway where her car's chrome gleamed in the moonlight.

Matt Cohen's most recent novel was the critically acclaimed *Last Seen*, which was a finalist for both the Governor General's Award and the Trillium Award, and was chosen by Margaret Atwood as Best Book of 1997 (*Maclean's*). In 1998 he received the Toronto Arts Award for Writing. He has been published in the US, the UK, Brazil, France, Germany, Korea, Mexico, Poland, the Netherlands, and Spain. He lives in Toronto.